50 WAYS TO
Ruin a Rake

JADE LEE

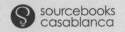
sourcebooks
casablanca

Published by Sourcebooks Casablanca, an imprint of
Sourcebooks, Inc.
P.O. Box 4410, Naperville, Illinois 60567-4410
(630) 961-3900
Fax: (630) 961-2168
www.sourcebooks.com

Printed and bound in Canada.
MBP 10 9 8 7 6 5 4 3 2 1

One

Make a plan, be sure of it, and do not deviate.

THERE ARE CERTAIN THINGS A WOMAN KNOWS. SHE knows what the weather will be based on how easily her hair settles into the pins. She knows when the cook has quarreled with the butler by the taste of the morning eggs. And she knows when a man will completely upset her day.

And right now, that man was walking up her front drive as easy as if he expected to be welcomed.

Melinda Smithson bolted out of her bedroom where she'd been fighting with her curls—again—and rushed downstairs. "I'm just going for a quick walk!" she said much too brightly to their butler as she made it to the front door. Rowe hadn't even the time to reach for her gloves when she snatched her gardening bonnet off the table and headed outside. She had to get to the odious man before he rounded the rock and came into view from her father's laboratory. If her papa saw him, she would be done for. So she ran as fast as her legs could carry her.

She rounded the bend at the same moment he arrived at the rock. One step more, and she was doomed.

"Oh no, Mr. Anaedsley. Not today. You cannot come here today." She said the words breathlessly, but she punctuated with a severe tug on her bonnet. So hard, in fact, that three pins dug painfully into her scalp.

Mr. Anaedsley had been whistling, but now he drew up short. "You've punched your thumb through your bonnet." He spoke with a charming smile that made her grind her teeth in frustration. Everything about the man was charming, from his reddish-brown hair to the freckles that dotted his cheeks to the rich green of his eyes. An annoyance dressed as a prince of the realm, for all that he had no courtesy title. He was the son and heir of the Duke of Timby, and she hated him with a passion that bordered on insanity.

Unfortunately, he was right. She'd punched her thumb clean through the straw brim of her bonnet.

"Yes, I have," she said as she stepped directly in front of him. He would not pass around the rock. He simply wouldn't. "And that is one more crime I lay at your feet."

"A crime?" he replied. "To poke a hole in that ugly thing? Really, Miss Smithson, I call it more a mercy. The sun should not shine on something that hideous."

It was hideous, which was why it was her gardening bonnet. "The sun is not supposed to shine on my face either, so it is this ugly thing or stay inside."

"Come now, Miss Smithson," he said as he held

out his arm to escort her. "I am well aware that you have dozens of fetching bonnets—"

"But this was the one at hand." She ignored his arm and stared intimidatingly at him. Or at least she tried to. But he was a good six inches taller than her. Average for a man, but for her he was quite the perfect height. Not too tall as to dwarf her, but large enough to be handsome in his coat of bottle-green superfine. It brought out his eyes, which were made all the more stunning by the sunlight that shone full on his face.

"Shall we amble up your beautiful drive and fetch you a pretty bonnet?"

"No, Mr. Anaedsley, we shall not. Because you shall not come to the house today. Any other day, you will be very welcome. But not today."

His brows drew together in worry. "Is your father ill? Is there something amiss? Tell me, Miss Smithson. What can I do to help?"

It was the right thing to say. Of course it was because he *always* knew the right thing to say. Her father's health was precarious these days, a cough plaguing him despite all attempts to physic him. She might have ignored his words as simple politeness, but she saw genuine worry in his eyes. She couldn't help but soften toward him.

"Papa is the same as before. It's worst at night—"

"The gypsy tincture didn't help then." He took her arm and gently eased her hand into the crook of his elbow. Her fingers were placed there before she even realized it. "I'll ask a doctor friend I know as soon as I return to London. He may—"

She dug in her feet, tugging backward on his arm. He raised a perfect eyebrow in query, but she flashed him a warm smile. "An excellent idea. You should go there right now. In fact, pray fetch the doctor here."

His eyebrows rose in alarm. "I shall write down the man's direction and a message. You can send a footman—"

"No, sir. You must go yourself. Right now. It is most urgent."

He flashed her his dimple. Damn him for having such a very attractive dimple. "Now why do I get the feeling that you're trying to rush me away?"

"Because the first thing I said to you was go away!"

He cocked his head, and his expression grew even more delightful. She would swear she saw a twinkle in his eyes. "Miss Smithson, I thought you were a scientist. The first thing you said to me was, 'Oh no, Mr. Anaedsley, not today.'"

"Well, there you have it. Go away. We are not receiving callers."

And then, just to make a liar of her, her uncle's carriage trotted up the path. Four horses—matched chestnuts—stepping smartly as they pulled her uncle's polished, gilded monstrosity. And inside waving cheerily was her cousin Ronnie. Half cousin, actually, and she waved halfheartedly at the wan fop.

"It appears, Miss Smithson, that we have been spotted. I'm afraid politeness requires that I make my bow."

"No, we haven't!" She'd used the distraction to pull them back from the rock. They were, in fact, completely shielded from all windows of the Smithson residence including the laboratory. "Ronnie doesn't count. And he certainly doesn't care if you greet him or not. The most powerful snub only seems to inspire him to greater heights of poetry."

"A poet is he?"

"Yes," she groaned. "A good one too." Which made it all the worse.

"Ah. Your suitor, I assume?"

"Suitor" was too simple a word for her relationship with Ronnie, which involved a lot of private family history. "He's my cousin. Well, half cousin, as my father and uncle had different mothers. But he has convinced himself that we are fated to be wed."

"And as a practical woman of science, you do not believe in fate."

She didn't believe in a lot of things, but at the top of the list was Ronnie's fantasy. He thought fate had cast them as prince and princess in a make-believe future. She thought her cousin's obsession with her silly at best, but more likely a dark and dangerous thing. "I do not wish to wed the man," she said baldly.

"Well, the solution is obvious then, isn't it? I shall join you today as an afternoon caller, and Ronnie will not be able to press his suit upon you."

"That would be lovely," she said sourly, "if you actually did as you say. But we both know what will really happen."

"We do?" he countered, all innocence.

She tossed him her most irritated, ugly, and angry look, but it did absolutely nothing to diminish his smile. "Oh leave off, Mr. Anaedsley, I haven't the time for it today."

"But—" he began. She roughly jerked her hand from his arm and stepped away to glare at him.

"Five minutes after greeting everyone, my father will be excited to learn about your latest experiment."

"Actually, it is your father's experiment. I only execute the task he requests—"

"Two minutes after that," she continued as if he hadn't spoken, "the two of you will wander off to his laboratory. Uncle will follow, and I shall be left alone. With Ronnie." She spoke her cousin's name as she might refer to one of her father's experiments gone horribly wrong.

"Perhaps your uncle will remain—"

"Uncle desires the union above all things."

Clearly, she'd flummoxed him. He didn't even bother denying his plan to disappear with her father. And yet the more she glared at him, the more his expression shifted to one of charming apology. That was always the way with him. She'd even taken to calling him Lord Charming in her thoughts, and as she was not a woman prone to fairy tales, the name was not a positive one.

"I see your problem, Miss Smithson," he finally said. "Unfortunately, when I said we had been spotted, I wasn't referring to your half cousin."

She blinked. "What?"

His eyes lit up with genuine warmth as he gestured behind her. Then, before she could spin around, he opened his arms in true delight.

"Mr. Smithson, how absolutely wonderful to see you out and about. Why your daughter was just telling me that she feared for your existence. Was begging me to bring in a London physician—"

"What?" her father said as he strolled down the drive toward them. "Mellie, I've told you I'm right as rain."

"Papa? Where did you come from?"

"Down at Mr. Wilks's barn. Been looking at the sheep to see if the lice powder worked."

Damn it all! She should have known he'd be inspecting the neighbor's sheep. They were the subjects of his current experiment, after all. And naturally he'd be there instead of in his lab where he'd *promised* to look at what she'd done. "But you have been ill," she said, rather than snap at him for ignoring her latest chemical experiment. "You complain of the rain. It makes your joints ache."

"Well, that's what old men do, my dear." Then her papa turned to Lord Charming and embraced him as if the man were a lost son. It had always been this way between them, starting from when her father had been Mr. Anaedsley's tutor more than a decade ago. The two adored each other, and it was so pure a love that she couldn't even be jealous of it.

Well, she *shouldn't* be jealous, but she was. Especially as she knew that her plans for the day were doomed. The two would go off with her uncle and leave her with Ronnie. And worse, the main purpose of the day—the sole reason she had asked for her uncle and cousin to visit this afternoon—was completely destroyed.

And it was all Mr. Anaedsley's fault.

❧

Trevor Harrison Anaedsley, grandson to the Duke of Timby, was not a fool, though he often chose to appear one in public. In truth, he had an engineering mind-set that led him to see how people fit together, one with another, such that society marched at a steady, appropriate, even mechanical pace.

And today, Miss Melinda Smithson did not fit. Her cogs were out of order—likely a female thing—and would rapidly be put to rights with the correct application of lubricant. Except, of course, he had already tried compliments and charm—his usual method of easing the social machinery—and she was even more out of sorts, glaring at him even as he embraced her father.

"Papa," she said with a false amount of cheer, "I know it's lovely that Mr. Anaedsley is here, but today isn't a good day. It's a family reunion of sorts, and he would be bored to distraction."

"What?" her father asked, blinking owlishly at his daughter.

"Family reunion. Mr. Anaedsley is *de trop*." Her words were heavy with extra meaning, and for a moment Trevor feared he was about to be tossed out. That would be a problem for him. A massive problem, in fact, as he could not return to London for two days at a minimum. Three would be better.

But he needn't have feared. Her father blinked dumbly at his daughter, then waved away her concerns with a snort of derision. "Don't be ridiculous. Honestly, Mellie, I don't know why you fuss so. I'll talk to your uncle while you younger folk entertain yourselves."

"A capital idea!" Trevor cried.

"A terrible idea," Miss Smithson snapped, her voice

much more strident than usual. "Papa, I wish to be there when you speak with Uncle."

"Nonsense. I can tell him all about your frippery."

"It's not frippery!"

"Of course not, dear. I shouldn't have suggested such a thing." And then in the way of a very absent-minded father, Mr. Smithson touched Trevor on the arm and guided him toward the house. "I'm so glad you're here, my boy. I want to tell you about my latest experiment. Do you recall my cream against ticks? I was just now inspecting the effects on the sheep, and I'm afraid the results are rather disappointing. I thought perhaps you could give my formula a once-over."

"It would be my great pleasure," Trevor answered honestly. He fell into step with the man while stifling the guilt he felt at Miss Smithson's glare.

Once, he would have found a polite way to delay her father, thereby restoring peace between the three of them, or at least to Miss Smithson. But his circumstances had become so desperate that a woman's temper barely caught his attention anymore.

How low he'd sunk to feel such a way. And how desperately he needed a solution beyond food and lodging for three more days.

But this was all he had right now, so he embraced it with good cheer, entering into a scientific discussion about sheep ticks and softening wool before it was even sheered. Ten minutes later, the discussion was so detailed that he barely noticed their arrival at his mentor's home. If it weren't for the interruption by something the size of a small bear, he might not have noticed at all. But a behemoth did push him aside, Mr.

Smithson's notebook went flying, and then the massive man abruptly pushed Miss Smithson right back out the door. His voice brooked no disobedience as he cried, "Quick! Outside. Right now!"

"Ronnie!" Miss Smithson exclaimed, and she might have toppled if Trevor hadn't grabbed her elbow. As it was, he dug his fingers too deeply into her arm, and she would likely sport bruises. But at least she didn't tumble into the dirt. Or become completely flattened by the beast of a man whom he now gathered was her cousin and suitor, Ronnie.

Meanwhile, the behemoth in question was tilting her head up toward his face. Miss Smithson gasped, and for a moment Trevor thought the man intended to kiss her. Right there, on the doorstep in front of family and servants.

"I say, Ronnie," began Mr. Smithson.

"Silence!" the man commanded.

Trevor felt his fists bunch as he calculated the most vulnerable spots on the beast's body. He might not have interfered, but Miss Smithson had made her desires to *not* wed this man quite clear. If this Ronnie intended to make inappropriate advances—and on the front step, no less—then Trevor intended to set the man straight.

Then another voice interrupted the excitement—a man's voice, deep and slow, but no less clear. "Oh, for God's sake, just let him look. He's been prattling on about the color of her eyes for three days."

"My eyes?" Miss Smithson cried.

"Yes," said Ronnie, the word clipped and his expression intent.

And sure enough, as everyone watched, Ronnie took hold of Miss Smithson's head in his massive paws and turned her into and out of the sunlight.

Back somewhere in the hall, Mr. Smithson snorted as he bent to recover his fallen notebook. The newcomer—presumably Ronnie's father—echoed the sound before asking after some new shipment to the Smithson's wine cellar. Trevor, on the other hand, didn't relax until he saw the butler calmly turn aside to hand off hats and coats to a waiting footman. Family might well discount the danger, but servants always knew. If the Smithson's butler saw nothing untoward, then Trevor could relax his fist.

He did, easing his grip on her elbow as well. But he stayed right by her side while her bizarre cousin continued to twist her head one way and the other as he stared intently at her face.

Meanwhile, Miss Smithson rapidly got tired of being manhandled. "They're brown, Ronnie," she snapped as she tried to pull away. She had more hope of pushing aside a boulder.

"Of course they're brown," her cousin agreed. And yet he continued to study her as…well, as Mr. Smithson studied his insects. "To the baker, they're brown. To a lovesick stable boy, they're brown. But to me, sweet Mellie, they are decidedly more interesting than *brown*." He actually sneered the color.

Trevor felt his irritation run away with him. Was the man a Bedlamite? "But they *are* brown," he said.

The behemoth shot him a triumphant glare. "Exactly my point."

Miss Smithson made a very loud sigh. "Ronnie—"

"You see," her cousin continued, riding directly over her words. "Your eyes are a kind of mink color in darkness—"

"You can't see them in the dark," she said. Exactly what Trevor would have said.

"In shadow then. But in the sun…" He twisted her head such that the light fell directly on her face. Then he exhaled as one might breathe when in the Sistine Chapel—with awe and amazement. "I was thinking mahogany, but that's not it, not it at all. They're like cat's eyes."

Miss Smithson pursed her lips. "Yellow and slitted?"

"Not a real cat. The stone. Cat's eye stones. Brown, but with striations of gold, not in a slitted line, but more like in a circle. A radiating circle. No, that's not right." He dropped his hands with a huff. "It's most difficult."

Finally released from her cousin's grip, Miss Smithson took a deep breath and straightened upright. She wasn't that tall, but she did have a fierce expression in her eyes—her golden-brown eyes, he reluctantly noted—as she glared at her cousin.

"Ronnie, you didn't have to grab me like that. You could have just asked me to step into the sunlight."

"What?" her cousin said, his brow furrowed in thought. "Your eyes are most difficult, you know. I would just call them cat's eye brown, but that's a double metaphor, you know. The stone is a metaphor for the animal. And the stone would be a metaphor for your eyes. Bad poetry, that."

"Yes," Miss Smithson said, obviously not caring in the least. "Very bad."

"I'd use the chrysoberyl and say damn to the boys who'd have to look up the word, but it would be impossible to rhyme. And besides, the word looks so odd on the page. No one would know how to pronounce it, and the moment they're thinking of that, they've lost the beauty of the poetry." Then he looked back at her. "Though, of course, you know what chrysoberyl is, and the poem is for you—"

"I also know what color my eyes are," she said as she turned to the house. Then she paused to shoot her cousin an irritated glower. "May I go inside now?"

Her sarcasm was lost on the bear suddenly looking at her bonnet. "There's a hole in your bonnet. Did you not notice?"

Which is the exact moment that Miss Smithson's anger shifted right back to Trevor. Her gaze caught his, and he would swear those gold and mahogany eyes shot darts at him. "Yes, Ronnie, I knew."

"Oh. Is it a new female style? To punch holes—"

"No, Ronnie." Stomping past Trevor, she ripped off her broken bonnet and handed it to the butler. "Come inside, Ronnie. You've seen what…" And then she took a quick step forward, her gaze shooting down the hall. "No, Papa! You promised I could be there!"

It took a moment for Trevor to realize what had happened. Looking far down the hallway, he saw Miss Smithson's father and uncle as they headed for the laboratory.

"You children amuse yourselves for a bit, will you?" came her father's answer.

Meanwhile, Trevor naturally took steps to follow

them. After all, the happiest days of his life had been spent in Mr. Smithson's laboratory. Not here, of course. The Smithsons hadn't come into their money until recently. But years ago, Mr. Smithson had been his tutor, and the laboratory had been on Trevor's estate. But here or there, the principle was the same: science, experimentation, and a place where a man could cut or boil or blow things up in perfect peace. And Mr. Smithson had said he was welcome at any time.

"Don't you dare," hissed the lady from beside him.

"But—"

"If you abandon me to Ronnie, then I swear I shall find a way to pour itching powder onto all your clothes. I'll bleach your cravats white. And... and I'll—"

He held up his hand before she could think of more dastardly things to do with his attire. "I believe your father said we should amuse ourselves."

She folded her arms right beneath her bosom. It would have been quite attractive if she weren't glaring at him. "Do not leave—"

"And I, for one, believe I shall be best amused in the laboratory."

"Of all the selfish—"

"You as well, I think. Isn't that what you wanted, Miss Smithson? To go into the laboratory with your father and uncle? To explain something to them, I believe. About a frippery?"

"It's not a frippery!"

He held up his hands, seeing that she had completely lost her temper. And no wonder, what with being manhandled by her cousin for her eye color. "Whatever it is, you will best be entertained in the laboratory, yes?" He held out his arm. "Shall we go?"

She hesitated, biting her lip before looking at him with disturbingly real tears in her eyes. "Please, sir. Please, I beg of you. Can you not just leave and come back tomorrow? You have overset everything!"

He huffed, disturbed that she seemed sincere in her distress. "What exactly have I overset?"

She pressed her lips together, clearly unwilling to tell. But in this, the mystery was solved by the no-longer-distracted Ronnie.

"Oh, she wants to show us her formula for a new women's cream. Big secret. Excellent market potential. Women by the scores will be buying it."

She spun around, her mouth ajar. "Ronnie!"

The bear simply shrugged. "Well, it's not as if the lordling is going to manufacture it himself."

A women's cream? Certainly not. But he didn't say that aloud, as he would likely learn more if he kept silent. And sure enough, the argument continued without him prompting it at all.

"That's not the point!" Miss Smithson exclaimed. "This is my formula. I should be the one who decides who gets to know about it. And most especially, how I will sell it."

Clearly, he was not to be included in her intimate circle.

The bear merely smiled as he leaned against the wall. "What she doesn't realize is that she doesn't need to prove her formula. Father likes the idea and thinks it a capital thing to take to market."

"He does?" she cried, clearly excited. "But that's… that's—"

"Capital!" Trevor completed when the appropriate word seemed to escape her. "It means you need not demonstrate your formula. Your uncle is ready to market it whether or not I find out about it." Which meant that she would go back to not throwing him out, and he could happily spend the next few days in the laboratory with her father.

"Not exactly," interrupted Ronnie. Irritating fellow.

"What?" Miss Smithson asked. "What do you mean?"

"Weeeell," answered her cousin, slowing down his words in the way of a natural-born storyteller. "We need the formula."

The lady shook her head. "Not until…until…" She glanced his way, clearly uncomfortable with speaking such personal details in front of him. Fortunately, Ronnie had no such qualms.

"She won't give over the formula unless the profits go to her."

"Well, that seems fair," Trevor said. After all, that was the point of creating a new product, wasn't it?

"Of course it's fair!" she said. "But Papa thinks a lady shouldn't have her own money. Shouldn't run a factory or be known to create formulas."

Trevor nodded. "Well, it is somewhat unusual. I wouldn't think you'd want to run the factory in any event. Nasty places, noisy and crammed full with unwashed people."

She rounded on him. "That's not the point!"

"But it is the point," interrupted Ronnie. "What you want is unnatural, Mellie."

Trevor heard her grind her teeth. It was quite audible. And then she spoke, each word spit out like tiny rocks.

"I won't give over the formula any other way."

"And neither of our fathers will put the money in your name."

She exhaled slowly. Loudly. "Ronnie—"

"But there is one way you can have what you want. One solution that will make everyone happy." He stepped closer, his eyes wide and his expression earnest. And he was such a large man that he by necessity shouldered Trevor aside even as he blocked the sun from the room.

"Ronnie," she began, clearly knowing what was about to happen. But Trevor didn't know. And he was suddenly very interested to find out.

"It's our destiny. Has been since the day I was born."

"No—"

The man dropped down to one knee. He went hard, the thud of impact on the marble echoed in the foyer, but the bear didn't even wince. His eyes were all for his cousin as he captured her hands.

"Marry me, Mellie. I could tell you as many romantic things as you want. I can talk about your beauty and write poetry—"

"You have been writing—"

"But that hasn't worked. So let me speak as my father does. Marry me, and the business will naturally come to both of us. I'll let you have all the money you want. You can run it or hire someone else to do it. You can have as large a laboratory as you like. Your own place, and you won't have to keep cleaning up your father's messes."

Trevor could see that she wanted to stop him. He saw her lashes blink away tears, not of love, but of frustration and despair. And yet, she didn't say anything, and the damned poet kept talking.

"I love you, Mellie. I always have. And even if you don't feel the same way right now, even you must see how very perfect we are for one another. Please," he said as he pressed his mouth to her knuckles. "Please be my bride."

Which is when—for no reason whatsoever—Trevor punched the man, knocking him flat.

Two

Rakes, like all men, are guided by their own bizarre code, incomprehensible even to themselves.

MELLIE SQUEAKED IN ALARM, AND SHE WAS NOT A woman who usually made animal sounds. Which made her all the more furious with the situation. Ronnie lay sprawled on the ground, a look of total shock on his face. Lord Charming stood over her cousin, his expression equally startled, though she detected a gleam of satisfaction in his eyes that belied his whispered, "Bloody hell."

She felt a hysterical giggle rise in her throat, but quickly swallowed it down. This was not a good situation. Not a good one at all, and yet how many times had she wanted to plant a facer to her cousin? Too many to count. That it had come during yet another of Ronnie's proposals was beyond perfect.

Except it wasn't perfect. Ronnie was likely to be her husband, and she couldn't really approve of people flattening him. So she schooled her face to be serious. "Mr. Anaedsley, I hardly think—"

"Sir, you are a cad and a…a monster!" Ronnie cried as he rubbed at his swelling jaw. "I was proposing!"

"I know," Mr. Anaedsley returned. "*Everybody* knows," he said as he looked pointedly at the servants dotting the hallway. What Mr. Anaedsley didn't realize is that Ronnie loved an audience for his romantic gestures. The more, the merrier.

"You haven't the right to interfere!" Ronnie gasped. Oh dear. He was exercising his righteous indignation, and that never ended well.

"Never mind that, Ronnie," she said as she reached forward to help her cousin stand. Or so she tried, but Mr. Anaedsley blocked her path. And when she attempted to move around him, he shifted to stop her. "Mr. Anaedsley, I assure you, this is not helpful."

He flashed her an odd look—part rueful chagrin, part gleeful miscreant. "You did beg me not to abandon you to your cousin's attention."

"I did not!" she said, though she wondered if perhaps she had.

Meanwhile, Ronnie was rising to his full and impressive height. His brows were drawn together, and his lips were curled back into a sneer. He looked fierce, and she took a step backward in surprise.

"Step away, Sir Monster," her cousin intoned, his tone dire.

Sir Monster?

The appellation obviously had no effect on Mr. Anaedsley. He simply raised his brows and shrugged. "I must insist that you stop importuning your cousin. She is not amenable to your suit, and—"

"Do we fight as gentlemen? Or as brutes?" Her

cousin's voice had dropped to a velvet threat, both soft and cold. It sounded very dramatic. And wholly unnecessary.

Melinda pasted on a placating smile. "Perhaps we should all retire to the parlor for some refreshments. Ronnie, I have especially requested those cakes you like—"

"I have no interest in cakes, my Mellie," he answered as he lifted his fists.

Damn it, this was spiraling out of control. First, she hated it when he called her "my Mellie." And second, it was clear he intended to brawl in the foyer.

Mr. Anacdsley must have seen it too. She watched him grimace in distaste, even as his fists came up in a defensive posture. Sadly, he had no way of knowing that Ronnie was extremely accomplished with his fists. And given his size advantage, Mr. Anaedsley was soon to be in a bad way.

Which meant she had to stop this now. Gathering all the strength she could muster in her voice, she snapped out her words like a sergeant issuing orders. "Ronald Gregory Smithson, you will cease this ridiculousness right now! You will not resort to fisticuffs in my hallway. Not in front of the servants and not with a future duke!"

Something flickered in Ronnie's eyes. Something wild and manic. It was in his gaze, in the pull of his lips back from his teeth, and in the way he suddenly opened his fists as if his fingers had springs. She didn't know what it was. Her cousin was prone to many romantic fits, but this was new. And she didn't completely trust new.

"Ronnie—" she began.

"As gentlemen then," her cousin said. And faster than she thought possible, he grabbed a pair of gloves off the table and smacked them across Mr. Anaedsley's face.

Whack!

The sound was floppy but no less loud as it reverberated off the marble floor and wood paneling. Melinda gasped, her gaze riveting to the red mark on Mr. Anaedsley's cheek.

"Oh no," she moaned, but Lord Charming smiled, though his eyes glittered menacingly. Melinda stepped forward. "Um, perhaps—"

"You're not supposed to use my gloves, you idiot. You're supposed to use your own."

Everyone looked to the pair of gloves in Ronnie's hand. Sure enough, they were Mr. Anaedsley's calfskin pair, not Ronnie's black leather pair.

Without a word, Ronnie set the calfskin aside, then moved for his own hat and gloves.

Mr. Anaedsley's voice cut cold and low through the hall. "Don't reach for those unless you mean it. Unless you mean pistols at dawn."

Ronnie would do it. Melinda knew without a shadow of a doubt that Ronnie would fight in some misguided romantic idea of a duel. And he would die that way. Or Mr. Anaedsley would, which would be especially awkward, as he was the grandson of a duke.

"Don't even think it," she said. "Either of you. Ronnie, if you so much as touch your gloves, I swear, I will…I will…" Damnation, it had to be something romantic, something appealing to his chivalric code. "I will drown myself in the lake."

That got both their attention. Ronnie's eyes widened and a softness came into them. "Would you? Would you really, my Mellie?" Lord, he actually sounded hopeful.

Mr. Anaedsley merely snorted. "There isn't a lake for miles."

Well, as if that was anything to the point! Didn't he understand she was trying to avoid backing Ronnie into a corner? "But there are streams."

"Not deep ones."

"They have rocks. I could dash my brains upon one."

"Of all the—"

"You won't if I win," Ronnie said, pulling himself up to his full height. "You'll see me defeat the monster and—"

"And jump from the tallest tree to dash my brains out upon the rocks. I despise violence. It is my guiding principle. If you fight, then I shall kill myself."

Mr. Anaedsley regarded her with a smirk trembling at the edge of his lips. "You do understand that killing oneself is still considered violence."

She glared at the man. "I am most determined."

"And what of my honor?" he challenged. "I have been insulted." He touched his reddened cheek for emphasis.

"You have no honor," bellowed Ronnie. And given his girth, he had quite a bellow. It made everyone in the hall flinch.

Meanwhile, Lord Charming straightened in mock

horror. "What a dishonorable thing to say! You, sir, are no gentleman!"

"Oh, stop goading him!" Melinda snapped. "He's quite serious. That's *his* guiding principle."

Mr. Anaedsley frowned. "Being serious? How is that a—"

"Deadly serious." She spoke it in accents of doom merely because she knew it would please her cousin and hopefully shift his thoughts away from duels. And in the meantime, maybe Mr. Anaedsley would take the hint. Ronnie was fully idiotic enough to follow through with an affair of honor if they didn't turn his thoughts aside. "Why I remember once when—"

Smack!

This time the sound wasn't floppy. It was the hard clap of something hitting a man's palm. It was loud and sharp, and it was Ronnie's gloves as Mr. Anaedsley caught them mere inches from his face.

"God, Ronnie," Melinda moaned. "Why would you do such a thing?" She knew the answer, and yet some questions had to be voiced, especially as the two men were now locked together—Ronnie's gloves gripped in Anaedsley's hand—while the two stared at one another like two tensing bulls.

Mr. Anaedsley spoke first. "I could kill you, you know," he said softly. "Pistols or swords, I can best you in minutes."

Melinda pushed forward aggressively this time. She knew better than to step between them, but she set her feet so both men could see her clearly. "And you'd have to flee to the Continent. Dueling is illegal. Good God, my father is the magistrate here!"

Ronnie's nostrils flared. "Fisticuffs then? I swear, I will not kill you."

Mr. Anaedsley's eyebrows rose, and his lips twitched in amusement. "What of my lady's hatred of violence?"

Ronnie rolled his eyes. He actually rolled his eyes at her. "Fisticuffs aren't violence. They're pugilism."

Mr. Anaedsley glanced at her. "Is that so? If we fight, you swear you will not dash yourself upon the rocks?"

She folded her arms in disgust. "I am more likely to cosh you both over the head while you sleep!"

The damned man did smile then. "That's not very sporting of you."

Ronnie seemed to agree. "And it would be violent. Really, Mellie, you don't truly abhor violence, do you?"

"Oh, I most certainly do. Otherwise you both would be dead by my hand at this very moment."

Both men nodded, apparently in complete agreement. And then by some secret man signal, they dropped their hands and straightened. Mr. Anaedsley thought to reassure her by flashing his charming smile. "See. All better," he said.

And Ronnie—damn his eyes—made so bold as to gesture to the parlor. "Shall we have some of those cakes, cousin? I'm suddenly feeling quite hungry."

❧

Trevor found her that night as she sipped brandy and stared out at the fireflies dancing across the back lawn. The other men had gone to bed, but she, as hostess, had remained awake—a constant, quiet presence who directed the staff and saw to their comfort. Once he might have discounted the skill it took to manage such a smooth-running household, but he knew what a hash his mother made of it, so he quietly marveled at her accomplishment.

"Shouldn't you be resting before your dawn *affaire d'honor*?" she asked, a bite to her tone.

He smiled. He should have realized she'd be aware of him standing at the door to her parlor. After all, he'd spent most of the day much too conscious of her. Even when deep in scientific discussion with her father, a part of him had tracked her movements with the staff, counted the minutes when Ronnie had trapped her in conversation, and even caught her frowning at him more than a dozen times.

"You have no need to cut up at me," he said as he moved into the delightful parlor at the back of house. "My sacrifice saved you from an unwanted proposal."

She shot him an irritated glare. "Ronnie proposes on every visit. I assure you, practice has made me skilled at deflecting his attention."

"But it's gotten harder, hasn't it?"

She didn't answer except to look out the window. He watched her profile in the moonlight, seeing her pert nose and long lashes. Her skin tended to a plebeian light brown, but in the moonlight, she nearly glowed. And with her hair curling around her cheeks, he saw how very beautiful she could be. That realization drew him to sit on the settee beside her.

"I do not want you to protect my honor," she said as he found his seat.

"You are worried about tomorrow's fight. I promise you, I shall not hurt your cousin overmuch."

"You? Hurt him?" She gaped at him. "Good God, you are a fool. You think because you are heir to a dukedom that no man can touch you. Ronnie will take great pleasure in touching you, sir. Indeed he will not stop pummeling you until you are sent to the hospital!"

"You are worried for me!" he said with no small amount of pleasure. "But there isn't any need. Ronnie did not hurt me this afternoon—"

"You caught him by surprise."

"And tomorrow will be no different."

She stared at him, her expression darkening by the second. "He has two stone on you and nearly six inches more reach. His feet are nimble despite his larger size, and you, sir, are blinded by arrogance."

He tilted his head, surprised by her yet again. "You know something of boxing?"

She pursed her lips in distaste. "I spent the afternoon in study of it."

"Indeed?"

"Yes, indeed. While you were deep in conversation with my father, I was with Ronnie prompting him to share his plans. He sees tomorrow's fight as an affair of honor—"

"And so it is."

"And so he intends to put you down." She shot him a worried look. "Those were his very words: *put the cheeky bastard down.*"

He leaned back on the settee, enjoying the rare experience of a woman worrying after his health. It put him in charity with her as never before. "It is a simple schoolboy fight. They happen all the time."

"You are both grown men."

"Who sometimes wish to revisit their childhood glory."

She sighed, and her attention turned back to the window. He settled in beside her, wishing he had his own glass of brandy, but loathe to leave her side. He didn't spend much time thinking about his reasons for sitting there. Instead, he studied the strange position of the furniture, occupying his thoughts with the odd way she had arranged the room.

The settee, for example, was angled so she could curl up near enough to the fire to read, but facing the window rather than the door. In truth, just about every table and chair in this small room turned its back on the door in favor of viewing the dark vista outside.

"This is not a very welcoming room," he mused aloud.

"Then you need not stay," she returned.

He chuckled, not at all put out by her ill temper now that he knew it stemmed from concern. "I do not criticize," he said honestly. "I simply note that this is a room that is not designed for company but solitary enjoyment of the view." He frowned as he peered through the window. She looked out over grass and then wood. "The autumn leaves must be quite spectacular."

"All the seasons are spectacular in some way or another," she answered more quietly. He was pleased the bite had disappeared from her tone. "And this is not the visiting parlor, but my own sanctuary."

"So you arranged things to please yourself. I quite

understand. I recall trying to do that with my bedroom once as a boy."

She tilted her head to look more closely at him. "What did you do?"

"Put my bed under the window, my toys within easy reach, and a chair to block the door."

"Ah."

"Yes, it was that last one that ended any wish to move furniture again."

"Well, at least you got to move your bed to the window."

"Oh no. It was all returned to proper order."

"Proper?" She tilted her head as she looked at him, and another one of her curls escaped her pins. It bounced quite distractingly against her cheek. "Is there an improper way to set furniture?"

"Oh yes. And as my father's heir I was to set everything in the darkest corner on a raised dais, and not have any toys at all to hand. Honestly, I didn't care about the window. I just wanted my toys."

"Did they belong in the nursery?"

"Naturally."

"And little boys—"

"Were not allowed to barricade themselves in their bedrooms. I was set to eat gruel for a month as punishment."

"Surely not."

"Surely so. That was always the punishment in our home." It was, in fact, his mother's way of saving on the food bill, but it was some time before he realized the truth. "It worked, by the way. To this day, I cannot contemplate gruel without total horror."

"And you never again rearranged the furniture?"

"Never." He was silent a moment, running through what he wanted to say. Was it smart? Was it his best option? He had no answers for those questions—only a burning need to find a solution to his difficulties. If it also aided her, then why not give in to the unusual idea? But first he had to have an answer to one very specific question.

"Miss Smithson, I have a question for you. A truly impertinent one, I might add, but I pray you answer it honestly."

She shifted in her seat, her gaze and her body disconcertingly direct. She faced him, she watched him, and she waited with an air of a scientific study. It most forcibly reminded him of her father when he dissected beetles in their various stages of development.

"Er," he began, pulling his thoughts together as quickly as possible. "I wish to know…do you intend to marry your cousin?"

She blinked…once. "I already told you that I don't love him. Most times I don't even *like* him."

He nodded. "Yes, yes, but do you intend to marry him?"

He watched her purse her lips in thought as her gaze turned toward the window again. "That is the question, is it not? Everyone seems to wish for the union. Even my father. His health is not the best, you know, and he worries what will become of me."

Yes, he had noted her father's pallor. "He did not cough overmuch today."

She nodded. "Five times this day. But then it

mostly troubles him at night when he tries to sleep. And that prevents him from resting as he ought."

He nodded, his concern for his mentor momentarily overriding his other thoughts. But a minute later, he returned to her. "You have no other suitors, then? No gentlemen whom you fancy?"

He watched her jaw tighten as if she bit back an acerbic comment, and no wonder. His questions were highly impertinent.

"No, Mr. Anaedsley, there is no other gentleman whom I could reasonably expect to marry." Then she sighed, and her gaze focused on the night scene beyond her window. There was nothing there. Even the moonlight had deserted it, but she gazed out and her words drifted between them. "As a child I dreamt of love and thought of princes who would carry me away to my castle. It was ridiculous, of course, because we had so little money, and you were the only male of my acquaintance even close to a prince."

Her tone of voice indicated he was a preposterous choice, and though his vanity was pricked, his mind agreed completely with her assessment. As a boy, he'd thought her gawky and completely untutored in the ways of what a real girl should do. Real females, in his young opinion, should wear ribbons and pretty dresses. They should not read books, and certainly not be better at his lessons than he was.

"I was a complete idiot as a boy," he said, "and so you are forgiven for not wanting me to carry you off."

She might have snorted in response, but as she was sipping her brandy, he couldn't be sure of her response.

"So you have not met any other princes?"

"Worse," she said in a dry tone. "Ronnie is determined to become my prince."

Yes, he could see that her cousin's romantic nature would attach to her childhood desire.

"And even more than that," she continued. "We made all this money. Suddenly I am managing a big house, we have all these servants, and we live here in the country."

"I like it here." In truth, he loved it here away from the bustle of London. A man could study science in peace without constantly being badgered to choose a bride and continue the family line.

"But no one here will marry up to a woman like me, and none of your set will marry down."

"That's not true," he said, thinking through her difficulty. "There are many who would marry a well-dowered girl."

"But you are the only aristocrat who comes here." Her tone said quite clearly that he was still completely off her list as a potential husband. "And I haven't the money to go elsewhere."

"That can't be right. You have gads of money." Her uncle ran a mill that brought in thousands of pounds a year.

She turned to glare at him. "My father has money. My uncle has money. I have nothing."

It took him only a moment to assemble the pieces, to fit the cogs into the wheels that turned this situation. She had been furious with him this morning for interrupting her demonstration of a new cosmetic, one that would garner them money. Or more accurately: garner *her* money.

"That's why you won't give over the formula unless you earn the money. You wish to travel then, in the way of Lady Stanhope?"

Her mouth opened in surprise as if she couldn't believe he'd guessed her plans. But her next words contradicted his guess. "Nothing so grand as an archeological expedition."

She was looking away from him then, curling her fingers about her brandy glass though she didn't drink. Clearly she had a plan, although she was loathe to tell him. But he had a very curious mind, especially when people didn't act as he expected. "Come, come. You must tell me what you want. Otherwise how can I help?"

"Why would you help me?" she challenged.

"Because I suspect we can help one another." She looked up sharply, but before she could ask, he held her off. "I will explain my thoughts in a moment. First, you must tell me—specifically—what you want."

"A lot of money."

"Why?"

"So I can travel. So…" She drained her brandy glass. "So I can meet men."

Ah. So it was as he suspected. She was desperate for a means to find someone other than Ronnie. "What kind of men, exactly?"

She shook her head. "Not men in general. I am looking for one man." Then she looked at him, and for a moment he saw the little girl he remembered from a decade ago. One who loved spending time with her father and hated that he was the not-as-bright interloper student her father adored. One who wore her heart on her sleeve and apparently wished for something all little girls dream of. And then, lest he miss it, she said the words out loud. "I want to fall in love with a man and him with me. I want children and a happy home. I want to live happily ever after."

"Well, you definitely won't get that with Ronnie."

She nodded morosely as her gaze went back out the window. Not just out the window, he realized, but in the direction of London. "Your father won't let you go to London? To have a Season?"

She lifted her chin, slid pretend glasses down her nose, and looked at him in exactly the manner that her father would take. "As a wealthy cit on display? You would hate it, my dear. All of them are gamblers and whoremongers. Best to marry Ronnie. At least poetry will not burn through your dowry."

His eyebrows rose. "Your father does not have a very flattering opinion of my set."

"Don't most gentlemen of your set spend their time gambling and womanizing? Discussing the cut of their clothing and planning elaborate amusements out of boredom?"

A true hit. "Not all gentlemen do such. Some run the country or the Exchange. Some are diplomats and scholars."

"And so I told him, but…" She shrugged. "He wants me to marry Ronnie. It will keep the money in the family."

"But you want to have money so you can go on your own?"

"I want my own money to go anywhere, Mr.

Anaedsley. Anywhere at all that has men who might love me."

"London has all the best men," he said, seeing how he could get her to fall exactly into his plans.

She dropped her head back against her chair. "But I have no sponsor. Even if I had the money of my own, I have no *entre* into society."

"On the contrary," he said. "You know me."

"You are hardly an appropriate chaperone."

"Quite true, but I have friends who would help if I asked." He flashed her his most charming smile. "I can be rather persuasive when I want."

She turned to frown at him, but hope sparked in her eyes. "You would do that for me? You would be persuasive on my behalf?"

"Of course I would," he said, excitement bright in his heart.

"But why?"

He grinned. If he was to do this thing, then he should by all rights do it completely. And so he dropped to one knee before her, imitating the exact pose her cousin had been in not twelve hours before.

"I would do it," he said, "if you would become my affianced bride."

Three

Rakes are tricky beasts who always have a plan.

MELLIE STARED AT THE MAN AT HER FEET, AND HER mind refused to comprehend. Mr. Anaedsley, the future Duke of Timby, was on his knees before her with a mischievous twinkle in his eyes. It made no sense. What he'd said... He couldn't be serious, and yet some part of her understood exactly what was happening and was beyond thrilled. Her heart beat in her throat, and the joy that tingled in her stomach was going to make her ill.

Lord Charming was asking her to be his bride.

"But...but..." she babbled.

"Yes?" he prompted, his grin widening. He had the attitude of a man making a joke, but this was no joke. Not to her.

"But you don't like me!"

"I know," he said. His eyes were definitely dancing now. "And you don't like me."

Well, that wasn't exactly true. She thought him mischievous and unfocused and...well, and an aristocrat.

Which meant he was generally a useless person living a life of selfish pleasure. He didn't study. He didn't lead. He simply gadded about doing whatever struck his fancy.

Useless. He was useless, and yet for the first time in her life, she thought that useless might not be so bad. Not when it came with a smile and a twinkle. Not when he could make her laugh and offered to save her from her cousin. Given that, useless might look like chivalry.

"Mr. Anaedsley…" she began, but she didn't know what to say. She didn't want him to sacrifice himself to rescue her. And yet, part of her did. Part of her wanted it most desperately.

He laughed, then lightly jumped back onto his seat. "Sorry. Couldn't stay down there long. It's too hard on the knee."

She blinked and nodded. She didn't want him hurting his knee. But…

He had just proposed to her! Her mind finally latched onto that one fact. Marriage. To Mr. Anaedsley.

"I—" she began, not knowing in the least what she wanted to say.

"Don't answer. Not until you've heard me out."

She closed her mouth. That was the least she could do.

"You suffer from a lack of options. You have not met enough gentlemen to attract the right man."

She barely heard his words. She kept thinking. He was the grandson of a duke. Why would he propose to her? Especially since he just said he didn't like her. It made no sense, and so she set her free hand to her mouth, pushing her lips hard against her teeth to prevent any sound from escaping.

"What you don't know," he said, "because I have taken great pains to hide the fact, is that I am woefully short on funds." He still held her right hand, and he began to idly rub her knuckles as he spoke. It seemed a casual gesture, one he did without thought, and yet she felt every pass of his thumb as if he were scraping against her open heart. "Do you remember my favorite mare? The chestnut one that I usually ride when coming to visit?"

She nodded, barely able to follow his conversation. "You said your father requested it for some hunt."

"I lied. I sold her. Broke my heart to do it, but she went to a good home."

"Oh. I'm sorry."

"Yes," he said mournfully. Clearly the loss of his horse affected him more deeply than the request for her hand. "My carriage went too, though I didn't mind so much. Always thought it a waste in the city anyway. I much prefer to ride."

Again, she bobbed her head as if she knew what he was talking about. Then it hit her. Her dowry. Of course! And how stupid of her. Many gentlemen would condescend to marry a cit if the dowry were large enough. She just never thought he would be one of them.

"So the dukedom has fallen onto hard times?" She could barely fathom it. Certainly many titles were struggling, but he always seemed so flush.

"Not a bit. The family coffers are quite full, truth be told. It's just that my grandfather has cut me off."

She blinked. Cut him off? "But why?" Was it gambling? That was the normal way of things, but he'd never spoken of gambling. And when he visited, his conversation was all about science and engineering.

He sighed, the sound coming from deep inside him. "Grandfather is all up in the boughs about me marrying. Have to carry on the title and all that rot. My father's as healthy as a horse, but as I don't have a brother, it's up to me to marry and produce a number three in line for the dukedom." He leaned forward. "My grandfather would die of apoplexy if he thought the title might go to my French cousin. That's something you and I have in common, by the way."

"What?"

"Difficult cousins. Though in my case, my cousin really is off in the head. Can barely tie his shoes. They've got a nurse on him and all that, so he's comfortable enough, but his brain never progressed to the point of…well, of a normal boy, much less a duke. Broke my aunt's heart, but there was a problem with the birth and he was hurt somehow."

"Oh," she said, her head feeling light. "How very sad for her. For your family."

Mr. Anaedsley shrugged. It was not important, apparently, except in that the duke would die of apoplexy if the boy stood in line to inherit.

"Please," she said, her voice very small. "If you would explain—"

"Oh yes. Of course." He was still rubbing her fingers, but this time he added a squeeze. "Grandfather's cut off all my money unless I find a bride. No allowance, no bills paid, not even the tab at our club. Not a penny unless I hitch myself to a woman."

Her mouth went very dry. Did he want her? Of all the ladies he knew, he picked her? A cit? She was certainly wealthy enough, but it sounded like his grandfather would start paying his bills again the moment he married. It made no sense.

"I thought I had it worked out," he continued. "Got an investment in an emerald mine. A friend of mine from school found the place, and together we worked out a new way to get them out of the earth. I thought we'd be seeing a profit already, but it's deuced expensive to begin and has taken three times as long as I expected."

"Oh. That must be most awkward."

He rolled his eyes. "It's been terribly awkward. I've survived by going to parties and the like, but a man can live off society for only so long before some enterprising mama snares him. I am set to inherit a dukedom, you know. Stirs female minds everywhere into heights of devious treachery."

Her patience was wearing thin, so she jerked her hand back from his distracting caress and glared at him. "Yes, well, I am not so devious, and you are the one who just proposed to me. So…so, what are you about, Mr. Anaedsley? I cannot believe you have suddenly tumbled into love with me."

"Certainly not!" he said with an insulting amount of shock.

"Then I fail to see—"

"I need time," he answered, "for my investment to come in. And you need a sponsor to meet other gentlemen. Second sons and the like. Ones who would be more than happy to wed you without writing poetry."

She wished she didn't feel so stupid around him. "And how does that lead to you on your knee before me?"

"Because we should get engaged. My grandfather will open the coffers, giving me time for my investment to profit. I know of just the person to sponsor you, and so you will be going to rounds, meeting all sorts of eligible men."

"But as your fiancée!"

"Well, naturally. But Lady Eleanor won't take you under her wing any other way but as a favor to me."

She frowned. Lady Eleanor? As in the daughter of the Duke of Bucklynde. Even Mellie had heard of that august personage. It had been in all the papers that her male relations had died of some fever, and a nobody seaman had inherited the title. "But why would she help me?"

"As a favor to me. And because she needs a spot of cash herself. So if we offer to pay her and bring her in on the secret—"

"What secret?" she nearly screamed.

"That you're going to cry off at the end of the Season. Don't you see how perfect it is? You and I become engaged. Grandfather allows me enough money to survive until my investments come in. You go round to the parties, meeting all sorts of gentlemen, while I remain completely safe from those nefarious females. And at the end—when my money arrives— you cry off, marry the gentleman of your choice, and

I can finally tell the duke to go to the devil. That I'll marry when and where I choose and not before."

She understood it now. This had not been a true proposal, he had no wish to marry her, and it was all a trick. That the trick was on his family and not on her made not the least bit of difference to her heart. She didn't even like the man, and yet she felt humiliated to be used in such a fashion. To receive a proposal and then be gleefully informed that it was a sham. As if she were of no more importance than his horse. Less importance, in fact, because she was simply a tool to evade matchmaking mamas and foil his father's plans.

"You are an odious man," she hissed out. "Absolutely odious."

He reared back, obviously shocked by her disgust. And that, of course, damned him even more in her eyes.

"But…but don't you see how it works? It is a perfect fitting—you and me."

"Not as an engaged couple!"

"But you don't like me and I don't like you. The two of us will never suit, and we have both said as much to one another. Repeatedly!"

Of course that was true. She had said as much and often. If not out loud, then at least in her thoughts.

"So that makes us the perfect pair for this," he continued. "I cannot do this with a woman who might develop a tendre for me. That would be too cruel, and I couldn't be sure that she would cry off at the end of the Season."

"Well, there is no need to fear. I will certainly not develop any tendre for you. I'd rather kiss a snake."

"Exactly!" he said as if she finally understood. "There is no fear of softer feelings between us. And as far as the scandal, my family will be in alt when you cry off."

"In alt!"

"Well, you are a bit of a step down for me. We'll have to claim a passionate love affair, overcome by our emotions and some such rot, but all they'll see is the mésalliance. So when you cry off, they will be so relieved as to not care about the scandal."

"And what about me? What about the scandal attached to my name? I will have cried off from a future duke."

He shrugged. "And how could a scandal bother you? You don't travel in the social rounds. Whatever man you choose will be thrilled to have a wealthy bride no matter the scandal. And won't that be a grand romantic gesture? You throwing off a duke's heir to marry a second son. Bound to stroke any man's ego."

She stared at him, appalled that his words were beginning to make sense. Setting aside the insult, he did have the right of it. She could meet scores of eligible gentlemen, ones that she could never touch any other way. It would allow her to find an alternative to Ronnie. And if they were all useless fribbles as she feared, then she could easily turn her back on Lord Charming and give herself to Ronnie. Her cousin would certainly take her back and likely see it as just the grand romantic gesture that he adored.

Mr. Anaedsley grinned. "You are thinking of it. I can see it in your eyes."

"You can see nothing but revulsion." She was

speaking too harshly to him, but she couldn't stop herself. Her heart had been twisted about too much for her to speak civilly just yet.

"Miss Smithson. Mellie…" He reached for her hand again, but she snatched it away. She couldn't think with his hands on her, so she stood to pace about her parlor. This was her sanctuary, the place where she came to be at peace. And now, as she walked back and forth by the settee, all she could see was Lord Charming sitting there like a veritable prince, his body calm and his expression animated. He was excited and obviously had no doubt as to her agreement to his mad plan.

Well, he was far out on that. She was an honest woman and a deception like this…

"Your only other choice is Ronnie. Do you really wish to chain yourself to him without even looking at other men? You could fall in love, Mellie. You might meet another man of science. I do know a few. One who might allow you to study and work however you want. I swear, I shall introduce you to every one."

Her steps slowed as her mind started churning. He was right, damn his eyes. This was exactly why she'd wanted her own money—so she could stop being a recluse with her father and meet eligible gentlemen. He was offering her the chance to go to London. And not just travel to the great city but to have a Season on the marriage mart, where ladies and gentlemen were thrown together with the hope of making an excellent connection.

But could she do it? It was all so devious. "What would my father say?" she wondered aloud.

"I'd think he'd be in the boughs with delight. Not every day a daughter gets engaged to a future duke."

She shot him a glare. "And when I cry off?"

"Then you shall introduce him to your true choice in husband and convince him that the new man is the better match. He will be, you know. A better choice for you. And your father is a man of logic. He'll see that you and I would never fit."

"Stop saying it that way." It made her feel like a toad, the way he so gleefully dismissed her.

Then he stood up and came around the settee. She would have resumed pacing away from him, but what was the point? He was here, and she was despicably aware of him no matter where she stood in the room. Which is why she didn't argue when he possessed her hands again.

"I see that I shouldn't have proposed like that, on one knee like Ronnie did. It put you too much in mind of him."

That wasn't it at all, but she didn't argue.

"I should have outlined the scheme logically. Shown you the advantage of it first, and then done the pretty as a nice touch at the end. But I couldn't resist the jest, you know. I thought you'd laugh when you understood it."

"I have never understood your amusements," she said.

"I know. That's another reason you are the perfect choice. If you can't laugh with a man, then there's no hope for a future."

She nodded. It was true. She saw that clearly even if her heart did not. Her heart was suffering from a lack of choices. With the only two gentlemen in her circle being Lord Charming and Ronnie, of course it would leap at him. But she was a thinking person, not a foolish girl led about by her emotions, and so she thought about his proposal.

"You are sure Lady Eleanor will sponsor me?"

"Absolutely."

"And I will meet plenty of eligible bachelors?"

"Scores of them. I vow it."

She nodded slowly and watched his eyes light with excitement.

"You'll do it?"

Could she? Did she dare?

"Yes, Mr. Anaedsley, I shall do it. I shall be your fake fiancée and then take great pleasure in crying off. I hope you are completely humiliated when I spurn you."

"Excellent!" he cried.

And then he kissed her.

❧

What was he doing? The question spun through Trevor's brain for about two seconds before logical thought completely stopped. All he'd really seen was how pretty she looked in the moonlight, how her hair curled so perfectly by her ear, and how her lips were moist and inviting. So he'd taken the invitation without thought to the consequences.

It started in the usual way. The lady gasped in surprise, and that naturally allowed him entrance. He deepened the kiss automatically, thrusting inside and pulling her closer. Her head had to tip back, which gave him the superior position as he dominated her head and body. He tasted, he toyed, and he took from her before she had the wherewithal to refuse. It was the way a future duke kissed, and he was well practiced.

Except, apparently, she was practiced as well. She closed her mouth—a little, just enough to threaten his tongue. His blood surged at the threat, and his fingers tightened, holding her to his will. She fought him for a moment, her hands hard where they clutched his shoulders. But as he thrust into her mouth, she arched into his body, dropping her head back.

In that small movement, she gave him dominion, and he set out to plunder her with a different mind-set. Where before he had taken, now he set to a skillful dance of advance and retreat. In and out, he played, easily besting her until he found himself burning with a fire wholly unexpected. His heart was pounding in his ears, his hands were shifting to support her so he could take her to the floor, and most damning of all, his organ was hot and hard where he rubbed himself against her skirts.

The speed of this inferno stunned him, and he broke from her in shock before he lost himself to her fire.

He stepped back harshly, his breath coming in great gasps. She was clutching onto him so she followed, though she didn't pursue the kiss. She too was breathing heavily, and that was the only sound in the room. Two people gasping in the most erotic of rasps he had ever heard.

He swallowed and made to straighten his jacket, but his hands would not move from her body. He was locked into supporting her until she found her legs. She did eventually, while he fought the hunger to pull her back to his kiss, and to a great deal more. He was just giving into his baser nature when she pushed herself away. His fingers were wrenched open, and he made a sound low in his throat. It was not a noise he had ever made before, and the feel of it—deep and guttural—appalled him. He was not a beast, for God's sake.

He looked at her, seeing the rosy flush to her cheeks, the wet red of her lips, and he nearly lost himself to her again. But then she turned her face away and half stumbled to the settee. She fell upon the cushion without grace, and he was flooded with images of her hair in a wild tangle, her skirts at her hips, and himself plunging into her again and again.

"What are you doing?" she gasped. Her tone was accusing, and he took that for a well-deserved remonstrance. After all, he was half ready to leap upon her and damn the consequences. That ought to give him pause. Some things could not be forgiven, and this was one of them. And yet, he looked at her with her wide eyes and disheveled skirts, and he wanted her as he had never wanted a woman before.

"You have done this before," he said, his words harsh. He did not intend to accuse her. Indeed, his fury was all for himself, but she took it as the words sounded.

"You attacked me!" she shot back.

"That was hardly an attack," he returned, a sneer entering his voice completely unbidden. Sometimes his grandfather's voice came out of his mouth at the worst possible times.

"Do not blame this on me!" she said, her voice growing stronger and her hands steadier as they smoothed her skirts.

He didn't. He couldn't. And yet, he didn't feel entirely to blame either. After all, her kiss had been incendiary. He took a moment to steady himself. He needed to take stock before he further aggravated the situation. He straightened his waistcoat, he fixed his cravat, and he did his best to hide his erection from her view. She didn't appear to be looking in that direction, but damnation…her kiss. That was no maiden's kiss.

"Where did you learn to do that?" He tried to keep the hauteur out of his tone and succeeded for the most part. But he had to know just how seasoned she was.

"Did you think I could age to four and twenty and not experience a kiss or two?" Scorn dripped from her words, a match for his earlier hauteur.

"A kiss or two? Balderdash." He had kissed courtesans who had less skill. "What the devil is your father about, letting you learn such a thing?"

She snorted—a most unladylike sound. "My father is about his bugs, as you well know. I have been in charge of my own education since I was eight."

"That is not the sort of thing a gently reared girl should learn." He didn't know why he was arguing the point. Only that he was unsettled, and harsh words were his only means of release. Which was ridiculous. Before today, he'd never really thought twice about her. This was the place he came for science, not dalliance. And she usually busied herself with other tasks when he visited. Since he and her father were wont to take their meals in the laboratory, he had barely been in her company at all since she was twelve.

How he came from barely noticing her to being a hare's breath away from ruining her on a settee was beyond his powers of understanding. And yet it was true. Indeed, part of him was insistently pushing him to finish what they had begun.

"Why did you kiss me?" she asked, her voice betraying true distress. "Especially if…if…"

He looked at her, seeing her beautiful mahogany eyes shining too bright in the moonlight. "If what?" he asked quietly.

"If you did not want me to kiss you back?"

He had no answer for that, and so he turned the conversation back in on itself. "How did you come by this skill, Mellie?" He used her father's nickname for her because he thought it would help ease the personal nature of the conversation.

"Was I…was I very good at it?"

How to answer that beyond the obvious? "Yes."

She nodded once to herself as if confirming a suspicion. "I have kissed three boys in total. Two are inconsequential. The third, however…" A fond smile played about her lips. He made a strangled sound, and she glanced his way, her cheeks heating. "I was sixteen, and he was the chandler's son."

"You kissed a candle maker?" The words were strangled as he fought an irrational fury.

"A great many times. It was summer and…and I don't know. He was fun. He called me pretty. I think I would have married him if he'd asked."

"He didn't?" Damned idiot boy. He could have

snagged himself an heiress. And a woman who kissed like she enjoyed it.

"Papa forbade it when he found out. And..." Her voice grew pensive as she stared out at the night sky. "Even then I knew I was just looking for someone who wasn't Ronnie." Then she shrugged. "Besides, as much as I liked him, he had the most minimal understanding of mathematics and was completely hopeless in natural history. That's why we spent most of our time kissing. There was so little else to discuss."

Thank God for idiot chandlers. And how awful that she'd spent so much of her life looking for an alternative to her cousin. Still, the whole thing soured his stomach even though he knew it shouldn't. After all, that was exactly what he'd offered her: a chance to find someone other than Ronnie. He couldn't blame her for using all her whiles to ensnare someone else. And yet, somehow he did. He blamed her even as he pushed for all the details.

"And what else did this chandler's son teach you beyond kissing?"

"How to make candles," she said. Her glare was venomous. "But that's not what you want to know, is it? Though I don't see why you have the right to ask."

"Because I am your fiancé!" he shot back. The words echoed loudly in the room, and they stared at one another in a kind of suspended horror. It was true. They were engaged now. He had asked, and she had accepted. It was all a ruse, but indeed...they were affianced.

He watched as she swallowed, her skin pale. Her

fingers entwined tight enough to make her knuckles white.

"Oh," she said softly. "I beg your pardon. Of course you have the right to know."

Except he didn't. Not really. Not when their engagement was a lie. He didn't say that aloud though. He was too interested in her answer.

"James and I kissed. Just…kissed. I knew not to go further, and he was gentleman enough not to press. And truthfully, it was only a few weeks before Papa realized and put a stop to it."

At least her father had paid some attention. But bloody hell, the dangers to an innocent girl wandering about the countryside were legion. He shuddered to think what might have happened. "What became of this chandler's brat?"

She shot him an annoyed look. "You have no cause to call him names. He married one of the local girls the very next year. They have three children now and are very happy."

Did he detect a note of longing in her voice? Or perhaps the better term was "loneliness." He had not stopped to think what her life must have been like here, secluded and waiting hand and foot on her father. The man had enough care to forbid the local men, but not enough presence of mind to be sure she met gentlemen other than her cousin.

"I beg your pardon," he said as he joined her on the settee.

She tilted her head and more of her curls escaped their pins. The whole mass would come tumbling down around her ears soon, and he found himself hopeful for the event. He waited while she looked at him, her eyes steady and no longer shiny with suppressed tears. He waited even longer, but she said nothing in response to his apology.

He deserved that, he supposed. He was the one to kiss her and the one to rudely demand she account for herself. Therefore it was up to him to make amends.

"I suppose I am unaccustomed to being engaged. I have behaved badly."

"By kissing me?"

Yes. No. Bloody hell, but he couldn't make himself regret that kiss. "By being impetuous. It's my gravest fault, you see. Sometimes I just act without thinking."

"Ah," she said. Nothing more. Damn, she was hard to read, and he was accounted a good judge of people and faces.

He shifted to look at her more fully. "You haven't changed your mind, have you? About our engagement?"

She shook her head, then looked at him. "Have you?"

"Lord, no. I've been casting about for a solution for weeks now. But..." He looked at her lips. He looked at the way she twisted her hands in her skirts. And he was excruciatingly aware of his still throbbing erection. "But no more kissing, I think."

"I assure you, James and I haven't kissed in years."

He frowned. "I, um, I meant us."

Her lips twitched. "Yes, I know."

She was teasing him. The minx had deliberately misconstrued his words. Damnation, how could she be so composed when his blood still ran hot with lust?

He dropped back against the cushions and regarded her darkly.

"It occurs to me that you and I don't know each other very well."

She quirked an eyebrow at him, but did not speak.

He felt his jaw clench. "You have been cutting up at me all day. Do not become taciturn now. It ill becomes you."

"Mr. Anaedsley, we have known each other nearly all our lives."

Perhaps. But he had only vaguely been aware of her. And now he wondered if he had missed something—someone—special. An odd thought to be sure. Meanwhile, she unclasped her hands and made an open gesture.

"What is it you wish to know?"

Damnation, this was ridiculous. He didn't know what he wanted to know. If he did, he'd know it already. He huffed out a breath, completely at a loss.

"Mr. Anaedsley—"

"Trevor. We are affianced, Mellie. At least call me by my Christian name.

She nodded. It was a rather regal dip of her chin. Quite refined, come to think of it. "Very well, Trevor. Might I make a suggestion?"

"I would welcome it."

"We shall spend a great deal of time together in the next few weeks. To start with, there is the carriage ride to London. Then the preparations for the Season, not to mention all the parties and the like."

He nodded, though he suspected she had no idea exactly how busy she would be during the Season. His sisters were not yet out, but he had friends who had told him of the military-like campaigns females waged during this time of year.

"Perhaps," she continued, "we should delay the personal inquiries until tomorrow."

He tilted his head. "Are you trying to be rid of me?"

"Dawn comes very early," she said softly.

"What of it?" He rarely went to bed before three.

"Fisticuffs at dawn?" she prompted.

The duel. "I'd completely forgotten." He studied her face, noting the fine lines of worry. "I swear I shall not hurt your cousin overmuch."

She sighed, the sound coming from deep within her. "Go get some sleep, Mr. Anaedsley. One can only hope that the rest will revive your brain."

Right. She thought he was going to lose. "I will not lose a fistfight to a poet. The very idea verges on insult."

She stood up from the settee. As he was still sprawled upon it, she looked very intimidating as she glared down at him. "You have promised to rescue me from my cousin. I shall be very cross with you if your injuries tomorrow prevent that from happening."

"But—"

"Oh, go to bed, Trevor!" she snapped. "Perhaps in the morning you will be less of a damned fool!" And with that she swept from the room.

"Impressive woman," he said to no one at all. "Definitely worthy of a second son. Most definitely."

He spent the next few hours musing on her charms and enjoying his host's fine brandy. Which is why,

a scant four hours later, he was squinting at the pre-
dawn sky and wondering why in the devil his valet
had woken him.

Four

Allow him a few masculine amusements, but in no circumstance should you participate.

MELLIE WRAPPED HER CLOAK TIGHT AGAINST THE morning chill. There was no mist, thank God, but the field was wet and the cow pies pungent. She had hoped that the fight would be a quiet affair. That was the whole point of having it at dawn, wasn't it? Except it appeared that half the county had come to see the spectacle of the duke's grandson fighting one of their own. That Ronnie wasn't one of the local villagers didn't seem to matter. Ronnie had been knocking about the place since she and her father had come to live here a decade ago. That made him one of the locals, though only in respect to a fight against a lord who had never been about at all.

Ronnie stood in the center of the crowd, enjoying the attention as he pumped his arms back and forth, stamped his feet, and generally milked up all the hubbub. He kept looking to her, standing with her cloak about her face, as if searching for her approval.

She wasn't going to give it, so he might as well look to the tavern maids prancing about. She'd even told him exactly that, in exactly those words, not ten minutes before when she'd tried to talk some sense into her cousin.

But the man loved the drama of an *affaire d'honor*—apparently it was more important when spoken in French—and that made him stubborn. The fight would proceed as planned. If only the opponent would appear.

Ronnie was in the midst of his third overloud speculation on the cowardice of the aristocracy when Mr. Anaedsley appeared. He looked well turned out as he always did, but the skin beneath his eyes was shadowed, and he shot annoyed glances at the bright sunlight.

Overindulged in her father's brandy, had he? Well, it served him right. She had told him to go to bed. She had warned him of Ronnie's intention to beat him insensate. If after all that, he chose to ignore her advice, then she washed her hands of him. Except, of course, she didn't. Her belly was knotted with anxiety, and her hands gripped the edges of her cloak tight enough to poke holes in the fabric.

"Ho, ho!" Ronnie called when he spotted his opponent. "Is it a little early in the day for you? This is the time when decent folk are up and about their business."

Loud catcalls greeted that statement, and Mellie watched Trevor wince even as he grinned with good-natured aplomb. "True enough!" he said. "I'm not one for an early day, never have been. But I'm here now. I acknowledge the grave insult I did to your person, stopping you from proposing to a woman who doesn't want you. But I was wrong, and so I am here to atone for my sin."

"Churl!" Ronnie said, throwing his arm forward to point hard at Trevor's face. "You know nothing of us here. You are an interloper and a cad!"

Trevor clutched his chest as if wounded. "Oh sir, I cry guilty to being an interloper. But as for me not knowing women…" He turned and winked broadly at one of the more notorious bawds in the county. "On that mark, I say I am well versed."

Good God, they were acting as if this were a performance at a theater. Even the bawd—Grace was her name—knew to blush prettily as she dropped into a curtsy. "Lawks, sir, but he does."

There was a rush of bawdy comments after that, and Trevor played to every one of them. He acted like a bored roué, and Melinda found her teeth grinding in annoyance. Apparently, Ronnie didn't like it either as he tried to regain control of the crowd.

"Fie, sir! You speak of the base pleasures of the flesh."

"That I do!" returned Trevor.

"But I refer to the lofty expression of love. Of man and woman in the pure state of godly adoration."

"Oh, I adore. I assure you, I adore."

The crowd roared at that, but Melinda felt her body tense for an entirely different reason. These two men were playing a game here. It was all a farce of fighting, of Ronnie's proposal and her godly adoration, whatever that was. They acted as if her marriage was a stage play where all the county got to watch and laugh.

She hated it, and she hated both men for subjecting her to it.

So with a grunt of disgust she started to turn away. But she had forgotten that everyone here knew who she was. She was covered in a cloak, but that did nothing to hide her identity among people who had known her for half her life. The minute she turned away, she found the path blocked. No one wished for her to leave, and it took only a moment's commotion to attract Ronnie's attention.

"My fair darling, pray don't abandon me in my hour of triumph!"

She gave up trying to push between the baker's wife and his three daughters. So she turned around and threw back the hood of her cloak. She might as well enjoy the sun on her face while she was made a laughingstock. "You clearly have no need of me here, Ronald."

"Nay, fair maiden, but—"

"Leave off, Ronnie. You weren't insulted by Mr. Anaedsley. You barely even have a bruise."

"This is an *affaire d'honor*!"

"Then I say, your honor be damned."

There were gasps all around at her language, but she didn't care. She wasn't a lady, and she certainly wasn't someone who enjoyed this type of spectacle. Meanwhile, Trevor came up beside her.

"It's just good fun, Mellie. There's no harm in it."

Good God, he still didn't understand! Ronnie was enjoying prancing about now, but in a few minutes, her cousin was about to bloody Trevor. And then what type of good fun would it be?

She turned to her cousin and spoke earnestly. "He's the grandson of a duke. You cannot hurt him."

Ronnie actually grinned. "Oh, I mean to hurt him quite a lot, my love. Quite a lot."

She bit back a curse, but it was Trevor who kept her from really speaking her mind. "Don't take this so to heart. I had meant to let him have his fun for a bit longer, but for you, I shall end it quickly now."

"Good Lord…"

"Hush and step back. You have to trust me." He led her to a spot beneath a tree near enough to see clearly, but far enough away so as not to interfere. Or so she presumed. And right as if this had been rehearsed, the crowd parted to keep her and the combatants in view.

Clearly Ronnie didn't like Trevor acting the gallant. But given that he never thought to escort her anywhere, Mellie hardly cared, especially as it gave him yet another public jab.

"Play the dandy all you like," he taunted. "My lady fair will know her true heart before this morning's work is done."

Trevor executed an elaborate bow, pitching his voice to the crowd. "If it were done when 'tis done, then 'twere well it were done quickly." A nice touch, she thought, quoting Shakespeare's *Macbeth*, though the reference was likely lost on most everyone there. Everyone, that is, except herself and her cousin. Ronnie just grinned, apparently liking that Trevor had cast himself in the role of betrayer. That cast Ronnie in the role as the king.

"The love that follows us sometime is our trouble,"

quoted Ronnie from the same play. "Which still we thank as love. Herein I teach you!" Then he took up a position in the middle of the field.

Trevor stripped off his coat and jacket, ready to set it down in the grass, but Grace stepped up. "I'll keep it nice and tight for you, me lord."

Trevor grinned. "I have always felt safe in your arms," he returned as he delicately set his clothing in her arms. Grace grinned while the rest of the crowd jeered. And then Mr. Anaedsley took up his position before Ronnie, his fists raised.

Except, apparently Ronnie wasn't satisfied. "A little to your left, if you would, sir."

Trevor frowned. "What?"

"Just a step, if you would."

Trevor's expression flattened into a grimace of distaste. "If you insist."

"I do."

With a resigned shrug, Trevor took the requested pace to the left and then readied his fists. The baker stepped forward and raised...good God, had he brought a cowbell? Apparently so, because he lifted it high before striking a single loud clank with a small hammer.

The crowd began to scream, Mellie felt her breath squeeze tight in her lungs, and then she watched in horror as Trevor threw his arms wide and lifted his face to her cousin. It was well timed if he intended to be flattened. Ronnie had drawn back his ham-like fists and had begun a slow but obvious blow. Even she could see it coming, and Trevor adroitly put his chin in its direct path.

She gasped, too horrified to speak. And then it happened. Ronnie's fist connected, Trevor's head snapped back and spittle went flying, and then Mr. Anaedsley, grandson to the Duke of Timby, went flying backward to land in a rather large and obvious pile of cow dung.

So that was why Ronnie wanted him to step to one side. So Trevor would land there. Of all the dishonorable, despicable—

The crowd roared and surged forward, carrying her with them, but Ronnie didn't stop. He stepped forward, dropped to one knee in the muck, and raised his fist again. Trevor was just coming back to himself, groaning as he raised a hand to his jaw. He'd barely managed to open his eyes before Ronnie grabbed him by the collar and lifted him into better striking position.

"What?" Trevor asked, but there was no time as Ronnie's fist landed again with a sickening thud.

Trevor's head snapped back, and the crowd roared its approval. Mellie saw blood splatter and smelled the stench of the offal. She was furious at Ronnie, and yet wasn't this exactly what she'd known he would do? What he'd said he would do? He was going to beat Trevor senseless, and from the way he was lifting the man up and readying his fists, that's exactly what he was about to do.

Trevor managed to rally. He raised his arms and blocked the punch as it descended. But he was slow and clumsy, obviously still reeling. At best he managed to grab hold of Ronnie's lapels and use his arms to keep his head clear of the blows. In retaliation, Ronnie grabbed his opponent's arms, gritted his teeth, and tensed his whole body. With a bestial roar, he hauled backward, lifting them both off the ground much to the crowd's approval.

They made it to their feet, both men staggering. But a moment later, they recovered, though Trevor looked a great deal worse for wear. Nevertheless, he raised his fists, though his expression was still somewhat confused.

"You have the won the bout," he said through his bloodied mouth. "There is no need—"

Apparently, there was need because Ronnie swung again, but Trevor was prepared this time. He ducked, he weaved, and he staggered about the field while her much larger cousin pursued.

The crowd started rumbling, disgruntled that no blows were landing. Ronnie was certainly throwing them, but Trevor was lighter on his feet and managed to avoid everything.

"Hit him!" screamed Grace where she still clutched Trevor's clothing. "Show 'im what for!" The sentiment was echoed all around until Mellie actively hated them all.

Then Trevor struck. The jab was quick and drew nothing but a surprised grunt from Ronnie, but the crowd thought it wonderful, especially as he followed it with a half dozen more in rapid-fire succession.

Ronnie might have been surprised, but that didn't last. He soon started punching, each blow heavy, now with increasing speed. The fight was on in earnest, and Mellie watched in horrified fascination. Her cousin had size and power. Trevor had speed, connecting twice as many times as Ronnie. Though his blows were not as powerful, the cumulative effect was beginning to take its toll. He also had a fox's speed as he ducked and twisted all over the field.

It was after ten more agonizing minutes of this that Mellie finally began to relax. It's not that she was enjoying the fight like so many of the crowd. Far from it. But she understood finally what Trevor had been trying to tell her. It was boys fighting in the school yard. Bloody and violent, to be sure. Especially since they were grown men. But no one was likely to die or even end up needing a surgeon. The two were well matched. At least that's what she saw with her very limited experience. Which is when things went horribly awry.

Trevor stepped in a hole.

It was Ronnie's doing, she was sure of it. He probably thought himself clever, but Melinda thought him a beast for it. After all, he knew this field. Had played here as a boy. He'd no doubt arranged for other pugilist matches on this very location. He likely knew every hole, every rock, every cow pie in a quarter mile and must have maneuvered Trevor to step in exactly that spot.

Trevor cried out in surprise and pain, crumpling quickly—in part from being off balance, in part because he was ducking to avoid Ronnie's fist. Thank God he was wearing boots, otherwise his leg might have snapped in two. As it was, he was perched precariously, one leg ankle deep in mud while the crowd roared in bloodlust.

Trevor held off Ronnie as best he could, blocking blows aimed at his head. He needed enough space to regain his footing. He found it a moment later, lucky that Ronnie was a big man who tired quickly. Her cousin couldn't keep up his rain of blows for long, especially with his lungs working like great bellows. Ronnie paused, pulling back his arm for another blow, but obviously slow from exhaustion.

Trevor took that moment to wrench his leg free, but when he stepped down on it he continued to fall. Damnation, his leg had given out! He must be hurt in earnest.

Mellie saw the realization hit both men at once. Trevor grimaced in dismay, doing his best to roll with the fall. Ronnie, on the other hand, saw his moment of triumph. His lips pulled back in an ugly grin, and she knew what he intended to do.

Trevor was down. Ronnie was going to finish the fight. But he hadn't reckoned on Melinda. She'd been an unwilling participant in this whole disgusting display. Well, if her cousin wanted a Cheltenham tragedy, she would bloody well give him one.

She surged forward, having no need to fake the desperation in her voice. "Stop it! Ronnie, stop it now!" And when he didn't hear her, she said the words she'd never thought she'd utter in her entire life. "My love!"

That got his attention. His fist was raised, but he looked to her, his eyes alight with excitement. "Mellie!"

She flung herself forward. Dropping to her knees, she slid in the mud, coming to a stop just where she'd intended—right beside Trevor's head. Ronnie reached for her, but she pushed him away as she wrapped herself around the fallen lord.

"Stay away, you brute!" she practically spit at her cousin. Then she used her cloak to dab at the blood on Trevor's face. "My love, my love, are you alive? Oh God, someone fetch a doctor! Please, someone!"

Her words were ten times more dramatic than were needed, but she'd learned that the best way to deliver a message to her cousin was in the most theatrical tone possible. So she cradled Trevor in her arms and crooned like any heroine in the most lurid gothic romance.

Trevor's face was indeed a battered mess, but not so unrecognizable that she didn't see the gleam of appreciation in his eyes or the mischievous smile that pulled at his swollen lip.

"Are you an angel?" he asked. "Have I died?"

The man was lying in the mud, his ankle nearly snapped in half. His face oozed from a myriad of cuts, and yet he still had the wherewithal to give the crowd a good show. It was enough to make her contemplate dropping him in the mud. She didn't, of course, but she hoped her glare would suffice.

Meanwhile, Ronnie just stood there poised, his fist still raised as he gaped. "Mellie?"

She looked up, shooting a venomous look at his bloodied fist. "Do you mean to trounce me as well? Lay me out in the mud and the shite like last week's garbage?"

"What?" Ronnie took a moment to understand while she gestured with her chin toward his fist. Then he abruptly gasped and shook out his hand, dropping it helplessly to his side. "But I won. This was an *affaire d'honor.*"

"Congratulations," she mocked. "You beat a man half your weight."

"Hey!" muttered Trevor. "I'm not that small."

"Oh shut up. I'm making a point." Then she turned her attention to her cousin. Best make the situation absolutely clear. "You were right, Ronnie. You have made everything so clear to me. I could never love a brute like you. It's him I want. A man of elegance, not violence."

She watched her cousin absorb her words, his mind obviously working slowly, and no wonder. Certainly, Ronnie was an accomplished fighter, but he'd never in his life been called a brute. He was a poet, for God's sake. And his father was wont to call him a useless fribble with no starch whatsoever. Of course, both appellations were completely wrong, but truth didn't matter here. Not when he'd wanted drama. And so she stretched the truth—she outright broke it—and she felt no remorse.

"I love Trevor," she said loudly enough for everyone to hear.

"Since when?" her cousin demanded.

Since never. She had a thorough disgust of them both. Especially as Trevor began to speak in a quavering voice.

"Oh, to finally hear those words, now in the moments before I expire. My life is complete."

"You're not dying," she hissed. Unless he was hurt more than he appeared. The thought shot her with alarm until he started speaking again.

"I am dying!" he cried. "Kiss me, my love. Kiss me, and mayhap your love will keep me tethered to this mortal coil."

"I will not," she said between clenched teeth.

He pitched his voice to a plaintive wail. "Then I shall die for sure!"

Damnation on all bloody arrogant, ridiculous men! One glance about her showed that the crowd was hanging on his every word. She didn't really care until she looked at Ronnie's face. He wasn't stupid. He could see that Trevor wasn't really hurt. It wouldn't take him long to remember that she'd never spoken of Trevor with anything but disdain. And from there it was a small step to realizing that this entire display was a sham. So she had to do something quickly. Something that he'd never forget, even if he did suspect the lie.

So she did it. She kissed Trevor.

She more than kissed him. She lifted him in her arms and gave him the kind of scorching kiss that every woman dreamed she'd received from the grandson of a duke. And he—horrible roué that he was—wrapped his arm around her shoulders and kissed her right back.

And he kept kissing her, with tongue and teeth and a growl of hunger so wonderful that she hated him even more. Even as she lost all thought to propriety in this very public place.

Five

Keep your composure at all times, even if he has lost his.

"MELINDA SMITHSON!" RONNIE EXCLAIMED AND probably not for the first time. Trevor barely restrained his irritation. The idiot apparently thought taking a parental tone would endear him to Mellie. Sadly, the tone did have an effect on Trevor. It cooled his ardor just enough for him to realize they were kissing in the mud in full view of the entire county.

Romantic? Yes. Appropriate behavior for a gentleman of good breeding? Decidedly not.

So with a reluctant sigh, he drew back, taking the time to stroke her cheek and admire the silky texture of her skin. Damn, but she was a beautiful woman. Especially since their ardor had pulled the pins from her hair and tumbled her mahogany curls down her back. The sunlight brought out the red highlights and turned her mink eyes golden. And her lips—her wet, red, plump—

"Melinda Smithson!" Ronnie cried again. "You forget yourself!"

many entertainments offered in London. "I shall take you to the Royal Theater. You will love—"

"London!" squeaked Ronnie from a step behind them. "Whyever would you go there?"

Trevor grinned, relishing the idea of putting the man in his place. With his most arrogant expression, he shot Ronnie a glare. "She is my fiancée, man. Did you think I would hide such a jewel in this backward county? We are to London where she will learn how to be a duchess."

"A duchess!" Ronnie squawked.

Did the man know nothing? "I am grandson to the Duke of Timby." He barely held back the "you idiot." It was a second later when he realized that of course Ronnie knew who he was, but apparently, he wanted to be sure everyone else knew the supposed reason Mellie had chosen him over her cousin.

True to the drama in the man's head, Ronnie's mouth flattened into a disapproving line. "How could you, Mellie?" he asked in a loud hiss. "How could you betray everything—destiny, love, everything—for a title? You are nothing but a money-grubbing—"

His hurt ankle be damned. Trevor lifted off Mellie and punched Ronnie right in the mouth. The crowd had started to disburse, but at his action, they all halted and turned back. If Ronnie wanted a passion play, then by all means, let them have it.

"I am Trevor Harrison Anaedsley, grandson to the Duke of Timby," he said in ringing tones. "And after my father, I will be the duke. Miss Melinda Smithson is to be my bride and in good time a duchess. If any man dare insult her again, be assured I shall do more

"Yes," she said, her expression still gratifyingly dazed. "Yes, I suppose I do."

Trevor grinned. "Love will do that, you know," he said as he stroked his thumb across her plump lower lip. "Makes one forget everything else…" He stretched toward her, and she brought herself in reach. But then there was Ronnie, grabbing hold of Trevor's shoulder and muscling him back.

If the idiot had dared to touch Mellie, Trevor would have punched him hard right in the knee. It would be enough to cripple the man, potentially for life. But as the bastard chose to exercise his physical prowess on Trevor, his knee was spared. Sadly, the same could not be said for his own ankle. Now that he wasn't kissing Mellie anymore, other painful sensations were pushing to the forefront of his brain. His ankle, for one, was swelling by the second. His jaw was already three times as large as it should be, or at least it felt that way.

He dropped his head forward, touching his forehead to hers. All around them, their audience was cheering, jeering, or simply making ribald comments that were getting more and more obscene.

"We need to get you home," he said to her softly.

Her eyes had widened at some of the things being said. No more sexual daze. Just a growing pinkness in her cheeks and not from his attentions. "Can you walk?" she asked.

He nodded. "It'll hurt like the devil, but I think I can manage it."

"Should I send for the carriage?"

"Heavens, no!" The last thing he wanted to do

was sit in here in the muck waiting. "If you support me—"

"Of course. Lean on me, Mr. Anaedsley. I'm a great deal stronger than I look."

He squeezed her fingers, only now realizing that he was holding her hand. "I'm beginning to realize that, Mellie. Indeed, I wonder at how blind I've been."

Her mouth opened in surprise at his words, and this time he knew that the pink in her cheeks was because of him and not the buffoons around them. He meant to keep it that way. The more he distracted her from everyone else, the less mortified she would feel.

"Yes, cousin," pressed Ronnie. "Do get up. This is most unseemly."

She shot the man an irritated look. "You wouldn't say that if I'd been kissing you."

Trevor didn't think it was possible for Ronnie to look like an offended princess. The buffoon was too big to pull off the dainty, nose-in-the-air look. Apparently he had a little dandy in him. Ronnie pranced backward, stepping on his tippy toes as he gasped at the insult.

"You wound me, cousin. I have thought nothing but for your happiness. I only wonder what this roué has said to sway you from your normal common sense—"

"Oh, owwwww!" Trevor groaned loudly as he pushed to his feet. In truth, it wasn't that bad, but he would play a dying invalid if it shut up Ronnie.

Mellie scrambled to help. "I'm right here. Lean on me."

"Oh, for goodness sake—" Ronnie exclaimed.

"No, no!" he said over her cousin. "I can manage it." He'd made it to his feet, then leaned his weight

onto the bad ankle. He wasn't faking his gasp when pain shot like fire all the way up his spine.

"Don't be foolish!" she snapped as she quickly pulled his arm around her shoulders and bolstered him. Damn, she wasn't lying. She was strong, sturdy enough that he didn't fear he'd break her. Made a man think of all sorts of potential acrobatic feats.

"Damn," he muttered. "I'm getting my stink all over you."

She chuckled. "I've been in worse, I assure you."

He glanced at her, wondering how that was possible.

"When you're not here, whom do you suppose helps my father with his experiments? Who holds the sheep while he applies his tick cream? Who—"

"Good God," he exclaimed, truly appalled. "I'd assumed it was the servants."

"Only sometimes. He says I have the keener eye for detail—"

"But—"

"And a scientific mind to help him analyze the progress of his work."

She sounded proud of the fact, and well she should. After all, praise from her father was rare indeed, and he recalled beaming for a whole month after one of the man's compliments. "But he still should hire someone else to hold the sheep."

She chuckled. "He shall have to now, if I am to head to London with you."

Trevor smiled, liking the idea of her in London with him. He wanted to see her in silks and jewels. And he should like very much introducing her to the

than toss them into the shite. I shall run them through with my sword." He lifted his gaze and looked all around. "Do you all hear and understand?"

One by one, he saw people dip their chin and nod. A few even said, "Yes, Yer Grace," as if he had already inherited the title. His last heavy stare was for Ronnie, who had just regained his equilibrium.

With the sun at his back and his fists bunched, it was never more clear the differences between the two. Ronnie was two stone heavier and had a great deal more skill with his fists than Trevor ever guessed. Worse, the skill came not only from size, but from intelligence. He'd wager Ronnie was smarter than the average buffoon and a good deal cagier as well. And from the look of absolute hatred on his face, he wasn't going to give up Mellie without a fight.

It didn't matter. Mellie was never, ever going to marry this man. Trevor swore it on everything he held dear.

"Do you understand?" he repeated, his gaze locked on Ronnie's. "She is my affianced—"

"I understand." Ronnie's gaze slid with angry disdain to Mellie. "And I am disgusted."

Beside him, Mellie sighed. "Ronnie—"

Ever the dramatist, the man spun on his heels and stalked away. Just as well. That left him alone with Mellie as they hobbled their way back to their house. But after a few steps, Trevor realized that his fiancée was indeed bothered by what her cousin said. Her eyes were downcast, and her mouth had tightened into her own straight, quiet line.

"Mellie, what is the matter? Don't be concerned

about Ronnie's nonsense. I assure you, everyone will think you have done enormously well for yourself."

She jerked beneath his arm as if she wished to throw him off her but had stopped herself at the last moment. Then she twisted to face him. "That man is my cousin," she said in an undertone. "And quite possibly my future husband."

"Don't be ridiculous."

"I am being practical. There is no assurance that I will find a husband in London, and then what? I will have publicly thrown over Ronnie, and it takes the devil of a long time for him to get over imagined slights. Imagine a lifetime of apologizing."

"You will find a husband in London," he said, irritated beyond measure with her anger. She thought nothing of the sacrifice to *his* reputation. That he— grandson to the Duke of Timby—had just declared a grand passion for her. He liked her well enough. Lord knows a certain part of her anatomy couldn't get enough, but she was a cit. A woman from commerce with no pretense to good breeding. His family would have a collective fit when they heard. It might very well put his grandfather in the grave.

He understood that she was not used to this type of manipulation or deviousness. It was awkward enough for him, and he had been swimming in society's viper-strewn waters all his life. Did she truly not understand?

"You will be sponsored by a ducal family, you will be fêted as my fiancée, you will be society's newest morsel to be met and entertained. Everyone from the Prince Regent down to the smallest bootblack will be discussing you."

She looked horrified, which only went to prove how very green she was about society.

He sighed and tried to make it plainer. "Debutantes strive all their lives for just that kind of introduction into society. Women have been known to proffer all sorts of bribes and promises for the reach you will have merely because you are my fiancée. Mellie, don't you see? It will be the easiest thing in the world to find you a husband."

"But—"

"Enough!" he snapped. He did his best to keep his voice low despite the way he'd just wrenched his damned ankle again. "If you do not trust me in this, then our endeavor is doomed from the start."

She blinked a moment, her expression clearly troubled. He waited, his ankle and jaw a throbbing annoyance, but nothing compared to the pain of having his word questioned by a green chit who knew nothing about anything. In the end, though, she dipped her head in acknowledgment. "I trust you," she whispered.

"Good. Then trust this. I swear upon my honor, upon my family name, and upon that stupid sword my grandfather keeps perched above the mantle: I will find you a good husband. A man who is decidedly *not* Ronnie!"

She looked at him a long time, obviously unaware of what it meant for him to swear by his family's sword. He was about to curse her for her stupidity when she again dipped her eyes.

"Thank you," she whispered again.

"You're welcome," he managed, doing his best not to sound surly.

"And now, perhaps we should get you home to a bath."

Yes, because—as he was now very aware—the future Duke of Timby stank of shite.

⤙❧⤚

"This is just so unlike you."

"You've never done anything like this before."

Melinda didn't respond to her father or her uncle. They were pacing about the room, shooting furious comments at her every second step, but her mind had gone far, far away. Normally, she would wander about in her chemical recipes, mentally playing with ingredients and speculating as to the results. It had been a favorite game of hers for as long as she could remember. But this time, her thoughts were locked inexorably on kisses. A thousand kisses in an infinite variety but all from one, mischievous aristocrat.

"Your mother, of course—"

"But you don't want to be like that."

"No. Not like your mother."

"I'm just so concerned, my dear."

"This is so unlike you."

Then *he* walked in. His hair was wet and slicked back, but as his curls dried they started to spring about his head in a casual wildness she found very appealing. His expression was guarded, but his smile was as wide as the morning sun. She focused there—on his mouth—because he was infinitely more interesting than anything else at the moment.

"Well, I feel much better," he said. "And I wager that I smell infinitely more appealing." He crossed to her side, drawing her lax hand to his mouth for a kiss. "How about you? Are you recovered from my stench?"

She smiled because he seemed to want her to. "Of course, Mr. Anaedsley. It was only a little bit of shite."

He chuckled. "It was a great deal more than a little. Your cousin aimed me exactly."

She nodded. "And you let him do it. Did you know at the time what he intended?"

He shrugged. "I did. And I thought a single blow that landed me there was adequate recompense for his wounded pride."

If only Ronnie had thought the same. "I did warn you," she said softly.

"So you did. And I have learned my lesson."

"Not to underestimate Ronnie?"

He chucked her under the chin. "No, silly. To heed what you say. You are of an uncommonly level-headed nature."

She winced, knowing what was coming. After all, her levelheaded nature was exactly what was in question here. And her uncle lost no time as he pounced on Trevor's words.

"And just what have you done, you whoremonger, to turn her head so? Good God, do you routinely make a spectacle of the women of your acquaintance?"

Far from being insulted, Mr. Anaedsley appeared to be amused. "Only those who enjoy the spectacle, sir."

"Well, I assure you," inserted her father, "she did not enjoy it. She did not enjoy it one bit."

Her fiancé arched his brows as he turned to her. "Is that so, my dear? Not even a little?"

She felt her body heat under his gaze, warming from the frozen place she'd existed before he'd walked into the room.

Meanwhile, her uncle was making disgusted noises. He was rather good at them actually. He combined outrage and a snort to a loud sound that never failed to draw everyone's attention. Well, everyone, it seemed, except Trevor. He was busy teasing her knuckles with his thumb while his eyes sparkled with a dark mischief she found completely mesmerizing. Especially since his lips curved upward in a secret promise.

"I think we should be away to London with all speed," he said. "Have you directed your maid to pack?"

She nodded. He had reminded her twice of this plan before heading to his bath. But she had not had a chance to tell her father, who was right now sputtering with rage.

"L-London? What? Good God, Mellie! But I have my experiments, and you must help. And—and— London? Why?"

It was Mr. Anaedsley who answered with a cordial tone laced heavily with aristocratic arrogance. "Because she is my promised bride, sir. She must be introduced to society with all haste. The Season is barely a week away."

"I don't understand any of this," her father said. He stopped walking to drop into a chair by the fire. His entire spirit seemed diffuse, as if he hadn't the strength or the will to support his own body.

Mellie's uncle put a comforting—or a condescending—hand on his brother's shoulder then shot a glare at Mr. Anaedsley. "What is there to understand, Gregory? He seduced her. He came into your house, crept into her bedroom—"

"Have a care, sir. You are speaking of my future wife."

"I am speaking of you, sir. How could you abuse—"

"Enough!" Trevor had been standing, but somehow, the man appeared to grow taller. She was looking right at him so she saw him draw the mantle of his heritage about him. His shoulders straightened, his chin grew hard, and his words became clipped and cold.

"I will answer this once because you are her family. She is as pure as the day I arrived. I have neither seduced nor debased anyone here, and you do her no credit to think such a thing." Then he turned to her father, and his body softened a bit. "Sir, I know I should have spoken with you first. In truth, this…connection with your daughter has caught me by surprise. But I think you would wish us happy."

Her father slumped even further in his chair. "It's just so unlike her."

And there it was. The words that had damned her from the beginning. She could tell that Trevor had no understanding of what those words meant in this family. He lifted his hands in a helpless gesture. "A woman's heart is a mysterious thing, sir. I can barely fathom my own actions except to say that your daughter is a prize among women."

His words heated her enough that the final frozen part of her began to move. She spoke for the first time in over an hour, her voice filling the room for all that she spoke in a whisper. "What he means, Mr. Anaedsley, is that such an impetuous action is something my mother would do."

Trevor frowned, obviously trying to remember her parent. "I'm sorry. I don't understand. Isn't it the most natural thing in the world for a daughter to resemble her mother?"

Three exclamations of shock greeted his words. And no wonder as he'd just voiced everyone's secret fear. With a sad smile, Mellie finally found the strength to stand. A moment later, she had crossed to Trevor's side as she stood before her distraught father.

"Mama was somewhat impulsive," she said neutrally.

"Somewhat!" her father exclaimed. At least he didn't snort like her uncle.

Meanwhile, Trevor cocked his head to one side as he looked upon the three of them. "Impulsive? Or prone to dramatics like Ronnie?"

"How dare you, sir!" Ronnie's father exploded. "My son is entirely sane!"

Trevor drew back in surprise. "I don't believe I suggested otherwise. Just that he's prone—"

"Mama killed herself," Mellie said softly. "I believe my family fears I might have inherited her madness." There. She'd said the words. Now it remained to be seen if he would end this scheme for fear of her mother's taint. "I suppose I should have told you earlier, but…"

"No, no," he said, shaking his head. "Perhaps I already knew. Something about a bridge?"

"Yes—"

"This is outside of enough!" bellowed her uncle.

And looking at her father, Mellie knew the man was at the last of his strength. She hadn't realized how much of a blow her engagement would be to him. So she went to him, sinking down on her knees to be level with his eyes.

"Papa, is it all so very odd? You have been singing Mr. Anaedsley's praises since the first time you tutored him."

Her father shook his head. "And you have had nothing but disdain for him."

She sighed. It was true. "Perhaps I have changed, Papa. Maybe I finally opened my eyes and looked at him."

Her uncle made an ugly sound. "What you saw was a title, my girl. And a—"

"An alternative to Ronnie?" she said, shooting him a heavy glare.

Her father took her hands. "But Ronald makes sense. He's only your half cousin, you know. And if you two marry, we will keep the mill in the family."

She sighed. "Yes, I know, Papa. But perhaps I can look higher."

"Don't be foolish, girl," interrupted her uncle. "You won't be accepted into his world. You'll be reviled by everyone you meet, called an encroaching mushroom, and criticized at every turn."

From the corner of her eye, she saw Trevor stiffen. "I will see that she is not."

"As if you could promise that," her uncle said with a sneer. "No man is that powerful, not even a duke. She belongs with us."

"She belongs where she chooses to be." He

lifted his chin. "And where I have invited her. Mr. Smithson, we have declared our intentions. It is up to you now whether you choose to accept it or fight—"

"No," she interrupted in a low tone. She could tell he meant well, but Mr. Anaedsley was still a man and had little understanding of how to ease her father into a situation. Some things required a woman's touch. And so that's what she did. She took her father's hands and kissed them. "I wish to go. Will you truly stop me?"

His eyes grew watery, and she could feel the tremor in his hands. "This is all so sudden."

"Even so, Papa."

"Gregory—" her uncle began, but she shot him an angry look. It was seconded by Trevor who made a growl akin to her uncle's, except that it was lower and more threatening. Apparently, it was the only way to silence her uncle because after a single furious glare, he stomped to the sideboard and poured himself a brandy.

Meanwhile, she laid her cheek against her father's thin hands. When had they gotten so frail?

"Papa, do not toss me aside."

"As if I could, Mellie."

She lifted her head then and looked into his eyes. "You will let me go?"

"If you are truly engaged, I cannot stop you."

"Papa," she whispered, cut to the quick by the defeat in his eyes.

He looked at her then. "You have been scheming for years for a way to go to London. You have finally found one I cannot fight."

She swallowed, knowing now how stupid she'd been to hope he would understand. "I have to grow up, Papa. I cannot be home at your beck and call forever. I am a woman grown."

His eyes grew watery, and he looked away. The fire grate was cold, and she thought to light it despite the warmth in the room. But when she moved to do just that, her father clutched her hand. "Mellie," he said, his voice cracking on his words. "Do not...don't do anything impulsive."

What he meant was: don't do anything mad. Do not act crazy. Except this whole escapade was insane, and so she wavered, abruptly unsure of what she should do. Were they right? Was this her mother's illness coming to the fore?

Then Trevor was beside her, his hand warm on her back as he supported her. She would not topple with him beside her. And when he spoke, his voice was pitched low, soothing to her father. "This is not insanity, sir. You know me. You have admired my mind and my sense since I was a boy. Do you think I would affiance myself to a madwoman?"

Her father lifted his gaze slowly—not to her, but to Trevor. It rose until the men looked each other in the eye, and then finally, her father nodded. "Very well. Go to London, Mellie. But just the Season, yes?"

"Yes." She had to work to push the word out of her mouth. If all went according to plan, she'd return with a husband and would never live here again.

"You'll write me, won't you?"

"You could come up and join me," she offered, all the while wondering if that were even possible.

"No, no. I have my experiments, you know."

She knew.

"And your uncle has some excellent ideas about your formula."

Her uncle spoke from behind his brandy glass. "You still need to give that to me."

She looked to her uncle, noting that his expression was as bland as possible. But what was more interesting to her was the way Trevor took a step back, his narrowed eyes jumping from her to her uncle in rapid succession.

"Of course," she said as she rose to her feet. "I can write it down—"

"No need to bother with that now, my dear," interrupted Trevor. "You should get your valise. The day is rapidly escaping, and we have a long ride to London."

She didn't suggest they wait until tomorrow. It would only increase her father's agony. He did not adjust well to change, and the anticipation of an event was often worse than the adjustment itself.

"Papa," she said softly. "May we take the carriage?"

"And what of a chaperone?" her uncle demanded.

"My maid will do fine," she said, hoping it was true.

Finally, her father released a long sigh. He deflated even more in his seat, but when he looked at her, his eyes were clear and strong. "You may take the carriage, my dear. But if you ask me to bless this marriage…" He shook his head. "I cannot."

"What? But Papa—"

"No, my dear." He stood then, his movements bizarrely normal. He had his normal strength, his usual crispness in speech. "Go if you must, but I do not approve."

Then he turned and headed for his laboratory.

Six

Reward him for being solicitous. Once you have his attention, do everything to keep it.

Trevor sat in the most well-appointed carriage he'd ever had the pleasure of traveling inside. The springs were new, the cushions plush, and there were even decorative lamps in case one wished to read after dark. It was the height of modern luxury, and yet he'd never felt more uncomfortable in his life.

He sat alone on his seat. Across from him was Mellie and a sour-faced prune of a maid who obviously took her position as chaperone much too seriously. Every time he tried to touch his fiancée—even the accidental brush of knees—she glared at him as if he'd just tried to lift Mellie's skirts. Even conversation was stilted as the woman glowered at all discourse, clearly blaming him for her sudden removal to London.

Well, to hell with it. Mellie was his fiancée, and more important, she was clearly suffering. He would talk to her and do what he could to ease the pain of her father's defection.

But how to start? How to broach the subject when the lady didn't wish to converse? She sat as still as stone, her gaze vague, and her hands clenched tightly together in her lap. He'd already tried the normal conversation starters. He'd discussed the weather and the length of the drive. Noted various interesting sights, which frankly were nothing more than, "Oh, there's another handsome cow." In the end, he decided on direct speech. It had always worked best with her anyway.

"Mellie, you no doubt feel rather unsettled. I know this is sudden—"

"I have made my choice, Mr. Anaedsley, and am well content."

Her words were spoken in clipped, almost acerbic tones, but he could see the anxiety in her tightened fingers. "I'm sure you are," he said trying to be soothing, "but that cannot have been an easy conversation with your father."

For the first time in over an hour, her gaze cut to his and held. It was too dark to see any glisten of tears, but he knew that she'd been on the verge of crying ever since her father had walked out on her. How could she not? It had been just the two of them since she was a child. In many respects, her father was her whole world.

"He will adjust in time," she said softly. "It is all for the best."

"Yes, it is, but…" He leaned forward onto his knees. He didn't dare take her hand because of the damned maid, but at least he could reach toward her without actually connecting. "Mellie, in twenty-four hours you have become engaged and now left your home." He didn't mention the viper's nest called London society. She'd learn the horrors of that soon enough. "Please, ask me questions about what is to come. Or rail at me. Hit me even, if you like. Do something to ease the pain."

Her lips tightened, but her words came out calm. "Will that help? Will it force my father to forgive me or make the insults to come easier to bear?"

So she did have an idea of what would happen in London. "I have found that women who discuss things find everything easier to bear. Or so they have claimed."

He could not shake the memory of how white her skin had gone when her father refused his blessing. Or that she became stone while her uncle cut at her some more until Trevor put a stop to it. No more tragic a figure had ever appeared on stage than Mellie standing still while her only family voiced their disgust and walked away.

Meanwhile, she shook her head, keeping her lips resolutely shut.

"You are thinking," he guessed, "that to speak of such things aloud will surely cause your heart to break in two. That the pain will cripple you, and you will curl up into a ball and sob until you cannot move again. Do I have the right of it?"

Again her gaze locked on his, holding it without wavering. And then she opened her mouth, but not a word came out. She tried twice. He saw her draw breath, but not a sound broke through.

So he reached across and took her hands despite her

maid's angry cough. He could not entwine his fingers with hers because Mellie's were curled into tight fists, but he could wrap his two hands around hers where they strained in her lap.

"You are not alone, you know. I am here, and I have many friends in London. They will stand by you as well. It is only that it is so sudden that you feel turned around."

Her mouth was working again, but this time she managed to whisper one question, barely heard, though there was little noise from the carriage. "What if they're right?"

He frowned. "Who is right? About what?"

She blinked her eyes, clearly fighting the tears. So he squeezed her hands and tried to silently reassure her. In the end, it must have worked because she took a deep breath and spoke, her words louder if not yet steady.

"This has happened so fast. I am never impulsive, and yet here I am. It has only been a day."

"You have been looking for an alternative to Ronnie for a very long time. Months, even."

"Years," she said.

"Then that is the opposite of impulsive."

She nodded, but she did not appear convinced. "My mother..." Her words were cut off. Stopped, and this time he could not get her to start again. Not by squeezing her hands. Not even by touching their knees together.

"I do not remember much of what happened," he said. "I believe my mother told me, but it was so long ago."

She looked away. "Mama drowned herself. She was pregnant at the time."

"Good Lord," he breathed. "How old were you?"

"Six. It was very confusing."

"And you——" He cut off his words. This was absolutely not something to discuss with a servant sitting right beside them. Not the question of why her mother would do such a thing or how her father handled the loss. "You were so young." And now her whole family obviously lived in terror of her repeating her mother's madness. "But you are nothing like your mother." Indeed, he suspected that she had been raised since that very day to be the very opposite of her mercurial parent. He just wished he could remember the details of the event.

"Not generally, no," she said. "But——"

"Not at all." He flashed her his most charming smile. "Remember, I am well acquainted with impulsiveness. And given the example of my mother and two younger sisters, I can also firmly state that you are not prone to fits, moods, or even the normal female range of excitation."

She blinked at him. "Are you saying that I am not a normal female?"

He snorted. "Of course you're not normal! Good Lord, do you think I would engage myself to a normal female? They are the most impossible, unmanageable, and difficult creatures on Earth. You, my dear, are nothing of the sort, and I revere you for it."

It was the absolute truth, but he feared she didn't take it as the compliment he intended. She stared at him in open-mouthed horror and slowly drew her hands back. He sighed. He knew from experience with his most irrational sister that some women would take an insult no matter what one said. But he had never counted Mellie as one of those types.

"Surely you see I mean it as a compliment," he said.

"Surely you see that calling a woman an unnatural creature is nothing but an insult, no matter how it is intended."

He dropped back onto the squabs, seeing that she was determined in her mood. "You are just worried about what is ahead and grieving what you have left behind." He shrugged, though inside, his belly tightened with frustration. "Tell me what I can do to ease your mind."

She opened her mouth to speak—once, twice—and then she dropped her head against the squabs and stared at the ceiling. "I think I should prefer to…"

"Grieve?"

She shrugged. "Think in silence."

"As you wish."

So the three of them sat with their own thoughts. It should have been a peaceful trip, but he quickly realized that silence was not his natural habitat. He was so rarely quiet that this silence felt deuced awkward. There was always chatter in his life: with his friends, with the society he often was forced to endure, and even in his own mind. To sit without speaking now was to allow his mind to run rampant with noise. He realized then that his attempts to soothe her had been—at least in part—a way to distract himself from his own fears.

After all, he was now engaged to a woman far

beneath his station. They were about to enter the social fray where he had vowed to protect her when they both knew there were distinct limits to what he could do. And yet he had promised. He would do his utmost to see the process through, but it was a daunting task. And if he were honest with himself—which in the silence he was forced to be—he feared he wouldn't be able to do any of what he intended: protect her, gain his own independence, even so simple a thing as to find her a husband. Herculean tasks.

And in this silent misery, they made their way to London.

∾

Mellie was nearly dead inside by the time they made it to Lady Eleanor's Grosvenor Square residence. It was a curious thing how her thoughts and body stilled to the point of total hibernation. In truth she hadn't even realized how little life remained in her until her fiancé had woken her. In the last twenty-four hours, he'd brought her to brilliant life with kisses and caresses, but then it had all died as they rode in silence toward London.

She didn't blame him, of course. It wasn't his fault that she was an unnatural woman, her mother had been mad, and her father lived only for science. But she blamed him for showing her what feelings were, how life could be expressed in laughter and in lust, such as she'd never thought existed before.

And now, as all that awareness died, she learned about pain. Not physical pain, but an ache as that brimming understanding slowly quieted. She was once again sitting without moving, watching silently as life passed her by. It was all she could do to muster the strength to stand and face the home of the esteemed Lady Eleanor.

Meanwhile, Trevor stepped out of the carriage, groaning slightly at his stiff muscles. His jaw had swollen to an ugly and no doubt painful degree. And she was sure he had a myriad of other bruises about his person. And yet he had endured the long carriage ride in silence without a word of complaint. She couldn't imagine her father doing such a thing. Or Ronnie, for that matter. She hid a small smile. Her uncle was in for a miserable ride back to his home with Ronnie in the carriage.

Meanwhile, Trevor was extending his hand, and she felt awkward as she alighted. Her own body was stiff from the travel, and she winced as her knee popped when she straightened it. She was sure that Lady Eleanor's knees never made noise.

"No worries now, my dear," said Trevor as he tucked her hand into the crook of his arm. "Everything will be right and tight, you'll see. By the morrow, you'll be buried in dress shopping and party invitations. You won't have a second left to worry."

She didn't answer. She hadn't the life inside her to speak, but the feel of his hand and the heat of his body gave her enough strength to begin the stately walk to the door. It was an impressive house in an impressive neighborhood. She'd never been in Grosvenor Square, though of course she'd heard of it. As it was near dark, there were no other people on the walk, but the ever-present murmur of the city beyond kept the place from being quiet. At least until Trevor banged the huge brass knocker carried in the beak of a fierce eagle. The ducal crest, she presumed, and she felt appropriately intimidated by it.

The door opened on silent hinges by a butler with a large frame and immaculate salt-and-pepper hair. Trevor greeted him warmly.

"Seelye, you're looking in excellent health."

"Mr. Anaedsley. A pleasure to see you this evening." By not even a flicker of an eye did he acknowledge Melinda, but he did step back to gesture them inside. "Please step in out of the damp air. I shall inform His Grace that—"

At that moment, a woman's low throaty laugh vibrated through the air before they heard the words, "Radley, that's wicked!"

"Is it?" the man answered, humor lacing through his words. "I thought it would be fun."

Melinda looked up to see a couple descending the stairs, the woman a bit faster than the gentleman, her eyes alight with laughter as he reached forward and missed her arm. There was nothing untoward in their actions, except that anyone with eyes could see that the two were playing with each other. Nothing so childish as tag, but still a game of run and catch though neither went faster than a quick walk.

"Slow down, minx," the man called, but he needn't have said it. The woman had stopped abruptly on the second to last step, her gaze finally catching the party in their front hallway. Since the man hadn't noticed yet, Mellie feared a collision, but at the last second, the gentleman stepped nimbly aside, taking a small leap around his companion to land sweetly on the main floor. Which was when Seelye cleared his throat and everyone—the couple included—looked to the butler.

"Your Graces," Seelye intoned. "Mr. Anaedsley and Miss…"

Mellie remembered at the last second what was required. She hastily dropped into an awkward curtsy. "Miss Melinda Smithson, Your Grace. Er, Your Graces."

"A pleasure to meet you, Miss Smithson, Mr. Anaedsley," said the duke as he stepped forward and executed a smooth bow.

Meanwhile, Her Grace frowned, obviously searching her memory. "Mr. Anaedsley. Mr. Trevor Anaedsley, grandson to the Duke of Timby. Goodness, I stitched quite a number of gowns for you, sir."

Beside her, Trevor chuckled as he pulled off his hat and gloves. "For me, Your Grace? I assure you, I have never worn a gown in my life."

"No, sir, but countless ladies have ordered them just to please you." She smiled as she joined her husband's side. "I must know, is yellow truly your favorite color?"

He frowned. "Yellow? No, Your Grace. I favor purple instead."

"Very royal of you," she said. "And I always did think Miss Atterberry somewhat addled. Didn't stop me from selling a dozen or more yellow gowns last Season."

"Very clever, Wendy," her husband said with a smile, "but we shouldn't keep them standing about in the hallway." Then he grinned at Trevor. "Do you know what the best part of being a duke is?"

Trevor laughed. "I can think of a thousand things."

"Well, other than my lady wife, there is but one: excellent brandy. Would you care for a glass?"

"With pleasure," he answered as the four of them crossed a pristine marble foyer to enter a lavish parlor. His Grace went directly to the sideboard, and as he poured from a crystal decanter, he glanced at her. "And for you, Miss Smithson?"

"I should love a glass of brandy, if you please."

The duke's eyebrows rose in surprise, but he didn't say anything. Which left it to Trevor to enlighten her.

"As a general rule," he said in an undertone, "ladies find brandy too strong."

"Oh," she whispered back. But she'd always drunk brandy. It was one of her favorite... Well, no matter, she was in society now. "I'm sorry. I suppose I meant...um..."

"Sherry for her, please," Trevor finished.

The duke was just turning around with a glass of brandy when his duchess lifted it from his hand. "Let her drink what she wants." She pressed the snifter into Mellie's hand. "You'll find we're not the typical duke and duchess."

Mellie looked at her drink, unsure what to do now. "Is there a regular type?" she wondered aloud.

"That's a question for Eleanor," the duchess replied as her husband passed another brandy to Trevor. "She's Radley's cousin and takes great delight in correcting our misguided notions. But for now, you should eat and drink as you like in our home."

Mellie smiled, feeling her insides ease a little. The duke and his duchess were of a warm sort. They smiled often—usually at each other—and took pains to set her at ease. She hoped that she wouldn't muck things up so badly.

Meanwhile, the duke had leaned back against the sideboard, his brandy glass held out to Trevor. "À votre santé," he said gravely.

Trevor raised his own glass in salute. "To your health as well."

The duke flashed a broad grin at his wife who groaned. "Yes, yes, you said it right. But it loses its effect if you grin like that." She settled on the settee next to Mellie. "He just learned that phrase from Eleanor and thinks he's the cat's cream whenever he says it."

His Grace chuckled. "It's French, you know. Never had the chance to learn the Frog's lingo. And I refuse to even try Latin or Greek. But I've got Spanish well enough, plus a smattering of Egyptian and Arabic. I'm not bad as languages go, but I knew a ship's mate who only had to hear something once before he could spit it back like a native. Terrible navigator though, and that more than anything hurt his chances aboard ship."

Mellie nodded as if his words made complete sense. Oh, his meaning was clear enough, but his general manner and casual speech didn't fit with her idea of a duke. Didn't they all speak Latin and converse about politics?

As if sensing her confusion, Trevor gave her a hasty explanation. "His Grace is the newest sensation in London. A seaman elevated to a duke."

"Gracious," Mellie breathed. So this really was the

man she'd read about in the papers. "That must have been overwhelming."

The duke chuckled. "Most would say exciting."

A woman's dry voice cut through the air, the words coming from the doorway. "Or tragic."

The duchess's expression turned wry. "Good evening, Eleanor. Pray join us."

A statuesque blonde entered the room. Her gown was of the finest cut and fabric—a blue silk that shimmered as she walked and emphasized the pure color of her crystalline eyes. Her hair was expertly coiled in a design that made Mellie's eyes hurt as she tried to trace the locks. And the expression on her flawless skin was polite, if not especially warm.

"Seelye mentioned that I had visitors." Her gaze stumbled for a moment on Melinda who was suddenly aware of the stains on her travel dress and the uneven texture of her skin. But then Trevor stepped forward, executing a deep bow.

"Lady Eleanor, it has been too long."

Her face suddenly shifted. Her eyes widened, and a polished smile curved her perfect lips. "Trevor! My goodness, when did you get back in town? And what has happened to your face?"

"Just today, as you can see." He made an expansive gesture at his creased clothing. "And I came directly here to speak with you."

"To see me?" She pressed a hand to her lips, a gesture that brought even more attention to the flawless color of her skin below those blue, blue eyes.

He reached forward, gently tugging at her hand until he could press a kiss to her knuckles. Mellie watched the whole exchange as she would an opera sung in a foreign language. They were actors on a stage performing perfect roles in their dance. Beautiful in a way, but so distant that she felt no connection to them, or even to the world around her.

"Sweet Eleanor, I have come to beg a boon from you. You did promise me one long ago."

"I did not. I would never."

"I believe I rescued your kitten from a tree."

She frowned a moment then huffed out a breath. "That was years ago."

"Nevertheless," he said as he straightened. "I should like to collect on that promise."

"I was seven!"

He arched a brow, and she tilted her head, exposing the long column of her white neck.

"You always were a scapegrace, Trevor. Very well, what is it that you'd like?"

His grin broadened, and suddenly Melinda became part of the opera. He swept his arm toward her in a perfect arc. "First, may I introduce you to Miss Melinda Smithson, my fiancée."

Mellie rose to her feet, knowing at least this part of the performance. She dipped her chin and bent her knees, dropping into a curtsy, such as would be expected when greeting a lady.

But when she straightened, she didn't see a cool greeting on the lady's face. No, Lady Eleanor's jaw was slack with horror. Then she turned to Trevor, her body trembling with the enormity of her revulsion.

"Stop this, you idiot. Stop it now!"

Seven

If he ignores you, be patient. Revenge will come in time.

TREVOR WATCHED IN DISMAY AS ONE OF HIS OLDEST friends insulted his fiancée. Eleanor didn't mean to, of course. She was just reacting to the mésalliance of himself with Mellie—a natural reaction for one of her station. As the daughter of a duke, she understood what so few did of the personal and cultural divide that separated the aristocracy from new money cits such as Mellie.

But it wasn't an unbreachable gap, and it certainly didn't warrant such a massive reaction as Eleanor's pale face and dramatic pronouncement suggested. And damn it, she kept doing it.

"Trevor, you have to reconsider. Think about what you are doing." Then her gaze narrowed on his face. "Were you forced? Is that why you were beaten?"

And all the while, Mellie stood there unmoving, her face composed into a cold, flat mask.

"I was not beaten," he snapped. Then he took a breath. "Please calm yourself." Then he took her by the elbow and turned her toward the door. "Perhaps we had best take a walk in the garden."

"Oh yes," drawled the duchess from behind him. "Do wander off with Eleanor. I'm sure your intended will feel so much better, being abandoned like that."

He shot her an irritated look, but then caught himself before he insulted the highest-ranking woman in the room. Damn it, Mellie would feel that much worse if he had it out with Eleanor in front of everyone. Fortunately, his fiancée was of a more practical mind-set.

"No," she said softly. "He's right. Some discussions require privacy for frank discourse."

The duke stepped forward. "Not to take sides here, man. Your marriage is your affair, but don't you think Miss Smithson should be part of your frank discussion? Wendy and I can take ourselves off, can't we, love?"

The duchess pushed to her feet, ready to leave with her husband, but Trevor looked to Mellie for guidance. Did she want to be part of what looked like a humiliating argument with Eleanor? Or would she rather he simply deal with it himself? Unfortunately, she gave no clue as to her thoughts. She'd simply folded her hands before her and looked down. Like a damned servant in front of her betters, which he supposed he couldn't blame her for. But hell, it gave him no idea how to proceed.

In the end, it was up to him to decide, and frankly, this was not something he wanted said in front of Mellie. "I won't be but a moment. I swear."

She looked back at him, her eyes nearly blank as she nodded. "Of course. I'll just wait here."

Trevor stifled a curse and nodded, then he allowed Eleanor to guide him out the parlor door and to the back of the house. They didn't go outside but moments later walked into a cozy room meant for intimate family discussions. It was stately; this was the residence of the Duke of Bucklynde after all. But it had a tad less velvet, a great deal more browns from the wood, and none of the impressive knickknacks of history that were placed about the receiving parlor.

Sadly, it wasn't in the least bit comfortable, but at least it was private. He took a breath, trying to feel his way into the conversation. He needn't have bothered. Eleanor took that on herself. She grabbed both his hands, squeezed them warmly, and spoke in a sincere voice.

"We have known each other practically since the cradle, traveled in the same circles, and shared the same friends since the beginning. No one knows better than I the stresses you face as the heir to a dukedom. It is a daily struggle of appearances and moderated words and not a single moment to think on what we want. On what we require as people who laugh and love and wish just like the lowest bootblack."

"Eleanor," he began, but she shook her head, revealing a desperation he hadn't seen in her before.

"Hear me out. I know the pressure and the constant pain of biting one's tongue, of wishing to scream at the unfairness of it all. You are a man and have more freedom to fight back, but that means very little when the usual pleasures don't satisfy."

He frowned. "Usual pleasures?"

She huffed. "Come now, Trevor. You're not the

kind of man to lose himself in drink or women. You don't gamble, and you hate politics. What is there left but your science experiments?" She said "science" as if she were speaking of a hobby like embroidery or gardening.

"Don't be insulting," he snapped.

"I'm not trying to be!" she shot back equally irritated. "I know you want to prove something to your family. God knows I don't know how you've held off for so long. But Trevor, that's no reason to throw away your entire future for a science chit." This time she said the word "science" more like she might speak of kitchen scraps.

"She's not some experiment," he shot back. "She's a girl. A human being. And what makes you think she enjoys science?"

Eleanor rolled her eyes. "Well, I have eyes to see, don't I? She's got no pretense to class, curtsies like a housemaid, and doesn't speak unless spoken to. The only way that she could have come into your awareness was through your hobby. So who is she? How did you meet her?"

"She's the…" He sighed, knowing he was simply proving her point. "She's the daughter of my old tutor."

"Mr. Smithson. The one who first got you excited about all those bugs."

He nodded, not even bothering to challenge her thought. "It doesn't matter how I met her—"

"Of course it does."

"What matters is that we're engaged, and I want you to bring her out."

"*What!*"

He held up his hands. "Listen to me—"

"I don't care what you say, I will not help you destroy your future. Marriage to her would be a disaster!"

He was beginning to become irritated by her absolute certainty that Mellie would be a disaster. Mésalliance, yes, but a disaster? "Eleanor, she's a very nice person."

"I don't care if she's Mother Mary!" Then she pressed her hand to her mouth, obviously realizing the sacrilege she'd just uttered. Neither had sat down, and so she plopped on the nearest settee, only to jump up a second later. "You don't know how hard this is, Trevor. I am daily confronted with the…the disaster that is my family name. We used to be an honored and respectable title, but all we are now is a joke. He's the sailor turned duke, and we are a laughingstock."

"Hardly a laughingstock." Certainly the duke had been the wonder of last season. Still was a conversation item, and his wife was no help as she was a seamstress by trade. But things had quieted down. "They seem to have adjusted well enough." Especially given what he'd heard about the duchess's extra family affiliations.

"And whom do you think is responsible for that? Certainly not those two. They think it entirely appropriate to run squealing through the house."

Trevor frowned, his thoughts on the sight that had greeted them when they'd first stepped through the door. The duke and duchess had seemed a tad casual, of course, with a marked lack of consequence in their manner, but nothing so crass as what Eleanor implied. "I'm sure any respectability is due to your influence.

Which is why I came to you, my oldest friend, and the one most capable of helping in my hour of need."

"Don't try to butter me, Trevor. You don't know how hard it is."

"She can pay for her own come out, you know."

"As if that matters—"

"And I will add in extra for your troubles. I understand you're without great resources. Not to put too fine a point on it, but extra income probably wouldn't come amiss."

She whirled around, her hands on her hips as she glared at him. "I am very well situated, Mr. Anaedsley. I only remain here in this house as an example of proper breeding. If it weren't for me here, they'd likely have livestock to dine!"

She was exaggerating and they both knew it. But she was speaking the truth from her perspective. Anyone could see that the duke and duchess were a little rough about the edges. Their ability to adjust to their new status obviously came from her guidance. But that was exactly why he'd come to her in the first place.

"Tell me what I can say to convince you."

She folded her arms. "Not one thing. Forget about the Season, and forget about her mysterious science ways. Imagine instead a lifetime with her across the table from you every day. Does she clutch her fork in her fist? Reach for the wrong glass?"

"It's not that bad—"

"Does she insist on making friends with the wrong people? Embarrassing you if you ever have someone appropriate to visit? You cannot live on science. Her conversation is all well and good for now, but what will happen year after year when she simply does not live up to the name?" She stopped and gestured angrily at his jaw. "And what has happened to your face?"

He touched his swollen jaw and shrugged. "A ridiculous brawl." He wouldn't call it a duel because with Eleanor, she would think pistols or swords. And this morning's affair had not been nearly so elegant.

"A brawl. Trevor, look what she has brought you to! Think of the daily strain of it all. Believe me, it wears on a person."

He winced because he knew she was right. Though he'd likely never tire of Mellie's scientific conversation—she'd learned plenty from her father over the years—a lifetime of the constant reminder of their mésalliance would certainly become tedious.

He sighed. He would have to tell Eleanor the truth. He'd hoped to avoid it, but could see now that she had his best interests at heart. She would never agree to help him if she thought that he truly was set on this marriage. So ignoring propriety, he dropped into the chair nearest the fire.

"Pray come sit down, Eleanor. If we're going to talk plainly, I'd rather not do it on my feet."

"There is nothing you can say to sway my—"

"It's not a real engagement."

She stopped with her mouth ajar. He watched her frown, then snap her mouth closed before she quickly dropped into the seat across from him. "Tell me everything."

So he did. He told her about his grandfather's scheme to see him wed. He explained that he needed time for his investment to prosper, and that Mellie needed an alternative to Ronnie. He explained it all step by step in logical detail. And when he finished, he looked at her and asked the most important question. "So will you help me?"

She shook her head slowly, not in denial, but in apparent shock. "I never thought you capable of such deviousness."

He grimaced. "It is not my natural path."

"Don't cut up stiff. I mean it as a compliment. I just..." She leaned forward, catching his hands. "Are you sure you're not bamming me? This isn't a grand passion?"

He laughed at the idea. Loudly, and for a very long time, just to prove the point. Though he was remembering the kisses. The very wonderful, very exciting kisses he'd shared with Mellie. If he were of a silly frame of mind, he could easily form a grand passion for her. And that was what made this scheme so perfect. He could pull it off. He could pretend to the world that he'd fallen desperately in love with Mellie. Or, at least desperately in lust, and that was enough.

Apparently, his mirth was enough to convince Eleanor because she sat back and looked at him with the kind of expression he'd learn to respect. It was a female look and indicated a devious mind at work.

"Eleanor?"

"So you haven't found a wife?"

"Absolutely not. In fact, if you could help me find Mellie a husband, I would be beyond grateful."

She grinned. "How grateful? Just how much money has your grandfather promised when you become engaged? And how much will he pay afterward to make you become un-engaged?"

He cocked his head, startled to realize that she was haggling. There was a decidedly mercenary gleam in her eye. "I believe the new duke and duchess have had an effect on you."

She sniffed and drew back. "No need to be insulting."

"It's not an insult. My recent experience with poverty has shown me just how important it is to mind one's coins. I cannot see that it is any different for a woman."

"It's more important for a woman. Especially one who isn't as yet wed and who is sick of hiding in her rooms whenever Radley comes home." She leaned forward. "Do you know they are most disgustingly in love? Constantly kissing in dark corners throughout the house." She shuddered. "My mother is likely rolling over in her grave."

"Surely it isn't as bad as—"

"It's worse. And I would desperately love to be established in a house of my own."

He waited, his brows lowered as he watched the wistful expression cross her face. Dreams chased one after the other in her eyes, but he hadn't a clue what she wanted. Eleanor was likely as open with him as she was with anyone, and yet he still had no clue as to her true thoughts. What did this woman dream of? He didn't know, and he found that sad. After all, they'd been friends from the cradle, and yet she was always the Elegant Lady Eleanor. What did a woman who defined the best of his class think of in her private moments?

He touched her hand. "What do you want, Eleanor?"

"Money," she said bluntly. "Lots and lots of money."

Well, that was clear enough. So with a grin, he set about the negotiation.

❧

Mellie watched Trevor disappear with the extraordinarily beautiful Lady Eleanor and tried not to groan. They were two peas in a pod, those two: beautiful, titled, and of longstanding acquaintance. She had no way to compete with that, and so she simply had to accept it, though fear churned in her stomach. They were deciding her fate, after all. And clearly, she had no part in the discussion.

"It's nearly dinnertime," the duchess said into the silence. "Do say you'll stay to dine. I should very much love to hear the tale of how you trapped the Unassailable Duke."

"The what?"

The duchess laughed. "Mr. Anaedsley. That's what they call him. It's a play on the word 'unavailable' because he is always available. Enjoys going to parties and the like, especially during the Season. So he is available, but no woman has been able to catch him. So he's 'unassailable.'"

Her husband frowned. "I don't believe unassailable is quite the right word."

His wife laughed. "Probably not. No one said that society girls were smart. Only that they're marriage-minded."

The duke gave a mock shudder. "Don't remind me."

The two shared an intimate chuckle. It was then that Melinda noticed they were touching. Though the duke stood and his wife sat, he was near enough to stroke the back of her hand, which she stretched out for him. As Melinda sat, their fingers entwined, folding and caressing each other in such a way as to make her blush. It was ridiculous. They were just interlocking their fingers, and yet it had her thinking the most carnal things.

Meanwhile, the duchess had turned her attention back to Melinda, though her cheeks were pink and her eyes bright. "So how did it happen?"

"What?"

"You and Mr. Anaedsley. You must know that everyone will want the tale."

"Oh. Well, my cousin challenged him to a duel."

"What!" cried the duchess.

"That explains the jaw," said the duke.

Mellie twisted her fingers together, her mind not on the fight but the kiss they'd shared afterward. "It… um…it wasn't a real duel. Fisticuffs, but it was a long fight. All the county will be talking about it for years to come." Given their little village, she would likely be the subject of gossip for generations.

"That sounds like a tale."

She shook her head, feeling mortified all over again. And angry. Mostly angry at the silliness of men. "It happened so fast," she said. "Yesterday I was thinking of different scents to add to my creams. Today…" She gestured vaguely to her surroundings. "Today everything is different."

The duchess smiled. "Sometimes love is like that." Then she looked to her husband, and the two exchanged so soft and intimate a smile that Mellie was transfixed.

So that is what love looks like, she thought. Entwined fingers, shared smiles, long looks. She would have to remember to do such things with Trevor. But the idea of stroking even the back of his hand twisted her belly to a tight knot of anxiety. Or perhaps she was feeling something different. Something hot and needy. She didn't know. She wasn't used to these emotions at all.

She needed to change the subject. She needed to distract herself and everyone else from this confusing discussion until she had time to sort through her thoughts. But when she looked back at the duke and duchess—both watching her with disconcerting attentiveness—she realized she had no idea what to say. Her father was easy to distract. A simple scientific question, and he could be occupied for hours. And neither Ronnie nor her uncle had ever needed her to do more than nod and agree as if she had been listening to their every utterance.

But this, she realized with a growing sense of panic, was polite conversation, and she had none. There had been no need to learn it in her father's household where she was mistress and almost no one ever visited. But now, she was in society as the fiancée to a future duke. And she had absolutely no idea what to say or how to make the growing silence anything but uncomfortable.

She looked to the duke and duchess, realizing that

of all the people she would meet, they were perhaps the kindest. Unusual on their own, they would be more accepting of her oddities. That should have been reassuring, but it wasn't. If she could not speak with them, then how would she handle anyone else?

She abruptly stood, her mind whirling as she searched for a solution. But this was not a chemical recipe. There was no way to add an ingredient or set a mixture on a fire to heat. This was society, and she'd been a fool to think she could manage such a place.

"Miss Smithson?"

"This was a mistake. A horrible, horrible mistake." She headed for the door. "I cannot be here."

"Oh Lord, she's bolting," the duchess said, dismay in every word.

"Seelye, bar the door please," the duke called. "I fear we've insulted our guest, and now we must trap her here until she forgives us."

It took a moment for her to understand what the man had said. That, and the sight of the butler, looking like a kindly uncle as he held out his arm to gesture her back into the parlor. She tried to take a step around him, but he somehow managed to be directly in front of her no matter how she moved. And then she processed what the duke had said.

She whirled around. "Oh no! You haven't insulted me. I just…I just…"

The duchess came forward. "Never been to London before, have you?"

"Well, yes, I have. For shopping and the like. A few times." Exactly twice.

"And here we are confusing you. We're terrible

that way. No one ever knows how to talk to us. We're just too odd."

"Oh no, Your Grace."

"Tut, tut. I know it's true."

"Oh…oh…" And that was it. Just that ridiculous sound over and over as the couple firmly escorted her back into the settee. It was embarrassing. They were treating her like a lunatic child, and she didn't blame them in the least. But what was she supposed to do? How was she supposed to act?

His Grace pressed a brandy into her hand and encouraged her to drink. She did, nearly swallowing the whole in a single gulp.

"Good girl," he said as he might to a dog. Then he looked at the butler. "I think it's time that we request Mr. Anaedsley join us to dine."

"I shall do so directly," the man intoned.

"And you and I shall talk fashion," Her Grace said with a smile of encouragement.

Oh Lord. She had no idea about fashion. None whatsoever.

"Don't worry," the woman said as she patted Melinda's hand. "I know just how to set you up right. Make all the tabbies jealous when you appear. We'll get you dressed like a queen."

Melinda didn't know what to think. She certainly had no idea what to say. Somehow, in the few minutes away from Trevor, she'd been reduced to an idiot. And this time she couldn't blame it on anyone but herself. How had she come here so unprepared?

And how would she manage her escape?

Eight

Revenge must be plotted carefully. Observe the lay of the land first.

TREVOR WAS DEBATING THE NEWEST TREND IN FASHION fabrics with Eleanor when Seelye coughed discreetly at the door. Trevor didn't really care much for fashion one way or another, but he'd learned young how to discourse easily with a woman such as Lady Eleanor. And truthfully, there was comfort in knowing the pattern of a conversation even if the individual steps were beyond boring. But they knew their duty when Seelye appeared.

"We should continue our discussion with His Grace," he said to Lady Eleanor. They both knew which conversation he meant—Eleanor's sponsorship of Mellie—but the lady chuckled happily.

"Radley couldn't care less about the different choices in cotton."

"The Philistine."

She laughed and took his arm. "It's been very odd, you know, seeing him wear the title. But I think I have learned how to manage him."

Trevor didn't comment. He very much doubted that Eleanor had learned to "manage" the man at all. She had simply found a way to make peace while residing in his household. Fortunately, their bargain regarding Mellie's come out would go a long way to seeing her established in her own home where she could do as she liked.

So it was in companionable accord that they ventured back to the receiving parlor. His gaze found Mellie immediately, and what he saw was enough to make him slow his steps. To anyone else, she looked composed and quiet. Too quiet, actually, because her body was absolutely statue-still, an image reinforced by the stark pallor of her skin. The only sign of life was when her gaze cut to his and held. Panic. That's what he saw there: an angry, wide-eyed panic.

"Mellie?" he said carefully as he pasted on his most friendly smile. "Don't fret. I'm here now. Everything will be fine."

At which point her panic turned murderous.

He swallowed, somewhat at a loss. What could possibly have happened in the bare half hour that he'd been talking with Eleanor? He looked to the duke and duchess, but saw no help there. The man appeared genial as he sipped his brandy, and his wife studied Eleanor with a quiet, serious expression. No one appeared interested in talking. No one, that is, except Eleanor who had been reared since the cradle in handling tense social situations.

"My goodness, it's gotten late. Cousin, would you mind terribly if Trevor and his fiancée stayed to dine?

I have an exciting idea that I'd like to pursue, but it requires your permission."

The duke's eyebrows raised. "My permission? Eleanor, in my experience, you do exactly as—"

"Yes, yes, but you are head of the family now, and we must see to the proprieties."

The duke's mouth flattened as he set aside his glass. "Then by all means, let us see to the proprieties."

The duchess flashed a canny smile. "I have already sent word that we would have two more to dine. You can't say no, Mr. Anaedsley, because I've already sent down the order."

"I wouldn't dream of it," he answered, not liking the expression in her eye. He'd seen that look before on merchants and aristocrats alike. It saw advantage and was ready to seize it. Not evil or even cruel, but he'd be a fool to underestimate the woman.

Meanwhile, the duke wandered forward and set a gentle hand on his wife's shoulder. It was a small gesture—definitely an intimate one—and the lady's expression softened as she turned to her husband.

So the stories were true. The two were definitely a love match, their strengths and weaknesses clearly complements, one to the other. He pegged His Grace as the genial one—Her Grace would be the one to measure advantages. Together they would make a formidable couple. But what could they possibly have said to upset Mellie?

He looked to his fiancée and drew on his vast experience dealing with his mother and two sisters. Settling near her, he took her hands in his and patted them as he might a small child's. His mother especially appreciated this gesture.

"You'd like that, wouldn't you dearest? Dinner with the duke and duchess?"

Mellie's eyes narrowed, and her fingers stiffened into claws. Hell. That was not the reaction he'd hoped for.

"I…um…" He swallowed.

Meanwhile, Eleanor released a musical laugh. "Don't pester her, Trevor. Can't you see she's nervous? It's not every day she dines in such exalted company. But if my cousin is agreeable, I should like to make it a commonplace occurrence."

"Oh?" Her Grace asked, her voice polite in the most casual way. But the gleam was back in her eye.

"Why yes. Trevor and I are old friends, you see. Similar stations and the like. He has just asked me— well, begged me, truth be told—to help him smooth things with Melinda." She glanced over at Mellie. "May I call you Melinda? I think we shall become the grandest of friends soon. At least I hope so."

"My lady." Mellie's words were clear and precise. She even dipped her head as was entirely appropriate—in a servant. She appeared completely docile except, of course, beneath his fingers her hand was still rigid with fury.

"Oh, excellent!" Eleanor cried as if she had just been given a treat.

Meanwhile, Radley released a loud sigh. "Out with it, Eleanor. What are you asking?"

"Well, nothing so very terrible. I thought it would be nice if I had a companion, so to speak. For the Season."

Trevor stiffened, but it was nothing compared to the jerk that went through Mellie's hand. Though tiny, he felt her reaction all the way to his toes. "Not a companion, Eleanor," he said coldly. "As a friend."

"Well, what is a companion except a friend?" She turned back to the duke and duchess. "You see, I thought Melinda could stay here with us for her come out. She and I will have the grandest time. We could go together to balls and such. Don't worry about her attire. She's going to get completely outfitted. I thought we'd go to your dress shop, Wendy. And then—"

"Stop." The one word was soft, but no less clear, It came from Mellie like the single ring of a bell, and all eyes turned to her.

Trevor's fingers tightened on her hand, alarm shooting through his body. "Mellie, dearest, you must trust me."

"I am not accustomed to trusting others with my life," she said simply. "Nor am I a beggar to be thrown at their doorstep like a lost child."

"Of course not—"

She didn't stop to allow him to finish but turned directly to the duke and duchess. "Your Graces, I apologize for intruding into your home. The thought had been to seek Lady Eleanor's sponsorship during the coming Season, but I see now that it won't work."

Trevor patted her hand, desperate now for the gesture to soothe her even though it had already failed. "It *will* work, my dear, if only you would allow me to—"

"Why won't it work?" asked the duchess. There

was no animosity in her tone, but neither did she allow others to speak over Mellie. When Trevor turned to her, she waved him to silence with an impatient gesture. Her gaze was on his fiancée as she waited for her answer.

Beneath his hand, he felt Mellie wage an internal war between honesty and prevarication. He knew because he recognized the symptoms. Her breath accelerated, her fingers twitched, and her gaze dropped to the floor. The changes were subtle, but he was watching her closely. Sadly, he couldn't help her in this. If their scheme were to work, she would need to face the duchess regularly. And yet, he still tried.

"It has been a long, exhausting day, hasn't it? You're feeling quite overwhelmed and probably would like a lie down." That is, after all, exactly the suggestion his sisters would adore.

Her expression broke, and she shot him a glare. "I began the day fearing for your life, Mr. Anaedsley. Then I wallowed in the mud with you before being cast out by my father. What exactly do you think is overwhelming about sitting in a parlor with pleasant people?"

The duke barked out a laugh as he settled on the arm of his wife's chair. "Sounds like a lively tale."

"It isn't," Mellie said in exasperation. "It's an embarrassing tale. Just as this conversation is rather..."

"Humiliating?" offered the duchess. "Feeling like a piece of rubbish being tossed about on the wind?"

"Yes." Mellie's body tightened then released, her breath coming out in a soft sigh. Exactly the reaction he'd wanted, but he hadn't expected the duchess to understand what he had not.

"But there's nothing to be embarrassed about," he said. "I've got it all handled."

The duchess snorted. "She's not the type to want to sit quietly while others do everything for her. If you don't understand that about your own fiancée, then the two of you don't suit."

Trevor rounded on the woman, outrage at her statement overruling his good sense. "On the contrary," he said coldly, "it is one of the things I most admire about her."

"Really," drawled the damned seamstress. "Then why did you just go off with another woman to arrange things on her behalf? Did you think she'd appreciate being left with strangers while you bartered her future behind her back?"

"I wasn't bartering!" Except, of course, he had been. And the guilty flush that heated his cheeks showed him for the liar he was. "I was…I was arranging things. But that's what we wanted, isn't it dear?"

Mellie didn't comment. She'd gone mute. Even her hand had stopped moving, which was a sure sign that she'd locked herself up tight. In fact, he'd bet his fortune this was exactly how she acted when Ronnie got out of hand. But he wasn't Ronnie to blather on in ignorance of her wishes. "Damn it, Mellie, we discussed this and agreed." She'd even kissed him in full view of the entire county.

Her gaze dropped from his. "I know. But I hadn't realized…I didn't know you'd meant here. With…" *Them.* She didn't have to say it, but her gaze encompassed the house and all its exalted occupants.

Good Lord, didn't she understand? "I am the grandson to the Duke of Timby. Did you think I spent my days with merchants and a baron or two? You wanted a Season. This is what it means to have one." *With me.* He didn't say the words, but she had to understand them. He was a peer.

The room settled into an uncomfortable silence until the duke apparently got impatient. "So as I understand it, Eleanor, you want to sponsor Miss Smithson. Introduce her to society, but what exactly does that mean?"

Eleanor immediately brightened. "Well, I should like her to live here," she said. "We've plenty of room, and she does need some education."

"Actually," Trevor cut in, wondering why he was suddenly so irritated by his childhood friend. "She's had a better education than you. Certainly a better grounding in the sciences."

Eleanor huffed. "Well, what is that to the point? There's not a soul who will ask her anything about that."

Surprisingly, Mellie spoke up next. "She's right, Trevor. There are things I should learn before I enter society."

Eleanor beamed at her as if she were a particularly bright child. "See, she understands."

"*She* has a name," he growled back.

"But she hasn't given me leave to use it. Not really."

Trevor frowned. Hadn't she? Damnation, why was the conversation so hard?

"You have my leave," Mellie said woodenly, which was even more worrisome.

Meanwhile, the duke was apparently trying to keep things moving. "So you'd like her to live here, and then the two of you would go to parties and such."

"Yes, exactly," Eleanor answered.

Meanwhile, the duchess entwined her fingers with her husband's. "I expect it will take a great deal of Eleanor's time and attention."

The duke frowned as he thought. "Keeping her busy, you mean? So she can cease nattering at us?"

His wife smiled. "Well, I doubt that will ever truly stop."

"Truly spoken." But he did smile. "I should like a little less of Eleanor's attention."

Eleanor released a puff of disdain. "If you would but listen closer when I speak, I would be happy to instruct you less."

The duke proved Eleanor's point by roundly ignoring her. "There are plenty of rooms in this house. We could put her next to Eleanor's bedroom."

His wife's expression turned indecently intimate. "And if you are not called upon to chaperone all the time—"

"Sold!"

The duchess grinned, but Trevor did not like the tone of the conversation. "Mellie is not at auction!" he snapped.

"No," the duchess agreed, "but we have a bargain. Miss Smithson, it is my greatest pleasure to welcome you to our home. Eleanor, pray make sure to keep yourself and her well occupied. And in the meantime," she said as she pushed to her feet, "I should very much like to eat." She looked over their shoulders at the butler. "Seelye, that is why you are here, is it not? Is dinner served?"

The man bowed in a most proper form. "It is indeed."

The duke was also on his feet. "Excellent! My lady?" he said, extending his arm to his wife.

"My lord," she answered as she touched her fingers to his forearm.

Eleanor stood as well, though her expression was sour. "You are 'graces,' not lord and lady." Then she turned to Trevor as she waited for his arm. "They make an effort in public, but at home everything scatters to the wind."

Trevor had been busy helping Mellie to stand. She was clearly still angry, but there was more to it than that. Panic seemed to rest on her shoulders like an ugly cloak, but there was no time to address the problem. Propriety demanded that he lead Lady Eleanor to the table.

"Mellie—" he began, but Eleanor cut him off.

"Begin as you mean to end, Mr. Anaedsley." Then when he still hesitated, her voice became sharper. "Trevor, you came to me for a reason. Trust me to know how to polish a raw girl."

"She's not a raw—"

"In this she is." She glanced at Mellie. "You understand precedence? Who goes in to dine in what order?"

"Yes, my lady."

She nodded. "Excellent. Come along, Trevor." Then she grabbed his arm, sank in her talons, and began pulling him toward the door.

He had to go or appear completely rude, not to mention gauche and ridiculous. One did not fight with a lady, and certainly not with Lady Eleanor. So he turned his back on his fiancée, feeling like the lowest heel. He listened as they walked, every cell in his body attuned to Mellie, trying to discern her thoughts, her emotions, her…anything. But she was as blank to him as a darkened room.

Meanwhile, Eleanor began to prattle. "Now here is what I plan…"

And so began the most bizarre dinner of his life.

Nine

When the opportunity appears, do not hesitate. Strike swiftly.

MELINDA TRAILED IN BEHIND THE GROUP, FEELING LIKE a small child. She hadn't been the last to go into dinner since…well, since ever. Her mother had passed when she was young, so on her very first formal dinner—at the age of eight—her father had extended his arm, and they had walked in together like the King and Queen of England.

It was that memory—and not the sight of her fiancée leading Lady Eleanor to her seat—that brought her emotions to heel. She was not a woman who felt small. And she was definitely not a child to be overcome by feelings best left in the nursery. Therefore, she would do as she had been taught. She would analyze the situation like a scientist and come to a logical conclusion.

She began with the easiest. She would observe her environment. The ducal London home was well apportioned, had an excellent staff, and a first-rate cook. She had not yet been served, but the scent was tempting enough, even for her stomach, which was currently tied up in knots.

She'd already formed her opinion of the duke and duchess as warm and welcoming people, and Lady Eleanor as decidedly not. Especially now that the woman began speaking quite drolly about Lord Somebody and Lady Other with her attention completely centered on Trevor. It took another two seconds of quiet observation for Melinda to conclude that Lady Eleanor was unwilling to allow a low-class usurper like her to be part of the circle that included Trevor. The woman barely tolerated the duke and duchess. A cit like her couldn't possibly compete.

For his part, Trevor chuckled in the exact same manner, though he kept darting worried frowns at her. Melinda concluded that he was either concerned about her silent demeanor or disappointed by her lack of polish.

And therein ended her conclusions based on observations. Not very useful after all, until Lady Eleanor paused in yet another anecdote to glance at her. "I do hope you're listening, Melinda. These are names you should memorize and information you should keep in your pocket."

She looked at the woman, acute dislike welling up through her belly. But she forced it down even as she curved her lips into something she hoped appeared to be a smile. "I have come to a decision," she said. In her experience, nothing exasperated an egoist more than having their comments completely ignored.

"Oh, excellent," crowed the duchess. "I do so enjoy decision at the dinner table."

Mellie took a moment to study Her Grace, unsure whether this was a criticism or a simple statement of fact. "Duchess?"

"Goodness, call me Wendy. After all, you shall be with us for the whole Season."

"Your Grace!" Lady Eleanor cried.

"Of course, Wendy," Mellie responded.

"Now, what have you decided?"

"That if I am to have a Season, everyone will be talking about the gross mésalliance between myself and Mr. Anaedsley."

Trevor cast her a soft smile. "It's not so gross nor so unusual."

"Truly?" Mellie challenged. "Then your family coffers need an infusion of my dowry?"

"Don't be ridiculous. The title is very well heeled."

"Exactly," Lady Eleanor inserted. "Mésalliance."

Mellie didn't wish to be supported by that woman at all, but she couldn't disagree. "Therefore, if we wish to distract everyone from that story, we must provide a different one."

The duke snorted. "I shouldn't worry about that. Something else will come along. Someone will have a scandalous affair. Someone else will drop dead of an interesting illness."

His wife shook her head. "No, no, she's right. She's talking about the story around *her*. And that won't be replaced by the usual tidbits."

Lady Eleanor nodded. "Not unless we do something to change it."

Good. They were all smart. Meanwhile the duke finished off his soup. "Well? Don't keep us in suspense. What do you mean to do?"

"I believe we should talk about my unusual scientific abilities. I'm quite accomplished. It was my discovery that bleaches muslin so white. And I've developed a new formula for an exciting new cosmetic. I should think that appeals to the women at least."

Total silence greeted her words, and Mellie had a moment of satisfaction. Perhaps she could manage this task after all. But it was a brief moment before an explosion of sound. In truth, the laughter wasn't more than chuckles, but it sounded like a cacophony. They clearly thought her life's work thus far was a subject of humor—that was insulting enough—but it was the softer expressions that truly hurt: pity. The same expression that appeared whenever someone referred to her dead mother, when anyone spoke about her odd father, and now, it was extended to her work as well.

Pity. And if that was the way of things then—

"By Jove, that's incredible. You must have been a child. Were you doing chemistry even when your father was tutoring me?"

Mellie blinked, focusing on Trevor as she nodded. "Yes. I was nine and had gotten grass stains on my dress. I didn't have that many dresses then and didn't want to tell Papa. So I thought of a way to use chemicals to lift it out."

"And did it?"

She shrugged. "Dissolved the thing into dust. And I burned my fingers trying to stop it." She held up her hand as if the mark was still there, but she'd been young, not stupid. As soon as the pain had hit her fingertips, she'd plunged them into cold water. And then stood by in misery as her favorite dress dissolved in front of her eyes.

"You don't bear scars from it, do you?" he asked.

She put her hand down. "No. Fingertips grow back quickly."

"Lucky that," Trevor laughed, "Or I'd have to stuff cotton in my gloves to fill them out. Especially after my experiments with combustibles."

She smiled at him, her humiliation easing, but was rapidly beginning to learn that everything moved faster in London, including the pace of conversation. She had no more than found a smile for Trevor when Lady Eleanor stepped in to destroy the peace.

"Well, that story won't serve. Really Trevor, you know better than to encourage that line of talk. Stuffed gloves. Science—"

"Wait now," interrupted the duchess. "I know about your mill's muslin. Whitest in England."

"Thank you—"

"Which is all very well and good inside a dress shop," Eleanor corrected. "But we're planning her come out. Adding 'bluestocking' to the story will in no way stop talk of the mésalliance. In fact, it will only increase it."

Mellie looked to Trevor, waiting for him to support her. After all, he understood what she'd accomplished. But he shrugged and gave her *that* look. Pity, damn it, from the one man who understood.

"She's right, I'm afraid," he said. "We need

something better. How about the duel I fought for her?"

Lady Eleanor gasped in horror. "You fought a duel for her?" She might as well have said, you had dinner in a pig wallow?

"Fisticuffs. But the entire county was there as witness," continued Trevor.

Meanwhile, Mellie was anxious to put an end to that tale. "I've already told the tale."

"But not to me," said Eleanor as she smiled at Trevor. Obviously, she wanted him to tell it, but then a second later she waved it off. "I'll want full details later, but again…that will only increase the talk of the mésalliance. After all, who would fight a duel with fists? That's a bout, not a duel."

"Fair point," said Trevor. "Though the man was a giant, and he had fists like granite."

Ronnie was big, but not a giant. "It's a wonder you survived at all," Mellie said, her tone sarcastic.

Trevor flashed her a grin. "Allow me a little exaggeration. It is my jaw that he pummeled, you know."

"And yet you are eating and talking with no ill effects."

He barked out a laugh, and she felt her tensions ease. But she knew by now that a moment later things would be bad again. Oddly enough, the next suggestion came from the duchess who had been mostly content with her food until now.

"Dress her outrageous."

The duchess was soft spoken, but her words seemed to carry, and again there was a moment's silence in response. Mellie tensed, waiting for more humiliating laughter, this time directed to the highest-ranking woman in the room. But instead Lady Eleanor paused in the act of reaching for her wine.

"Pray go on."

"Helaine can manage it. Something outré without being déclassé." She flashed her husband a smile at her French words.

Her husband frowned, then grinned as he translated. "Something wild without being vulgar. But would that work?"

"That all depends," said Eleanor as she frowned at Melinda. "Do you have any Russian heritage?"

"Russian?" Mellie asked.

"We can't do German," she returned. "There's nothing outrageous in the entire stodgy lot. French is out, of course, and you don't really look Spanish."

"What about Turkish?" asked Trevor.

"With a hookah pipe? Hmmm." Then Eleanor waved it away. "Too dirty with the smoke and all. And not very outrageous either. I think it shall have to be Russian."

Mellie set her hands tightly in her lap. "But I don't know any Russian." She didn't even know *anyone* Russian. "Perhaps we should return to my scientific work."

"No, no, I told you. Bluestockings are boring, not outrageous. We need to make you fun." She suddenly snapped her fingers. "I know! You must sing badly."

"What?"

"Very, very badly. Such that we all laugh."

Trevor was just being served the mutton when he shook his head. "But she has a lovely singing voice."

No, she didn't. Mellie frowned at him. "Why would you think that?"

He shrugged and gave her a mischievous smile. "Your father told me that once, I think."

Mellie shot him an irritated look. "Papa meant that I have perfected his cricket calls."

"Cricket?" the duke asked, using his fork to gesture. "As in with a ball and a bat?"

"Er, no, the insect. My father studies them, you know."

"So it's like bird calls only for insects?" the man pressed.

"Yes, exactly," she said, only belatedly realizing how odd this must sound to anyone outside her father's circle of friends.

The duchess set down her fork, apparently not liking the mutton. "But why would anyone want to call crickets?"

Good question. She'd asked her father the same thing at the time. "He believed the cricket's chirp was indicative of a mating ritual. He wanted to test the theory with calls, but he hadn't the knack of it."

Lady Eleanor beamed at her. "But you did. Can you do one now?"

"Er—"

"Can you, perhaps, make it into a song of sorts?"

"What?"

Eleanor suddenly brightened. "I know, make it a bit like 'Greensleeves,' but for crickets. You know the tune, don't you?" Then she proceeded to hum a bit of the song.

"What are you about?" That was from Trevor, his voice a mix of outrage and laughter.

The humming stopped, and Eleanor turned wide eyes on Trevor. "It's perfect, you know. We'll call her a poor Russian princess, so lonely she only had the crickets as playmates."

Mellie set her fork down with a click. "But I am not a poor Russian princess."

"No one will know that. And besides, you do have an eccentric father, right? We'll say he got his madness from his Russian side."

"But we're not Russian!"

Eleanor huffed. "We've been over this. All the other countries won't suit."

"Stop, Eleanor," Trevor said. "I won't have my fiancée made into a laughingstock."

"But that's the point, don't you see? To make her outrageous in a fun way." And when Trevor just stared her down, she added in a tiny pout. "You needn't frown at me like that. It was her idea. I was simply making it work."

Meanwhile, the duchess waved the footman to withdraw her plate. "We still need a story for her."

Trevor finished off his mutton with a last large bite. "Love match won't do it?"

Both society women spoke at once. "No." And, "Certainly not."

Which is when Melinda made her decision. Right there, between the mutton and the pheasant courses, she looked at the white gloves of the footmen who were trying to hide the gravy stains, the impassive expression of the butler who was nonetheless listening to every word spoken, and most of all, to the flirtatious glances of Lady Eleanor as she systematically made Mellie an object of fun. She saw the silly pageantry of it all, and she finally understood that Ronnie hadn't been the only one obsessed with creating a Cheltenham tragedy out of everything. Everyone wanted a pageant—tragedy or farce made no difference. It was the game of society, and if she wanted to be part of it, she needed to play her roll exceedingly well.

"Very well then," she said. "I shall be the Cricket Princess."

"The what?" Trevor gaped.

"Well, it's somewhat true, isn't it? My father is an eccentric entomologist. We are rich beyond Croesus—" Not true, but this was a play, after all. She might as well exaggerate. "And he has taught me some very odd things."

Trevor reared back. "He has taught you science."

"No, no," interrupted Eleanor. "She has the right of it. Science is only interesting if it's bizarre."

Trust the woman to call her right and bizarre in the same sentence. Meanwhile, she continued to speak to Trevor. "And as your love of bugs is well established—"

"Science," he reiterated, a heavy note to his voice. "And you know damned well that I believe there is a link between insects and disease."

"Well, what is that to the point?" she said, in exactly the tones that Eleanor had used earlier. "We shall make you the Buggy Duke and me the Cricket Princess. Everyone will believe a love match then because it's a perfect pairing."

"It is no such thing!" Trevor cried.

"Oh yes, it is," she said, her voice dropping to a low a threat. She had no idea where such a venomous sound came from, but it held all the frustration and embarrassment of the last twenty-four hours. And it laid all of it at his door. "Because if you believe I shall be trussed up and paraded around as an object of fun alone, then you are sadly out, Mr. Anaedsley. This was your mad idea, and I shall not be pranced about like a dancing bear without you right by my side as a monkey jumping to the same tune."

For the third time that evening, the room descended into silence. She could not tell if the reason was shock, horror, or appreciation. It didn't matter. Her gaze was on Trevor, as his was the only opinion that mattered. His expression was tight, but it slowly eased as he looked at her. In his lengthy silence, he seemed to be testing her resolve, so she kept her expression firm.

In the end, he puffed out a breath. "How will this work? I am not the least bit buggy."

She picked up her fork and gestured much as the duke had done. "Be sure to open your eyes very wide."

"Mellie!" he cried, the sound conveying both outrage and laughter.

"And no more of that," she said coldly. "I am a princess from now on."

Eleanor chose that moment to insert herself. "Can we at least make you Printsessa? That's Russian for—"

"No." This time it was Trevor and Mellie who spoke at the same instant.

❧

It was past midnight when he knocked on Mellie's door, half hoping that she wouldn't answer. Trevor had spent much of the evening in congenial drink with the duke. He found the man to be wise in the way of a practical man and pleasant in the way of the best drinking companion. So the two had stayed up late, and then—thankfully—the man had extended his hospitality enough to give Trevor a room for the night. Good thing, as there were likely creditors sleeping outside his usual rooms. Fortunately, he wouldn't need to live with a straightened purse anymore. His grandfather would be settling a nice sum on him the minute the engagement was announced.

But even pleasant masculine evenings had to end, and so it was that the duke went to his lady wife and Trevor turned his mind to Mellie. In truth, he'd been thinking of her for much of the evening—or avoiding thoughts of her—but it was time to face her fury. Or her gratefulness. Or her logic. Truth be told, he had no idea what she was feeling, and he was not a man who liked to walk blind into a woman's parlor. Two sisters and a petulant mother had taught him that. And yet he still felt the driving need to see her, so he scratched at her door and tried not to fidget in anxiety.

"Come in," came her soft reply.

Awake then. Steeling himself for whatever came on the other side, he quickly slipped inside her room, shutting the door behind him.

She'd rearranged the furniture. The duchess certainly wouldn't have placed the chair facing the window. But she'd put it and herself there, looking out the darkened panes while an empty brandy snifter rested by her elbow. He had a moment's pang that there was no bottle resting nearby. He suspected she was as affable a companion as the duke had been.

"Mellie?" he asked.

"Don't you mean *princess*?"

She spoke lightly, humor in her tone, so he smiled and dared approach. "Princess, then. I came to see how you fared."

She glanced at him, and he saw the moonlight caress her skin to a pearly glow. "So you haven't come to your senses, then?"

He was lost for a time in her beauty. God, the moon loved her face. But then he shook himself out of his reverie enough to blink at her. "What senses?"

"I have been thinking of writing down a fairy tale. The Cricket Princess and the Mad, Bad Buggy Duke. What do you think?"

"I think it shall be a marvelous tale."

"It is a ridiculous tale, and you know it." She adjusted her seat so that she faced him directly. "I thought you'd stayed away because you were steeling your resolve to tell me such."

"I have no need to steel myself to talk to you," he said with vehemence. And as the words left his mouth, he realized it was true. She was not an emotional woman, thank God. The fact that she could speak rationally, today of all days, told him that. So he dropped on the nearest seat—the edge of her bed—and breathed a sigh of relief. "Mellie, it will all work out. You just need—"

"If you tell me to trust you one more time, I think I shall hit you."

"But…um…oh." He had no counter to that because in his experience, it always did work out. Maybe not perfectly, but well enough.

Meanwhile, she arched a brow at his silence while he felt like an errant schoolboy caught doing mischief. Then she sighed. "Do you imagine that I have grown to adulthood in my father's house, managed servants and Ronnie, plus stopped my uncle's interference, by leaving it to someone else to bring things right?"

"Of course not. I'm sure you were the most responsible adult in that household within a year of your mother's passing," he said. Then he gripped his thighs rather than reach for her because what he was about to say would not be pleasant to hear. "But that is in the country, and this is London. You have to rely on someone. You're an outsider here."

"I can rely on advice, Mr. Anaedsley, without surrendering my reason completely."

She had a point, but rather than allow her that, he quietly chided her. "We are alone and affianced. You must call me Trevor."

"Are we?" she challenged. "Are we still engaged? Trevor—" She stressed his Christian name, and not in a nice way. It was more an angry, irritated, frustrated way. "This whole plan is ludicrous."

"It will work," he said firmly, though in truth, she had echoed his thoughts exactly. It was a delicate line to tweak the *ton*'s interest without crossing over into total revulsion. The mood of the aristocracy was capricious at the best of times.

"Well, it has already worked for you, hasn't it? With our engagement, your grandfather will release your money, and you are saved from the duns. Whereas I am to find a suitable alternative to Ronnie while acting as your fiancée and hailed as the Cricket Princess."

He tilted his head, seeing for the first time how careful she was. Obviously, she'd spent her life having other people see to their needs with never a thought to hers. In short, she expected to be overlooked and so had no qualms in accusing him of such a crime.

"You are far out on that, Mellie. Far, far out."

She took a moment to study him, then slowly shook her head. "I don't think so."

"Then I shall make it clear. We shall begin with the simplest. Our engagement isn't real until it is published in the papers."

She brightened. "Then there is still time to stop this nonsense."

"No," he lied, "there is not. Second, I made a bargain with you to see you wed, and I shall stick to it. You insult my word as a gentleman to suggest anything different."

She rolled her eyes. "Do you suggest that no gentleman has ever gone back on his word? That no bargain was actually a cheat or—"

"I say I am a gentleman, and I would never do such a thing." He was rather insulted that she entertained the idea. But then she had grown up in the country, and they had all sorts of ridiculous notions. "Besides, I am the one at risk here. I have proposed. You have accepted. What if you change your mind and suddenly post the banns at your church? If you set a date, we must perforce wed. A neat way to trap a future duke, don't you think?"

Her lips narrowed to a flat line. Obviously, she liked being called a cheat no better than he did. Except her words were entirely unexpected. "You cannot convince me that you would marry me in such a circumstance."

"Of course I would. Or face the rest of my life as the man who stood you up at the altar for no reason whatsoever. There are some things a gentleman doesn't do. I have pushed for this engagement, ruse though it is. You have accepted. Unless you murder someone or make me a cuckold before the vows, I cannot in honor refuse to appear on the day you choose." She blinked at him, obviously mulling over his words. Good Lord, he couldn't have just given her an idea. Of course not. She was Mellie. She didn't think that way. But it didn't stop him from hastily adding, "I am relying on you to not change your mind. To not put my honor to the test in such a malicious way."

"Do you know," she said, "I find your gentlemanly code as ridiculous as Ronnie's romantic one?"

He reared back as if struck, though his reason couldn't deny her point. "I am insulted to my core."

She arched her brow. "Truly? Insulted to your core?"

He shrugged. "Well, I should be."

"Then you understand my point."

"Of course I do. But you must acknowledge mine. I adhere to my code as firmly as Ronnie holds to his. I have made you a promise to find you a husband, and I shall stick to that no matter what."

She shook her head, not in denial, but in apparent awe of his stubbornness. "You would attach your honor to finding the Cricket Princess a husband. Do you not hear how ridiculous that is?"

"Well, I do acknowledge that it will be a challenge. But never fear, with Eleanor's sponsorship I am sure we will find a way."

She studied him again, her expression serious even though the discussion had hit unprecedented heights of silliness. "Your code—Ronnie's code—both are set to make me an object of fun."

"I disagree. In truth, our codes have very little to do with you except that you are affected by our behavior. Our codes are meant to manage ourselves, not others. And before you poke another accusing finger, recall that you have a code of your own."

"I do not," she said haughtily. Then she seemed to change her mind. "Unless it is science. The rule of logic."

"Well you need to toss that aside. You are in society now."

She snorted, and he liked the indelicate sound. "I gathered that at dinner, Mr. Buggy Duke."

He laughed, but he could see she was resigned to their charade. And for that, he was enormously grateful. "It will come out all right, Mellie. I have sworn it."

She looked up at him, and at this angle, the light fell upon the creamy skin of her bosom. Her night rail had come untied, so he saw beautiful skin and the swell of her very lovely breasts. "You are daft, Mr. Anaedsley. But I have given you my promise, and so…"

"And so?" he prompted when she fell silent.

"Must I really be a Cricket Princess?"

"Yes," he said in mock seriousness. "Much more a compliment than it sounds, you know. Men go mad for crickets. Just look at your father."

"Do not hold him up to me as an example."

"The Beetle Queen made a spectacular match last season."

"I lived in the country, Mr. Anaedsley, not Siberia."

He frowned, searching through his memory for his geography lessons. He'd been terrible in that subject, his interest much more in the construction of canals.

"It's part of Russia," she supplied.

"Ah yes, of course it is," he said. He couldn't stop himself. He touched her chin. "You are a very clever girl, you know. Much more clever than I, it seems, in matters of geography."

"You are better in entomology."

"And you in chemical recipes." He stroked his thumb across her lower lip, pleased when the flesh heated and swelled beneath his caress. "But in this—in society, and what attracts a gentleman—pray allow me to be the wiser one."

"I believe I have gambled my entire future on just such a thing."

He smiled. "So you have." Then his smile broadened. "There is only one thing left to do, you know."

Her lips had parted, the heat of her moist breath flowing over his thumb like a beaconing wave. "What?"

"We must seal this bargain with a kiss."

Her eyes told him she'd expected such a thing. The way her breath caught told him she'd hoped for such a thing. But it was her lips that he was most interested in as she formed these words.

"We have already sealed it with a kiss," she whispered.

A great many of them, in fact—kisses that burned in his memory as splendid events. As the best damn bargains he'd ever made purely because of the way they made him feel: alive, happy, and desperate to kiss her again.

"I feel the need to ensure your promise again," he said as he leaned closer.

"You have it."

So he took it: her promise, her mouth, and a great deal more besides.

Ten

You must overwhelm his senses while keeping your own.

SHE KNEW THIS WAS WRONG. UNMARRIED LADIES DID not entertain gentlemen in their bedrooms. Not while in their night rail, and certainly not with brandy and kisses. She knew it, but she found herself unable to stop. After an entire lifetime of being demure, Melinda found herself tossing every scrap of logic and decorum aside.

She blamed him completely.

She blamed him for charming her out of her anger. She blamed him for leaning close and being so handsome that she ached to touch him. And she blamed him most especially for being so good at kissing that she wanted to do it again.

Their lips touched. His were warm and tempting. Like hot chocolate on a cold morning. She wanted to lick him slowly before relishing tiny sips. But she never had control with him or chocolate. She knew she'd start gulping him down while his touch still burned her tongue.

She kissed him full and deep. She thrust her tongue into his mouth, then quickly lost that duel as he dominated her. She was stretched awkwardly in her chair. He had the room to push forward and to wind his fingers through her hair as he took control of her mouth and her kiss.

She tried to stay dispassionate. After all, she'd kissed other men. What made this man's caress so much better than another's? Was it the way his one hand was firm as he cradled her head and the other hand a sensuous stroke as he brushed down her neck and across her shoulder? Was it the way his tongue was unpredictable, first thrusting then stroking? A push then a nip while she scrambled to keep pace? Actually, it seemed that his total command of the situation was thrilling and...

He touched her breast.

She knew he would. While their kiss had gone on and her mind had spun its distraction, she had allowed his fingers to slip the shoulder of her night rail down before his fingers stroked over her bare breast. She had allowed it, and yet, everything seemed dizzyingly beyond her control.

He broke their kiss, dropping his forehead against hers while their breath mingled hot and sweet. But his fingers did not stop as he brushed the rounded swell of her breast, then slipped quick as a wink beneath it. She felt him lift her slightly, and his thumb brushed her nipple.

Lightning tingled up her body, lingering in her jaw for a second. Bizarre, she thought, and then he did it again. His thumb, back and forth across her nipple.

This time the sizzle went low, heating her belly and weakening her legs.

"You must trust me," he said as he pressed a kiss to her nose.

"I do," she answered, though she'd meant to say, "of course not." Of course she did not trust a lustful man in her bedroom at night. She was a proper girl and not a fool. But then he pressed his lips to her shoulder. A kiss. Another. Then the scrape of his teeth against her skin.

It was so delightful she shivered. What an odd reaction, she thought, but as soon as the idea formed it slipped away under the steady thrum of his thumb across her nipple.

"Trevor," she whispered. She lifted her hand, meaning to push him away. Instead, she feathered her fingers into his hair, feeling the soft caress of his locks across the back of her hand. Soft curls. Sweet kisses, now on the curve of her breast.

He shifted until he was kneeling before her. He pressed his mouth against her skin and pushed her backward in the chair. Her head dropped against the ornate chair, and her pulse rushed close to the surface. She felt it in her throat, and yet she also felt the stroke of his thumb as if he touched the deepest center of her body.

Then he lifted her breast higher, bringing it to his mouth.

She had heard of this before. She wasn't completely ignorant, and she often overheard ladies whispering together. Gentlemen liked breasts, they'd said. "Sucking on tits" was the phrase they'd used. She never guessed that she would enjoy it too.

That the press of his lips would set her to gasping. That her pulse would jump as his suction pulled at her. Or that she would grip his shoulders and hold him so that he would never stop.

He sucked. Sometimes he stopped, and his fingers twisted her nipple. Not painfully. Or yes, a little painfully, but in the most wonderful way. On the other breast. On both breasts. And then, yes, he took her nipple into his mouth again.

Her heart hammered, and she shifted restlessly. She wanted to draw him closer, but she hadn't the thought. She felt his pull. Every stroke. Every caress. She felt it…

Everything tightened unbearably.

So tight. Like everything drawn in and held.

Until it broke.

Her belly convulsed, and her mind sputtered in shock.

Everything pulsed and writhed and rushed inside her. And it was wondrous!

It continued for a while, with her body throbbing, while everything else tried to grab hold. Her mind tried to understand, her breath tried to catch up, and even her belly, which quaked and quivered, tried to gather its dignity and pull her legs closed. Nothing worked except this flight of pleasure powered by the contractions of her belly. And in the end, she surrendered herself to the sensations, only to have them fade into a pale tremor inside her.

Which was when she opened her eyes to see him watching her. His eyes were wide and his mouth slightly parted. His expression seemed dazed, but beneath it all was a clear excitement. Not lust, but giddy joy.

Or was that her?

"Has that ever happened to you before?" he asked, his voice hushed.

She swallowed. "N-no."

He smiled. "And what did you think of it?"

Think? She couldn't think at all.

His smile widened into a grin. "That was the most amazing thing I've ever seen. I feel quite accomplished, you know."

He was laughing. She could hear the delight in his words, but she didn't understand his meaning. Accomplished?

His expression gentled, and he lifted his hand to stroke her cheek. "You're beautiful, you know. Every time I see you, it seems that I find something more remarkable about you."

She grabbed hold of her reason and formed a word. "What?" Sometime later, she managed to pull herself together enough to straighten in her chair. She meant to pull her knees together, but he was pressed against them, keeping them wide. It was only the fabric that kept him distant from her full body.

And then, while she sat there desperately trying to gather her wits, he straightened up. She still fought to control even the smallest aspect of her body while he slipped an arm underneath her legs and the other behind her back. Then he lifted her out of her chair.

She gasped in surprise, managing to wrap an arm around his broad shoulders as he maneuvered them to her bed. Then he set her down, his touch gentle, even as his eyes sparked with delight.

"Lord," he murmured, "the things I could show you."

She ought to object. She had enough awareness to know that. But the words didn't form. She didn't have the wherewithal to do more than grip his sleeve as he drew away, his expression regretful.

"This wasn't well done of me," he said with a sigh. "I should have left that to your husband, lucky bastard." Then he flashed his mischievous grin. "But I can't regret it. God, the way you looked. Surprised. Delighted. I haven't the words, Mellie, but I was awed."

She didn't understand what he was saying. She was coming to grips with the basics as her logical brain pulled the facts together. She had come. That had been an orgasm. Contractions and pleasure—she understood now. Women could take delight in their bodies. That was good to know.

But he was leaving her, and so she clutched his hand, trying to hold him still. She needed to comprehend what had happened. And she wanted to process the information while he explained. And provided more examples.

"Mellie—"

"Not yet," she managed. "Don't leave yet."

He paused. "You tempt me too much. Do you understand? I'm barely holding onto my honor as it is."

She did understand, and yet… "This is so new. I want to…"

"Explore more?" he asked.

She nodded. "Oh yes."

He chuckled, the sound tight for all that it was filled with good humor. "Then I must leave. Mellie, I have had too much brandy." And yet, he lingered and still held her hand. His thumb stroked her skin, and her nipple tightened in memory.

She watched what he did, and she felt her belly tighten again. She licked her lips and heard him groan.

"Mellie—"

"Does that happen every time?"

"With me it does," he answered, pride in his tone.

"No wonder the ladies flock to you."

He blinked. "What?"

"I read about you in the society papers. I know you are a favorite. Now I know why."

She tugged on his hand, and he obliged her by settling on the edge of the bed. She felt his heat against her thigh and idly brushed her fingers through the hair on his forearm. He had such lovely arms. Corded with strength, but still soft enough to stroke.

"The papers have me bedding every female in England. I assure you, that is far from the truth."

She shrugged. "But I understand it now."

He sighed, and the sound seemed to come from deep within him. "Mellie, I cannot. I will not debauch you."

She bit her lip. She wanted to be debauched. How had she lived this long without having that experience? How had she not even known it was possible?

But the more time passed, the more she knew he was right. She risked everything by having him here touching her. There were too many things set against her on the marriage mart already. She had to be sure to stay a virgin. She knew this, and yet it was so hard to stop touching him.

Then she looked at him, seeing a way to satisfy her curiosity. She rushed the words out, whispering them before she could stop herself.

"Will you teach me?" she asked.

She felt her words jolt through his body. A jerk of his hand, but a sudden heat in his eyes. "Teach you what exactly, Mellie?"

"Show me how to do that…to feel that way again. By myself."

She watched him swallow, and his eyes seemed to fire suddenly bright, but then his expression abruptly closed down. He looked hard. And very remote.

"Don't be angry," she said, though—God in heaven—why she had formed those words, she hadn't a clue. It was only that he suddenly looked so forbidding.

"I'm not angry," he said. "I'm trying to hold onto my honor."

"But—"

"Yes." The word was hard and clipped, but there was no anger in his face.

"You will?"

"Yes. But not tonight. I'll… We'll… Tomorrow night maybe. Or…Jesus." He rubbed a hand over his face. Then he abruptly straightened and stepped away. He gently disentangled their fingers and left the bed. "Another time, Mellie."

"But—"

"Not. Tonight." Then he gave her a stiff, awkward bow and headed for the door. "I—" he began. Then he shook his head. "Jesus."

Then he slipped away.

༂

Trevor stumbled to his room, his mind reeling. What an undiscovered jewel Mellie was! All men longed for a passionate, responsive wife. Sadly, there was no way to tell before the wedding night exactly the kind of sexual creature one had married. Most men discovered they'd tied themselves to a frightened virgin who eventually became a cold fish.

Mellie wasn't that kind of woman. She was sensitive. Good Lord, he'd never seen someone who could come just from nipple play. Add to that her naturally curious mind, and she could become a goddess in the bedroom. It only required some simple encouragement.

Her husband had better not be a clod. What a waste that would be!

He hastily stripped out of his clothes before collapsing naked onto his bed. He couldn't bear the thought of Mellie with an idiot for a husband. Which was why he'd promised her he'd teach her. If nothing else, he'd make sure she knew how to pleasure herself. He almost taught her right there and then, except he knew himself. If he got one hand between her thighs, nothing would stop him from completing the deed. He'd embed his cock so deep, she'd never forget him. And he'd surely end up releasing his seed without even the forethought of a sheath.

He knew that about himself, so he had run from

her like an errant coward. He had awakened her to the possibilities of her body and then abandoned her.

He released a litany of curses, but it was really a distraction. Easier to damn himself for a fool than to think of the way her skin had flushed and her body had writhed during her awakening. She had been so shocked, she hadn't even cried out. It had been more of a gasp and the sweetest mew of delight as her body shot from her control.

He closed his eyes, remembering that moment. Replaying it in his mind's eye over and over while he wrapped his own hand around his cock. And how ridiculous was this? He hadn't pleasured himself in years. Even under his current restricted finances, there were always women happy to entertain a future duke. But the idea of any other woman repulsed him.

So he took himself in hand and dreamed of the surprising Mellie. Of her smiling, her eyes languid and her body soft. She was so rarely soft with anyone, but with him, she had sighed in delight and shivered like a newborn colt. She had gripped his shoulders and arched into his caress.

He pictured himself repeating what he had done while slowly spreading her legs. He would slip in, taking his time so that she could adjust to him. She would be virginally tight. She would grip him as he plowed her, and her lips would form that perfect *O* of delight.

And he would…

While she…

Images flew through his mind, each more graphic than the last. He wanted them all with her. And when he exploded in his hand, it was almost an afterthought. The ideas continued, the thoughts consuming him, of what he could do with her. It would take years to accomplish them all, and by that point, he would have thought of some more.

He lay in the bed, his mind drifting through scenarios. And for the first time ever, he allowed himself to contemplate marrying her in truth. Many a man would happily trade his title for a lifetime of passion between the sheets.

No, that was a lie. Else there would be dozens of courtesans now named Lady This or Countess That. And even if that did happen, could he truly pick his duchess simply on her prowess in bed?

Of course not. He owed more to his family name. Mellie was a cit. He didn't like the term, but it was appropriate. She could certainly trade her dowry for a title, but his family was neither disgraced nor impoverished. There was no reason for him to stoop to her class for his bride, and every reason to make sure that his wife understood what was required of a woman who would become a duchess.

Mellie did not know these things, as Eleanor had made pains to point out. And even if she could learn them, there was no escaping the rest: her birth was common, her mother a lunatic, and her father an eccentric. Certainly, he adored both Mellie and her father, but that was no reason to bring them into the family.

The gossips wouldn't stop with poking at her true history. They would make up all sorts of nonsense, and it would continue every day of their lives, renewed each Season, and brought out with extra imagination on special occasions.

Mellie would crumple under the strain. No woman could handle constant criticism, no matter the training. Besides, he wasn't anxious to become the man who failed his title.

In short, marrying her wasn't proper behavior in a gentleman. There were well-founded reasons to marry within one's class, so as delightful as Mellie was in the bedroom, he could not hurt her so deeply as to subject her to a lifetime of being reviled by his family.

He could not.

He'd never despised being a gentleman more.

Eleven

*Be careful of other women. They can be your greatest
allies or your worst enemies.*

MELINDA LIKED TO SLEEP IN. CERTAINLY SHE ENJOYED
morning sunshine, and everyone liked the early song
of birds at the window, but late-night brandies and
even later visits from future dukes left her lingering
long in her bed. Or at least that had been her plan.

Eleanor knocked politely on her door then saun-
tered in. That was bad enough given that Melinda was
buried deep in the covers and hadn't bid her enter.
But the woman started talking as if they had been in
the middle of a conversation, which was decidedly not
the case.

"I don't mind telling you that this is a task I begin
to relish. It has been ages since my own come out, and
one forgets how exciting firsts can be. The first ball
gown, the first dance."

The first orgasm.

Mellie felt her face heat, and she buried herself
in her pillow. She'd spent the first half of the night

waiting for Trevor to knock on her door, and the second half reliving every second of the way he had touched her. She had thought sleep would bring an end to her salacious remembrances, but instead it had given fodder to a host of erotic dreams that still had her wet and throbbing in places that had never throbbed before.

"Tut tut. None of that."

Mellie had to bite her cheek to keep from giggling. "None of that" was right. No proper girl would allow what she had done last night, and yet she knew that if Trevor so much as winked at her, she would be rushing off to do whatever he suggested.

"Come, come," Eleanor continued as she came to the head of the bed. Melinda burrowed deeper. "No hiding from this. We're going dress shopping. You cannot say you'd rather laze in bed."

Good point. Mellie frowned into her pillow as she thought about it. Did she love dress shopping? It was fun to pick out fabrics and the like. And she had a rather good time with the seamstress at her local village. They would discuss clothing in an academic way, mostly about her uncle's fabrics and how women used them and why. It was basic information from someone who had learned that Mellie valued her opinion. And that was fun.

"Trust me," Eleanor continued as she tugged at the coverlet. "I have it all planned out."

Melinda groaned. Another smart plan from someone who didn't know her or understand the least thing about what she wanted. But in this case, that was probably the point. After all, Melinda had no idea how to appear a prancing bear in front of the *ton*, so she might as well leave that in Eleanor's hands. The image of the elegant Lady Eleanor leading a bear by the string had her smiling enough that she peered out from beneath the covers.

"That's it," Eleanor encouraged. "Perform your ablutions. The duchess will be here in a moment to take your measurements. She used to be a seamstress, you know, though we don't speak about it. And then Lady Redhill is joining us for morning chocolate before we head to the shop to look at fabrics."

Mellie pushed up from the covers. "In a moment? How much of a moment?"

"Five minutes, ten minutes, an hour? Who knows? Though she does have a shopkeeper's attention to time, so probably five minutes. Or less."

Bloody hell. She was not dressed for a duchess! Meanwhile, Eleanor was apparently pleased to have roused her, but not so pleased as to give a smile. Instead, she inspected Mellie's features closely, even going so far as to tug open the curtains such that the room was flooded with sunlight.

"Hmmm. I shall tell her to give you fifteen minutes, but not a second more. I take it the cosmetics you've designed is to fade your freckles? Or was it to ease the wrinkles?"

"I don't have wrinkles," Melinda said. At least she didn't think she did.

"Not yet, but I do see the beginnings of one right between your brows." To make her point, she lifted up a hand mirror to show her. And right there were two lines already bracketing her brows. And to make matters worse, they weren't even symmetrical. The one on the right was a fraction deeper and longer. Damn, she couldn't even wrinkle normally.

She rubbed her hand between her brows to smooth things down. It worked for about a second. She tried pulling at them, arching her brows, any number of things while Eleanor watched in silence. And then, about when Melinda had given up, Eleanor spoke gently.

"I have a potion that might help, though in my experience, it is a losing game. The best plan is not to allow lines to appear in the first place. That is done by adopting a serene expression at all times. In truth, that is the source of an aristocratic bearing."

"No wrinkles?"

"Total serenity. At all times. No matter the provocation."

Melinda stared at the woman, studying the flawless perfection that was Lady Eleanor. Her skin was pristine, almost translucent. No wrinkle, no freckle, no unsightly blemish or unattractive lump marred the perfection of her features. And given that she'd lost practically her entire family to disease not more than a year before, Lady Eleanor's perfection indicated she was either the very definition of serene or a cold-hearted shrew.

No, Mellie thought, that couldn't be true. Shrews, in her experience, had tight expression and pinched brows. Which meant that Eleanor managed a serenity beyond comprehension.

"How?" she whispered, awed by the woman before her.

"Practice. A great deal of practice."

Melinda shook her head. "I don't think I can do it."

To which the lady allowed her lips to curve just enough for a smile, but not too much to create lines. "Good. Because in your case, it isn't necessary. Remember, the plan is for you to be outré."

"But—"

"That means you are expected to have lines and wrinkles young. If you were outrageous *and* beautiful, the ladies of the *ton* would turn on you like rabid dogs."

Which, she supposed, meant that she wasn't beautiful. That wasn't much of a surprise, yet it still stung to hear it spoken so baldly. But she wasn't given time to ponder that as Eleanor paused enough to narrow her eyes—slightly—before smoothing them out and speaking in a low tone.

"That is your first and most important lesson, Melinda," she said, her words almost too quiet to hear. "Everyone in the *ton* has a plan, and I do mean everyone."

"A plan?"

"A stratagem. A way of acting. A reason they do things."

Mellie suddenly understood. "Like the gentleman's code."

"Ah yes, but you will soon learn that one gentleman's code is vastly different from another's."

That she'd already discovered.

"You must use that prodigious mind of yours to figure out their code and circumvent it. Unless of course, it aligns with yours."

Melinda nodded, though her heart rebelled at the

idea. "But that means I shall be constantly looking for hidden meanings behind every action and every word." That would be exhausting.

This time, Lady Eleanor beamed at her enough that a faint line appeared about her mouth. "Excellent. You understand. Now hurry! Our stratagem begins in ten minutes." And with that, she flowed out of the room. She didn't seem to walk, but just rippled her way out the door, moving like air over water.

Serenity personified. Mellie was impressed and suitably intimidated. Because that was not something she could ever do. She had always known she had no halfway point. She either retreated into herself such that she became a statue, or she invested herself fully. In her scientific pursuits. In her father's experiments. Or...

In what she and Trevor had done last night.

Full sensuality, full engagement in absolutely every aspect of their exploration. Which meant that it was a good thing she was set to become outré. She would have to commit to it, of course. She would have to learn and act her part as devoutly as she might some new chemistry exploration. But that was something she could do.

So with renewed determination, she cleaned up and readied herself to become something entirely different than the woman she was now. It was strangely easy. All she had to do was stop thinking and allow everyone else to do exactly as they pleased.

❧

Trevor woke with a raging headache and a stiff cock such as hadn't happened since he was a teen. Dreams of Mellie, of course. One after another until he couldn't breathe without thinking he'd explode. So for the second time in a matter of hours, he indulged himself in dreams of her while stroking himself to the inevitable conclusion. And just like last night, it wasn't enough. He clearly wanted the real woman.

So with that thought in mind, he cleaned himself and dressed with more care than he had in ages. It was a difficult task to strike that balance between personal perfection and casual insouciance. After all, he didn't want to look as if he'd made an effort. Matters were made all that more difficult since he had no valet and half his body was stiff or discolored from his bout with Ronnie. His clothes were crushed, his hairbrush was missing, and he had the distinct fear that his breath was strong enough to make a dog run. Not a very auspicious beginning to the day.

Still, he managed and was rather proud of the result. Then he went down to luncheon with the happy expectation of greeting his fiancée. He found Eleanor instead. She was calmly stirring her tea as she stared out the window at the most boring garden he'd ever seen. Exactly two bushes of a hardy variety and neither faring too well. Not surprising. It was London after all. It was impressive enough that there was any patch of green outside this back parlor.

"Good morning, Eleanor. Is Mellie—"

"Good morning, Trevor. I trust you will be removing yourself from this household today."

"I slept well, thank you. And you?" He frowned. Wait a moment. "What did you say?"

She set down her teacup and looked at him directly.

He could detect no change from her normal placid expression, and yet there was a hardness in her eyes. "I love this house. It is one of the few remaining jewels in my family's crown. There is actual jewelry, of course, and the estate is lovely. But it is this home in London that I love. Perfectly substantial for a ducal residence, and exquisitely placed in the most exalted area of town."

Having no response to that, Trevor found a seat and wondered if his friend had gone mad.

"It does have its quirks, though, as all buildings do. You understand, don't you, Trevor?"

No, he really didn't. "Quirks," he echoed. "I'm sure they're delightful."

"Not generally. Certainly not the thin walls. They are drafty, you understand, and I can hear the smallest peep of a mouse at all hours of the day. Or night."

Oh damn. Her bedroom was right beside Mellie's. Which meant Eleanor had heard him last night. Good God. His face heated, and he was grateful for the distraction as Seelye brought him a cup of tea. Good man, that butler. Remembered his likes. But then a moment later, the man set down a hearty plate of eggs and toast, which was definitely not his favorite way to break his fast.

"Actually, Seelye, I prefer—"

"I ordered this specifically for you, Trevor. I hope you enjoy it."

Trevor narrowed his eyes. "You know I dislike…" His voice trailed off as Eleanor regarded him calmly. Right. First off, it wasn't done among his set to argue in front of the servants. Secondly, she knew that he had a distinct dislike of eggs in the morning, especially ones such as this: thin and runny. Which meant this was his punishment for his nighttime roaming.

"You were saying?" she prompted.

"Hm? Oh yes, that I dislike, um, waiting for my food. Such a gracious hostess you are."

Eleanor dipped her chin in acknowledgment. The translation was clear: you are forgiven for your transgression.

He tucked into his eggs with an inward sigh. A good guest always ate what was set before him. "So has Mellie risen yet?"

"Hours ago. She is busy with Her Grace right now. I doubt you will see her before you depart."

There it was, the blithe assumption that he would be leaving. But he had no interest in departing just yet, for a myriad of reasons. First and foremost was the desire to be sure things with Mellie proceeded smoothly. This was all very new to her, and he would not abandon her to it. Certainly not to the tender mercies of Eleanor, who could be high-handed at times. And that was the nicest compliment he could think of at the moment.

"Oh, my plans aren't so cluttered as all that. And the duke has been so kind as to—"

"Is she to be married honorably or not?"

No need to belabor. Obviously, the question was about Mellie. "Married. How could you think—?"

"Then you shall be leaving directly, Trevor. You have put her in my charge. I do not chaperone mistresses or ladies of loose morals. I have the strictest standards, as you well know."

"Of course—"

"Then you will be departing directly."

Trevor shut his mouth with a hard clip. It took him a moment to get past his anger, but in the end he had to admit the truth. She was right. She was ten thousand times right, damn her eyes. But that didn't mean it sat well. "This is a delicate situation, as you know. I am the only one of Mellie's acquaintances here. You are strangers to her. I'm thinking of her comfort." It wasn't a lie. But he was also thinking about other things as well, not the least of which was her desire to be better educated in certain carnal experiences.

"I don't doubt it in the least," Eleanor said, her tone of voice indicating anything but. Then she looked up, her gaze on the butler. "Thank you, Seelye. If you would please deliver a message to the mews, we shall be needing the carriage directly."

The butler bowed deeply. "Right away, my lady."

Eleanor waited until the servant had withdrawn, then she turned her gaze to Trevor. But she didn't say a word. She didn't need to. He was squirming from just the force of her gaze and the weight of his own guilt. He was in the wrong. He had snuck into Mellie's room last night. He had behaved as no gentleman would. And yet, he was loathe to simply give up his position without a fight.

"She needs me here."

"She needs a protector, and you need to be whipped."

He blinked. She had spoken the words so calmly that her meaning was nearly lost. But he had understood, and he reared back with appropriate shock.

"You are doing it much too brown, Eleanor. I have known her almost as long as I've known you, and she was unsettled last night. I was merely…helping." God, he hoped his words sounded better to Eleanor than they did to his own ears.

Apparently not, because her words were delivered as if he were the blackest roué in the city. "You are charming, Trevor. And because of that, you think you can blind everyone to your faults, and everything will work out in the end. For you, that is mostly true. But someone always pays the piper, and it is usually the woman. And Melinda is more vulnerable than most."

"We just had a short conversation," he lied. It wasn't for his own protection, but for Mellie's. He could not have Eleanor thinking the worse of his fiancée. And certainly not because of something that was entirely his fault.

Her stare was heavy indeed, but he did not flinch. The secret to holding a lie was total adherence to it. And in the end, she dipped her chin in acknowledgment. "Good. I think better of you then."

He exhaled, though the guilt seemed ten times worse now. "Thank you—"

"But you are still leaving."

Damned harridan. "Be reasonable, Eleanor. She needs all of us, myself included."

It was at that moment that they were interrupted. The door didn't open. Naturally not. This was an efficient household, but as Eleanor had said: the walls were thin. He heard women coming down the stairs. Three to be exact, if he judged the voices correctly. The duchess's voice, another woman's, and then the soft, subtle murmur of Mellie. His entire body went tight, stretching for another sound.

A moment later, Seelye knocked quietly on the door before entering. "The carriage awaits your convenience, my lady."

Eleanor pushed back from the table. Trevor had already abandoned his runny eggs to rush out to the main hallway. Mellie would be there, and he suddenly had a desperate need to see her. He didn't question why. He simply acted.

As he suspected, she was coming down the staircase. The duchess was in animated discussion with the other woman, whom he now identified as Lady Redhill, the other owner of A Lady's Favor dress shop. And trailing behind—though clearly listening closely—was his Mellie. Her skin was pale, her eyes a little wide, but it was unmistakably her. Just as he saw how absolutely beautiful she looked with her hair pinned artlessly back and her brows narrowed in thought. Then she spoke, and his body adjusted to her tone. Like an instrument tuned to her note, he shifted his position to greet her the moment she stepped upon the main floor.

"But crickets aren't only green. They have lots of different colors."

He smiled, seeing his entry into the conversation. "Are we determined then to dress you as the Cricket Princess?"

Her eyes locked on his, and he was pleased to see the strain ease around the edges. She said something of which he only heard half. Something about telling the others that she could wear colors beyond just green. He might have had an opinion if he hadn't been so mesmerized by the way several locks of her hair tumbled out of her pins to bounce onto her shoulders. And when she stepped into the sunlight, the contrast between the auburn strands and her pearly white skin was delightful.

"I shall commission a necklace for you," he said. "One of a cricket with a crown."

"Don't you dare!" she cried. "Not unless you wear a matching one with buggy eyes."

"Nonsense. On a man, it would need to be a signet ring."

"I will not wear such a necklace," she declared.

"Then I will appear decidedly strange with my new ring." He held out his hand, and she descended the last step with her fingers in his. She felt warm. Much more alive than yesterday when she was more statue than person, but still a far cry from the woman he had brought to completion last night. And yet when he took her fingers to his lips in greeting, he knew the flash of fire in her cheeks—and in his groin.

Damn the thoughts she inspired in him.

And as he kissed her fingers, he saw her pink blush heat to bright red.

He stood there, kissing her hand and watching the shifting colors of her skin. A minute. Maybe more. It didn't matter. He was fascinated, and his memories were rapidly mixing with fantasies.

It was the duchess who brought him out of his reverie. She chuckled and turned to her friend. "Does your husband greet you in such a way, Helaine?"

"If he did, I doubt I'd ever leave the house."

"Or the bed."

The two women laughed, and it took him a moment to realize their meaning. Oh damn. Oh thrice damned. His thoughts were obvious, weren't they? And even if his weren't, Mellie's certainly were.

He straightened and proceeded to greet the other two women with as much charm as he was able. When he was done, he was all but assaulted by Eleanor's steady regard. It was a moment's stare. Or perhaps a minute's. But in that time, he knew what he had to do. As an honorable gentleman he had no choice. If he remained behind, he would have Mellie debauched within a week. With an inward curse, he turned to Seelye.

"Would you call a hack for me? It's time I returned to my rooms."

He felt the surprise hit Mellie. They weren't even touching, but the air around her seemed to jerk. Then she spoke, her voice high and tight. "You're leaving?"

He nodded and tried to put an apology into his words. "Generally, affianced couples do not reside in the same home. It's not proper."

Lady Redhill frowned. "Well, that's not entirely true," she began, but Eleanor cut her off.

"It is in this house. I will not tolerate anything less than total propriety here."

To which the duchess released a loud sigh. "She says that a lot, you know. But we have plenty of room, Mr. Anaedsley. And I know my husband enjoys your company."

"As I enjoy his," Trevor said with complete honesty. He found the duke quite refreshing. Unfortunately, the idea of debauching Mellie was completely dishonorable, and so he sighed. "I will visit every day."

"You will escort us to Melinda's first ball and nothing beforehand," said Eleanor with irritating finality in her tone.

"But—"

"I insist, Trevor."

He glowered at his longtime friend. "Letters then, Eleanor. There is nothing untoward about a man writing letters to his fiancée."

To which Lady Eleanor dipped her chin in a regal nod. He barely noticed as his gaze returned to Mellie. He saw immediately that she understood the subtext. She might be green in society, but she was far from stupid. But beyond that he could read nothing. Did she regret their actions last night? Did she hate that he was leaving and yearn for him as he ached to hold her again? Or was she resolved to her role in their charade?

"Mellie?" he whispered.

"Never mind, Trevor," she said in an undertone. "There will be plenty of time to…" She swallowed. "Plenty of time after my wedding."

Her wedding. Not *their* wedding. Which was exactly as it should be.

And yet he never felt so robbed in all his life.

Twelve

Ruination is a game of rigid appearance and flexible mind-set. Do not confuse the two.

Melinda was starting to lock herself down. She could feel the slow creep of icy stone as it expanded through her body. Trevor was abandoning her. She knew it wasn't really true. She understood exactly why he had to leave. After all, the last thing his gentleman's code would allow were the things they'd done last night. And she did her best not to think about them or how they might continue. She was in a carriage with three perceptive women, and she'd blushed enough already this morning.

So he was leaving, likely due to Lady Eleanor's interference. Mellie understood his reasons, but she could not stop the irrational feelings of abandonment. It wasn't like her, this emotional upheaval in defiance of all logic. But that's how she felt, and so her soul was beginning to lock down. Soon she would be watching the world again as it passed her by.

"No, no!" Lady Redhill was saying. She was the

clothing designer, and even in the carriage she had out pencil and paper as she sketched possible attire for Mellie's come out. "I will not give her wings."

Lady Eleanor huffed out a breath. "But crickets have wings, and she's the Cricket Princess. Do you not understand the plan?"

"I understand it completely, but I will not make her or any of my dresses look ridiculous. Unless she's going to a masquerade, she will not wear anything that gives her wings."

Well, that was something, at least. Mellie tried to thank her with a silent look, but Lady Redhill had her head down as she sketched something new. The duchess was peering over her shoulder and nodded approvingly.

"That might work."

Lady Eleanor leaned forward. "What? I can't see in this dratted carriage." She was seated with Mellie facing the other two, but she now tried to stand as she peered at the paper. It didn't help her in the least as Lady Redhill pulled the pad close to her chest.

"No, you can't see. Not yet."

"But—"

"I want Miss Smithson's opinion first."

Eleanor dropped back into her seat with a huff. "Very well," she said. She might as well have said, whatever for? Meanwhile, it took Mellie a moment to realize that they were all looking at her.

"I beg your pardon?" she said.

Lady Redhill passed her the pad. "These are just rough ideas, but they are vastly different. Eleanor said you wanted Russian—"

"No. Not Russian."

Beside her, Eleanor released a snort of disgust, but didn't make any further comment. She was busy looking over Mellie's shoulder at the designs.

Lady Redhill raised her brows but agreed. "No more Russian influence."

"Good," inserted the duchess. "We don't have time to outfit her properly, and all that fanciness would take too much."

Then again, everyone was looking at Melinda. It was ridiculous. She knew nothing about clothing or fashion, and here they were all waiting for her opinion. So she spoke without even thinking about her words first. "Crickets aren't fancy. Their wings are simple and clean."

Eleanor leaned back. "But they do have wings, don't they?"

"Well, yes, of course. Two pairs actually. A forewing and a hind wing."

Once again her words were greeted with silence, and Mellie squirmed in discomfort. Good Lord, she already knew she was odd. Did they need to stare at her like that? But a moment later, Lady Redhill was reaching for her sketches again.

"Two wings," she murmured.

"Two skirts," the duchess echoed.

"Both green, but one lighter, the other—"

"Darker. Trimmed in veins of gold perhaps?"

"Just a hint," Lady Redhill said, her fingers flying as she rapidly drew more designs. "Do you know the fabric I mean?"

"I don't know that we've more than the one green

silk," the duchess returned. "Can't fashion a dozen gowns out of one bolt of green."

"Irene will manage. And there is more than one. We've got a green velvet for a cloak."

The duchess clapped her hands. "That will be her signature! That dark green cloak with threads of gold shot through it like veins. Everyone will know it's her. At least until the others start copying her."

Melinda blinked. People would start copying her? What a silly thought. Except beside her, Lady Eleanor was nodding as she thought. "Excellent," she murmured. "Do you think we can fashion a tiara that looks like antennae?"

This time everyone stared at Eleanor, and to her shock they burst out laughing—Eleanor included.

"Yes," the woman said ruefully. "A tiara might be a bit much. But perhaps some stitching on the cloak's hood?"

To which Lady Redhill once again looked at Melinda. "Miss Smithson, you must direct me. Just how much do you intend to embrace this identity? You are a lovely woman. I cannot think that this elaborate game is necessary."

"But that is just the point, isn't it?" she said, her voice starting out weak but growing stronger with each word. "My Season, the fashion, the way we preen about ourselves, it is all a game. Even in animals and insects, there are elaborate rituals in the hopes of mating, though it is usually the male who does most of the preening."

"Oh, never fear about that," drawled Lady Eleanor. "You will witness a great deal of male preening soon enough."

"But you must decide," pushed Lady Redhill. "Just how much are you willing to *play*?"

That was the question, wasn't it? And while she was still thinking about the question, Lady Eleanor spoke up.

"It is all about confidence, Melinda. If you are not completely at one with the role, we shall never bring it about."

Confident? In being a prancing cricket princess?

Then the duchess spoke, her voice kind but no less assured. "They're right, Miss Smithson. You cannot sit like a bump on a log in these dresses. You must play with the role—"

"Play with *us*," stressed Lady Redhill.

"Play with *them*," corrected Lady Eleanor. "The men, the society women, the whole of the *ton*. Play, Melinda, and be pleased that you are smarter than all of them combined."

And that's when she finally understood. Each of these women, in her own way, was asking her to join in a game. This was how they had fun. Just as when her father asked her to help with his experiments, he truly believed he was offering her an enjoyable experience. He was playing with science and inviting her to join. These ladies were inviting her to join them in a game of society and wondered if she would participate like a child joining a game of marbles.

She stared at them, thrown as the meaning dropped like water between cracks into her consciousness. "London is a most peculiar place," she finally said.

To which all three ladies burst out laughing. And

before they could catch their breath, Melinda found herself chuckling.

"I can play," she said, somewhat shocked to realize that she could. She would. And she might even enjoy it.

"Excellent," Eleanor crowed. "Now do we add antennae to the cloak or not?"

She thought about it seriously for a moment. She thought about all the different types of sensory equipment on insects. She pondered strict adherence to science and immediately discarded it. This was fun, not fact.

"Many species of cricket have the most elegant long antennae that can sweep wide or drape elegantly down their backs." She gestured for the paper and was immediately offered pad and pencil. "Perhaps this?" she asked as she drew a pair of curving lines down the back of the cloak, vaguely suggestive of a woman's form.

"Oh, excellent!" cried Eleanor.

"I know just how to do it," added the duchess.

But it was Lady Redhill who summarized things exactly. "Oh my, this is going to be so much fun!"

They discussed their plans in earnest until the carriage arrived at A Lady's Favor dress shop. Mellie was feeling significantly better as she disembarked, finally stepping foot in the most fashionable shopping district of London. It's not that she hadn't shopped before. In London even. But she'd never felt at ease among the elite until now. Heavens, right now, a duchess and two ladies surrounded her!

The moment that the duchess opened the shop

door, they heard an argument. In truth, it could be heard from the street, but Mellie hadn't paid much attention. It was just more noise among the call of hawkers and the like. But once inside, they all realized the shrill voices were coming from the shop's back room.

"What the devil?" Lady Redhill murmured as she headed straight through the welcoming parlor. The duchess was barely a step behind, which left Mellie and Eleanor to exchange startled glances before following.

They entered what was obviously the work area. Mellie saw tables throughout the room, each set up as a workstation. Fabric was everywhere, as were dresses in various states of completion, along with buttons, pins, thread, and other baubles that often decorated clothing. It was so chaotic, in fact, that Mellie had trouble finding the source of the commotion. Until she stepped farther into the room and saw a second doorway, one that clearly led to an alley.

The workers' entrance, except that it was barred by a furious looking young woman who stood with her arms crossed and her glasses perched on the end of her nose as she glared at the man attempting to enter.

Mellie focused on him because, in her experience, it was usually the man who was the problem. He was thick set with brown hair and broad shoulders. She supposed he was handsome in a rugged way, especially as he hadn't shaved yet this morning, so his skin cast a shadow on his clenched jaw. But it was his eyes that made her wary. They were a familiar pale brown, almost as if he had an inner light that softened the darkness of every other aspect of his body, and they were narrowed in a sleepy kind of fury. And worse, his hands were clenched into fists where they perched on his hips.

Melinda had plenty of knowledge of large, dumb men. Brutes were dangerous in a raw, powerful way, but this man was large and smart—a dangerous combination—especially since he was clearly angry.

Meanwhile, the duchess pushed her way forward. "Bernard? What are you doing here?"

"Exactly what you asked me to, sis."

So that's why his eyes looked familiar. He had the exact same eyes as his sister. Eleanor came to the same conclusion as she whispered in Mellie's ear.

"That's Bernard Drew, the duchess's brother. He's running the businesses."

Mellie frowned. "I thought the duchess and Lady Redhill ran A Lady's Favor."

"They do," Eleanor all but hissed. "He's running the *other* businesses. The ones where *men* go." She spoke in clipped tones with clear emphasis. Mellie knew she was supposed to understand a great deal more than the words themselves, but she had little context for it. Men frequented many other establishments. She could be talking anything from haberdasheries to whorehouses.

"I will not let whores and thieves in here!" cried the bespectacled woman.

Ah. Whorehouses then. And perhaps a thieving ring. Goodness, she had no idea that any member of the aristocracy owned such things, much less the duchess herself.

Meanwhile Bernard gestured behind him to a man

and woman who stood quietly awaiting their fate. "It's only one whore and one thief."

"Bernard!" the duchess groaned. "Don't antagonize her. And Tabitha, you have no idea what these people have done. We discussed this. We need the help. Orders are piling up."

"You heard him. A whore and a thief."

"Yes," Bernard growled. "But *he's* the whore, and *she's* the thief!"

To which the man cried, "I am not!" and the woman shook her head. "Not anymore, gov. And only for me bread."

It would have been funny if not for the desperation hidden behind the words. Both thief and whore—for lack of better words—were gaunt and hungry with sunken eyes and sallow skin. Their clothing was threadbare, but clearly someone had made an attempt to clean it. The stains were faded, as if someone had tried to wash them out, and there were patched places that could not be disguised no matter the skill of the seamstress.

The duchess gestured the woman forward, then tugged at the sleeve of the woman's dress. She held it up to the sunlight, tilting it one way then another. Mellie couldn't guess why she did it. That appeared to be the one place on the dress that had no damage. Or so she thought.

"Did you mend this?" the duchess asked.

"I did, Yer Grace. The other bits weren't my work." She pointed to the patches that Mellie had seen. "It's not my dress, you see. But I had time to mend the tear here."

"Good work," she said as she tilted the sleeve toward Tabitha. The blonde woman adjusted her spectacles then peered closer.

"But she's a thief."

"No, miss. I just had some hard times, is all." Then she swallowed. "Please, Your Grace. Without this work, I will have to turn to… To become…"

She clearly couldn't say the word, but Bernard could. "It's this or the workhouse. But she's got a weak chest. She'd have a better chance as a whore. Or an excellent chance as a seamstress." Bernard's voice was hard, but his eyes stayed kind and sad. At least until his gaze settled on Tabitha, who naturally bristled in anger.

"We can't have a thief or whore here! It'll dry up the orders quicker than snip." She clipped her two fingers together like a pair of scissors cutting.

Meanwhile, Lady Redhill was looking about the workroom and shaking her head. "They'll dry up anyway if we don't get help. We're behind on every order."

Tabitha grimaced. "Then hire some girls. Just not from *his* place. There are plenty of good girls out there looking for work."

"But they still need to be trained," the duchess said. "And she does have a fine hand."

"Every thief does."

Eleanor clearly agreed as she said, "Listen to the girl. You're running a business, not a charity house." She spoke in an undertone, the words obviously meant for Melinda and no one else. But Eleanor's voice had a way of carrying, and everyone turned to look at them—Eleanor and Melinda—where they stood witness to what was clearly a private debate.

"I-I beg your pardon," stammered Melinda. "Perhaps Eleanor and I should look at the pattern books in the front parlor."

"Unless you enjoy blood sport," returned Bernard in a dry voice.

"Bernard!" the duchess cried. "Stop being crude! And don't threaten Tabitha. She's worth her weight in gold, and I'd be loathe to lose her."

"Thank you, Your Grace—"

"And I would be sad to see you go over something this trivial. This woman sets a fine stitch. If she cuts as well as she sews, then—"

"Er, that's my job," said the man who'd said he wasn't a whore. "I cut, she sews. We'll make a fine team."

"No!" cried Tabitha.

Beside her, Eleanor heartily agreed as she whispered, "Don't. Just...don't." Again, Eleanor's words were overheard. Lady Redhill shot them a glare over her shoulder, emphasizing to Melinda that they should not be here. So she took Eleanor's arm and began backing away.

Fortunately, Eleanor did not fight her. But once out of the room, she wasted no time in expressing her opinion. "Good God, how could Wendy be so stupid?"

"To hire a woman who needs the work? And who would be good at it?"

Eleanor huffed out a breath. "I thought you were beginning to understand, but apparently, I was wrong."

Melinda didn't bother to respond. She knew that Eleanor would enlighten her soon enough. It took only a few more seconds for the woman to speak.

"Society is about appearances. It is all for show. That's why we're making you into the Cricket Princess."

"Yes, I know, but what does that have to do with them?"

"People flock to this shop because they can then say that a countess and a duchess stitched their gowns. It makes them feel special and allows this shop to charge exorbitant prices."

Melinda frowned. "Perhaps they come because Lady Redhill designs beautiful clothing."

Eleanor rolled her eyes. "Of course she does, as do a hundred other designers throughout London. They come here because she is a countess, and Wendy is a duchess. People want them, not a whore."

"But it is clothing."

"It is about status. There is nothing elevating about wearing a dress stitched by a whore. Or a thief."

Mellie thought about that, rapidly stacking up everything she had heard about London society. In the end, she made no comment. Instead, she picked up a pattern book and perused the sketches. But Eleanor, apparently, couldn't leave it like that.

"You think I'm wrong."

"No," Melinda responded honestly. "I fear you may be right."

"You do?" Clearly she'd shocked Eleanor.

"I do," she said. "But that doesn't mean I think it's right. In fact..." she said as her gaze fell upon

Lady Redhill's sketchbook. The woman had set it here before rushing into the backroom. Grabbing the pencil, Mellie found a blank page and quickly wrote down an address as well as some detailed instructions. But before she did more, she looked at Eleanor.

"Do you find the duchess to be a smart woman?"

Eleanor frowned. "Of course I do. It is the only reason I bear any hope for my family name. Her problem is stubbornness, not idiocy."

Mellie waved that aside. "What about her brother? Do you know anything of him? Can he judge a man or woman accurately?"

Eleanor took longer to decide on that, and Mellie was impatient by the time she finally spoke. "I have little knowledge of Bernard personally, but in the months that I have been guiding Their Graces, he has managed to quietly and consistently bring in money to the title." Then she dipped her chin. "I'm not supposed to know that, and we should not be discussing money, but—"

"So you have no understanding of his character then?"

"On the contrary. I said he *quietly* brought in money. Which means he is likely not only smart, but discerning. Anything else would be noisy."

Obviously, a grave sin. But that was enough of a reference for her. So she tore off the sheet and headed for the workroom. She wasn't surprised when Eleanor followed. The woman might be discreet, but she was still nosy.

Apparently, Tabitha had lost the argument. She stood mutinously by as the two newcomers were shown about the room. But everyone paused as

Melinda entered. She crossed directly to Bernard, who stood with his arms crossed in the doorway, his eyes on the furious Tabitha. But when she approached him, his expression shifted to bland neutrality that others might mistake as ox-like placidity.

"I have a solution," she said to the room in general. "But it's not ideal." Tabitha looked up eagerly, but Bernard spoke, his voice rich in its low rumble.

"No solution needed. These two are settled here."

"Yes, I can see that," she said with her eyes on Tabitha. "But in case these two would like another option, I could find them employment in the country. My father's house needs a new maid who is handy with stitching. And my uncle owns a mill that could use a man with sharp cutting skills and brawny shoulders." This man did not actually have broad shoulders, but with steady food he would probably grow stronger. "I have written down instructions on what to say to my father and uncle. They're in different counties—"

"Leave London?" the man asked, his gaze going to Bernard.

"Different counties? How far apart would we be?" asked the woman.

Bernard simply raised his hand for them to be silent. "That's a generous offer, Miss…"

"Miss Smithson. And I'm counting on you to vouch for their honesty."

"Oh, I do. I most certainly do," he said, his gaze cutting hard to Tabitha. "But these two are needed here at my sister's shop."

Melinda knew better than to argue. She could see the determination in Bernard's eye. And though

Tabitha sputtered and complained, Melinda saw the duchess study her brother in a long silence. And when Tabitha finally ceased with her litany of objections, it was the duchess whose voice slipped soft and quiet through the room.

"What aren't you telling me, Bernard?"

"Nothing, sister. Only what you already know."

"Which is?"

"That I swore to your husband that no harm would come to you or yours from the…the other businesses."

The duchess rolled her eyes. "He's overprotective."

"No, Wendy, he's not. And these two are here to make good on my promise."

"But—"

And finally, his expression broke. Finally, the man who had looked nearly ox-like in his calm, suddenly threw out a snort of frustration before running a hand through his badly shorn brown curls. "Damn it, Wendy, when will you trust me? Haven't I earned that these last months?"

The duchess reared back, her eyes wide with shock. "Of course I trust you. I've always—"

"Then these two stay here. They're honest workers, and they are best as a team."

Tabitha drew breath to argue, but at a glare from the duchess, she wisely shut her lips. Meanwhile, Bernard wasn't done. He turned to Melinda, who had thought she was no more important than the nearest chair, but suddenly, he was touching her hand as he tugged the foolscap from her.

"There are others though, Miss Smithson. Others who would be happy for the work."

She nodded slowly, wondering at just what kind of protection the duchess needed. And what this unlikely pair could do should the worst happen. But it wasn't her business except to offer good work to another pair, perhaps.

"It's hard work, and as I said—"

"I'll see that you get two good souls, Miss Smithson. They won't turn on you, I swear."

Tabitha still couldn't keep silent. "And how would you know that, Mr. Drew? How can you be so sure—"

"Because they know better than to turn on me." The words were spoken simply enough. There wasn't even an underlying ugliness to the tone. A straightforward sentence, but it nonetheless sent chills through Mellie's body. Despite his placid appearance, there was cold steel beneath Bernard's words, and everyone heard it, including Tabitha.

Then suddenly, he was all smiles as he bowed to Mellie. "I grateful for the directions, Miss Smithson. Now if you'll excuse me ladies, I haven't yet slept this night, and I'd like to seek my bed."

"Haven't slept?" said his sister. "But it's nearly noon."

"Even so." With another bow to the room in general, Bernard disappeared into the alley. For such a large man, he moved quickly. And quietly too. There hadn't even been a sound to his footfalls as the workroom door clicked shut behind him.

And all was silent.

Except for Lady Eleanor. "If I may make a suggestion?" she said to the room at large.

Melinda all but groaned. Eleanor's opinion wasn't

needed in this taut situation, but no one had the wherewithal to silence her.

"If you must employ these two, then I suggest you give them simple names and call them...well, call them Miss Smithson's friends from the country. At least that way, you have a hope of keeping their, um, previous occupations secret."

To which the man replied, "There's nothing complicated about our names. I'm Charles, and that's Mary." Everyone waited a moment, and eventually, he gave a charming smile. "Jones. Charles and Mary Jones."

False names, perhaps, but it hardly mattered.

"Excellent," Eleanor said, as if she were in charade. "Mr. and Mrs. Jones."

"No, no," the man corrected. "Brother and sister."

The two couldn't look less alike. Whereas she had dark hair and an olive cast to her skin, he was sandy-haired, somewhat tall, and sported freckles. They were definitely not brother and sister.

"Very well," the duchess said slowly. "Brother and sister from the country. Friends of Miss Smithson."

Eleanor nodded briskly. "Melinda, pray acquaint them with some details of your home life in case someone asks. Lady Redhill, I believe you mentioned some green silk that needs to be discussed? Duchess, if you wouldn't mind speaking with your head seamstress, I'd appreciate it. Though I agree with her sentiment, it appears we have been overruled. In which case, the only alternative is to press on without a frown. Can't have the wrinkles, you know." Then she took a deep breath as she looked about the room. "Really," she drawled, "it's a good thing I'm of a flexible mind-set. Otherwise, I believe I should have gone mad when Radley first ascended to the title."

And the startling thing was that absolutely everyone agreed with everything she said. Well, everything until she began pointing at some decidedly *not* green fabrics.

"Are you sure we can't add just a touch of Russian ornamentation?"

Thirteen

Ruin him in small ways with a nickname, a token, or an intimate promise.

TREVOR WAS NOT A MAN WHO WROTE WELL. HE HAD friends who were great orators, others who could craft a sentence like a sculptor shapes marble. When he had promised to write Mellie daily, he had imagined himself sending missives filled with reassurances and clever anecdotes. Simple stories to buoy her spirit and make her smile.

He envisioned her smiling a lot when she read his letters. It was one of his favorite fantasies. Well, one of his non-salacious fantasies.

But when it came to actually creating these gems of written correspondence, he failed utterly. They contained statements like: "I went to the tailor today. He says I am a fit man." Short, simple sentences less eloquent than his tailor bill. Clearly, she'd engaged herself to a dullard.

At least he had accomplished something. In the two weeks that he had been prevented from seeing Mellie, he had sent the announcement of their engagement to the papers. It had been published the next day with more eloquence than he could manage. At which point he had been flooded with invitations and visits from friends all wanting to know about his mysterious love affair.

He'd promised Eleanor to keep his answers short, giving only the barest details, all in anticipation of tonight's first ball where Mellie would be "revealed" to the world at large. Or at least to the *ton*. Lady Redhill had been prevailed upon to give the ball. And as she was also the woman who designed Mellie's clothes, everyone anticipated a grand theme. Or at least a spectacle.

What Mellie thought of this was a complete mystery to him, for as bad as he was at writing, she was arguably worse. She told him in equally simple sentences about this fitting or that visit to the milliner. She spoke in numbers more than words, as if life were some sort of mathematical formula.

"We had three trips today. I bought four hats and a pair of new walking boots. The cost is the equivalent of two downstairs maids for a year. Or a month's worth of my father's chemicals. I cannot think this is necessary, but Eleanor told me twenty-two times this morning that it is."

There was only one missive from her that raised her above her normal level of accounting. In desperation for something to write to her, he had asked about her choices in dress. Her answer had been vague. She had indeed said that she enjoyed the process, which surprised him as much as it appeared to surprise her.

And then he was subjected to two pages of detailed notes on the chemical treatment of fabrics. Apparently, she and the duchess had found a common interest in the creation of cloth. Mellie had recorded a small portion of their discourse, and he had to dredge up all he remembered of various chemicals and cotton to follow her missive. In the end, he had encouraged her to record her thoughts for the next time she spoke with her uncle about their mill. And then he had asked her about her new boots. Thankfully, her comments on footwear were easier to understand: she disliked footwear that pinched. Fortunately, dancing slippers did not have this problem.

Good God, would they ever be able to convince anyone that they were in love? If their letters were proof of anything, it was that the two of them were the most unloving couple in London. And given the level of animosity between couples in the *ton*, that was a bleak assessment indeed.

Or so he thought until he presented himself at the ducal mansion at precisely five of the clock. They were to have a light meal before the ball began at seven. But when he arrived, no one was about. Not even Seelye. Apparently, the man had been recruited to help supervise the extra staff hired for the Redhill ball. A mottled-skinned maid too young to be anything but an apprentice opened the door. She'd shown him into the main parlor, forgot to take his hat and gloves, and then ducked away without saying a word.

And then he'd stood there in the parlor, fidgeting with his hat brim while worrying about the coming hours. Would Mellie be up to the task? Was he up to the task? Or would everyone see that they were complete frauds the very first moment they were seen together? What if Eleanor had exhausted her? What if—

"Good evening, Mr. Anaedsley. I see that your tailor was correct. You are indeed a very fit man."

He spun around at the sound her voice. It was richer than he remembered. Her vowels were smooth, her expression even more so. She stood there at the entrance to the parlor looking like…like…

He blinked.

"What are you wearing?"

"Don't you like it?" she asked, a tremor of worry in her voice. She raised her arms and spun slowly before him. "The duchess was adamant that this was the perfect thing to wear. Eleanor thinks it will become all the rage. And Helaine—that's Lady Redhill—said it was her greatest design. Do you think…I mean…is it too much?"

He stared, completely at a loss for words. She was wearing feathers. She was wearing a lot of feathers. As in, from birds. He was sure there was fabric beneath the plumage, but he couldn't see it. Which meant she looked as if a stiff breeze would leave her completely naked. Worse, the feathers were of a smallish sort so they seemed to hug her body. It would be suggestive enough if she had a waifish appearance, but Mellie was sturdier than that. She was *curvier* than that. In truth, her body was more of the lush, Rubenesque variety. Full breasts, neat waist, and the kind of hips that made a man think of grabbing hold and thrusting like a beast in heat.

Good God, he wanted to pull off every one of those feathers with his teeth before he—

"There's a cloak for travel," she said, "and it's hard to sit down without crushing things." Then she flashed him a shy smile. "But it's fun. Or at least...I thought so." Her voice trailed away on a mournful note, and he rushed to reassure her.

"No, no," he said, his voice coming out thick with lust. "I mean, it's..." *Suggestive. Indecent. Licentious.* "I...um..."

She dropped her arms and stared at the floor. "I know it's awful," she said.

"Er...what?"

"Crickets don't have feathers. I told them that, but they kept saying that no one would care. And it's mostly brown and green feathers."

Yes, that was certainly true. Not that he'd noticed. He was too busy thinking of ways he could accidentally brush across her breasts. Would the feathers break? Fall off? What would be revealed beneath?

"Tabitha suggested we use real cricket wings, but I thought that was too much. Feathers are bad enough. I didn't want to wear real wings."

"I can certainly understand that."

"Trevor?"

"I think you are going to be quite the sensation tonight," he said in all honesty. "I think the men will flock to you, and I am very grateful to have already announced our engagement. That gives me an excuse to stand by your side and keep the blighters away."

"But not all of them right?" she pressed. "I still have to marry one."

Like hell—oh, right. Their ruse. Of course. Suddenly, finding her a husband didn't seem like so daunting a task. Except he had the most desperate urge to hide her upstairs and never let her out. He didn't want any other man to see the treasure he'd found in her. And the idea of handing her over to one of the lust-addled men she'd meet tonight made him physically ill. It didn't matter that he was one of the lust-addled in question. He simply did not like the idea of anyone else seeing her as such a...a...

"Bloody hell, you're a beauty. Worse, you're to be a sensation as well." He rubbed a hand over his face. "This is going to be damned difficult."

"What?" she said, her word more of a quiet gasp. "You don't think they'll want me?"

He looked at her horrified expression and cursed himself for an idiot. Then before she could run, he took her hands and squeezed her fingers. She hadn't yet put on her gloves, so he could touch her skin to skin, and he once again marveled at how soft she was. How dewy fresh and innocent she seemed, even in that scandalous dress.

"Didn't you hear me, Mellie? I said you're beautiful. I wanted to find you a quiet man of science. But it'll be damned hard for such a person to get to your side now. Darling, you will be surrounded ten deep in men."

She flushed, the pink of her cheek nicely accented by the dark green and black feathers. "But we're engaged, Trevor. The men won't flock to me. I'm already taken."

She didn't understand the *ton*. "The decent men

will respect that, Mellie. It's the indecent ones that I'm worried about it."

"Oh."

Oh indeed. He looked at her, seeing the anxiety in her expression though she tried to hide it under a nearly placid expression. How had he ever thought her uninteresting? He found every nuance in her expression fascinating. And right now, he saw a myriad of emotions in her eyes. Or perhaps that was merely a reflection of the jumping, contradictory feelings inside his brain. Either way, there was only one way to stop such destructive thinking. A simple thing, but he had been aching for two weeks now to do it.

He stepped forward and kissed her. He did it badly. On some level he knew that. A girl such as Mellie should be approached with reverence and care. She was green in the ways of the body, and yet he had none of his usual skill with her.

He simply kissed her because she was there, and they both seemed to want it. She didn't seem surprised. Her mouth parted on a sigh, and she stepped into his embrace in the same motion that he used to pull her tight.

The feathers were smooth, letting his hands glide sweetly down her back to her bottom. But her lips were silkier, her taste more delightful, and best of all was the sound she made as he thrust inside. No cricket chirp, but a soft, delighted sigh. He would make it a moan, he swore. A needful cry when he thrust into her, and then a keening moan as she came around him. It would happen. He needed it to happen, so he deepened the kiss and allowed his hips to thrust shallowly against her.

Easy now, deeper later, until—

"None of that now! You'll crush the feathers."

He leaped back, or at least he meant to. All he did was jolt backward a bit while keeping one hand firmly planted on Mellie's hip. She, on the other hand, jumped like a startled colt. And even though she didn't move far from him, he could feel the anxiety rippling in the muscles beneath his hand.

Meanwhile, the duchess stood in the doorway looking like a living flame in a gown of orange red silk. Her arms were folded, but her eyes were dancing with laughter.

"I'm not one to stop an engaged couple's fun, but Mr. Anaedsley, that dress took forever to stitch. I'll not have you crushing it before Melinda's big moment."

She was right. Trevor knew it, and so he slowly withdrew his hand. Especially since they weren't truly an engaged couple, and what he had been planning to do wasn't considered gentlemanly, even if they had been ready for the altar. Some things were meant for a marriage bed, but damn...

"She's too beautiful, duchess. This gown is too... too..." Damn it, now was not the time to lose his words! "She cannot be so beautiful," he repeated, knowing how ridiculous his words sounded. "She's a wealthy woman. When she looks like this..." He shook his head. "I won't be able to keep her safe."

"Which is why you have friends, Mr. Anaedsley. And even if you didn't, Miss Smithson has become very dear to me. No one will harm her."

"Certainly not," inserted Eleanor as she stepped into the parlor. "She's my charge. Everyone will treat her with the utmost respect or risk my displeasure."

He shot a look at his childhood friend. Did she truly believe her dislike would have any impact on a randy man? Apparently, she did, so he said nothing. Fortunately, the duke chose that moment to appear in the doorway a half step behind Eleanor. Trevor met his calm expression with a desperate one of his own. Only to have the man burst into laughter.

"In love with a beautiful woman? Nervous whenever she appears in public?" the man taunted. "It's a trial we lucky few must learn to bear." He said the words to Trevor, but his eyes were on his wife. She visibly preened as his gaze took in her body. The two flowed toward one another, as if gravity simply pulled them close. They were about to kiss when Eleanor snorted.

"Good heavens, must you do that everywhere? We've no time for it especially since Trevor is behind schedule."

Trevor frowned at her. "I was here at five of the clock. Exactly as you said. It was you—"

"Not that, you dolt. You are behind time with Miss Smithson."

"What?" He looked at Mellie who seemed equally baffled.

Then Eleanor held up Mellie's green gloves, which she'd brought into the room. "For an engaged woman, her hand is distinctly bare."

Now he remembered. It wasn't that he'd forgotten exactly, but he hadn't wanted to do this with an audience. "Eleanor—"

"Hurry up, Trevor. It's not as if this is a *significant* gesture."

No, it wasn't. Because this was not a real engagement. Still, the matter required delicacy. Especially since...

"It's all right," Mellie said, her voice soft, but so easily riveting his attention. "If you haven't got one with you—"

"Don't be silly," he said at the exact same moment that the two other women in the room made their opinion known.

The duchess snorted. "Of course it's significant."

"Don't be embarrassing," Eleanor said as she tugged her own gloves further up her arms.

Trevor did his best to ignore them as he captured Mellie's hand. He tried to draw her apart from the others, but she didn't move beyond allowing him to raise her arm.

"Mellie, look at me please," he said.

Her gaze leapt to his, and he watched the color deepen in her cheeks.

"You should be wearing the signet ring of the Duke of Timby," he said. "All the Timby brides wear it for their first presentation. Usually for the whole of the engagement, before it goes back to my grandfather."

Her eyes widened, and she looked slightly horrified. "Oh Trevor, I couldn't," she whispered. By which he took it to mean she couldn't wear it when they weren't truly engaged. But he shook his head.

"My grandfather didn't respond to my request for the ring. And he wasn't at home to me when I visited."

He watched as her lips formed a perfect *O* of

understanding. It was exactly as they'd predicted: his grandfather was opposed to the match. That was, after all, the plan, so that it would be easier when she cried off. But it still infuriated Trevor that he hadn't been able to get the signet ring for his fake bride.

"It's better this way."

"The hell it is. I'll not have you slighted, Mellie. I…" Damnation, he was doing this wrong. He fumbled to remove the jewelers pouch from his pocket. Then he held up her hand and pressed it into her palm.

"Trevor—"

"Wait. Please." He covered her hand with his, preventing her from looking at the contents of the pouch. "Before you look, understand that I meant it as a bit of whimsy. Once I realized that my grandfather wouldn't give me the ring, I thought…I thought this would be funny. But now I realize how silly the idea was." This was her engagement ring, after all. People would judge her by the ring she wore. "There are two rings in there. One for me and one for you. To let you know that you are not in this alone."

She looked at him, wariness in her expression. Except when he looked closer, he realized she did not seem worried. More…well, there was a misty kind of smile on her lips. Far from reassuring him, that made him feel all the more anxious.

"Mellie, I swear, I wasn't making fun of you. I'd never make—"

"Oh, for God's sake, man, let her look." That came from the duke who was standing close enough to overhear every word. Along with the duchess and Eleanor.

Trevor shot them an annoyed look. This was meant

to be a moment between him and Mellie. But there was no help for it, especially as a gong sounded, no doubt to signal their supper was ready.

"Mellie—"

"Trevor. Let me see them."

He had no choice, did he? Not only Mellie, but everyone else in the *ton* would see it tonight. Might as well get it over with. So he withdrew his hand and waited with his belly knotted as she carefully opened the pouch and let two rings fall into her palm.

She looked at hers first. It was an emerald set in gold, but fashioned to look like a cricket. Sweeping antennae flowed over the stone, then back and around to encircle her finger.

His ring was equally fanciful. It bore two round diamonds, fashioned to look like enormous fly eyes. In this case, the wings of the fly became the circle of the ring.

"It's the Cricket Princess and the Bug-Eyed Duke," he said, worried when she hadn't spoken. "I thought—"

She laughed. A musical chuckle that became a full trill of laughter. It was much like he'd imagined she'd react when reading his letters, and yet it was so much prettier than he'd pictured. The sound flowed strong and happy, and he could not believe his eyes when she held both rings up to the light.

"These are wonderful, Trevor!"

She started to put hers on, but the duchess stopped her with a loud, "Tut tut!"

And when Mellie paused to look at their audience, Eleanor explained.

"He's supposed to put it on your finger."

Normally, he hated such silly formality. What did it matter who put the ring on her finger so long as she wore it? But in this, he agreed with tradition. With as much gravity as he could manage, he took the ring from her, then lifted up her hand and slipped it onto her finger. She looked down at it while he looked at her.

There was laughter in her eyes, he was sure. And a smile played about her mouth. "I love it," she whispered.

"But it's too small," said Eleanor in disgust.

Mellie held up her hand. "It fits me perfectly."

"But it's supposed to go over your glove, not underneath it."

Trevor shook his head. "No. The signet ring goes over the glove. This is Mellie's ring. I hope you will keep it forever."

The duchess snorted. "Well, of course she'll keep it forever. It's her engagement ring."

Which would be true if they were going to get married. He and Mellie shared a look of silent misery. Who knew what her real husband would think of such a thing? But it didn't matter as Mellie then held up his hand.

"And shall I put on yours, Mr. Buggy Duke?"

He groaned, but he extended his finger. "I do hate that name, you know."

"That's what makes it perfect," she said as she slipped it on. "There now. We're a pair."

And he felt it. He felt as if they were well matched. For better or worse, they were in this together. So he lifted her hand to his mouth and pressed a kiss first to her ring, then again to her palm. In that one gesture, he tried to express all of his better nature. He wanted to say that he was a gentleman and would treat her as the lady she was. He would honor her and stand by her side no matter what happened.

But even as he pressed his lips to her palm, he realized the futility of it all. He was not a gentleman, because this engagement was a lie. He was not honorable because he still intended to teach her the joys of her body as soon as he could find a way.

And no matter how beautiful she was, tonight's guests would make it their mission to make her feel odd, outcast, and wholly unworthy.

Fourteen

Be hard and calculating like a man. Do not let feminine emotions enter your head or worse, your heart.

MELLIE TRIED NOT TO PACE IN THE UPSTAIRS PARLOR OF the Redhill home. Normally she would sit quietly with her hands composed in front of her. Her father had trained that position into her from her earliest memory. He believed hands folded in quiet repose was the best position for a quiet mind. The two of them had practiced it every day until she could sit in silent meditation for nearly an hour. And yes, it usually did quiet her mind.

But to sit now would crush the feathers on her dress. To sit now would be to suggest that this riot of emotions in her mind was a bad thing. And truthfully, she rather enjoyed it. She had never felt more alive in her life.

Well, never felt more alive when doing something proper.

And that thought naturally brought her to Trevor and the wonderful things she still wanted to do with him. She reached for the ring on her finger, but couldn't truly see it because of her glove. Still, she felt it on her finger, solid and whimsical at once. The idea that he wore a matching ring on his finger made her grin. She'd wanted so desperately to kiss him when he'd given this to her. She'd wanted…well…those were not the thoughts of a proper woman, so she tried to put them away.

She tried to quiet her mind while standing, but failed utterly. She was about to be presented to the *ton* and in a spectacular fashion. Never in her wildest dreams had she thought this day might come.

Lady Redhill had stated two weeks ago that the Cricket Princess wearing a feathered gown needed an equally dramatic presentation. So while everyone entered the ballroom in the usual fashion—Trevor included—she was to wait upstairs until Seelye came to fetch her. It was to be just before the dancing began. At that time, Seelye would escort her downstairs and hand her off to the Redhill majordomo, who would announce her to the *ton*. And then Trevor was to climb the stairs to escort her down to Lord and Lady Redhill.

After the greeting there, Helaine and her husband would open the ball with a dance: a waltz. Trevor and Mellie would be the second couple on the floor. Everyone would be looking at her, everyone wondering who was this strange cit in feathers who had captured the heart of a future duke.

She ought to be terrified. She ought to be embarrassed. After all, she was wearing feathers, for God's sake. But she wasn't. She was elated and excited and filled with a giddy terror. It was wonderful, and all she wanted to do was spin around and laugh before falling into Trevor's arms.

Joy. Oh, such joy as she had never felt before. If only time would speed up and Seelye would knock.

Knock, knock.

She gasped and spun around. Was it time already?

The door opened, and a man stepped in. He wasn't Seelye. He wasn't even the Redhill majordomo, or any servant that she could tell. He was tall with dark, curling hair and a physique most handsomely displayed in his black evening clothes. His face was cut in angular lines, which emphasized the bump on his nose from where it had been broken at some point. And his dark brown eyes were particularly handsome, though it was his mouth that drew the eye. Full lips when she might have expected severe, and a curve at the edges that grew when he looked at her.

"Goodness, but you're not Redhill," he said. His voice matched the angles of his face—gravelly and sharp. But his smile softened the tone. And the frank appreciation of her dress made her flush with embarrassed pleasure.

"No, sir," she said, belatedly remembering to curtsy. "I believe his lordship is downstairs greeting guests."

"Well, he would be, wouldn't he? Except he seems to have disappeared, and as I had some urgent matters to discuss with him, I thought I'd catch him. But of course, I seem to have caught you instead."

She had no answer to that, so she lifted her chin. She wasn't supposed to tell anyone her name. Not until she was announced. At the time, she'd thought

Eleanor's dictate ridiculous. After all, who would see her but the servants? This man, apparently. So she smiled and folded her hands before her, secretly pressing her ring against her finger. This was her first true *ton* meeting, and she needed the reassurance of Trevor with her, if only in the form of a hard cricket ring.

"Allow me to present myself. Mr. Carl Rausch, at your service," he said.

She dipped her chin. "I am pleased to meet you, sir."

"No need to tell me who you are. You're the mysterious Miss Smithson. And I must say, you're living up to expectations."

She arched a brow. "We've only just met, sir. I cannot have lived up to anything."

"On the contrary," he said as he leaned negligently against the door frame. "You are indeed beautiful. I believe the betting books were in your favor on that. Trevor was never one for ugly girls."

She kept her expression calm, but internally, she winced. Part of her couldn't help wondering if that was one of the reasons Trevor told her they wouldn't suit: because she wasn't beautiful enough.

"And Miss Smithson, I'm afraid I have a secret source. You see—I know your uncle."

She blinked. "What?"

"Yes, he and I have had some dealings regarding his mill."

"But I have nothing to do with the mill."

His smile widened to the point that it appeared nearly wolfish. Angular face, wide smile that showed teeth, and those rakish black locks. Mellie silently revised her estimate of him. He was not handsome, but he was vastly interesting. Especially as he spoke of her greatest accomplishment with admiration.

"I know that you are the one responsible for the bleaching process your uncle uses. I also know that you have continued to work and have an exciting new formula. And that, my dear, makes you brilliant."

She felt her cheeks heat. Finally, someone who understood that she was smart. As fun as it was to wear a gown covered in feathers, this was true pleasure. This was someone who appreciated the years of dedicated effort she had put into science.

"Do the betting books also list me as a bluestocking?"

"Strangely, no. But I believe that is the work of Lady Eleanor. Bluestockings cannot be of the first stare of fashion, and so she has likely downplayed your intelligence." Again his smile widened. "I believe I shall win a great deal of money when your true talents are revealed."

"You bet on my intelligence?" She ought to be insulted, but she wasn't. He was obviously a discerning man, and so why shouldn't he make money by learning the truth about her?

"I did." He pushed off the wall to fully enter the salon. "Do prove me correct by allowing me to introduce you to my chemical society friends. I believe you and they will have a great deal to talk about."

"You are not a student yourself?"

"Not of the sciences, though I enjoy a mathematical discourse or two. My interests lie more in the realm of economics."

"Money," she said.

"And how to make a lot of it."

He was completely unabashed in his mercenary desire, and in this he reminded her of her uncle. Though her uncle was never this handsome or this refined. While she stood there mentally comparing him to her uncle, he stepped directly before her, possessed her hand, and pressed a kiss to her knuckles. Then he continued to hold her hand as he gazed into her eyes.

"Do say yes," he said. Only he didn't just say it. He smiled it. He teased it. No, he *persuaded* it. And her.

"Yes," she said before she even remembered what she was agreeing to.

"Excellent," he said as he lifted her hand even higher. There, dangling on her wrist, was her dance card. "I shall find you for our dance and then lead you to supper afterward. Most of my friends can join us then."

"Oh no," she said. "I'm sure I'm supposed to go into supper with Trevor."

He arched his brows as he wrote his name on her card. "Trevor should join us then," he said. "He always enjoys a lively scientific debate."

"Of course he does," she said, feeling rather dazzled by the way he simply took possession of her hand, her dance card, and her activities. It was the last part that annoyed her the most. So she pulled her card back, but not before he'd scrawled his name on the last dance before supper. "He and I are affianced, and this is our first ball together. Wouldn't it be odd if I made plans without him?"

He straightened, pursed his lips, and seemed to

consider her thoughts. "I can see your point, but I'm afraid it betrays your country upbringing. *Ton* couples do not live in one another's pockets." Then he shrugged. "But do as you wish. I have no interest in making things awkward for you. I simply thought you would enjoy my friends' company."

Put like that, she felt like a shrew. He had only been trying to give her some scientific conversation. And given that she had spoken only of fabrics and fashion for the last two weeks, not to mention dance lessons, French lessons, and lists of names she had to memorize, she would sorely love some simple scientific discourse.

"Very well, sir. I suppose I didn't understand."

He brightened considerably. "Excellent! I'm sure my friends will be delighted to hear about your newest formula." Then he leaned forward, close enough for her to see the striations in his dark eyes. "I don't suppose you'd like to give me a hint. What exactly is this new recipe of yours?"

She blinked at him, making sure her expression was wide and innocent. "My uncle didn't tell you?"

"He was about to, but I'm afraid we were interrupted. We're to meet later in the month, but it would save me some time if you simply explained it now."

Of course it would. Especially since she was sure her uncle could absolutely not have told him the recipe, as she hadn't shared it with him yet.

"Oh my," she declared. "It's really a simple skin cream. Designed to be mixed in with a man's shaving soap. Makes the beard stand up straighter, so that it can be cut more easily."

"Really?" he said. "I'm fascinated."

"Would you like me to write it down for you?"
She looked around then sighed. "But I have no pen
or paper."

"No matter. I have an excellent memory. Just tell
it to me."

"Mind you do it exactly." Then she began to recite
it in specific detail. Except the formula she gave him
was not for a skin cream to make a man's beard stand
up. It was one to make him stink. Horribly. And for
days on end.

Though on the up side, it would likely kill any
sheep ticks that lived on his face. That was how they'd
discovered it. It was one of her father's concoctions to
destroy sheep tick larvae, but they had to discard the
formula because of the awful stench.

"Do you have it?" she asked.

He repeated it verbatim.

"Excellent! You should try it in your hair as well,"
she said. "It makes the strands fuller. We plan to make
it into a soap for balding men."

"An excellent idea. You are most definitely
brilliant."

"And you, my lord, are…" A trickster. A seducer.
"…a very clever man."

"Nonsense," he said. "I merely recognize cleverness
in others. And now, I should leave. I'm sure Lady
Eleanor has a grand entrance planned, and I shouldn't
like to damage that."

"No, Lady Eleanor wouldn't like that you are up
here now."

"Then I will bid you adieu until our dance."

She smiled and dropped into a small curtsy. By the time she straightened, the door had already shut behind him. Which left her alone to think of the man. To analyze—

"Miss Smithson? It's time."

"Seelye. I didn't even hear you open the door."

"Silence is highly prized in a good butler," he returned.

In more ways than one, she should think. She wondered if he had seen Mr. Rausch as he ducked back to the ballroom. And if he had, would he tell anyone that she'd been alone and unchaperoned with him?

"Don't be nervous, Miss Smithson. Lady Eleanor knows just what she's about."

She had no doubt about Eleanor. It was her own performance tonight that she worried about. But she didn't allow that to show on her face. Instead, she lifted her chin.

"Well then, Seelye. I suppose it's time I made a spectacle of myself."

The butler gave her a rare smile before holding up her dark green cloak with the stylized antennae on the hood. The plan was to pull it off at the top of the stairs, thereby revealing her in all her feathered glory.

Just as she stepped into concealing garment, she heard Seelye speak.

"Mr. Anaedsley is a lucky man." The words were spoken quietly, almost too soft for her to hear. And when she finally straightened and turned to look at the butler, his face was its usual impassive expression.

Oddly enough, the sight reassured her as nothing else. They all had their rolls to play, didn't they? Seelye was the stoic butler. She was the blushing innocent. Even Mr. Rausch was the mysterious distraction.

But what was Trevor? Was he the ardent lover? Or merely another clever schemer? She supposed she would have to get to the end of the play to find out. So she descended the stairs, belatedly realizing she was leaving a small trail of feathers in her wake.

Just how much of her dress was she going to lose before the night was done? She didn't really care about the answer. She was distracting herself as she walked the long corridor to the top of the ballroom stairs. And then she was there. Seelye passed her off to the Redhill majordomo before fading back into the shadows.

Now was the moment. She stepped to the top of the stairs, keeping her head down and fully covered beneath the cloak. She wasn't to look up until she was announced.

"Miss Melinda Smithson."

The murmur of the crowd silenced. Someone whisked her cloak off. Then she lifted her chin and looked...

Oh my.

Oh goodness.

She hadn't expected the number of people there. She hadn't realized how high the steps were before descending into the ballroom. She hadn't thought everyone would gape at her like that. Or that she'd feel like a prancing bear dressed in feathers.

This was a mistake.

A horrible, ridiculous, stupid—

Trevor started climbing the stairs. She focused on him as she might have looked at a shield or a wall that she might hide behind. If she weren't frozen in place, she would have run to him like a child trying to crawl behind a rock.

But then he smiled at her. That familiar face. Charming. Freckled. With warm brown eyes that held her gaze. She'd once hated that face because it meant he was taking away her father and leaving her with Ronnie. And before that, he'd been the spoiled prince who tugged her hair before running off to chase frogs.

She had a history with this man and a shared secret, not to mention that solid, whimsical ring about her finger. This was Trevor, and when he smiled at her, she felt herself come alive. She felt her belly soften and her shoulders ease. She was no longer frozen in place, so she moved for him, meeting him two steps below the top.

He bowed to her as she curtsied. Not so easy on the steps when her knees were still stiff. But she managed it as he took her gloved hand and pressed a kiss to the back. Well, that's what his mouth did. But what mattered was that he managed somehow to wink at her just as he was acting the most formal of greetings.

"My Cricket Princess," he murmured, too low for anyone else to hear.

"My Bug-Eyed Duke," she returned.

She thought it was too quiet for anyone else to hear, but she'd forgotten about the Redhill major-domo. Out of the corner of her eyes, she caught his start of surprise. He twisted slightly to look at her, and then recalled himself.

Trevor saw it too. His eyes danced with merriment

as he gently set her hand on his arm. "Allow me to introduce you to our host and hostess."

"Of course—"

"And it's Buggy Duke. Not Bug-Eyed."

She giggled. She couldn't stop it. "I think your ring speaks for itself. Bug-eyed."

"Oh blast. I knew I'd fashioned that thing wrong."

He hadn't done anything like that. He was simply talking nonsense with her as they often did. And he was distracting her from the fact that the silence that greeted her appearance was now filled with the steady murmur of talk. Whispers, chatter, outright giggles.

They were laughing at her. Her father and uncle were right. She was a laughingstock. And yet, with a cricket ring on her finger and her duke at her side, she couldn't bring herself to care. Not at this moment. Not as she curtsied to the Earl of Redhill and his countess.

Helaine pressed a kiss to her cheek, whispering into her ear. "We've almost done it. Just keep a brave front for a bit longer."

Mellie didn't have a chance to respond as Lord Redhill turned to the musicians and gave the nod. The opening notes were struck, and immediately the center of the ballroom appeared. People slid backward as if simply pushed away.

Lord Redhill took his wife's hand, then pulled her indecently close, and together they began to dance. Melinda would normally have wanted to watch. The couple moved so beautifully through the steps, but it was her turn now. And if she was a bit reluctant, Trevor seemed to be eager.

In one motion, he took her hand and slipped his

other about her waist. A moment later, he had her on the dance floor. If he hadn't held her so securely, she likely would have stumbled, but he braced her. A few notes later, she was able to relax into the motions of the dance.

Of the waltz.

In his arms.

Sweet heaven, it was glorious.

In all the excitement of the preparations, she'd nearly forgotten what it was like to be held by him. To feel the grip of his fingers and the muscular bunch of his thighs. They weren't supposed to touch leg to leg, and they didn't for the most part. But even at a proper twelve inches apart—which truthfully, they weren't—she was still aware of the strength of his legs and the thrust of his steps. Forward. Backward. Sweeping her about the room until she began to smile from the sheer exhilaration of it.

"That's better," he said as he smiled at her.

It took her a moment to realize that he meant her expression, not the motions of the dance. "Do I look terrified?"

"No. Do you feel terrified?"

"I did. I was."

"And now?"

Now she wanted him to kiss her. Now she was thinking of brandy in her bedroom and the press of his body against hers. "Now I hope this dance will never end."

He tightened his arms around her, drawing her even closer. She went easily, abandoning herself to the heat of his body as he moved them about the room.

She found his rhythm, she matched his steps, and then she laughed. How had she lived this long without dancing? How had she ever preferred a book in her laboratory to spinning about a room in Trevor's arms?

He slowed. His steps faltered, and then they stopped. But he didn't stop staring at her. And she did not step away from his arms.

The music had ended. Some part of her was aware of this, but he was there, and she was so close to him that she knew when he breathed. When *they* breathed.

Her heart stuttered, her chest squeezed tight, and her breath caught.

Something was blooming inside her. Something tender and horrifying and powerful all at once. It was there, swelling in her though she was terrified at the change in her soul. She was a quiet girl. A country girl of science, and yet... And now...

She felt it burst through her consciousness like a blow to the head. Or perhaps a blow to her heart because that organ abruptly lurched inside her.

Love.

She was in love.

And while she stood there gaping at him, he turned his eyes to the crowd. It took some moments before she heard what he did, before she saw what absorbed his attention.

Clapping. The crowd was clapping.

Apparently, she was a success. Everyone was smiling at her, the newest sensation of the *ton*.

"That's done it," Trevor said with pride.

"Done what?"

He extended his arm, ready to escort her to her

position on the edge of the dancing floor. Already there were a dozen gentlemen lining up to greet her.

"You're a success. And now the real work begins."

"What?" She stumbled slightly, but he held her safe. "What work? I thought this was the hard part. This launch that made me a sensation."

"That was Eleanor's hard part. This is mine."

She looked at him, too many conflicting emotions rioting inside her. She was still reeling from this burst of love. She had no understanding of what he meant.

"Trevor?"

He turned her, lifting her hand to press yet another kiss onto the back of her glove.

"The hard part," he explained. "Helping you pick one of these gentlemen to be your husband."

"Oh," she said. *That* hard part.

"Don't worry. Just pay attention tonight, and let me know if you think you could love any one of them."

And then before she could say anything—before she could burst into tears—he began to make introductions.

Fifteen

Women gamble with hearts. Men gamble with money, for they have no hearts with which to wager.

"AND THIS IS LORD…" *TINY PRICK.* "…TULLOCK. WE were in school together."

"A pleasure to meet you, Miss Smithson."

"And beside him is another old friend, Lord…" *Smells like Fish.* "…Lowes. He was a genius at Latin."

"*Quam pulchra es!* That means—"

That you try to bugger every female you meet.

"That I am beautiful. I am well versed in Latin, Lord Lowes," Mellie said with a smile. "*Blandiris me.*"

"Not flattery at all, Miss Smithson."

Trevor held his tongue while Lord Randy Bastard scrawled his name. Probably in Latin. And then he introduced the next pair of idiots.

"Do say that we can have the honor of a dance. Do you have any left?"

Do you mean to tup her together? Or just make her watch the two of you?

Trevor did his best to remain congenial, but as each

man stepped forward to ogle his fiancée, his thoughts became cruder and crueler until he was appalled at himself. It was not like him to think such black thoughts, and yet the parade of men bowing over Mellie made him murderous. It wasn't logical. He knew that. Damnation, he was supposed to be pondering them as potential husbands for Mellie. But the very thought of someone else touching her turned him vile.

"So sorry. Her card's all filled. Try your luck with the dowagers."

"At last, we finally meet!" cried a too high, too sweet voice.

Bloody hell. Gargantuanly bloody hellfire cocked damn. "Oh look," he ground out. "It's my mother."

Mellie turned, her expression sweet and open. And all he could think was: lamb to the slaughter.

"Darling," he said in desperation. "I think this is my dance." He grabbed her hand and started pulling, but she remained steadfastly where she was.

"I'm not dancing this set so I can meet your friends."

"You've met them. They're all terrible people. Come along—"

"But it's in the middle of the dance."

"We'll join late."

"What…"

"Trevor!" cried his mother. Bloody hell. She said his name in that tone that shot ice down his spine. Part warning, part syrupy sweet. It was like the taste of spoiled fruit that was a little too strong before it made you gag. Or worse.

All his friends—the bloody traitors—backed away.

His mother was well known in the *ton*, and no man young or old stayed around if they could avoid it. She was apt to force them to dance with a buck-toothed lackwit or do the pretty at her latest afternoon tea. Or *pay* for her next afternoon tea, which had been her recent campaign until his grandfather cut off all his money.

"Well hello, Mother," he said dryly. "Fancy meeting you here." It was a stupid thing to say. Of course she would be here. But some madness had made him block the idea from his brain until confronted with her face to face.

"Fancy meeting your fiancée at someone else's ball!" she cried. His mother always cried. In fact, she even whispered in exclamation points.

"I wasn't aware that you were hosting a ball this Season. Has that changed? What are your ideas this year?" It was his only hope: distract her with her plans, her ideas, her anything but him. Or Mellie.

Sadly, she wasn't completely stupid. And she'd set her sights on his fiancée.

"You are the most unnatural of sons! To think that I had to wait to meet this dear woman!" She reached out to Mellie. "Come, my dear, let us converse without—"

"Oh no!" Damnation, now she had him talking in dramatic accents. "Mother, Mellie and I are about to dance. You cannot drag her away now."

"Drag her away? Drag her away! How you think!"

Which was a sure sign that she had absolutely intended to drag Mellie aside and eviscerate her somehow.

"Mother—"

"You must tell me, Miss Smithson, how you managed to trap my son! All the ladies—"

"Mother!"

His mother blinked innocently at him.

"She did not trap me. We are in love."

She patted his cheek. Like he was still in short coats, she patted his cheek and then made it worse by leaning forward to kiss him. He couldn't back away without appearing completely obnoxious—not that he didn't consider it—but he knew his duty. He stood still as she condescended to him in front of the entire *ton*. Then when she finally straightened, she turned a dazzling smile on Mellie.

"Trevor has always been prone to wild flights of fancy."

"Really?" Mellie interrupted. "I've found his mind to be extremely logical. His scientific papers are very sound, especially his Elementary Histological Study of Sheep—"

"Good God, don't say that in public!" his mother gasped.

Mellie looked taken aback, but no more than he. She'd read his paper? She thought it very sound? Damn, but she was a smart woman. Sadly, that had little impact on his mother.

"We should have met earlier," his mother said with a dramatic sigh. "That way I could have educated you on polite discourse."

Then the delightful Mellie tilted her head and looked politely confused. "Which word do you object to? Elementary? Sheep? Histological—"

"Don't say it!"

"—means relating to tissue."

His mother puffed herself up as large as the woman could make herself, which given that she was of slightly above average height was merely…puffy. Then she deflated with an exhausted sigh. "My dear, if you are to be my daughter-in-law, I insist you come to me for lessons. Tomorrow afternoon. We need at least four days of education before Trevor's tea party."

His mother then nodded as if that settled things, but Mellie simply frowned at him. "Are you having a tea party?"

He shook his head slowly, knowing better than to argue, but doomed to say the truth nonetheless. "I am not aware of a party."

"Of course you aren't!" his mother cried, heaving her admittedly way above average bosom. "It's because you refuse to read my correspondence. I have been trying and trying to gain your attention since the announcement in the paper. And to think that is how you treat your own mother!" She turned to Mellie. "I must warn you now because your blessed mother cannot: if you wish to know how a man will treat you after you're married, just look to how he responds to his mother." She pressed a handkerchief to her lip. "You are doomed, my dear. Doomed to a forgotten and neglected—"

"I should be happy to attend Trevor's tea party," Mellie said, smiling up at him.

Oh damn. Not the thing to say, but she didn't know that. Because his mother would take that one small admission and run with it until it spiraled out of control. "Er, Mellie—"

"Excellent!" his mother cried, clapping her hands. "Thursday afternoon. All the important people already know, but invitations will be sent tomorrow. It will be so much fun! Really, the event of the season. I think I shall set my butler to catching crickets in your honor."

"God, Mother—" Trevor began, but the woman just kept talking.

"Come tomorrow precisely at two. Invitations and the like don't write themselves. And we must discuss your dress. I'm sure feathers are all the rage in Russia, but we can't have you trailing the things around. The dogs will eat them and then…"

"No," Mellie said. She had yet to learn that his mother appeared to be deaf to that particular word.

"Don't worry, my dear. I'll make sure you understand everything you need to know about society—"

"No, regarding your dogs."

Trevor had learned early to just let his mother ramble on and then mitigate the disaster afterward. It was the best he could manage. Except with one word—a word his mother was an expert at ignoring—Mellie had managed to completely thwart his mother's conversation.

"No dogs?"

"No feathers. With dogs. The two make a vile and rather explosive combination."

His mother blinked, but she'd been in society a long time. She wasn't one to be thrown off track easily. "That's exactly what I was saying," she said.

"And you are most correct. I wouldn't risk harming your dogs. But I promise to be there at the party, assuming Trevor sends me an invitation." She smiled sweetly up at him.

"I have terrible penmanship," he said solemnly. "My mother tells me so frequently."

"So no invitation?" she asked.

"Not from me."

"Ah." She turned back to his mother whose mouth was hanging open in shock. "I'm so sorry, Lady Hurst. The tea party was such a fun idea."

And then finally—like a miracle from heaven—the next set was forming. He didn't care which blackguard had scrawled his name on her card. Trevor was going to take the excuse to leave the conversation.

He grabbed her hand and set it firmly on his arm. "Our dance, my dear."

"Really? I thought—"

"It is," he interrupted. Then he took her hand and walked as fast as he could manage. His mother took a step after them, but she knew better than to appear like she was chasing them. Which she would be. And then…escape! A miracle, and all due to Mellie. "I could kiss you right now," he murmured into her ear.

"Even I know that would be improper."

"I've never seen anyone get the better of my mother like that. Never! And I've been trying for years."

"That's because you are too honorable to circumvent her," she said. And for a moment, he wondered if she meant it as a compliment.

"Well, not in public," he finally admitted.

"Exactly."

They took their positions in the country dance,

side by side with their hands linked. "It won't last, you know. Right now, she is plotting how to get her tea party."

She shrugged, and his attention was pulled to the shift and pull of the features across her bosom. Damn, but it was the most distracting gown. "I know. In truth Eleanor heard about the tea days ago, so we have already planned for it."

"You did?"

"Of course. But I had no wish to become your mother's secretary and no time either. Eleanor has me scheduled from dawn until …well, dawn."

"But…did Eleanor warn you about my mother?"

"Goodness, *everyone* has warned me about your mother. She is famous as a managing woman."

Very true. "Then you don't mind?"

"The tea? Not at all. Though it was rather bad of you not to introduce us earlier. She's right about that."

He frowned. "I was trying to save you from her."

"She's your mother. She's due a little courtesy."

He took a moment to absorb that, and realized to his horror that his mother had somehow won again. Because no matter what conversation he had with her, no matter that Mellie neatly put her in her place regarding the invitations, he had once again ended up in the wrong. And, apparently, he was going to a damned tea as well.

"Have I just been managed?" he mused, not at all pleased by the thought. Surprisingly, he was not horrified either. It might be fun to watch Mellie and his mother fence with one another. He'd thought his fiancée akin to a lamb to the slaughter, but she'd just proved she had teeth of her own. Just so long as he could watch from afar. From very, very far away.

"So you'll let her have her tea?" Mellie asked.

"If you want it."

"I think it's only polite."

It would be a nightmare, but she didn't realize that yet. Fortunately, he would be at her side the entire time and could protect her. Or so he planned as the steps of the dance began.

Then there was little time to talk as they skipped and hopped through the patterns of the dance. She moved easily, neither the worst nor the best dancer he'd ever been partnered with. But what made this moment so much more delightful was the way she seemed to relish dancing. She enjoyed a pattern that had become routine to him. She smiled brightly at him, she laughed happily when one lady was particularly dashing, and she held his hand and looked at him as if he had given her the moon.

And he wanted to. He wanted to give her the sun, moon, and stars and anything else her heart might desire. He wanted to swing her around and pull her into his arms, then kiss her senseless. And after he laid her down in a bed of silk sheets, showered her with jewels, and made her come a thousand times? Then he would sink into her and find such bliss between her thighs that—

The dance came to an end. The dance ended, and she was looking at him with a furrow between her eyes. He swallowed, forcibly bringing his mind back to the present. Then he bowed in his most respectful fashion before leading her to the edge of the ballroom where every male in London was standing and waiting for her.

"They are waiting for their time with you," he said, his voice tight. It was an effort of will to keep his hands from becoming fists.

"Should I refuse them?"

"No," he forced himself to say. He saw Eleanor standing nearby. He had no idea where she'd been during that blighted conversation with his mother, but she was here now, entertaining the men while they all waited for Mellie.

He turned to Mellie, choosing the brutal truth for the first time in a long time. "I cannot watch you dance with them."

"What?"

"I'm sorry, Mellie, but they are thinking things that make me want to run them through with a sword."

She blinked at him. "Do you even own a sword?"

"A pistol then. I own a pistol." A fine pair he'd won in a game of faro. He hadn't the slightest idea where they were at the moment, but he remembered winning them. "Or my grandfather's sword."

She laughed, the sound rich and fine. How had he not seen how refined she was on every level? "You quite turn my head when you speak so romantically."

"Really?"

She laughed a little louder. Then she sobered. "No silly, because I know you are teasing me. But I thank you for the effort. I feel…" She took a deep breath and turned her sparkling eyes to the room at large. "I feel alive, Trevor, and it's wonderful."

"Then you should enjoy it. And like the besotted

bridegroom, I will stand on the side and glower at any man who dares touch you."

"They are only trying to pluck the feathers off, you know."

"I know," he growled. "And that makes it ten times worse."

"Shall I tell you a secret?" she whispered as the gaggle of gentlemen began to surround her. Trevor had made sure to stop far enough away to have their conversation, but the blighters had moved to her.

"Please," he said. Anything to distract him from how beautiful she was.

"There is a design on the gown underneath. The feathers are meant to flake away to show the colors and stitching below. The duchess predicted the pattern will be revealed by midnight."

He gaped at her. Good God, did she not understand what that did to the male mind? To know that he is *supposed* to undress her? It would be quite the surprise tonight, but after that? Every man would be determined to destroy her gown whenever she appeared.

"I shall have to carry pistols and hire guards to protect you," he said.

She simply laughed, too innocent to know that he was serious. "It's to make me exciting, and I must say, it's working. I feel like a mysterious package soon to be opened."

Good God, he was going to have a word with the duchess. He was going to tell the woman to alter Mellie's gowns immediately. Dark, heavy fabrics and a hood from now on. Even knowing the idea was ridiculous, he couldn't help thinking it. And before he could think of anything charitable to say, he lost the chance. Men surrounded her on all sides, and she was smiling at her next dance partner. Sweet heaven, she was a success, and he was going to be a raving lunatic within the week.

"You always did have a good eye," a familiar voice drawled in his ear.

Bloody hell. First his mother, now his father.

"No," he said, hearing the regret in his voice. "I'm just lucky. I had no more idea that she was a beauty than anyone else."

"So it was Eleanor who was the making of her?"

Trevor nodded, feeling ten times the fool.

"Good, then she'll be fine once you break it off."

He jolted turning around to stare at his father. "We are engaged."

The man gave him a sour expression. The one reserved for especially bad faro hands and miscreant sons. "Come along, Trevor. You need a drink."

He was parched, but that didn't mean he would walk willingly into a tête-à-tête with his father. "I think I'll stay here and watch—"

"Your grandfather is in the card room. He thinks you might enjoy a few hands of loo."

Trevor did laugh at that. He found loo to be a particularly vicious card game, especially when played by vicious people like his grandfather, the Duke of Timby. "Thank you, but I'm content here."

His father sighed and weariness appeared on his suddenly haggard face. "Don't be childish, Trevor. I'm only trying to help. You will have this audience with him, and it's best if it's done in public."

"Have you gone daft? This is not a conversation to be had in public."

"On the contrary, the more people who know the true reason for your impetuous engagement, the easier on both you and the girl when it dissolves. This way when she cries off, she'll be seen as an honorable gel since you weren't truly engaged to her in the first place."

Trevor ground his teeth. Damn the man for simply assuming the engagement would dissolve. "And why would you think—"

"Because I'm not an idiot," his father all but hissed as he grabbed his son's elbow. "Once I heard about your grandfather's plan, I knew you would do something like this. It was a ridiculous gambit on his part. I told him so, but you know how impervious he is to any ideas but his own."

"Father—"

"Just talk to the man. Do it in public—politely, of course—and let's get this resolved in the most equitable way for everyone."

Trevor had no choice but to agree or cause a scene. It was a hard choice given his already foul temper, but his father was right. Best do this now and in a way that required some sort of restraint. So with a last look at Mellie, who was currently enjoying a dance with a handsome future earl, he followed his father as they maneuvered their way to the card room.

It was slow going. Every few feet someone wanted to congratulate him on his engagement. Only a few were truly happy for him. Most wanted gossip. They tried every conversational gambit they knew to get salacious details of his courtship out of him. But as he'd already been playing this game for two weeks, raising anticipation for tonight, he was able to deflect everyone with an expansive gesture toward Mellie and the words, "I am a lucky man."

Eventually, they made it through the ballroom and into the parlor for gentlemen to play cards. The duke dominated the largest table and had one of his fellow septarians on either side. Two other seats were occupied by his father's friends. Trevor's own friends were too smart to sit at a table with these cutthroats.

"There you are, my boy," his grandfather boomed. "Been waiting for you to grow tired of that nonsense out there and join the men. Eddie, get up. Let my grandson have your seat at the table."

"No thank you, Your Grace," Trevor tried, but Baron Edwin Waite had already risen from his seat. "Please sit down. I haven't the funds right now to cover your stake." He turned his gaze on his grandfather. "I'm a bit to let right now since someone has refused to pay his vowels." His meaning was clear. He'd applied several times to his grandfather's man of affairs for the money owed him due to his engagement. Each time, he had been refused.

Meanwhile, the baron visibly started. "Refused to pay. The blackguard! Give me his name. I'll be sure to see him banned from all the London tables."

"Hmmm," he mused. "What do you think, grandfather? Should I tell the blackguard's name?"

"Don't be ridiculous. You don't possess any vowels from anyone. Everyone knows you don't gamble."

That wasn't exactly true. His whole venture with Mellie was one huge gamble, but the duke was correct. He'd always thought money bet on a turn of a card was a waste of time. "Gentlemen wagers happen all the time, grandfather. And only a blighter would cheat on such a thing."

"Quite right," said the baron. "I'm feeling rather parched. Wouldn't have sat down at all, but your grandfather insisted. Here's a thought. Trevor, play my stake, and we'll split the winnings. We all know I'm bollocks at loo."

That was certainly true, and so with an internal sigh, Trevor took the baron's seat. But something happened as he settled into the chair. Something dark and angry that had been brewing for a while bubbled up. It was probably Mellie's influence. Once he'd accepted all the machinations of the peerage as the normal course of affairs, but now he saw them in a different light. He saw that it was pure maliciousness— and greed—that had his grandfather putting the affable baron at the table. And meanness in dismissing the man so cavalierly.

So he turned and touched the baron's sleeve. "How much has my grandfather taken you for tonight?"

"What? Oh. Well, I should know better than to sit at the table with him. But I can't dance anymore. Gout, you know. So what is a man to do to pass the time while his gels enjoy themselves?"

Trevor thought back. The baron had a daughter he was launching this year. He made a mental note to spread a kind word around about the girl. "Get something to drink. I'll be sure to get your money back."

The man gave a hearty laugh. "That's kind, but don't worry. I don't stake what I can't lose."

Which made him a smart man. But it didn't lessen his grandfather's maliciousness. Or Trevor's intention to win back every penny of what the baron had lost.

So he settled into his chair and nodded at the dealer. Trevor's father, it seemed, was not to be given a seat, so his pater hovered nearby looking anxious. Just as well. The man was miserable at both mathematics and the understanding of one's opponents, which made five-card loo a terrible game for him.

Meanwhile, Grandfather's best friend began the opening salvo. "Tell me about this gel you've brought tonight."

"Miss Smithson is my fiancée and a brilliant woman on a variety of different subjects."

"I don't doubt that in the least," the man responded with a lascivious sneer. "I myself love a mistress with a variety of talents."

The others at the table chuckled, but Trevor kept his expression cold as he looked at his hand. "Insult my fiancée again, and I will challenge you. Your hand isn't so steady anymore, my lord. That would make you terrible with a blade and even worse with a pistol."

His grandfather's eyes narrowed. "And yet she dresses in feathers that fall off."

Trevor smiled, his darker emotions easing slightly at the memory of Mellie. "She does have her own unique style."

"No doubt," returned his grandfather.

"Athletic?" the friend said with a laugh. "Or does she practice something more exotic? With those feathers—"

"I believe I just won your stake, Lord Barr," Trevor interrupted.

The man blinked, then looked at the huge pile of chits before him. Trevor laid down his hand, winning the modest pot, but not the markers in front of the man. Didn't matter. Trevor kept his eyes steady and his voice cold.

"Your choice, my lord. Your stake now, or we meet pistols at dawn."

Lord Barr reared back. "You can't be serious."

"Shall I start a rumor that your wife is…athletic? No, no one would believe that." The woman weighed as much as a small cow. "Your granddaughter then. I shall provide details. I've visited her brother, you know. Had plenty of time—"

"You will cease this nonsense!" growled his grandfather. And it was a growl filled with phlegmy vehemence.

At this point, Trevor would usually laugh off the whole thing as a joke. It was a delicate balance with the oldest generation. The threat of a duel was enough to make his point. The laughter now would allow Lord Barr to maintain his pride. And then all would go back to normal, hopefully with fewer jokes about his fiancée's possible skills.

But he wasn't in the mood to let anyone off, much less a seventy-year-old roué who thought he could insult whomever he wanted with impunity.

"I did warn him," Trevor said. He pulled out his

gloves from his pocket. "Shall I slap you? Whom would you have as your second? I assure you, my grandfather won't rise from bed before eleven. He wouldn't bestir himself at dawn even for you."

And by saying that, he pointed out that his grandfather had been using Lord Barr just as clearly as he'd used Baron Waite.

"Your move, Lord Barr."

He could see the man's mind work, see the knit in his brow as he tallied up his level of sins. First off, he'd insulted a man's fiancée, even after a warning. That would put him on the wrong side of the gentleman's code, especially since they had an audience here. Second, he knew that in the court of *ton* gossip, he was not nearly as well loved as Trevor. That came from being his grandfather's friend. They were known to be cruel at times. Third, and this was most telling, he loved his daughter and doted on his granddaughter. The girl was probably the only person in his life that he valued over the duke. Given that, the outcome was entirely predictable.

He pushed his chips over to Trevor. "I apologize for my rudeness. Must be the brandy."

"I would think it's the company you keep, but by all means, blame the French drink."

Lord Barr didn't answer as he bowed to the table at large and withdrew. Meanwhile, Trevor's grandfather narrowed his eyes.

"You'll regret that."

"No, I don't think I will. Your deal."

The man took up the cards, his aged hands still able to deal with crisp efficiency. "You've become impertinent, Trevor. Your manners are common, and your judgment questionable. Even so, that girl is beneath you."

"Terribly sorry that your memory is flagging, Grandfather. Nothing to be ashamed of. It comes with age. But with the ducal estate at risk, you really need to leave matters to father and your man of affairs. You've been bungling lately, and you know it."

Trevor's words were beyond the pale. They were not only rude, but they hit at every aging man's most vulnerable spot. But since even Trevor couldn't threaten to skewer his grandfather in a duel, all he could do was make his point in another fashion. Especially as this next hand did not go to his grandfather, but the other crony. Trevor managed to keep a portion of the pot, but only barely.

And then his grandfather leaped to his usual form of attack with Trevor. "I'll have you cut off," he hissed. From a growl to a hiss. Trevor was making progress.

"You already have, sir. How unfortunate that the estate is entailed, and you would have to disown my father to disown me. And then where would the title go upon your demise? Did you ever legitimize your French bastard?"

"How dare you!"

"Ah, I thought not."

His grandfather won that hand. He might be furious, but he still remembered his cards. Trevor was looed, but that was inevitable in this game.

Meanwhile, his father set his hand on Trevor's shoulder. Ever the peacemaker, the man squeezed his son and tried to moderate the emotions. "The duke is simply worried for you. We all are."

"My grandfather need not worry. I have my affairs well in hand. It was his bumbling machinations that started this whole chain of events in the first place."

The duke slammed his fist down on the table. Finally, Trevor had pushed him into an unseemly display. And it hadn't been all that hard to accomplish. The man truly was aging.

"That girl is beneath you. She is beneath all of us, and she will not have my name or title."

Trevor arched a brow. "No, she won't. She'll have my name and my title. You will be worm food soon enough. I only need wait a time."

"I'll disinherit you!"

Trevor rolled his eyes. "Your memory again. We've already had this discussion. You'd have to disinherit my father, and we both know you won't do it." And then he played a trump, winning the lion's share of the pot.

But his father wasn't nearly as calm. His face was pale, and he squeezed Trevor's shoulder harder than a vise. For a moment, Trevor feared that he'd have to moderate his plan if only to prevent his father from having a seizure, but to his surprise, the man came down squarely on Trevor's part.

"I warned you this nonsense wouldn't work, Father. Trevor has your stubbornness. He won't be managed like I was."

"Trevor needs to learn his p-place!" the duke sputtered. "He will marry a girl of my choosing or starve."

Trevor tsked loudly. "Your memory again, sir.

You have already proved how bad your judgment is regarding women."

"The devil you say!" the man exploded.

Trevor didn't answer at first. He was too busy winning the next hand. When he spoke he knew he was crossing not only society's rules, but also the law within his own family. It didn't matter. For the first time in his life, he saw exactly how ridiculous it was to maintain a system of bride-choice that had proved so disastrous time and time again.

So he won the hand, then he looked squarely at his grandfather. "Your choice in bride was bad enough," he said. "Grandmother was frail and unable to conceive adequate sons. So much that you went to France to father half a dozen bastards."

The man gaped at him, too furious to even draw breath. And then, Trevor made it worse. He turned on his father who had just a moment before supported him.

"And your bride is even worse. I know Grandfather picked her. How much in debt are you, Father? And not just because of Mother. Did I see your mistress sporting a new diamond bracelet? How expensive was that? But I am thankful that you've been careful. At least I have not had a dozen illegitimate brothers to contend with. Only the one girl."

His father paled. This was not something spoken of publicly. Ever. And yet, here Trevor was pouring it out in an open card room at a party attended by the whole *ton*. But it was the truth, and everyone here knew it.

The duke pushed up to a stand, his eyes hard, his

body trembling in fury. "So you marry for money?" He spoke as if that wasn't the choice of hundreds of aristocrats.

But Trevor shook his head. "I pick the woman I want."

"Even if she's a common cit? With a mad mother and an idiotic father? Good God, boy, *think*!"

Trevor smiled. He hadn't thought he could. It was a devastating thing to humiliate both father and grandfather, but the darkness in him spilled out. He laid down his last card, winning the pot.

"I am thinking. And I think you owe me a great deal of money. Unless you plan to forget this as well."

"I forget nothing."

"Then you will pay your debts, cease prattling about disinheritance, and stay the bloody hell away from my fiancée."

Then Trevor stood, waiting with fists pressed against the baize. Did his grandfather cower? Did he give in gracefully?

"You are dead to me, boy," the man spat.

Trevor waived a hand in dismissal as if that meant nothing. It was a lie. The words cut at him. A part of him still loved his grandfather, but it was clearly a one-sided love. "Do you forget your debts? Do we turn the financial reins over to Father?" He gestured at the table. It was so much more than a pile of chits here. The man either had to pay or admit he was unable to handle money. It wasn't enough to legally declare him *non compus mentis*, but it was a start. Especially as there were at least two barristers in the room listening closely.

Then his grandfather gave in. His hands shook, his eyes blazed in fury, but he did as honor bid. He threw down bank notes as he might throw away bad meat. "You may apply to Oltheten," he said, his voice thick but clear. "He will give you the last penny you will ever see from me."

Trevor simply shrugged. "Between you and my parents, sir, I never expected to inherit a penny anyway." That was a lie, but everyone here took it as truth.

Trevor had just thrown away the fortune of a lifetime. He was well aware that the entailed properties wouldn't support themselves. He would be in a bad way if he inherited a title with no means to support it. But that was a worry for another day. For now, he'd beaten his grandfather. He'd declared his independence from a domineering old goat, and…and…

And he wanted to see Mellie.

He *needed* to spend some quiet moments in her arms assessing exactly what he had just done. She would help him sort through the facts logically before he planned his next step.

She would help him.

And so it was with absolute horror that he stepped out of the card room to see her on another man's arm. Not just any man, but Lord Rausch, the slimiest damn German in London. And she was laughing while he unobtrusively plucked a feather from her bodice.

Bloody hell, this night might just end with a challenge after all.

Sixteen

Listen carefully so you can use his own words against him.

MELLIE DIDN'T NOTICE WHEN TREVOR APPEARED AT the edge of the ballroom, or so she told herself. She kept her gazed fixed on the gentlemen who surrounded her, so she couldn't possibly have seen when he stepped out of the card room with an expression more appropriate to a boxing match. Lord, she'd never seen him more furious and that included when Ronnie had punched him hard enough to land in a cow pile.

Damn, she was looking at him when she shouldn't be. Her attention was supposed to be on Mr. Rausch who was especially charming right now. And his friends were very learned. She'd spoken more natural history in the last fifteen minutes than she had in years of living with her father. She usually got her information from published papers, but it was immeasurably more stimulating to speak with like-minded scientists. She was so happy about the conversation that she didn't even care that they were mostly there to ogle her gown and try to learn gossip about her and Trevor.

She thought she could catch Lady Eleanor's eye. Perhaps she knew why Trevor would look that angry upon leaving a card room. Did the man gamble to excess? Had he just lost a lot of money?

Unfortunately, Eleanor was surrounded by her own circle of admirers. Somehow the two women had become separated by all the gentlemen, which meant that there was no female to moderate Trevor's attitude when he shouldered his way into her circle.

Mr. Rausch responded first. "Mr. Anaedsley, I must say you've been sadly neglectful of your fiancée. She's absolutely fascinating—"

"Thank you, sir. When I need advice on my intended, I'll be sure to turn to you." Then he held out his hand. "Mellie, if you wouldn't mind…" It was clearly not a request. It was also not a statement of what he wanted. Just an outstretched hand and an expression as dark as pitch. And she had no idea how to respond.

"Um, I'm supposed to partner Mr. Greenfield in the next set." The musicians had started tuning again, so it wouldn't be long.

"Perhaps Mr. Greenfield will forgive you," he said, his tone softening, but not his expression. "I would like to speak—"

"Come now, Anaedsley," Mr. Rausch interrupted. "The girl is allowed some fun, don't you think? We're having the most stimulating conversation." He gestured toward Mellie, but froze as Trevor's voice cut through hard and cold.

"Touch my fiancée again, Rausch, and I will meet you at dawn."

"Trevor!" Mellie gasped.

At her cry, Trevor blinked, then his eyes widened, as he must have realized what he'd just said. Suddenly, he was grimacing as he pulled his hands back to his sides. "Forgive me, everyone. I'm in a deuced foul temper."

"Then perhaps you should leave the ladies alone," said Mr. Rausch, his voice cold as he stepped protectively between her and Trevor.

But that was ridiculous. Trevor would never harm her. And if he was in a foul temper, it was incumbent upon her to find out what had happened.

So it was that she touched Mr. Rausch's shoulder. She saw a muscle tick in Trevor's jaw, so she made her intentions very clear.

"Mr. Rausch, would you mind stepping aside? I find I need to have a word with my fiancé. Gentlemen, my apologies. I fear I'm otherwise engaged for this set."

Fortunately, Mr. Rausch was protective, not stupid. Seeing that she would not be deterred, he slid aside but not before catching her eye.

"If you ever have need of anything, pray do not hesitate to call on me. Day or night, whatever—"

"She has no need of you, Rausch," cut in Trevor.

Mellie just sighed. What was it about men that they had to push themselves to ridiculous displays to prove they were men? Affairs at dawn, protective statements. Really, she already missed the rational discussion of chemicals. Well, part of her did. The other part worried that something serious had happened in the card room.

So she stepped around Mr. Rausch and took

Trevor's hand. "Let us take a walk in the garden, shall we?"

She made her words especially loud as a way to draw his attention away from staring hard at Mr. Rausch. It worked. Trevor blinked and flashed her a grateful look. It was a small tick of his lips upward and a general lowering of his shoulders, but she had studied his gestures closely. He was grateful for her understanding, and so she set her hand on his arm and maneuvered toward the French doors that led into the tiny back garden.

"What has happened—" she began, but he squeezed her fingers.

"Not yet. Let's get outside, and I'll tell you everything."

"Of course," she answered, but it was easier said than done. After all, they were the couple of the hour. Everyone wanted to speak with them, and more than a few had watched his dramatic confrontation with Mr. Rausch.

Still, she managed to do it, mostly because Trevor was a master at responding politely before pushing them forward. It took forever, but eventually they crossed to the cooler air outside. She was able to take a deep breath and lift her face to the night sky. She'd never realized how much she relished the simple space to breathe even the fetid London air.

"Finally, Mellie," said a too familiar voice at her side. "I've been waiting an age."

No, no, no, no, no! Ronnie couldn't be here. Not in London at her first ball. And yet, the voice was unmistakable. As was Trevor's response.

"Mr. Ronald Smithson, what an unpleasant surprise."

"You, sirrah, have no right to speak to me!" Ronnie answered, his tone surly.

Mellie finally located her cousin standing at the edge of the brick porch as it led out to the garden. There were a few others here as well, but her cousin took the whole of her attention. As well as the brunt of her temper. "Ronnie, you're the one without any rights. You were *not* on the guest list. I could have you tossed out—"

"Mellie, please. I came to you with an urgent matter."

"Every matter is urgent in your mind, and do you know what? Not a one of them is."

"Your father is sick."

She swallowed, a queasy feeling twisting in her gut. But this was Ronnie, and she'd been fooled by his dramatic statements before. "How sick?"

"Desperately."

She waved that aside. "Is he sleeping?"

"Barely a wink. Paces the house all night long. Doesn't eat. Coughs like the very devil. And all because he's sick with worry over you."

"Oh thank God."

Her relieved pronouncement brought Ronnie up short. It even seemed to surprise Trevor. She felt his forearm twitch beneath her hand, so she squeezed him slightly to reassure him. And then she launched into her own dramatic statements.

"I've been trying to kill my pater for years. If I'd known all it took was an impetuous trip to London, I would have done it years ago."

Ronnie blinked at her, then his expression darkened. "Good God, London has driven you insane! Just like your mother—"

"One more word, Ronnie, and I will stab you with my hairpin. And not in your chest where it won't do any good. I'll go for your ability to father children."

To which Trevor dropped her arm. "I'll hold him still for you, love."

"Thank you—"

"Mellie!" Ronnie exclaimed, backing toward the edge of the brick. Mellie would have continued the charade longer, but the other five people in the area were listening with great attention.

"Ronnie, my father takes to his bed when he's upset. *You're* the one who paces all night long. Which means you made up my father's illness out of whole cloth—"

"He's *worried* about you! We all are!"

Trevor stepped forward with a low growl. "You should be worried I don't kill you—"

"Good God, *stop it!*" If they hadn't caught everyone's attention before, Mellie's bellow certainly did now. "Why does everyone keep threatening to have duels? Is this some London infection of which I'm unaware?"

Both men turned to her, equal expressions of outrage on their faces. "It's how gentlemen express their most vehement displeasure," Ronnie said stiffly.

Trevor started to nod and then abruptly seemed to catch himself. "It's…it's a silly, empty threat. I shouldn't have used it. I beg your pardon."

Ronnie turned to Trevor, his eyes narrowed. "It's not an empty threat with me."

Mellie sniffed. "And that's why I'll never marry you, Ronnie. Because you have no sense."

Ronnie stepped closer, and for the first time in the conversation, the light fell full on his face. What she saw there stunned her. He looked…haggard. There were bags under his eyes and a gaunt look to his haphazardly shaved face. Even his clothes were wrinkled, though he'd obviously made some attempt to fit into her ball. He was in his best attire even if it hung awkwardly on him.

"Ronnie? What has happened to you?"

He looked down at himself and then shrugged. "I fell in love, Mellie, you know that. And now you're engaged to him, and it's all wrong. Why can't you see that? He's all wrong for you."

"Why? Because he's going to be a duke? Because he's a man of science, and I adore science?"

"Because he will bring out the madness in you. With me, I am the mad one, and you are forced to be sane. With him…" He held up his hands beseechingly. "Your worst impulses will claim you. Tell me that you haven't been dreaming of doing things you know you ought not."

The problem with Ronnie—aside from his obvious romantic delusions—was that he'd known her from childhood. He knew just the words to say to strike deep at her heart. To make her question everything she believed about herself.

She had been thinking—almost constantly—of giving in to her baser desires. Of doing things with Trevor that she knew respectable women did not. So in that, he was absolutely correct. And while she was still grappling with her cousin's words, Trevor released a snort of disgust.

"You know nothing of this woman you pretend to adore. You don't know what she wants, what she needs, or even what would make her happy. Do you think this—" He gestured to the growing group of people collecting on the terrace. "This public display will make her happy? Romantic gestures disgust her, and you live by them. Can you not understand the truth? You. Disgust. Her."

Well, that was putting it a bit too strongly. Or maybe not. Maybe deep down, everything her cousin represented—the exhausting emotions, the grand romantic gestures, the aggrandizement of his own personal dramatics—truly did disgust her. And that he came here with a make-believe statement of her father's health, professing to worry about her own madness put the final cap on her fury.

Meanwhile, Ronnie had heard Trevor's words, gone deathly pale, and dropped to his knees before her. "Do you not see?" he said with a gasp. How he could gasp and make himself heard was beyond her, but he must have practiced it. "He separated you from those who love you the most. You are filled with emotions that are not your own. And now, he publicly decries me. I am your cousin! I love you! Mellie, come back to your senses before it is too late!"

She almost did it. She almost gave into her growing fury and resorted to violence. After all, fisticuffs were all that seemed to get through his brain. But in the end, she knew she had a more potent weapon at her disposal. After all, he'd cast her in the role of a princess in need of rescue. But she could just as easily be the evil queen. So she'd fully embrace the role.

It began with a discounting of his feelings for her. That always insulted him. "You only think you love me. I'm easy for you. You have never had to do anything hard to win me."

"That's a lie! Every day without you is agony!"

"That's laziness, Ronnie. What have you *done* but write poetry to me? I'm sure I could have four men in the ballroom composing sonnets to me before supper."

Trevor nodded. "A dozen at least. Shall I make a list?"

Ronnie was not impressed. "Bah! Sonnets."

She waited. He would get there in a moment, she was sure of it.

"Very well," he huffed, "if you discount my poetry—my epic poetry written in iambic pentameter—then give me something else to do. Let me prove my worth."

She waited a moment more. He would say the word. She only had to wait a moment more...

"Give me a quest."

There it was. A quest. And he was already in the perfect position for it: on his knees before her. She had no need to move beyond a simple bend at the waist. She touched his face, startled anew by the thin feel of his skin on such a large man. He truly had been suffering. Which made it all the easier to lean down and bestow a tender kiss to his lips. He clutched at her then, trying to draw her deep into his embrace, but she was prepared. She dug the thumb of her free hand into the juncture of neck and shoulder. She knew just the place to make him rear back in pain.

"Very well," she said. "I am lost in madness. I have given myself over to my mother's disease, and you cannot reach me."

"Mellie!"

"I am committed to this path of self-destruction, and now, your only hope is this quest."

"I will prove myself to you!"

"Bring me a dodo bird. A live one loved and nurtured by your own hand."

She feared for a moment that he hadn't heard her, but then his eyes narrowed. "Wasn't the bird killed by sailors? In Madagascar?"

"Every quest is impossible."

He was thinking hard. "I can do it, Mellie. You think I can't, but I—"

She'd had enough. She'd played the evil queen, she'd given him an impossible quest, and now she was done. Hopefully, the time he spent searching for a dodo bird would bring him some sanity. And if he took a very long time at it, she would gain some measure of peace. So she stepped back. "Mr. Anaedsley?" Mellie said as she held up her hand. "I believe I should like a walk around the garden."

Trevor was looking at them with a thinking man's frown, but at her words, he immediately stepped up to her. Ronnie's hands had gone slack, so she was able to slip through his arms to join her fiancé.

Ronnie had one last plea. A low moan that might have been interpreted as her name. It didn't matter. In order to be the evil queen, she had to be cruel. And what she'd just done was the cruelest thing of all. She'd finally refused him in terms he would understand.

They were off into the garden when Trevor finally spoke. His words were quiet, but attuned as she was to every noise around her, his words came to her clear with concern. "You know the dodo bird is extinct, don't you?"

"I gave him a quest. It's grand and romantic, and it will take him far away from me." Her words were strong, but her mind was elsewhere. She was thinking over Ronnie's words. Had she just descended into madness as he accused? It was possible. What sane woman talked about quests? And Trevor was smart enough to see the flaw in her plan.

"Aren't you encouraging his delusions?"

"Maybe." She sighed. "But I'm not sure he's deluded so much as fanciful. Either way, the romantic part of him won't deny the quest. The practical part knows that a long sea voyage will help him find another lady love."

"But the bird is extinct. And it wasn't from Madagascar. I think it was Mauritius."

"Maybe the place has pretty girls."

He chuckled. "Do you think he'll really go?"

"I don't know. What's more surprising is that I really don't care." And that—said her logical mind—was a sure sign of madness. That's what her father always said. That he'd known her mother was beyond his reach when she ceased to care. For herself. For the young Mellie. And for the unborn child she carried.

Meanwhile, Trevor's thoughts were going along their own path. They were walking out of the garden now, and as they left the small patch of greenery, he posed the next logical question. "What happens when you and I don't wed? Will he come back to bother you?"

A chip of ice twisted in her chest, but what she said was forced into a casual tone. "I will send him on another quest. Maybe make it three quests like in the fairy tales. Or twelve like Hercules. It doesn't matter. I will do it until he understands." She took a deep breath, and finally put words to the fury she was feeling. "I've finally found some measure of freedom from my family, and I don't care what they think or do. I'm not going back." Just as her mother had never looked back when she ran to the bridge. Or so the tale went.

They continued to walk in silence. She used the time to wonder what it was like to be at peace. To have no family showing up at balls, no threatened duels, no gossips surrounding her on all sides. In the end, she decided her life at home had been very boring. Which perhaps explains why her mother descended so easily into madness. It was invigorating. It stirred her blood. It made her wish to never return to the bleak life of reason she'd been raised to embrace.

So there it was. She was mad, and she didn't care. And while she tried to absorb that thought, her words ran somewhere else entirely. "What happened in the card room?" she asked.

Beside her, Trevor slowed his steps, his words starting out as a groan. "I was a fool. I lost my temper with my grandfather and did something unforgivable."

Her gaze cut to his, but in the darkness it was hard to see. "Your grandfather, the duke? What happened?"

He looked up at the sky. As it was overcast, there were few stars to speak of, but he wasn't really looking to them. "I told the truth, Mellie. And now, I think I will be cast out completely."

For such a dire prediction, he didn't seem that upset. But then she remembered that he'd been in a devil's temper when he pushed his way into her crowd of admirers. "As bad as that?"

"Maybe. Maybe not. But like you, I seem to find it hard to care."

Two people in the grips of madness. This was not a good combination. Or rather, since she was a student of chemistry, it was an explosive combination. "Then we are two of a kind," she said, liking the sound of her words. "We are both unfeeling outcasts from our families."

He was silent for a long moment. Long enough to have her searching for his face through the darkness. There was a quarter moon tonight, so there was some light, especially with the gaslights a dozen feet away. But that only gave her enough to see the shadow of his features—the dark circles that could be his eyes and the full line that might be his mouth.

"Mellie," he said as he brought her hands to his lips. "When I hatched this mad scheme, I never thought it would hurt you."

"I'm not hurt, Trevor. I feel free. I feel alive." She said the words, but there was a tightness in her belly that belied her statement. Then, as if to prove it, she kept talking. "I was a success at the ball, had admirers on every side, and if it weren't for Ronnie and whatever happened with your grandfather, I would say it was a perfect evening."

"Then why do you grip my fingers so tightly? Why do I hear desperation in your voice?"

How did he know her so well? How did he hear when her voice was tight and her mind at war with itself? She didn't know, but she knew an easy way to distract him. Or perhaps she meant to distract herself. Either way, her path was easy.

"Because I want you to kiss me, Trevor," she said. "Because I want so much more than that tonight."

He stepped closer, and though she couldn't see it, she knew his eyes had blazed hot and hungry. She knew the cadence of his breath before he kissed her. And the tension in her belly that anticipated his touch.

"Mellie, this is madness."

She smiled. Finally, he understood. "Kiss me, Trevor. Teach me what you promised."

He dropped his forehead to hers. She was not the only one waging an internal war, she realized. So she ended the agony for them both. She ducked under his head just enough to come up from below. Then she claimed his mouth with hers.

His kiss set fire to her blood. She had started the motion, pressing her lips to his, but he finished it, opening her mouth with his tongue before thrusting inside. She surrendered without protest. She opened herself to him and let her body press forward, anxious for his attention.

He let go of her hands, slipping them forward to grip her hips. She thought for a moment that she could feel his member then. Hot and hard as he thrust once against her. But then he set her back.

"I'll not take you in a London back alley," he growled.

"So take me somewhere private, Trevor," she said.

His fingers slid up her body. Just his right hand, but the trail was a long caress the left fire in its wake. "So reasonable," he murmured.

She wanted to laugh at that. She had embraced her madness now, not run to reason. But his fingers had found her breast. Sometime during the evening, her bodice had become completely denuded of feathers so there was little between his fingers and her taut nipple but the smooth caress of silk. She moaned at the feel— the rasp of his nail across the hard bud. And she ached for him to do more.

So she pressed her hand against his on her breast, trapping it there. Then she took his other and slid it from her hip to the juncture of her thighs and held him there. "Now, Trevor. Please."

He answered with one word, but it was all she needed right then. "Yes."

Seventeen

Novelty is the key with every rake. Do something new with him.

TREVOR HAD NEVER BEEN MORE GRATEFUL FOR BEING too poor to afford a regular servant. As he whisked Mellie through the London streets—trailing feathers like breadcrumbs—his mind filled with all the things he wanted to show her.

The sexual explorations were one thing, but the idea that she would see his rooms—in all their haphazard, disastrous glory—had him thinking of what he should hide. That brought him to the startling realization that he wanted to show her everything.

His notes on her father's work. The latest paper on the newly discovered bones of a massive lizard. Even his rather complex research on the possibility that insects carried diseases, and his friend's recent gift of knitted pants. He wanted to show her everything, and that startled him enough that he slowed his steps.

Turning to her, he searched her face. Her eyes were wide, her lips red and moist, and she was smiling.

"Mellie…" he began, unsure exactly what he meant to say. It didn't matter because she silenced him with a kiss. She was too quick in her approach, and he had to catch her even as he slanted his mouth across hers. Then it was thrust and parry with tongues and teeth. All else was obliterated.

Then she pulled back. "You promised, Trevor," she whispered against his cheek. "I will never forgive you if you go back on your word."

"I won't," he promised. At that moment, he would promise her anything and then do his damnedest to see her every wish fulfilled. "Come upstairs."

He rented bachelor rooms in a house loosely run by a widow. She fed him and the other tenant occasionally, kept the main parlor clean, and was in bed by dark. She was also nearly deaf.

He pulled Mellie in the back door and up the stairs. A moment later, they were inside his rooms, stumbling past a pile of papers he intended to read and skirting a pile of mending meant for his valet as soon as he could afford one again.

"So this is where you live," she said, her steps slow as he tugged her into his bedroom.

"Yes." He decided against lighting a candle. The window had no curtains, and so the partial moonlight streamed in. He could see how her skin glowed like alabaster especially as she pulled off her gloves.

He stripped off his coat and waistcoat, wanting full use of his arms. Meanwhile, she wandered through his tiny room, stepping into the only open place near the window. While he set his clothing aside, she stood looking out at the street below, at the expanse of rooftops, and perhaps, at the indifferent moon. He, on the other hand, got to look at her.

The feathers were nearly all gone, and the moonlight highlighted the silver stitching along the silk. A design that...

"Are these wings?" He couldn't stop himself from tracing the line along her back. She shivered as he touched her, and her eyes drifted closed.

"Yes," she whispered. And in that word, there was so much more than an answer to his question. It was gratitude, anticipation, and need all compressed into that single sound. And it was all the permission he needed.

He kissed the skin along her neck. Her hair had mostly tumbled down, and so he used his fingers to pull the tendrils aside. She let her head drop to the side to give him better access as he nipped her sweet skin.

Her scent was stronger now than earlier. Or perhaps away from the cloying atmosphere of the ball, he could sense her more clearly. She'd used lemon on her hair. She tasted of salt and strawberries. He had no idea how, but that's what came to his mind.

And then there was her musk. Not something he usually appreciated, especially on a woman. But her scent filled his nostrils, and his body began to take over. His hips pushed forward, grinding his erection against her. Her bottom tightened against him. For a moment, he thought she was appalled by his base actions, but then she pressed backward against him, rubbing herself enough to make him insane with want.

His hands were shaking as he tugged at the shoulders of her gown. It took him a moment to realize that the dress had to go over her head or be ripped. He almost did it anyway, but he wouldn't shame her that way.

So he pulled her backward—away from the window—and began to gently tug her gown up. Her skirt lifted, and she gasped.

"That feels…the silk feels…decadent," she whispered.

Decadent was good, so he took his time, swishing it against the silk of her stockings. She seemed to like it, making a sound that was as much a moan as a purr.

"I am going to teach you such things," he whispered. It was a vow he made to himself. Tonight she would know what she could experience. What lovemaking could be.

So he made a sensuous dance of lifting her dress off. She was out of the moonlight, but he could still see her in his mirror: a woman ripe for the taking with silk stockings gartered at her thighs, a corset that cinched her waist and pumped her breasts, and a chemise so fine it was nearly translucent.

"You're beautiful," he whispered. "Look in the mirror," he said as he angled her to see. "Watch what happens when I touch you."

He didn't loosen her corset yet. Instead, he tugged apart the thin straps of her chemise and let the edges drift down. The skin of her bodice had flushed rosy, but in the mirror, he could see that she was watching him. Steady. Calm. Too quiet, in fact. He resolved to make her scream.

So he stroked across her chest and then dipped a finger beneath the fabric to pop across her nipple. She gasped, her body momentarily tightening. And then when she relaxed, her body settled a little more deeply against him.

He played that way with both her nipples. Brushing underneath, pinching them as best he could, before pulling away. He learned that when he pinched hard, she gasped, but she moaned when he managed to twist them a little. And she sighed sweetly whenever he brushed his fingers across her chest.

But soon she began to get restless. She reached behind herself to tug at the ties of her corset, and so he pressed another kiss to her shoulder. "Allow me," he said.

Even in the dark, he had no trouble untying her laces. He quickly divested her of the tight garment, and then she pulled off her chemise. That left her standing before him naked except for her stockings and slippers.

She looked lush there in the half light. While he was untying her corset, she'd gathered her hair, pulling it to the side so that a riot of auburn curls draped across her right shoulder.

He grabbed a candle, lighting it with shaking hands. He was much too eager for what was to come as he carefully set it so the light would hit her just right. "You are going to see the most beautiful thing."

Then he settled himself on the edge of the bed. His room was so small, there was little space between bed and the full mirror propped against the wall.

"Will you do exactly as I say?" he asked. "Will you follow my lead and…" He swallowed. "And stop me when I want more?"

She nodded, but he could tell she didn't understand.

It was up to him to remain honorable. To teach her just so much and not take more. It was going to be the hardest thing he'd ever done.

And yet, just then, as he pulled her to sit on the edge of the bed between his spread legs, it felt like the most wonderful thing in his life.

"Don't you want to take off your clothes?" she asked.

More than anything, but he needed the reminder. "It's better if I don't."

She twisted in his arms and tugged at his shirt-sleeves. "At least let me feel you."

He hesitated, wanting to give in. Then she took away the decision, unbuttoning his shirt with quick and clever fingers. Quick because he was nearly unbuttoned before his next breath. Clever because she used the backs of her fingers to stroke his belly as she worked. His muscles leaped beneath her fingers, and he closed his eyes to better appreciate the feel of her touching him so intimately. It was all he would allow himself, and so he would live it to the extreme.

Especially as she pressed a kiss to his chest followed by a lick to his nipple.

He gasped, his hands tightening where they rested at his sides. "Where did you learn that?"

"It was a logical guess. I like it. Why wouldn't you?"

He chuckled—or he tried to. It was more a strangled moan as her fingers continued to caress his belly and lower. While he sat there, his hands fisted in the blanket as she outlined the heat of him, pressing and stroking until his blood pounded.

Just one more moment.

Just one more…

"Enough!" he gasped as he grabbed her hand.

"But I want to learn," she said with the most adorable pout he'd ever seen.

He pressed a swift kiss to her lips. "And so you shall." He was insistent as he turned her back around such that she faced the mirror. She was seated in the V of his thighs, her silk-clad legs so dainty and erotic as they crossed tightly at the ankles. Above she was rosy skin, tight nipples, and wild abandon. Below she was covered, her knees closed.

"Lean against me," he said.

She did, and he rewarded her with a kiss to her temple. And then he began to stroke her. Petting caresses that started at her shoulders, went down across her chest and breasts, and spanned her rib cage. He took his time, rechecking her responses as he tweaked or pinched her nipples. By the time she was squirming against him, he flattened his palm across her belly. Then he let his right hand trail down her thigh. He couldn't resist the ribbon ties of her garters, pausing long enough to tug the bow open.

But then he slid his hand down the length of her inner thigh to her knee. Her legs were only slightly relaxed now, so he had to push his fingers between her knees as he pressed another kiss to her temple.

"I'm going to teach you what you want to know now."

She blinked, her expression wonderfully dazed, but a moment later, she nodded.

"Relax your legs."

She did. He slipped to the inside of her knee and lifted her leg. Up and over his own knee on the right. He kept his legs as tight as he could so as not to frighten her. But then he encouraged her to do the same on her left.

It took a moment, but she did as he wanted. Soon she had both legs draped over his thighs.

"Trust me," he whispered.

Then he slowly widened her such that her dark curls, and then her flushed pretty center was exposed to the candlelight. He had his hands on her thighs, his fingers always moving as he brushed teasing circles at the edge of her garters.

"Do you want me to do it first and then let you?" he asked, his voice a hoarse rasp. "Or do you want to go first?"

She swallowed, her body shifting restlessly as he held her open. "I—I don't know."

"I'll show you first, then." Good. He would get to touch her as he wanted.

He went slowly, seeing her eyes focus on his hands as he trailed up her thighs and to her core. He stroked through her curls, nearly coming from the wetness and the heat. God he wanted her. He wanted to plow himself inside her before he…

He shuddered. He wanted to plant his child and watch it swell inside her. He wanted such things in that moment that he was frankly stunned. And yet that did not slow his fingers as he separated her folds. Because he needed to be inside her, he pushed a finger deep into her.

She gasped, and he felt the muscles of her legs

quiver in resistance. In response, he spread her even wider, opening her to every touch, every invasion.

He was gentle, but he did not allow her to resist him. Something dark and primitive had claimed him. If he could not have her in the usual way, he would own her like this. She would forever remember his fingers, the thrust of his thumb, and the way he held her spread as he owned every part of her most intimate space.

He took his time, submerging his fingers in her body. Not just inside her, but covered in her moisture, opening her petals. He would have all of her.

Then when her breath shortened, and her legs trembled, he pushed his fingers higher. He found her clitoris and began to stroke it. Gently at first, but with increasing strength and a variety of motions.

Well, that was his plan. In truth, he was so absorbed in touching her, in hearing her moans and gasps as he tried different techniques, that when she suddenly arched and cried out, he was caught by surprise.

But then he looked up. He watched her body undulate, felt her flesh grip where his fingers pressed deep inside her, and he heard her startled, delighted cries. It was the most beautiful thing in the world, and he tried to prolong it for his own selfish pleasure.

Eventually, she made him stop. She grabbed his hand and pulled it away, tucking it tight to her breasts while she continued to shudder in his arms. He held her then, pressing kisses to her temple and stroking her white skin until she lay languid in his arms.

"So," he said lightly, "are you ready to try it yourself?" He was teasing her. He knew she was still too weak to do much more than lay against him. But to his shock, she nodded her head.

"Truly?"

She lifted her chin, catching his gaze in the mirror. Then she took a deep breath, lifting her breasts to his hungry gaze. "Yes," she said, though he barely heard her over the distraction of her body. "I want to try doing that to you."

"What?"

She straightened, using her body weight to push him backward on the bed. He fell easily, mostly because he was too startled to resist. And then he felt her fingers on his pants, and he jerked upright. Or rather, he tried.

She was prepared, holding him down easily with one hand. He could have set her aside. He should set her aside. Undressing him was not safe. He was too close to taking what he wanted. But she was insistent, and it felt too wonderful as the buttons eased around him. Then she was gently pulling away his falls, exposing his throbbing erection to the cool air and her tender caress.

He groaned. God, to be touched like this was heaven. Her fingers were gentle as she tortured the wet tip and sensitive ridge. She lifted him higher, apparently to touch his underside. She was too tentative, too uncertain, and yet he couldn't make himself stop her. Whatever she wanted to do with him—to him—he would allow it.

"What should I do?" she asked. "Show me."

He opened his eyes. Her expression was earnest, and her breasts were swinging near his left hand. So with one hand, he filled his palm with her breast. With his other, he took her fingers and wrapped them around his girth.

Oh God. Everything about it was wonderful. Her tiny hand in his as he showed her what to do. And all the while, her full, soft breast there for his enjoyment.

He began to thrust in her palm. He didn't stop it, though he tried to go slow. He wanted this moment to last forever. He let his own hand fall away from around hers, hoping that the release in pressure would make it last longer. But she had learned quickly. She squeezed him just right and even picked up the pace.

Or maybe he was the one thrusting like a beast. Hard and fast. A quake had begun at the base of his spine, clawing upward no matter how much he tried to slow its progress.

And then he felt her lean down right next to his ear and whisper something. Three words that had more than his body exploding.

"I love you."

Eighteen

Rakes are afraid of feelings. Never admit to having any.

MELLIE WATCHED AS TREVOR'S EYES WIDENED IN surprise. She heard his breath catch, and then the pleasure hit him. The biologist in her was fascinated by the ripple of his flat belly, the thrust of his hips, and his powerful ejaculation. The woman in her wondered at his panicked expression when she'd told him she loved him. Was he horrified by the thought? Or was she misreading an expression that might be a simple grimace brought on by his release?

She started to pull away, but he gripped her wrist, holding her close. His body was still quivering. His eyes locked on hers, but he clearly didn't have the breath to speak. So she waited, and she watched, mentally cataloging every minute movement of his body. She told herself it was for her scientific studies. After all, she'd never seen a man ejaculate before. This was an important piece of her education. But a tiny part of her realized that she was running away from the shock of her impetuous revelation. She'd only just now realized her feelings. She hadn't intended to tell him about them tonight. Perhaps not ever. And yet somehow, the words had just tumbled out.

And now... Now he was catching his breath and drawing her hand up to his mouth to press a long kiss to her knuckles. It was nice, surely, but what did it mean? She wanted to ask, but her mouth was frozen shut.

"Mellie," he breathed. "God, you're amazing."

Well, that was good, she supposed. But he didn't say more. Instead, he rooted one-handed into his undone pants and pulled out a handkerchief. He cleaned himself up with quick, efficient strokes all while keeping a tight grip on her with his other hand. She tried to judge his expression, but his eyes were on his task, and his face gave nothing away.

Then he was done. He pushed up to a seated position and tucked himself away. She made to get off the bed, but he still wouldn't release her. And the longer it took for him to speak, the more her emotions seemed to whither inside her. They became tinier and colder until she thought her entire chest would freeze.

"Mellie, have you ever experienced orgasm with anyone else? Alone even?"

"You know I haven't," she said, her voice tight. How could he ask that when she'd just told him she loved him?

He nodded as if she'd confirmed exactly what he'd suspected. "Biology carries emotions with it as well. And an orgasm brings intense emotions. When I was a teen, I fell in love with a whore my father had given me for my seventeenth birthday."

She blinked. "Your father gave you a whore?"

"I suppose she was more like a mistress. I had her for a month, and she taught me everything, even things I'm not sure I wanted to know. She pleased me in every way possible. Not just in the bedroom, but we talked about everything. She really listened to me, and that was such a rare thing in my life." He shrugged. "She even pretended to a fascination with beetles."

"So you loved her."

"I was seventeen. Of course I loved her. With every fiber of my soul. I was going to marry her. Even bought a ring."

She glanced down at the cricket ring on her finger and tried not to think about a teenaged Trevor giving something that special to a whore. "What happened?" she asked, dreading to hear the answer.

"My month was over. I went to the house where she lived and found my father there instead. He was furious with me."

"You told him your intentions?"

"Didn't have to. She'd told him herself. Said that she'd run off with me if he didn't pay her to leave me alone."

Oh dear.

"Five thousand pounds."

A fortune.

"She left for the Continent that very day."

Mellie realized that Trevor would never have let her go. Not sent away by his father without a word to him. He was too determined and methodical in his passions. It was part of what made him a good scientist. "You must have followed her."

He nodded, and she now saw how his lips were tight, and his gaze had canted away from her. Was he ashamed? He'd been a boy. She used her free hand and gently touched his face. Eventually, he looked back at her. "What happened when you found her?"

He swallowed. "She was with her true love. A footman in my father's household. They were taking my father's money and starting a new life somewhere else. And with five thousand pounds, they could live quite nicely. For a time."

She heard the bitterness in his tone. She didn't truly understand finances. Not like her uncle did. She knew that five thousand pounds was a good beginning, but not enough for a lifetime. Not without proper management. Which meant that eventually the money would have run out.

"Oh Trevor, did she come back?"

He squeezed her hand, and she was startled to see how severe his expression had become.

"You don't have to tell me," she began, but he shook his head.

"I truly haven't thought about this in years. It shouldn't pain me at all."

But it did. How could it not? "She was your first love. Of course it still pains you."

He looked up, his expression rueful. "First love? Goodness, no. Well, yes in that it was so intense, and I had been so sure. But Mellie, I'm a man who falls in and out of love relatively easily. By the time I'd met Francesca, I'd already loved half a dozen girls at school."

"Did you propose to them?"

"I certainly thought about it."

So he made a habit of this, then. Proposing to girls and not carrying through. In and out of love, and none of it real. Her hand went slack in his, but he continued to grip her as he finished his sad tale.

"Frannie came back a year later. She begged forgiveness, spouting a sad tale of woe."

"You didn't believe her." It wasn't a question. She could see in his face that he knew the woman had been lying.

"Honestly, I'm not sure. She certainly regretted life with a footman who couldn't support her as well as life as a courtesan. But it didn't matter."

"Because you didn't love her?"

He looked her dead in the eye. "Because my affections had moved on. Because I'd learned by then that my heart is a fickle, uncertain thing. And by the time she came back, I couldn't fully understand what I'd seen in her in the first place."

She narrowed her eyes, watching the tiny shifts in his body. A month ago, she wouldn't have seen it. Truthfully, she wasn't entirely certain now. But the tightness of his shoulders, the studied casualness of his gestures—all of it indicated a lie. When Trevor was in the depths of science, his body was focused and economical. He moved exactly as he needed to and no more. When he was with her in dalliance or even dancing, there was a simplicity to his body. His gestures were fluid, but still with a coordinated purpose. It was only when he lied that his body seemed to disconnect. His torso tightened, but his hands fidgeted. His mouth and jaw moved when he spoke, but his head was statue still.

"You still love her," she guessed.

His eyes widened in horror. "God no!"

Well, that was certainly emphatic. "But something about her appeals to you. Something makes her betrayal still hurt." She touched him. Their fingers were still entwined, but this time she touched his chin and forced her to look directly at him. "Don't lie to me, Trevor. I couldn't bear it."

His eyes softened, and she saw a flash of regret even as his words came out firm and painfully clear. "The truth is that there is a strong correlation between the body and the emotions. Surely as a scientist you understand that."

"That's not love," she said, though in her heart she wondered. And damn him, he knew just how to make her completely uncertain.

"Are you sure? I was sure when I was seventeen. And before that when I was sixteen. And before that—"

"I'm not a child."

"But you are young in this."

He was right. She knew he was, but inside, everything felt like it was calcifying to chalk. She felt white and hollow and so very brittle. "You loved her," she whispered. But the truth was, she wondered. And she might as easily have said, I loved you, but now, I'm not so sure.

"I *remember* her," he said clearly. And then his voice roughened as he released her and reached for his shirt. "As you will remember me."

Her gaze shot to his, but she only caught the side of his face as he began to dress. He wasn't leaving her now? He wasn't abandoning her—

"We have a plan, Mellie," he continued. "We shouldn't abandon it because of…of…"

Love? Biology? What?

He turned to look at her. "Of feelings that will pass."

She shook her head trying to deny everything that he said, but she couldn't. It was too well reasoned. "What if they don't pass?"

"They will." He took a deep breath. "You need to touch yourself, Mellie. You need to feel these things when I am not around. You'll see that it's just as intense when it has nothing to do with me."

His eyes were steady when he spoke, but his hands were jerky and disconnected as he buttoned his shirt. He stood awkwardly beside the bed even as his words came out with scientific precision.

"Will you do that, Mellie? Will you…explore by yourself?"

The very idea repulsed her. Do these things without him? She couldn't. And yet she still found herself nodding. If he wanted it, then she would try. She had to find out if it was true. Would she feel the same things when alone?

"We need to get you home, Mellie. Soon. But if you want to…" His voice broke, and he had to clear his throat before he continued. "If you want to explore on your own, I can step into the other room and wait—"

"No!" she gasped when she realized his meaning. Did he truly want her to do it *now*? With him on the other side of the wall?

"It's a simple biological process, Mellie."

So he kept saying. But if she were to do as she'd promised, she would do it somewhere else. In secret. Sometime when she didn't feel so utterly wretched. So she reached for her corset. She thought her chemise or gown might be destroyed. There had to be some outward reflection of the way she felt. But everything appeared fine. Crushed, perhaps, but nothing that couldn't easily be set to rights.

"I'll just be a moment," she whispered.

He sketched a quick bow. "I'll find us a hackney. There's a lady's cloak in the hallway that you should use."

"Whose is it?"

His cheeks flushed slightly, and he shrugged. "This is a bachelor household, Mellie. It's there for general use."

For ladies who wanted to leave anonymously. Of course.

Meanwhile, he pulled on his coat. "I'll just be a moment."

And then he was gone.

❧

Trevor was shaking as he hailed a hackney. The depth of his perfidy was overwhelming him. To suggest, even by implication, that what he shared with Mellie was nothing more than sheer biology was like calling the Bodleian Library nothing more than a place where some scholars kept a few books. The scale was completely wrong, and the feeling was totally absent. Every moment with Mellie blazed in his mind as a nearly reverent time. What they had shared tonight was as holy to him as the library was to the Oxford dons who maintained it. And he had just pretended that she was no more to him than a fuck with a good whore.

He was nearly sick from his own lies. But what made it so much worse was the knowledge that he hadn't lied to her. He had spent a decade learning the joys of physical release. He knew how special Mellie was. But she was an innocent before their time together. Of course she would whisper that she loved him. Of course the feelings were beyond intense. Such was the nature of first times.

But he couldn't lie and suggest that what she felt was real. What she felt was sexual for the first time in her life. And that was so easily confused with love.

So he had done the honorable thing. He had explained as clearly as possible what was happening, and he had left her alone rather than ravish her, as he desperately wanted to do. And now, he would take her home.

He found a hackney quickly enough. It was the time of night for sordid liaisons to end and light skirts to be sent home. That anyone might class Mellie as that kind of woman made him ill. That he was the one who had done this to her made it even worse.

So he was grim-faced when he went back upstairs. He said nothing as he settled the cloak about her head and shoulders. And he was as courtly as he could possibly manage as he helped her into the carriage and slipped into the dark beside her.

She said nothing and try as he might, he couldn't find a way to break the silence. Every conversational gambit he thought of sounded stupid or insulting. So he remained silent. He didn't even touch her, though God knew he wanted to. But he didn't want to offer her more of an insult, so he stayed away. And in his head, he flayed himself alive for being a bastard.

Twenty minutes later, he discovered that he needn't have castigated himself so hard since Eleanor was more than happy to do it for him.

She'd been waiting up, even sending Seelye to bed so that she could open the door herself when he and Mellie knocked. She pulled open the door, gestured them inside, and quietly shut it behind them. Then she turned on him like a distempered rabbit.

"Did you violate her? Don't you dare think of lying to me, Trevor. Did you touch her? How could you do this? Damn it, everything played out exactly as it ought. A little faster than we planned, but perhaps, that's for the best. It all falls wrong if you touched her. All of it destroyed, Trevor, and I will never forgive you for it."

He had no answer, no way to mitigate the righteous fury in her eyes. So he stood there mute in his misery. It was Mellie—generous, sweet, *innocent* Mellie—who came to his rescue.

"Nothing has happened, Eleanor. Trevor was simply upset, and we walked. I'm used to living in the country, you know. It's the easiest way to talk—on a long, quiet walk."

"A walk in the city?" Eleanor huffed, though her tone was a great deal softer than before. "Don't be daft, Melinda. There are dangerous footpads everywhere."

"But we came across none of them. I am fine."

Then she made a mistake. She shrugged off her cloak, revealing her badly pinned hair, her dress without feathers, and the lumps caused by her badly tied corset. To anyone with eyes—especially someone as smart as Eleanor—she was exposed as a woman who had been ravaged.

"You fool!" hissed Eleanor, rounding on Trevor. "You damned—"

"She can still marry," he said, though even to him his words sounded like a weak excuse. The kind of thing said by immoral men who used women without conscience.

"My God, Trevor!" Eleanor cried, but again Mellie interrupted.

"I am still a virgin, Eleanor. Calm yourself."

Mellie didn't know it, but no one ever told Eleanor to calm herself. The woman was made of ice, her aristocratic heritage demanding nothing more than total nonchalance of the titled elite. To tell her to calm herself was akin to a slap across the face, and Eleanor reacted according to her training: with any icy fury that could destroy all of Mellie's chances.

She pulled up to her full height, she drew in her breath, and she…did nothing. Trevor was about to leap into the breach, to take all the blame onto himself—which is where it rightly belonged—but Eleanor simply stared, long and quiet. Then she spoke two words in an eerie kind of tonelessness.

"What happened?"

"We went for a walk—" Mellie began, but Trevor took over. It was best if Eleanor's rage was directed at him.

"I broke with my grandfather."

Eleanor sighed. "I know that, Trevor. *Everyone* knows that."

"We did go for a walk, and then…" He shook his head. He would not be made to report like a small boy confessing to an angry parent. "Eleanor, she is still a virgin. She can still marry whomever she wants. She is still totally and completely herself. Nothing untoward has occurred."

Eleanor spent a moment staring hard at him. Inside, he squirmed with guilt, but he kept his expression impassive. And then she turned her icy glare onto Mellie who looked equally impassive. Though she did break enough to give her confirmation.

"He has not lied, Eleanor."

The woman snorted. "You will learn, Melinda, that there is the truth, and then there is a *gentleman's* truth. Something momentous has occurred, and I should like to stand as your friend. Rest assured, whatever has happened, I will still sponsor you as I promised. I lay all ill things at his feet."

It took a moment for Trevor to understand exactly what she'd said. First, he realized that she was taking Mellie's part and would not abandon her. That was wonderful news, but the rest was rather painful to hear. What she said, in fact, was that she would take Mellie's part *against* Trevor, and as much as he deserved every word, it was still hard to hear. So when his words came out, they were more tart than he intended.

"So you won't abandon her *now*? What about this evening when she was all alone?"

Eleanor rounded on him, her eyes narrowed. "Whatever does that mean? She was never alone. Good God, do you know how many people were about her every moment—"

"You left her alone to Mr. Rausch and his friends. When I found her, she was dancing with him."

"What is wrong with Mr. Rausch?" asked Mellie.

Eleanor nodded complete agreement. "Of course I left her to dance with him. Apart from being Prussian, he is the perfect man for her. I hope they will make a match!"

"A match? Have you lost your mind?"

"He is not the sort for me, but they are of the same class. He has made his fortune and found way into society. They are perfect together. And now that she must cry off from you, I am sure he will come courting."

"Cry off?" breathed Trevor, shocked to his core.

To the side, he saw Mellie's eyes widen in surprise as well.

"Yes, cry off. That was the plan from the beginning. I had hoped to have more time, but you had that argument with your grandfather. And now everyone knows that he paid you to find a bride."

Trevor's gaze was on Mellie. She paled at those words, but the information wasn't anything surprising. Or even news.

"I told him that I intended to marry Mellie, and there was nothing he could do to stop me."

"You did a great deal more," Eleanor said, and he realized that the gossips had worked especially hard tonight. There had been a scant few hours since his disagreement with the duke, but clearly, some version of the story was already winging its way about London.

Meanwhile, Mellie spoke, her voice the cool bite of reason that was needed. "Exactly what is being said?"

"That the duke forced him to take a bride, so he selected you out of spite." Then she touched Mellie on the arm. "But don't worry. I have already let it about that you have been horribly used by Trevor. That you are an innocent in all this, and that I will continue to sponsor you."

Damn, Mellie had gone whiter than a sheet. She was withdrawing, and if they were alone, he would wrap her in his arms and kiss her until she stopped hiding inside herself. But they weren't alone, so he stood apart and tried to soften the blow.

"No one will turn from you, Mellie. Not with Eleanor's continued support."

"Exactly. Which is why you must now cry off. I have already hinted as much with Trevor's mother. We will make it public before her tea—"

Damnation! He'd completely forgotten the tea.

"But there is no reason to panic," continued Eleanor.

"I'm not panicking," Mellie said, her voice tight with irritation.

Eleanor just continued as if she hadn't spoken. "I shall tell you exactly how it will go. First, you will cry off tomorrow. I will cut Trevor and call him the most terrible cad, coming out firmly in your corner."

"Good," he said, though inside he was reeling. He wasn't ready for the engagement to end. His approval was because Mellie could have no better advocate than Eleanor.

"Lady Hurst will still throw her tea to show that there are no hard feelings. She has already begun, you know, decrying the manipulations of men. This whole thing truly is their fault anyway. Imagine paying your heir to court a woman and then disowning him because he'd gone and done what you instructed. It's madness."

Trevor heartily approved of anything that put the blame squarely at his grandfather's feet, but neither woman appeared to care.

"We will go to the tea to show that we are fast friends, and you are a perfectly eligible young woman. I believe I can convince Lady Hurst to invite some scientific young men. And then, between her and me, you will be launched most spectacularly."

Mellie frowned. "But what of Trevor?"

"Hmm? Oh, don't worry. Eventually, I will invite him to a ball or something, publicly forgiving him for being a man. That's what balls are for, you know. To show society that whatever their idiocies, we women will forgive them and still marry them. The men attend because it is the only way back into our good graces. And then we throw girls at them so they can marry and give birth to the next generation."

Good God, was that truly what happened? Was that…? It was ludicrous, and yet there was a certain twisted logic in it. He shuddered, but then refocused on the subject at hand. "I told my grandfather that I will not give her up."

Eleanor rolled her eyes. "Of course you did. That's

the gentleman's way. But as soon as poor Melinda heard that you only courted her to thwart your grandfather, her tender heart was crushed. She throws you over and declares to marry only for true love."

"What?" Mellie asked.

"Well, that's what we shall say. Society adores a true love story. Privately, you and I shall weigh the merits of each of your suitors closely, but once you have selected, the two of you shall fall madly in love. The wedding will be soon afterward because it must. People grow bored quickly, and so we shall keep them talking with the wedding. And then probably a month after you return from your wedding trip, you shall visit me, begging me to forgive Trevor. Everything will have worked out for the best, and then I will throw my ball, and everyone will see that he is back in my good graces."

She slapped her hands together to show how easy it would be. And truth be told, it would be that easy. She was a master at this type of manipulation. Add his mother to the mix, and everything would happen just as they said. Mellie's suitors and eventual marriage, the forgiveness ball, and mostly probably, his engagement to some woman of their choosing. In their minds, it was all a *fait accompli*.

He shook his head, feeling the pound of a headache beginning.

"What is it now?" Eleanor said with an annoyed clip to her words. "This is exactly what you wanted. You told me so at the beginning."

Had he? Perhaps. Well, yes. And yet, now that he was here, everything felt so very wrong. "I told my grandfather I would not give her up."

"Well, of course you *said* that—"

"I meant it." He looked directly at Mellie. "I will not give you up."

Mellie looked at him, her gaze steady, her body composed. Then she asked her question. "Why?"

Why? Damnation, he wasn't exactly sure why he was so determined. His thoughts were so muddled. So he said the easiest words to leap to his lips. "It's what I told my grandfather. A gentleman doesn't go back on his word."

"I know," she said, and he thought for a moment that she understood. If she would just give him some time, he was sure they could work things out with clarity. He just needed to think things through, preferably with her. But she simply lifted her chin and spoke. "That is exactly why I will cry off."

"No!"

"Yes. That was the plan, after all. Eleanor, how do I do this?"

Eleanor clapped her hands together, her expression both happy and relieved. "Well, as to that, there are a number of options. But we needn't have him here to discuss them. Good night, Trevor. Do understand that when I give you the cut direct tomorrow I shall eventually forgive you."

"What?" He reached for Mellie, but she had already moved toward the stairs, and he found he'd grabbed Eleanor's elbow instead. "This is not what I want."

"Yes," Eleanor said firmly, "it is." And then she handed him his hat, the damned cloak, and shoved him toward the door. Yes, she actually shoved him out, and he was too much of a gentleman to fight her.

Especially as Mellie started climbing the stairs offering him a halfhearted wave as she turned her back.

"Good-bye, Trevor. Thank you for everything."

He waited a moment, blocking the open door as he tried to think. But damn it, she just kept walking away. And Eleanor repeated the one thing he'd been thinking this whole time.

"This was the plan, Trevor. This is what you both want."

Well, given Mellie's last words, she was half right. It was clearly exactly what Mellie wanted. So he had to agree. He had to put his hat onto his head and step out into the darkness. It was what she wanted. And he had abused her too much to take that away.

Nineteen

Rakes expect grand emotional displays. Ruin him with regal disdain.

MELLIE HEARD THE FRONT DOOR CLOSE AS IF IT HAD shut something away inside her. The numbness didn't creep in as usual. It simply consumed her. One moment he was here, and she was alive. The next, everything in her was frozen, and he was gone.

She knew things were happening around her. Eleanor kept talking for one. Her feet were moving for another, and eventually, she found herself at her bedroom door. But nothing truly registered.

"Go to sleep, Melinda. Everything will feel better in the morning."

Would it? She nodded because Eleanor seemed to expect her to respond. Then her sleepy maid joined them, helping her to strip out of her gown. Eleanor shut the door and sought her own bed, leaving Mellie to random stray thoughts.

She'd lost all the feathers on her gown.

Trevor.

Her cricket ring felt heavy, but when she took it off, she felt its absence.

Her hair was knotted.

Trevor.

There was a spot of dirt on the wall by her dressing table.

Trevor.

She had danced a great deal tonight. Her feet should hurt. Her feet did hurt.

The sheets were cold.

Trevor.

Trevor.

Trevor.

❧

The morning was not better, which was why she rolled over and went back to sleep.

The afternoon was not better, but she had to face it as Eleanor was standing in her bedroom and waving a cup of hot chocolate at her.

She didn't want chocolate, but she thought it would be rude to refuse. Then she did want the chocolate because if she couldn't have Trevor, she could have chocolate.

And then Eleanor began to speak. An endless stream of words and plans and possibilities, none of which fully entered her mind, but some of it helped drown out his name. So she encouraged Eleanor to keep talking, to keep planning, and eventually, she began to focus.

The afternoon callers would be here soon. She had to dress and be charming. Eleanor suggested she not say much. After all, she was supposed to be a heartbroken former fiancée, though the official break would happen at the ball that evening. Their hostess was a friend of Eleanor's and beyond thrilled to provide the location for the dramatic scene-to-be.

Mellie agreed that she could manage a stoic look of dignified misery.

It all went off exactly as Eleanor planned. The steady stream of afternoon callers talked around her, often patting her hand in sympathy. The gentlemen were especially gentle as they kissed her hand once upon arrival and again on departure.

It was as if she were Eleanor's doll. She ate when Eleanor said, she dressed as Eleanor bid, and she even memorized a cluster of phrases to say. It was the easiest thing in the world to bring them out at random, speaking only when someone expected an answer. She had no idea if she made sense or not, but every time she caught Eleanor's eye, the woman was smiling encouragingly at her. And several times, she even whispered, "You're doing splendidly. Hold out just a little bit longer."

So she did. She held out. She dressed in her most sedate ball gown: dark blue velvet with gold trim. It settled on her shoulders like a shroud and cut off what little breath she had. Except, she still managed to move to the carriage and smile blankly at the milling crowd. She accepted dance requests with a smile then mutely held out her dance card.

And then he was here. She felt every cell in her body jolt painfully awake. He had just been announced, and her gaze found his figure before her ears registered why she'd turned to the ballroom entrance. He looked regal, she thought. His hat had casually crushed his hair, but the curls about his eyes were as charming as ever. His shoulders were pulled back, and his movements were slow. In truth, she'd never seen him with so little animation. But rather than making him appear wooden, it made him seem refined. Arrogant.

Ducal.

This, she thought, was the man who would become a duke, and truthfully, she didn't like him at all. There was no life in him. Not compared to the man who had kissed her so deeply. Not when she thought of how he'd looked as he stroked her or teased her or…anything.

And then he saw her.

She watched as he swallowed and nodded. A slow dip of his chin, which could have been for anyone, but she knew it was aimed at her. And then a slight curve to the right side of his mouth as he headed in her direction. It was a quick movement—that lift of his lips—but he might as well as written it on a sign above his head. *Let's get this over with.* She didn't need Eleanor's quick rasp in her ear to know what to do.

"Do it fast. That's the easiest way."

The crowd parted. The chatter died away. Or perhaps she simply couldn't hear over the noise in her head. It didn't matter. He was standing in front of her and bowing before she found the strength to draw breath.

"Lady Eleanor, Miss Smithson. Good evening."

Beside her, Eleanor was elegant perfection. She arched a sculpted brow, lifted her chin, and then turned her back on Trevor. It was all done in a single fluid move, and her words carried easily through the quiet ballroom.

"What a strange noise I've just heard," she said to the nearest person. "I think it's the sound of cruelty."

Trevor winced at that, but his gaze didn't waver. He'd been focused on her from the moment he'd entered the ballroom.

And now it was her turn. A simple shift of her body, a pivot on her toes, a twist of her head. Anything. *Move!* She stood frozen in place.

Trevor's eyes widened, and he seemed to lean slightly forward. Toward her. She should back away, but she didn't. From the side, Eleanor touched her elbow, tugging slightly.

"Melinda, I'm feeling parched. Would you join me in a stroll?"

She was supposed to nod. She was supposed to go with Eleanor, but she couldn't force herself.

"Mellie," Trevor said, but it wasn't a word. It was more of a rasp, or even a shaping of her name with his lips, spoken as a groan.

Suddenly, she remembered all the other times he'd said her name, and all the other ways. With desire, with hunger, with laughter, with any of a thousand emotions. And none were this near-silent anguish.

"Do you remember what I told you when all this started?" Was that her voice? Her words? Apparently so, because she saw his skin pale.

"I remember everything," he said.

So did she, and yet she kept speaking, the words flowing without restraint. "I said I wanted love."

How pathetic, she thought, to admit that out loud. She sounded like a schoolgirl in the midst of her first childish fantasy.

Trevor's lips compressed, and she watched his expression flash through torment before it settled into a bland frown. "My set doesn't look for love, Mellie. Not in their wives."

"I didn't think I was affianced to your set." She tried to stop talking, but it was like she was bleeding words. "I thought I was engaged to you."

He didn't respond, and for a moment she couldn't understand why. And then she realized he was waiting for her to turn around. It was time for the cut direct, but she couldn't move.

And when the moment stretched, he prompted her. "Was engaged?" he pressed. "So we are done then?"

She tried to say yes. She tried to nod or turn around or something, but her chest had frozen solid. No more words bled out of her. But inside, she was screaming.

Trevor!

He understood. She could see it in his eyes. He knew what she was thinking, knew that inside she was screaming.

Trevor!

"Everything will be all right," he said softly. "Trust me."

Fury—white and hot—blazed through her. She didn't even know if he'd said that on purpose just to make her angry, or if he really was that stupid. He had to know that she was done trusting him, done trusting any man to know anything about what was best. Because they were all cow-dung stupid.

"I hate you all," she said, and she truly, absolutely meant it. So she spun around, giving him her back. Then she focused on the one person closest to her, the one man who would most wound Trevor and best represented her disgust of his set. "Mr. Rausch, you were saying something about…about…"

Hell, she had no idea what the man had been talking about. Fortunately, he raised his arm and smiled as if she was the smartest girl on Earth.

"About bleaching creams. I understand you've been exploring their uses. But the air is foul in here, I think. Shall we step outside? The garden is quite lovely in moonlight."

She didn't bother answering. She remained unresisting as he took her fingers and set them on his arm. Then they strolled together to the French doors, stepping out to the night air. It was indeed cooler out there. And cooler inside her heart as well, as every step away from Trevor brought back the numbness. By the time they made it to the side of a sickly looking tree, her entire body was gone. A wooden doll again, though without the pat phrases from Eleanor. Her mind was filled with screams. First his name, then her anger, then a raw note that throbbed with every passing second.

She waited for the sound to fade, but it never did. It was there, at the edge of her awareness, never fully suppressed, but perhaps not as loud.

And then Mr. Rausch lifted her hand, pressed a kiss to the back of it while stroking the curve of her palm. On and on, just a slow circular stroke, until she finally, inevitably, looked up at him.

"Sir?"

"Ah. Welcome back. Are you able to manage conversation now?"

She flushed slightly at his words, knowing she'd probably been rude, but he didn't seem insulted. Merely concerned. "You are very kind to help me like this."

"No, Miss Smithson, I am not kind at all." He paused a moment, clearly waiting to see if he had her attention. She mustered what she could and gave it to him. His lips curved in a slow smile, and he spoke a little slowly as if she were a dim-witted child. Apparently she was, because she had a great deal of difficulty following his words.

"Plain speaking is best, do you agree?" he asked.

"Uh, yes. Yes, of course."

"I am not kind, Miss Smithson. I am greedy."

She stared, replaying his words. This was the usual patter of social conversation. "I'm afraid I don't understand."

He smiled at that, and it was an unusual smile. Neither cruel nor supportive, and not even lascivious, or not in the usual way. What she saw in the curve of his lips was...avarice. Polished, intelligent, and careful greed.

"I like to acquire things, Miss Smithson. Unusual things. And people."

"I beg your pardon, sir?"

"You have perhaps noticed that my circle of friends is selective, have you not?"

She hadn't, but now that she thought of it, the people that he'd called his friends were all unusual in some way. The brilliant chemist had caught her attention early, of course, even if he did speak in rapid sentences and pull on his hair often. But there was also the limping man who had a way of talking that drew one in and encouraged confidences. She'd intended to sit beside him at the supper table last night, but Trevor had pulled her away.

The others had less obviously unique qualities, but she could absolutely believe that they were each outstanding in their own way. And they all treated Mr. Rausch with respect and even admiration.

"It is rare that I allow a woman into my circle, Miss Smithson. But then again, you are a rare creature."

She tried to feel insulted by that. He'd as much as called her odd. But the way he said it had an intensity that startled her. "I don't know what to say." Then she pressed her fingers to her lips. She hadn't intended to say anything, and yet here again, words were falling from her lips even if they were inconsequential words.

"Yes, you do," he said. "Tell me you want to know more."

"About what?"

"About me. About how I find you exquisitely unique. About—"

"That would give you more information about me. You are asking me to reveal what I find most fascinating about you. And you are pressing me at a moment when—" Her throat closed down as that distant scream in her thoughts grew louder.

"When you are raw and unprotected. Yes, Miss Smithson, you are correct. But now is the only time I can say this and not have you slap me." He stroked a finger across her jaw. It was almost clinical in the way he touched her, and yet she didn't move away. "I want to have you," he said. "Not just your body, but your mind as well. And I can make it worth your while."

She stiffened and pulled back, her mouth separating on a gasp. He didn't react to her shock until he seemed to look over her shoulder. Someone was coming, and his next rushed words confirmed it.

"Money, pleasure, and freedom. You can buy these things from me."

"Buy them? With what?"

His grin widened. "Your mind, my dear. And your body. If you are bold enough. You give them to me, and I shall give you the rest."

She stared at him, her mind struggling to understand. "What—"

"Melinda, darling," Eleanor said as she came up beside her. "I've been so worried about you." Mellie gathered her wits and tried to look at her, but her gaze was caught by the quirk of Mr. Rausch's eyebrow. It seemed to taunt her—that lift of his brow—and she wondered if he could possibly deliver what he'd promised.

Money, certainly. Pleasure, without a doubt. But freedom? Now there was something to tempt her.

"Melinda?" Eleanor tried to pull her around, but when Mellie still looked at Mr. Rausch, she tugged sharply on Mellie's chin. "What has he said to you?"

When Mellie didn't answer, Eleanor rounded on the man. "I thought I liked you, sir. It turns out I do not. Pray excuse us."

His lips curved in a mocking expression. "Really? I find my opinion of you has not changed in the least."

Mellie's face jerked up at that. It was so bizarre to hear someone speak rudely to Eleanor that the novelty of it broke her out of her paralysis. "We were merely conversing, Eleanor," she said. The woman didn't appear to hear her.

"This woman is my friend. If you hurt her, you hurt me. And I assure you, I strike back."

His eyes changed then. They narrowed, even as his lips spread in a slow, lascivious grin. There was no avarice in that expression. This was pure sexuality, and Mellie found herself backing away. Not in fear. After her time with Trevor, sexuality intrigued her. But such a look was meant for two people, not three. Or rather, it was meant for Eleanor alone, who straightened to her full height complete with lifted chin and arched brow.

"Challenge me at your peril," she said.

"I accept," he answered, and then he bowed deeply before her. Was there mockery in his movements? Mellie couldn't tell, and one glance at Eleanor's face told her that the other woman was equally confused.

Fortunately, Eleanor recovered quickly. She tugged on Mellie's sleeve and gestured toward the ballroom. "The first set is forming." She spoke the words, but her gaze was still on Mr. Rausch.

"Is… Has…?" Damn, why couldn't she say his name? And her verbal stumble at last drew Eleanor's gaze to hers.

"Mr. Anaedsley has departed. The worst is over. You can relax now and enjoy the dancing."

As if she'd ever enjoy dancing again. Well, that wasn't true. There was some pleasure in it, but she'd only truly loved it when she'd waltzed with Trevor, but that was over now. He'd never take her in his arms again.

The scream in her thoughts grew louder again, so she focused on a new way to silence it. Or at least distract herself. Since dancing was an appropriate way to meet gentlemen, she would do it now. Perhaps someone else would be as successful as Mr. Rausch had been in temporarily grabbing her attention.

With that thought fixed in her mind, she headed inside to meet men.

❧

Four weeks went by. A whole month, and not a single man measured up. Each day, each ball, each conversation added one more layer to the encrusted boredom of her existence. At least at home she had her laboratory experiments. She could always lose herself in science, but not here. Here she was on a husband-hunting mission, and the entire process bored her to the point of madness.

Two moments lightened the crushing sameness of it all. The first had been a visit from her uncle and father. Her uncle had repeated his request for the cosmetic formula. She had merely shaken her head. She intended that to be her dowry if her father decided to throw her over entirely. Then her father had asked if she wished to come home.

She nearly said yes. At least at home, she had her lab. But in London she had hopes of something better.

At home, there was merely more of the same. And after her time with Trevor, she knew that she could never be content with the nothing of her existence before. Science could fill her mind, but she wanted something to fill the yawning blackness of her heart.

Once she had thought it would be love and children. Now she longed for something—anything—that would make it better. The only thing she knew for sure was that it couldn't be found at home. Which meant her only hope was in London at least for the rest of the Season. So she had sent her father and uncle home and turned her attention to yet another round of excruciatingly similar balls.

The second moment was more of a series of sparks of interest, like tiny flickers of possibility, before her raised hopes inevitably fell flat. And every one of those moments came from Mr. Rausch.

He had made a point of attracting her attention. He was unfailingly polite, unless Lady Eleanor was around. Then he was sarcastic and rude. But mostly he worked to entertain her with scientific tidbits, unusual people, and once, a trained dog.

She inevitably smiled at something that happened. Her mood lightened for perhaps as much as ten minutes. But in the end, she fell back into the sameness of it all. The people he called friends were interesting, but there was only so much one could explore in the middle of a society function without other people intruding. And even the trained dog was just…well, a dog. It performed nicely, but still sat down at the end and licked its own balls. She didn't even find that offensive, just very doglike in a very boring way.

So it was that on the return from her umpteenth ball with aching feet and a splitting headache that Mellie finally faced the truth.

She missed Trevor. More than that, she loved him, and he was an idiot for thinking she didn't know her own mind. And lest he suggest that her attraction to him was simply the novelty of sexuality, she had spent every night of the last weeks trying a different form of masturbation. It was nothing like what she experienced with him. It had its moments, certainly, but she wanted him.

She was in love with him.

And she'd be damned if she let him hold her heart without making some attempt to capture his.

The problem was that she never saw him. He was never at any function she attended. Never. That was probably Eleanor's doing, but it meant that she had only one choice. She had to go to his home at the only time she wasn't being shuttled from one event to the next. Which meant now.

Right now.

In the middle of the night.

By herself.

Odd how just making the decision sped her heart to a frighteningly excited pace.

Twenty

When you risk everything on a rake, be sure he makes an equal wager.

TREVOR WAS NOT A MAN WHO ENJOYED DRINKING. Well, that wasn't entirely true. He liked the taste of it. He liked the sociability of it. Some of his best memories were of sitting with his mates drinking brandy. Sometimes they smoked, but he'd never acquired an appreciation of it. Sometimes they gambled as they played cards, but he'd never seen the full sense in that either. He simply enjoyed a good drink with his friends without becoming stupid.

Tonight he was spinning drunk.

Tonight—and for the last many nights—he'd stumbled home while singing a German drinking song with his closest friends. One had helped him up the stairs. Another had helped him out of his clothes. Then they all left, but not before repeating the phrase they'd been saying for a month now.

"Forget her, Trev. Don't let a country cit be the ruin of you."

It was that last phrase that upset him. Mellie wasn't the ruin of him. At times he wondered if she might be the making of him. She had a way of making his path obvious. He thought more clearly when she was around. He could talk things through with her. He could sit with her in that beautiful house of hers and allow the quiet order of the place to clear the cobwebs from his mind.

For years he'd thought it was her father who did that, but Mr. Smithson was as cluttered as it was possible for a brilliant scientist to be. His lab was a mess, and his thoughts often skittered in different directions at once. But his notes and his experiments were usually pristine, the science behind them crystal clear. It was only now that he realized Mr. Smithson's notes were in Mellie's precise hand. Likely she helped her father organize his thoughts enough that everything else rolled out in neat lines.

Which is what she did. She made nice homes. She made people feel comfortable. She made him feel like he was a lazy, useless aristocrat because he'd had all the opportunity in the world but spent his days bouncing from party to party only sporadically doing his own research.

Hence the drinking. He'd known before that he wasn't worthy of her. Now he saw how very much he wanted her and couldn't have her. She had thrown him over and was daily courted by men who were smarter than him, whose family and friends weren't desperately trying to break them apart, and who had at least a courtesy title, if not the real one.

He'd lost her. And so he'd looked for solace in his friends, in copious amounts of brandy, and cigars. Yes, he'd tried cigars again because the thought of burying himself in any of the myriad light skirts who'd been thrown his way only made him want to weep.

But he really hated cigars. Made him want to gag and left a foul taste in his mouth. Which meant tonight had been about the brandy. And the wine. And ale. And anything else alcoholic that could possibly be consumed while lamenting his failures.

He closed his eyes, allowing the room to spin him into unconsciousness. Of course, the room might spin, but his mind always conjured up her face. Her voice. Her luscious body.

"Trevor?"

Bloody hell, he loved her voice.

"The door was open, and I…well, I just came in. I'd like to talk to you. Trevor?"

Damn that sounded close. As if it were real. As if…

Someone touched his shoulder, and his eyes snapped opened. "Mellie!" he cried, though it was more a hoarse croak.

She frowned down at him. Or at least he thought she did. Then she turned and quickly lit a candle. He winced from the light, but couldn't stop looking at her. Made for a bloody awkward position as he tried to stare and shut his eyes at the same time.

"Mellie?" he croaked again.

"Are you all right?"

"I'm bloody pissed, I am. Are you really here?"

"Yes, I'm here," she said, her voice rueful. "And I can smell the drink on you. Did you swim in it?"

"Tried to," he admitted. "Only way to stop thinking about you." Then he shrugged. "But it doesn't work."

"So then why do it?"

Well, wasn't that a bugger of a question. And right there was the whole damned point. She asked the right questions, which always led to the right answers. And here he'd thought all along it was him with the ideas. Well, it was, but only because she asked the right questions.

"Trevor?"

"Mellie, can I kiss you? I really miss kissing you."

She touched his forehead, stroking his brow. "I need to talk to you. Can you focus for a moment?"

He could focus on anything that was *her*. So he rubbed his eyes, pushed up on his bed, and sat facing her. But his hands…damn, he needed to touch her, so even as she sat primly beside him on the bed, he had to feel her skin. He had to outline the length of her thigh, to stroke the creamy softness of her arm, to know the round firmness of her breast.

"Trevor."

His gaze shot to hers. He noted with pleasure that her cheeks were flushed, her lips were moist, and most especially that her nipple had hardened under his caress. But then she trapped his hand, not pulling it away, but stilling his movements.

"Mellie," he said, putting all his feeling into these words. "I'm so sorry I failed you."

She smiled. "You didn't fail me. Everything you planned happened just as you said."

He shook his head. Not as he said. Or perhaps, maybe exactly as he'd said, but it wasn't what he wanted anymore. He didn't want to be estranged from her. He didn't want any of it.

He sighed, the drink clearing out of his mind a little. She was the more potent drug anyway. "You came to talk to me. What did you want to say?"

His hand had gone slack, so she drew it to her lips. She pressed a kiss to his fingers that sent fire straight to his cock. And her words—damn, they went straight to his head.

"Trevor, I love you. Don't tell me it isn't real love. I know my own mind. I love you, and I want to fight for you."

He gaped at her, his body and mind throwing him a thousand different reactions all at once. There was joy, stunned incredulity, even denial and shame, because he wasn't worthy of her. And most of all, there was his baser instinct, the one that said clearly: *possess this woman now.* Take her, and make her yours without doubt, without hesitation because…

Well, he never got to the *because.* He simply stayed with the growing *need* that became a *now.*

He kissed her. He wrapped his arms around her so that she couldn't run. She wasn't running. She was actually leaning forward and searching for his lips. That made it a thousand times easier to maneuver her into bed. To clumsily strip her out of her dress and rip the ties of her corset and shift.

Her breasts spilled into his hands. Oh yes. There were other words, he knew. Things he should be saying, but he couldn't grab hold of them. He was lost in the smell of her as his mouth went to her nipples. He suckled her breasts, then he tongued her nipples, and when she clutched his shoulders and cried out, he knew he had found heaven on Earth.

He'd already been undressed. His mates hadn't bothered putting him in any type of sleeping clothes, which was just perfect. Her dress was pooled about her waist as he nuzzled and sucked on her glorious skin. Thankfully, she helped him by tossing aside her corset. And when he tugged on the fabric of her gown, she lifted her hips to help him.

Good woman. Good, wonderful, luscious, amazing woman with the scent of the gods between her thighs. He found her curls, knew the dewy wetness there, and simply nuzzled her open with his chin. Her feet got tangled somewhere, but she fixed the problem somehow. He didn't care. He was too busy tasting her. He nipped at her skin, he gloried in her scent, and he spread her wide open.

His fingers were clumsy. That frustrated him, so he decided to abandon all use of them in favor of his tongue. He spread her and licked her, and the taste was like spicy cream.

She bucked beneath him, her cry echoing through the room. He thrust his fingers inside, needing to feel the greedy clutch and pull of her body. God, she was tight, but the wetness everywhere had him slipping in with ease.

But he'd been slow. Her contractions were easing. And her keening gasp, that he so adored, had faded to a breathy sigh.

"Don't stop," he murmured. "No, don't stop."

So he licked her again. He pulled his fingers aside and used his hands to spread her wider. He licked her just to hear that sound. And when she was pushing down against his mouth, he knew it was time.

She would be his now. *Now!*

He pulled himself up her body, stopping momentarily to worship her breasts. He sucked on her, tugging on her nipple until her special cry began. Not orgasm yet, but the nearness, the approach, the almost there.

And he was almost there.

He thrust.

Inside!

Her heat and her wet surrounded him. God yes. God glorious.

She stiffened beneath him, and belatedly he realized that she'd been a virgin, and there was pain for her.

"I'm sorry," he murmured. "It will get better soon."

He held himself still. Or rather, he held his throbbing cock in place, fully seated. He couldn't stop himself from raining kisses along her neck and her cheeks and her lips.

"It's all right," she murmured. "You're just… so much."

He dropped his forehead to hers, trying to hear her over the pounding in his head. "So much?"

"So big."

He grinned. The bigger his cock, the greater his possession of her. She thought he was huge, and that meant she would not forget him. She would remember that he was her man. He was the one who had taken her maidenhead and claimed her as his own.

Those thoughts spun over in an endless circle of glory in his mind. He tried to wait for her to catch up. He truly did, but without him willing it, his body began to move. First a shift that shot pleasure up his spine. Then a thrust in reaction to the joy that made her gasp in that sweet way of hers.

He looked in her eyes. He tried to apologize without words because he was moving too fast. She wasn't in that keening place yet. Her breath hadn't caught, and her body was so amazingly tight around him that he couldn't tell if she was clutching him.

But when he looked into her eyes, when the light caught the sweet pink flush of her skin and the rosy red of her lips, he saw her smile. It was Mellie's smile. It was the one she gave him when she learned something new, the one that wasn't a laugh, but a sweetness that was all her. It never failed to squeeze his heart tight and make him worship her. He'd do anything for that smile, if only she would give it to him again.

"I love you," she whispered.

He thrust. Her words had triggered a need so great, a welling of joy so powerful, that it took over his body.

She loved him.

He slammed in deep.

She loved him.

He slammed in hard.

She would be his. He would drill so far inside her that she couldn't possibly get rid of him.

Again and again.

Then he heard it. Her keening gasp.

And then, God, she became a wild thing beneath him. Pulsing and crying as her body fisted him.

Yes!

He exploded.
Mine!

❧

Mellie came awake slowly. She was spooning in Trevor's arms, her mind drifting, but her body entwined with his. Hours had passed. She knew it because the window in his room gave her a view of the sky. There were stars still, but fewer than before. Dawn couldn't be more than an hour away.

But that was her only thought as she felt Trevor's hands on her body. They were moving slowly, almost reverently. He stroked her skin, brushing her belly with heat, lifting her breasts as he brought fire to her nipples.

And behind her bottom, she felt his penis—thick and hot—as it pressed tiny pulses against her. The movements were so slow—above and below—that she wondered if he was even awake. Then she felt the press of his lips against her shoulder and the murmur of her name on his lips.

"Mellie."

"Ummm," she said in response.

"Mellie, it's almost morning. I need to get you home."

She knew it was true, but the way he touched her body mesmerized her into stillness. Or perhaps, not quite stillness, as she arched into the hand on her breast and pushed back against his cock.

He groaned as she did that, and she felt his teeth gently nip at the base of her neck right above her shoulder blades. She shivered in response, and he groaned again.

"Are you sore?" he asked.

"I feel wonderful."

"You don't regret—" he began, but she cut him off.

"Make me feel wonderful again." And lest he mistake her meaning, she lifted her leg and slid it over his. The hand on her belly stilled, but she knew what she wanted, so she took his wrist and pushed his hand lower.

He knew what he was doing. Lord, he always knew what she wanted. He slid his long fingers between her cleft and began to stroke her where she wanted.

"So wet," he murmured. Then more clearly. "Are you sure you're not sore?"

She hadn't the words as he stroked over her pulsing clitoris. She knew the medical word because she'd looked it up. She knew a great deal about sexuality now because she'd made a point to learn what she could. Sadly, there wasn't much information to be found other than the anatomical names. The rest she'd learned from him or from her own nighttime stimulations.

But none of what she'd experienced before had come close to last night's penetration. There was so much more to her time with Trevor than the contraction of muscles and the ensuing pleasure. With him, she felt a connection. As if he would die if he couldn't be deep inside her. As if she was fallow without his possession.

And now, when he stroked her clitoris, she felt the familiar build to pleasure. Her belly tightened, her breath began to stutter, but it wasn't what she wanted. Inside she was still empty, and she wanted to be filled by him.

"Not like this," she gasped as she pulled away his hand. Then she turned to face him. "Take me."

He blinked, his eyes bloodshot, but with intense focus. "Mellie—" He groaned, hunger in the sound. "It's too soon."

She flashed him a wicked smile, choosing this moment to echo his words. "Trust me," she said. "It will all be all right."

He knew that she was teasing him. She saw the rueful awareness hit his expression. But then she twisted her hips then reached down to grab hold of him. He'd taught her how to stroke him, and so she started with the head—a circle of her fingers—before she pushed down and around him.

He shuddered and thrust into her hold, but his words were clear. "What do you want, Mellie? What—"

"How deeply can you penetrate me?"

She watched his eyes widen, saw him swallow, but he answered calmly. "There's a position," he said.

She grinned. "Show me."

He nodded, then rose from the bed. She'd seen him naked before, but now she saw him like a god rising before her. Muscled chest dusted lightly with hair, broad shoulders and strong arms as he lifted her knees and, of course, the broad head of his penis between them.

"I will stop if it hurts."

She shook her head. Nothing hurt. Absolutely nothing at all.

Then he carefully lifted her legs, putting her ankles on his shoulders. She was spread before him, and he seemed to grow in size, his chest between her legs, his penis pressed against her curls.

Then he adjusted her even wider, helping her slide

her legs such that her knees lay in the crook of his elbows. She'd never felt more decadent in her life. Or more open. This truly was why they called it plowing a woman. His penis would be the blade that cut her open, and she couldn't be more thrilled.

He used his thumb to stroke her. His press started gently, but he rapidly built the tension because there was nowhere for her to go. She arched beneath him, she squeezed her legs against his arms, but there was no escape from the steady press and circle of his thumb. She pulsed beneath him, her hips lifted and lowered into his stroke, and her breasts ached with need.

"Touch your breasts," he said. He had one free hand to reach forward, but he wanted her to work her other side. She did as he bid, lifting her right breast to his view while he stroked her left.

"Pinch your nipple."

He did, and she did. And fire flared from her chest to her belly and sizzled in her spread thighs.

"Now," she gasped. "Trevor, now."

His hand dropped away from her breast, and he leaned forward.

"Please—" she began.

He speared her.

A thick penetration that burned with pleasure.

Oh yes!

"Mellie—"

"Again!"

He leaned forward a little more, pulling her legs wider as he moved. She felt his slow withdrawal, the collapse of her belly, the suction as she tried to keep him inside. But he was the man, and he did as he willed.

He pulled back, but he didn't escape. And then he thrust again.

Yes.

She was impaled, and the impact sent sparks of fire shooting through her body.

"Again!"

This time, she was the one who spread her legs further. She was the one who tightened her calves trying to pull him deeper. And she was the one who gripped his strong shoulders and held on.

Yes!

Yes!

Yes!

The thrusts were growing more rapid, the feeling of being split open repeated in escalating blows. She loved it. She loved every spreading, pulsating, pounding impact.

And when orgasm burst through her body, she allowed her consciousness to explode as well. She let everything in her become a gift to him. For his possession, for his adoration, for his seed.

She'd never known it could feel this primal. Or that this act could be so very…everything. Woman and man joined.

Yes!

He drove into her one last time. An impact that had him releasing with a warrior's cry—part triumph, part call to arms. His head was thrown back, his expression fierce, he looked like a god staking a claim.

She was his, and he would defend her unto death.

That's what she saw as he released. And that's what she heard in her soul: mine! So she answered in her heart: yours.

Then he fell to the side, barely catching his weight on his forearms before dropping heavily on top of her. She didn't mind. It felt right. And so she lay in blissful joy with his weight pinning her down.

And she nearly drifted back to sleep.

She might have if he weren't making her so hot. Sweat was beginning to form where he lay belly to belly with her. And worse, she needed to take a breath. So she shifted. Then she wriggled. And then, sadly, he groaned, and he slipped out of her as he rolled to his side.

She mourned his loss. Mourned the emptiness that came afterward as her belly hollowed out. But he was beside her, breathing into the sheets.

She pressed a kiss to his forehead. He answered with a kiss to her shoulder. And her eyes drifted shut again.

But she couldn't sleep. She had to get home before dawn.

She eased herself sideways. Her body was heavy with lethargy, but she knew if she gave in to it, she'd sleep until noon. She couldn't do that. She'd be compromised publicly, and that was a complication she wasn't willing to risk.

"I have to leave," she murmured, the words meant for herself as much as him.

His hand tightened, pulling her close, but then it opened. He knew she had to leave. He moaned as he rolled onto his back. His eyes were closed, his skin shadowed from his morning beard, but he still looked handsome.

She leaned forward and pressed a kiss to his lips.

His mouth curved into a smile, but he didn't move beyond that. And then a moment later, he groaned again, his words coming out muffled. "I've never felt more sated in my life."

She chuckled. She felt equally good, though she really wished he'd open his eyes. It didn't matter, she told herself. He was tired. So she pulled on her corset and shift. Her crumpled gown was there on the floor, but she smoothed it as best she could. She dressed quickly and somewhat quietly. She kept hoping he'd rouse. She wanted to make plans with him. She wanted him to say all those sweet things she'd read about in books. She wanted…

She sighed. He was snoring now. Which left her to grab the cloak and head home by herself. She paused at his door, waiting there. In the end, she chose to declare herself…again.

"I'm leaving now, Trevor. I love you."

A snore was his only response.

She sighed and let herself out. She was lucky and found a hackney quickly. The driver smirked at her, especially when he heard the address, but he didn't comment more. Ten minutes later, she was sneaking through the servants' entrance up to her bedroom. She was trying hard not to feel awkward, but her muscles were achy, and her clothing abraded her skin where his beard had made it tender, and…

And he hadn't said he loved her.

After all of that, he hadn't said a word.

Which made her start to cry.

She fought it for a while. She fought all the

damning, furious thoughts that crept into her mind. But in the end, she burst into tears.

But they didn't last long. She wasn't one to linger over tears.

By noon, she'd dried her eyes and took a frank look at what had happened.

A half hour later, she got angry.

Twenty-one

Use every tool in your arsenal, fair or fowl.

SHE DIDN'T SEE HIM AT ALL THAT DAY. THAT WAS IN part her choice. She declared herself ill, refused to go downstairs for afternoon callers, and barely made an appearance at that evening's ball. She kept hoping that Trevor would storm down her door and demand to see her. Or he would simply appear with a minister and a special license. Anything dramatic that would prove he wanted her as much as she wanted him. She needed that declaration because he hadn't made one last night. And she was afraid that she had thrown everything away on a ridiculous ploy to win him back.

She was a fool. A damned fool.

So it was that on the next day, she dressed herself in her best gown for an afternoon garden party. This was a green silk stitched with silver filigree meant to reflect the sunlight. It was her favorite gown, and she wore it as if the design weren't supposed to suggest veins. Veins in a cricket. She'd tried to explain to the duchess that crickets did not have veins as in a human, but the lady would have none of it. So she wore it and prayed everyone thought it an interesting design and not a scientific mistake.

Eleanor tried to talk to her as she stepped into the carriage. Mellie could easily believe that the woman had guessed the reason for her illness yesterday. She might have heard Mellie return early in the morning. She'd definitely seen Mellie's red-rimmed eyes. Fortunately, the woman didn't judge her. And in an uncharacteristic show of warmth, she had even patted Mellie's hand in the carriage.

"Are you sure you are feeling well enough for this?"

What she was really asking was, do you feel well enough to face society? The answer was obvious.

"Absolutely."

Eleanor gave an approving nod. "And you are in fine looks. Never fear, we shall find you a husband soon. A few more gentlemen have made inquiries into your financials. Radley told me he heard it from…" Eleanor chatted on, but Mellie stopped listening. She had no interest in any man except Trevor—only to scratch his eyes out.

Good Lord, didn't he know she could be pregnant? Didn't he realize…

While Eleanor prattled on about potential husbands, Mellie's mind circled with the same thoughts that had been spinning there for the last thirty-six hours: on all the ways Trevor had failed her. In truth, it wasn't a lot. It was simply that he didn't love her when she loved him. He had allowed her to stumble headlong in love with him while he remained damnably aloof.

By the time they arrived at the party, Mellie had worked herself into a fine temper.

As was typical these days, a group of her scientific friends greeted her immediately. She made her schedule known—or Eleanor did—and so those who wished to find her could. These gentlemen were among her possible husbands, and she found them pleasant but not especially stimulating.

She heard about one's newest anatomical drawing of a toad, another's unfortunate experiment with fireworks. She reassured him his eyebrows would grow back better than ever. And then there was the last man to bow over her hand: Mr. Rausch. He greeted her as warmly as ever, but there was a tightness about his face that was new.

He began talking, giving her some effusive compliment about how she'd styled her hair, which was especially annoying because she'd barely styled it all. The bulk of her hair was braided to the base of her skull before being allowed to fall free. So she held up her hand, stopping him mid-word.

"Pray, forgive me for interrupting, but what has you looking so pinched?"

She watched his eyes focus intently upon her face, and he abruptly frowned. "Pinched? I am never pinched."

She laughed and did as bold a move as an unwed girl could do in society. She stretched up on her toes and pressed her gloved thumb against the lines between his brows, smoothing away the tightness there.

"I meant pinched in terms of anxious. Not that your funds are lacking. I believe we are all aware of your wealth."

He frowned all the darker, but she did not flinch.

They were the same in their wealth. Newly minted as rich, they were not casual about their coin even as they relished every stitch of gold filigree in their attire. It declared to the world that they had something of worth.

So when he frowned, she merely shrugged. She could tease him about his coin, and he would tolerate it, or she would cut him. Such was her mood this day.

In the end, he was the one who relented. He took her gloved hand and pressed a kiss to it, holding her fingers overlong. "You make me laugh, Melinda."

"I have not given you leave to use my Christian name, Mr. Rausch."

"I know, but I am going to take a liberty before this afternoon is over, and I thought to ease the surprise with boldness."

"You are ever bold, sir," she retorted, but there was no rancor in her words. In truth, she liked a man who knew what he wanted and grabbed it no matter the consequences. "I intend to follow your example today," she said blithely. She was done with this prancing about for a husband. She would select one today and be done with it.

His brows shot up and a gleam entered his eye. It was his greedy look, and she was well used to it by now. "Miss Smithson, would you care to explain that last comment?"

"I do not believe so, Mr. Rausch."

"Then perhaps we should walk in the garden so I may pester you until you reveal your secrets."

She looked at him then. She thought of Trevor and her fury at him. And she thought of all the other gentlemen of her acquaintance. Mr. Rausch was the one who most intrigued her. Her heart might long for Trevor, but at least Mr. Rausch stimulated her mind. That was something when Trevor gave her nothing.

"I accept your challenge, sir. We may walk, and I shall work to ferret out the cause of your distress."

"Ah, well, that is no easy task."

"I have never been one to choose the easy path." She said the words, but in her heart she knew she lied. A careful look at her life revealed that she had always chosen the easy path of staying at home, caring for her father, and creating a place that was hers alone. It was only because Ronnie continually charged into her home that she was at last driven to seek an alternative. She might say that she'd chosen the difficult path in London, except that Trevor and Eleanor had arranged everything. She had performed, danced, and even spoken as she was told.

But no more. She was a woman reborn and would take her future in her own hands. And given that Trevor had spurned her, she supposed her best option was Mr. Rausch. So she allowed him to walk her through the garden. They greeted several friends, but never lingered. And when their path wended toward a more secluded corner, she allowed it to happen.

"Well, sir, we have had a lovely walk, haven't we?" she began. "But as we cannot expect to remain alone for long, pray tell me what is on your mind. Please don't say that I am the cause of your distress."

He smiled and possessed her hand. "On the

contrary, it is my business affairs that upset me because I must go away to Africa for a time."

"Africa!" she gasped. "Oh, I have often longed to go there just to see the animals."

"There are creatures there nothing like what we have in poor England," he agreed. Then he pulled her fingers to her lips. But rather than kiss them, he lifted her hand higher and higher until the button below her elbow was revealed.

"Mr. Rausch—"

He pressed a finger to her lips, telling her to be quiet. She raised her eyebrows at his impertinence, but didn't object. After all, she had decided to be amused by boldness today, right? But when he thumbed her glove undone and began to push it down her elbow, she wasn't intrigued as much as confused.

Then he brought it to his lips. Not her arm, but the glove as it slouched on her wrist. She felt the tickle of his lips and heard a slight sound as he sucked the button inside his mouth. He was…suckling her glove.

She looked at him, wondering if he meant to be erotic. Obviously, the answer was yes, and there was a certain wild thrill to be had when undressing in public so a man could fondle her arm. But she wasn't aroused. And when his tongue traced a circle along her skin, she shivered, not from excitement but a vague, wet revulsion. All she could think was that he was licking off her perfume. And then he looked into her eyes.

She expected to see a dazed hunger there. Some sort of sexual need such as on Trevor's face whenever they touched. Instead, she saw calculation. The kind of narrow-eyed inspection that her father gave rare beetles or something new and different trapped beneath the glass of his microscope.

This was not physical desire. This was analysis.

"Miss Smithson, you surprise me," he said. "And I assure you, I do not surprise often."

She tried to pull back her hand, but he held it still, idly stroking her bared wrist. "I don't know what you mean."

"Did you feel no desire then?"

"I—" She swallowed. "It was pleasurable," she finally admitted.

And it had been. Just not exciting.

"Damned by faint praise," he said as he straightened to his full height. "I suppose I shall have to persuade your mind then."

"I have always been impressed by the way your mind thinks," she said honestly. "You are not as educated as you pretend, but your thoughts are keen. And you know how to listen. That is rare, even among learned men. I find it quite stimulating."

His expression shifted into a genuine smile. It wasn't polite. Not the cultured shift of lips and chin to show amusement. This expression showed teeth and looked odd in this manicured garden. And yet it was the warmest she'd ever seen on him.

"Mr. Rausch—"

"I want to take you with me to Africa, Miss Smithson. I want to show you giraffes and rhinoceros."

She tilted her head. "Would that not be rhinoceri?"

He chuckled. "I have no idea, but I would show you them. And at night, I would teach you things that would excite you. I would show you ways to pleasure that can only be learned in the Orient."

She arched a brow. "Would we be traveling to the Orient?"

"Yes," he said, the word pitched lower and more seductive.

She began to think about the creatures to see in the Orient. She had never had a desire to travel the world before. Never thought to go beyond the streets of London. Her explorations had been reserved for chemicals and formulas, but now he sparked in her a desire to explore the world, and she took a step toward him.

"So you wish to learn?" he asked. "Shall I tell you about the creatures in China—big bears that are colored black and white and are the gentlest of creatures?"

"Bears? Gentle?"

"Usually."

She couldn't imagine it. "Tell me more."

His smile widened, and he began to touch her cheek. "There are such wonders in the world, I could not begin to describe them all." He leaned forward, his voice dropping to a husky whisper. "Or the things I have yet to try."

She knew he meant sexual things, and part of her tightened in curiosity. Perhaps even desire. So she did not stop him from caressing her jaw or brushing his thumb across her lower lip. His hands were different from Trevor's. Larger, more calloused. She wasn't sure she liked them.

Meanwhile, his greedy expression was back. He knew he had caught her. "It will cost you though," he said softly. "But I think you shall enjoy paying."

She nearly rolled her eyes. Men could be such single-minded creatures. "Sexuality is not so difficult a thing."

He chuckled. "Then you have a great deal to learn, and I shall enjoy teaching you."

She started to argue, but he pressed his thumb across her lips.

"I have a different payment in mind, Melinda."

She shook her head. "But I have nothing else to offer." Except her dowry, of course. But he had no need of money.

"You do. You have your cosmetic formula."

She blinked, pulling back. She hadn't thought about her clearing lotion in weeks, and wasn't that a surprise? Before Trevor, it had been the single most important thing in her life. But now, it languished in her notes. A forgotten recipe for a cosmetic for women.

"But...why?" He had no blemishes that she could see. No dark spots to remove or lessen.

"Can't you guess?" he challenged. "Give me the formula, Melinda. Let me sell it. You can even help, if you like. Advise me on the factories, tell me which shops would be best, which ladies would pay most for it."

She thought about it. She had no doubt that he could make a fortune with her formula. He had the skill and the resources to produce it. Meanwhile, he stroked his fingers along her neck. He slipped beneath her hair, and she knew he angled for a kiss.

"It is part of my dowry," she whispered, thinking aloud. "I should choose a husband who knows what to do with it."

She saw his lips curve, but there was no humor in the expression. "I have no intention of marrying you, Melinda. Only a mistress will do the things I imagine."

She jolted. "What?"

And now he did look amused, as one might at a very young child. "I have told you I am a man of greed. Why would I allow a woman—any woman—to load me with her debts? No, Melinda, what I offer you is the world."

"In exchange for the formula."

"And your body. Your luscious, innocent body to use for our pleasure."

Now she understood. Now she knew what he offered, and she was shocked. She shouldn't be, she supposed. What he said made sense. And damn it, she was considering it. After all, she hated this business of finding a husband. Why not throw it all to the wind and make a fortune besides? She could force him to share the profits with her. She could make a contract, couldn't she?

There was a name for what he offered. She'd overheard it before but only now began to understand what it entailed.

"Is this…" She swallowed. "Are you offering me carte blanche?"

"Yes," he said. "You strike me as a woman daring enough to make such a path enormously profitable. For us both."

"Daring? Me?" She nearly laughed out loud at that. She'd been the opposite of daring. And the one time she'd truly embraced recklessness, she'd given her virginity to the absent Trevor.

"Yes, you," he said, and there was a wealth of temptation in those two words.

She started to think about it. She tried to analyze her possibilities as she might a chemical formula. She tried to simply weigh options and costs, but despite all that intention, her thoughts were stuck on the night she'd shared with Trevor. And the horrifying idea of doing that with anyone else.

And while she stood there in awkward contemplation, a man appeared. A man who was so familiar to her heart and soul that her body was stepping toward him before her mind even registered his angry gaze and his raised fist.

"Bloody bastard!" Trevor bellowed. Then he planted a facer direct to Mr. Rausch's jaw.

Mr. Rausch rocked back on his heels, taken completely off guard. He had enough time to lift a hand in defense—but not recover his balance—when Trevor hit him again. This time, the man went down in the dirt.

Mellie rushed forward, grabbing Trevor's arm as she tried to pull him back. "What are you doing?" she cried. She could feel the fury in the man, felt it vibrating as he stood over Mr. Rausch.

"Name your seconds," he growled.

"What?" Mellie cried. "You are not going to fight another duel!"

Trevor turned to look at her. "He offered you carte blanche," he said as if that explained everything.

"Yes. So?" she pressed. "He offered it to me, not you. Damnation Trevor, how can you just punch a man like that?"

"He offered you *carte blanche*," he repeated.

"I know! And you have offered me nothing. So forgive me if I find his offer appealing."

"Mellie!" he cried. "I came here to propose, and I find him offering you—"

"Yes, yes," she interrupted. "But…what?"

He turned to face her more fully, though he clearly kept an eye on Mr. Rausch. "I had to get a special license. I had to make sure the money was there to support us." He rubbed a hand over his face. "Mellie, we need to get married."

She looked at him. She'd been caught off guard—by his punch and by his proposal—so she hadn't thrown herself into his arms. And now she stopped to take a breath. Now she waited for him to complete his proposal. And she waited.

And waited.

Until he frowned. "Mellie?"

Good Lord, did he think he'd just proposed? She wasn't expecting Ronnie's effusive poetry, but he had to know that she wanted more than: we need to get married.

"Why?" she asked.

He gaped at her. Then his gaze dropped significantly to her belly. "You know why."

Oh. He was afraid she was pregnant. That was it. That was the reason he was here before her, special license in hand. Then she looked at Mr. Rausch who was just now pushing to his feet, his jaw swelling and his eyes narrowed. But he didn't seem like he was about to attack. Instead, he was watching them closely.

"Do I understand this correctly?" she asked, her

voice tart as she turned to both men. "You, Mr. Rausch, are offering me the world in exchange for my formula, assuming I become your mistress—"

"Mellie!" Trevor hissed. "People are coming."

Of course they were. And she didn't give a damn. "And you, Mr. Anaedsley, are proposing marriage because you feel an obligation, and a duel because Mr. Rausch just insulted your possible fiancée?"

Mr. Rausch arched a brow at her phrasing, but he did nod his agreement. Trevor, on the other hand, took a threatening step toward the man.

"He was offering *carte blanche*."

Well, there it was. Her choices lay before her and not a word about love. She'd thought Ronnie ridiculous, but now she saw he had the right of it. Love was a great deal more important to her than she'd at first guessed. But in the absence of love, she would take… either of these two idiots and then make the best of it.

"Fine," she said coldly. Loudly, even, as she heard the rustle of people around them. They were staying just out of sight, but she knew they were there. "Name your weapon, Mr. Rausch, but let's make this a bit more exciting, shall we? The winner gets me."

Both men turned to stare at her. "What?" gasped one. She didn't really care who.

"I am done with this Season, the dancing, and the courtship. That is all nonsense anyway. I will go with the winner. No matter whom."

They stared at her, stunned that she was calling their bluff. Did they not think that women could descend to their level? If they hinged their sacred honor upon a duel, then why not a woman? She could be an honorable, unloved wife with Trevor or a dishonorable, unloved mistress with Mr. Rausch.

"Mellie," Trevor said, his voice hushed, and then another man came forward.

Just like before, she recognized him long before her brain registered a name. She knew the size and shape of him and recoiled on instinct. Though that might be because of the large bird that fluttered to the ground in his wake.

It was Ronnie, rushing forward, his fists raised and...

Bloody hell. He punched Mr. Rausch on the chin, knocking the man flat again.

"I accept!" Ronnie cried. "A duel for Mellie's hand!"

"Are you insane?" bellowed Trevor. Mellie wasn't even sure if the words were aimed at her or at her cousin, but it didn't matter. Ronnie didn't matter in the least, except that she felt bad for poor Mr. Rausch who had been decked now twice. Meanwhile, she was staring at the strange bird fluffing its feathers in irritation and emitting a strange "gobble" sound.

"Ronnie, what is this bird?" And why had he brought it to a garden party? But the minute she thought the question, she already knew the answer: his quest.

"I found it!" he cried dramatically, puffing out his chest as he turned to face her. "I have fulfilled my quest and brought you a rare and hitherto extinct dodo bird."

She stared at the bird as it stretched out its neck, shook a bright red comb that waggled under its chin, and trilled an annoyed, "gobble, gobble."

"That's not a dodo bird!" snapped Trevor.

To which Ronnie responded by decking him. Her cousin was fast, and Trevor had been glaring at the bird, so her former fiancé was soon sprawled in the dirt.

"You two do realize that dueling is illegal, don't you?" Mr. Rausch said from his place seated in the dirt. Apparently, the man had chosen to stay down this time as he fingered his jaw.

"And I'm already dueling him," added Trevor as he glared at Ronnie.

Mellie gaped at the men, wondering how seemingly rational gentleman could descend to such depths of idiocy so quickly. "Why not all three of you scramble together? Whomever comes out on top of the pile can have me."

She meant it as a joke. Her tone was laced with sarcasm as a way to point out how silly this whole affair had become. And yet, Ronnie took her words for complete truth.

"Exactly!" he cried. "A three-way duel!"

"Is still illegal," said Mr. Rausch. "Is it not, *Barrister* Creshe?" he said.

Mellie looked to where he gestured, and sure enough the barrister stood watching, his ponderous chins nodding their agreement. A half dozen others stood staring as well, and each one nodded. Yes, dueling was illegal. Sadly, Ronnie was a romantic, not an idiot.

"Which is why we shall do this duel the correct way."

"Ronnie, stop this now," she said, momentarily

distracted as the possible dodo bird strutted toward Mr. Rausch. Good Lord, she hoped it wasn't dangerous.

"To the death is traditional," Trevor said as he pushed to his feet.

"And—" began Mr. Rausch, but he needn't have bothered. Trevor finished it for him.

"And illegal."

"Not if it's a fight of yore. A fight of superiority not murder. A fight—"

"That's a fistfight, Ronnie—" Mellie said.

"With quarterstaves."

"And that's an American turkey," Mr. Rausch added.

"Lies!" Ronnie said as he prepared to punch the man again. But Mr. Rausch wasn't a fool. With a sudden kick, he knocked Ronnie's legs out from under him. Her cousin was now the third man to be sprawled in the dirt.

"Gobble, gobble," exclaimed the turkey.

"Unfair," moaned Ronnie as he clutched his ankle.

"You're an idiot," groused Trevor. "That's a turkey."

At which point, Mellie had enough. She had been moaning about the lack of love, and here providence had provided her with her last and final choice. A man who professed to love her to the depths of his poetic soul.

Very well then. Hadn't she said this entire Season would be a farce played out with her in the center? Then by all means, she should allow fate to have its way.

"Agreed!" she cried. "I shall be at Hyde Park

tomorrow morning at dawn. A melee duel with quar-terstaves. The man left standing wins me." She looked at the three men in turn, daring them to contradict. "And the turkey gets to compete as well!"

Then she spun on her heel and stomped away.

Twenty-two

Men like to prove their worth. Allow your rake to demonstrate his value in his own fashion.

TREVOR DIDN'T KNOW HOW HE GOT INTO THESE things. Before Mellie, he'd never challenged anyone to a duel in his life. And now? He was being roused before dawn by the Duke of Bucklynde and wondering if anything was more ridiculous.

He blinked, peered blearily at Radley, and managed to mumble a completely irrelevant question. "Where is Brant?"

"Asleep out there. Left this, though, with a note." He held up a flask.

Trevor blinked and tried to focus while the pounding in his head worsened. Thanks to Brant, he had spent too much time last night toasting to a good bout in the morning. Truthfully, he thought his best friend was trying to get him good and drunk so that he'd sleep through the duel. Er...fray. They'd spent some time discussing if a duel with three—or perhaps four—participants could be rightly called a duel. They decided that fray was the more accurate term.

"What does it say?" he managed as he pushed himself upright.

The duke turned the bottle toward the light and read in a dry voice. "I hope you sleep through the fray. I certainly intend to because she is not worth even one lost morning's sleep." The duke frowned at the couch in the other room. "That's rather severe, I'd say."

Trevor waved the comment away. "Brant doesn't think any woman is worth a morning's sleep. Or anything else for that matter. Though he has enjoyed my amorous misfortunes of late. As well as a great deal of bad wine and worse brandy."

"Hmm. Best mates, are you?"

Trevor shrugged. He'd known Brant since Eton. They certainly had some history, but they were more schoolboys who shared adventures every now and then. Except Trevor wasn't particularly enjoying this adventure or his friend. "I've gotten tired of him." His dislike began the first time Brant disparaged Mellie. By this point, Trevor wondered why he'd even allowed the man inside his home.

Meanwhile, the duke merely shrugged. "He's well out on the women. I've found an excellent one. I thought you had as well."

The man didn't have to finish the sentence. Trevor knew he'd mucked things up royally. But even he hadn't guessed that he'd have to fight a duel—or a fray—to win the woman's hand. The woman who might now be carrying his child.

"Hang on," said the duke as he flipped over the note. "There's more writing on the back."

Trevor didn't really want to know, but hadn't the interest to stop the duke from reading.

"He says to drink this before the fight for strength. What does he mean by that?" He opened the flask and sniffed. "It smells like tea."

"Brant likes to pretend he's an apothecary."

"With tea?"

"He adds things to it. Angelica and chives for a cough. Cloves to make an old light skirt pretty. That kind of thing."

Radley stoppered the flask. "Does it work?"

Trevor answered with a shrug, but he took the flask and tucked it into a satchel. Meanwhile, he pulled on his clothes with slow, resentful movements. "Why did she have to add the turkey? As if I don't feel ridiculous enough."

The duke had no answer. He seemed the kind of man who didn't bother with questions like why. He simply accepted and moved forward. He held out Trevor's cloak, and then paused before he passed him the quarterstaff that was leaning against the wall.

Damn the thing was huge.

"So you plan to fight for her then?"

What kind of question was that? "Of course I do. They can't have her. Neither man is worthy of her."

"It's the oversized chicken I'd be worried about."

"It's a turkey, but don't worry. I have a plan."

He'd thought long and hard about it last night and knew this fight wouldn't be easy. Trevor had fought Ronnie before and so had firsthand knowledge of exactly how powerful the big man could be. And that was with his fists, not a six-foot-long stick of hardwood. As for Mr. Rausch, who knew what the man planned? He wasn't *ton* even if he ran in the right circles to be. He hadn't been educated in the usual schools, but was generally known to be wily. Such a man was completely unpredictable, and Trevor wasn't anxious to see what he was capable of in a quarter-staff fight.

Fortunately, it hadn't taken Trevor long to figure out a course of attack. He meant to knock Ronnie unconscious first simply because the man was an idiot. A damned turkey was not a dodo bird! Next he would face off with Mr. Rausch. Though he'd like very much to beat the man for the insult to Mellie, Mr. Rausch had already been punched three times yesterday. That predisposed Trevor to be forgiving. If Rausch offered an apology, then Trevor would accept it and lay down his staff. If he didn't, well then Trevor planned to fight until he won.

He'd had a little experience with the quarterstaff long ago. He would be able to get at least a few blows in. That was all honor required. And then he would step away from the fight and appeal to Mellie. She needed to marry him. It was the only possible solution, especially if she was pregnant. As a logical girl, she would see that.

She had to.

So he grabbed the damn staff and began the long walk to Hyde Park. They were only a few feet out the door before the duke lifted the quarterstaff from his hand.

"I guess I'm your second now, so I should carry that."

Trevor took a moment to process that statement. Bloody hell, it was early. He wasn't thinking clearly. "That's right. Brant is my second. So why did you come to my rooms?"

The duke looked rather sheepish, his gaze skittering away before returning to Trevor. "I, um, came to tell you something."

Great. More bad news. "Spit it out, man. What's the newest disaster?"

"Well, it's my wife and Eleanor."

Dread twisted dark and hard in his chest. It was never good when women worked in concert.

"They've, um, decided to take Mellie's part in this."

"And see her wed to the winner of a du—fray?"

"And see that none of you gets her."

That sounded like Eleanor. And the duchess. And Mellie, for that matter. "How?"

"They've, um, decided to take up arms for the turkey. They've got truncheons. Their plan is to let you three knock one another out and then declare the turkey the winner."

"She's not going to marry a turkey."

"No. Cook is right now trying to decide how to best make it into a stew."

Of course she was. He had no witty response to that. No judgment on the absurdity of this entire affair. He simply knew that Mellie had set the course. He had to follow it or relinquish her forever. And that, he would never do.

Then they made it to Hyde Park. Trevor slowed

his steps, but made no comment. Which left it to the duke to express his awe with a low whistle. Every man, woman, and child in the *ton* had risen early to watch. There were even vendors selling sausages or meat pies. Plus a dozen tarts looking for their own business.

"It's like a hanging," the duke said under his breath. "Only with peers."

And him as the doomed man. Or the jester.

On that cheery thought, Trevor pushed his way through the crowd to the central clearing. Four posts encompassed by rope marked the edges of a square. The combat area, he assumed. It was hard to see through the press of people, but things soon became clear. To his shame, he was the last one there. But in his defense, his second had done everything in his power to sabotage his showing up at all.

He looked first at Ronnie, who was strutting in the center and waving his quarterstaff as if it were as light as a cricket bat. It was also bigger than Trevor's. By about three feet.

"Bloody hell, where did Brant get my staff?" How absolutely perfect that his second hadn't even bothered to get a correctly sized quarterstaff. The duke, naturally, had no answer to that, especially as Ronnie drowned out his words. The idiot was insisting that the last surviving dodo bird not be sacrificed on the altar of true love. Apparently, he had some scientific restraint to his poetic soul, and he chose to exercise it here.

"That's not a dodo bird," Trevor said, pulling two natural history books from his satchel. He had spent some time last night—while Brant was procuring his shorter-than-average quarterstaff—to visit one of his favorite scholars of natural history. Together they had found the appropriate volumes, and Trevor now set them out for all to see.

"This," he said pointing to a sketch of a bird with a huge hooked beak and a short, stubby yellow tail, "is a dodo bird. This is a turkey." He lifted a sketch of a bird with a huge dark fan of a tail, a small head with almost no beak, and a distinctive red chin called a waddle. He handed the sketches off to the nearest person, knowing it would make the rounds of the crowd.

Ronnie, of course, didn't even look. "After generations some differences are expected. Changes in environment would certainly cause greater variety in the creature."

"Pretentious bugger," said a voice beside him. He recognized the voice as belonging to Mr. Rausch.

Trevor turned, almost afraid to see what the man looked like this morning. Would he be in full battle armor? Would he be riding a horse as he whacked them with his quarterstaff? No. Mr. Rausch looked exactly like himself. Tall with a calm expression and a perfectly groomed face, assuming one discounted the bump in his nose where it had once been broken. His clothing was well tailored, and he carried…

"Bloody hell," Trevor groused.

Not only was the man's quarterstaff bigger than Trevor's, it had silver tips on each end. The better to stab and maim his opponents, one would assume. Because bludgeoning each other wasn't enough.

Meanwhile, Ronnie continued to prose on about a tenderhearted Portuguese sailor who had rescued a dodo bird from a Chinese island and brought it to be raised and nurtured by his mother in Leeds. Leeds, for God's sake.

"No one in Leeds grows up to be a sailor," said Mr. Rausch.

"No one in Leeds would save a dodo bird. It'd be whacked for supper before it came out of the sack."

"I say we whack him first, then discuss this like gentlemen."

It was exactly Trevor's plan, so he was pleased that Mr. Rausch had the same thought. Sadly, there were two other people they had to convince. "We might have a problem with them," he said as he gestured to the far corner where the turkey sat in a large cage.

There they were—Lady Eleanor and the duchess— looking like fierce Grecian maids as they stood on either side of the bird.

"What are they carrying?" Mr. Rausch asked, a note of admiration in his voice.

"Truncheons. They intend to have us battle it out so they can declare the turkey the winner."

"The devil you say."

The duke was standing near enough to overhear. "Don't underestimate them. My wife is most determined to clobber someone today. Pray one of you allow her to get in a good hit, otherwise she might turn that thing on me."

Trevor made a mental note to stay on Eleanor's side of the turkey.

"Well, I suppose we best get to our places," said Mr. Rausch. He gave Trevor a genial tip of his hat before sauntering off to another corner of the roped-in square. Cheeky bastard. He sounded like he was off to a show, while Trevor was beginning to feel decidedly ill.

And where in all this milling mass of elite humanity was Mellie? Surely she wouldn't miss this. Or maybe she would. Maybe her logical side finally convinced her that this display was unnecessary, that London was filled with fools, and she would be better off at home with her father, never to see the light of day again.

That thought depressed him even more than hearing a prominent member of their government declare that he believed the bird truly was a new form of dodo.

"Give me that flask," he said to the duke.

"Are you sure?" asked the man as he handed it over.

"Course not." But he unstoppered it and tipped it for a full draught. It tasted vile. Worse than vile for all that Brant had obviously added honey in an attempt to sweeten it. He only managed to drain about half the flask before he passed it back to the duke. "Definitely not sure."

"You need to get to your corner."

Yes, he could see that. The others had reached their places and were looking expectantly at him. But he'd be damned if he joined this display before Mellie got here. He was doing this for her, damn it, and…

There she was.

She'd drawn a cloak about her head, but he knew the shape of her even in that ugly shroud. She was at the edge of the crowd, waiting for something. He took a step forward, and she turned toward him. Her face was shadowed beneath the hood, but he could feel her gaze on him. It was a heat that brought everything inside him to life. He felt a surge of emotion, an enveloping wave that said, "She's beautiful."

He couldn't even see her face, but that word echoed though him. Her soul was so beautiful that he couldn't stop until he had her. Even if it meant fighting her giant of a cousin, a turkey, and...well, whatever Mr. Rausch was. He would fight for her until his dying breath.

"Steady on, mate." An arm gripped his elbow.

He frowned at the duke. "What?"

"You were swaying. Are you all right?"

Swaying? "I'm fine." He took a step forward and felt as if the ground had turned to sea. He gripped his quarterstaff, using it to keep himself upright. What was wrong with him?

Two more steps had him listing like a drunk. No. Oh no. He needed only another breath to realize the truth. Brant. "For strength, my ass," he spat.

"What?"

"I've been drugged," he muttered. "I'm going to kill him."

"You can't fight, then. Damnation, you can barely stand."

Then he saw Mellie move. Or perhaps that was *him* moving and her standing still. He couldn't tell. She tossed off that ugly cloak—good—and shook out her hair. It was tied back in a simple braid, but that was all that was simple about her.

Her hair shown like auburn fire in the morning light, a perfect complement to the rich green of her gown. Her skin was dewy fresh, and her eyes— Sweet God, her eyes were bright with the sheen of tears. He was sure of it. There was anger in every abrupt slash of her gaze, fury in the way she pushed aside an offered hand before she stepped on her own over the rope to cross to the center of the square. But there were tears in her eyes. A well of sadness that reached to him through his drugged haze.

She hated this. He could see her disdain for the mockery her life had become, and he wanted to take her in his arms and carry her away. He would give her a laboratory filled with all the chemicals she wanted. He would build her a house and furnish it however she liked. And he would give her children. A thousand children if she wanted.

"You better sit down," said the voice beside him.

"What?"

"You're giggling."

"What?" Though it might have come out as a wha—?

"Jesus, what was in that tea?"

Good question. But it didn't matter. "I'm going to fight."

"You can't."

"For her. I fight. Just…get me to the ring."

He felt the duke's supporting arm. Felt the grip of his fingers and the push as he half guided, half carried Trevor to his corner. Then there was the awkwardness of trying to get over or under the rope.

There was a strange roaring in his ears. The wave of an ocean punctuated with bawdy suggestions. It took him a moment to realize that he was hearing the crowd jeering him. He had in mind to give them a rude gesture back, but he needed all his concentration to crawl under the rope without getting sick.

Bloody hell. Maybe he should get sick. That might get the damned poison out of him.

Sadly, there wasn't time. Things looked like they were getting ready. His love was saying something. She had turned away, and his heart lurched in his chest. This is just what it had felt like when she gave him the cut direct.

His insides had hollowed out, and there was just a yawning emptiness where she had been. An aching hole that expanded and grew with every day that passed without her. He swallowed, feeling the tears threaten to choke him.

"Mellie!" he cried as the darkness threatened to overwhelm him.

She turned at his cry, and he dropped to one knee before her. Then to his horror, he watched as her lip curled in disdain. He looked down at himself, seeing the mud on his pants. He tried to brush it away, but that only smeared it into a disaster.

Never mind. He had to speak. He had to tell her his heart. Whereas words and images flowed through his brain he couldn't quite form them into words. All he managed was, "Cricket. Beaut. Beuuu. Tt." Damnation, he couldn't even say the full word. His mouth wouldn't form the *y*.

He watched her eyes narrow. The sheen of tears was gone, and now she was a towering goddess of fury.

"Beauuuuttt," he garbled.

And then he went down. Toppled like a tree. He landed face-first in the mud.

He clutched his staff, trying to use it to lever himself upright. But what before was a too-short stick was now a towering tree of unwieldy wood. All he managed was to roll onto his side so that he could see the fight.

Apparently, his collapse signaled the beginning of the fray. While he was trying to use arms that had gone numb to push himself upright, Ronnie had lifted his own massive stave up to the sky with a roar.

Backlit as he was by the sun and the crowd, the man looked impressive. Like a giant of old with a really big stick. But off in the other corner, the ladies were busy as well. They opened the turkey's cage door. The bird would likely have just sat there, content in his cage. Turkeys—or even dodos—were not contentious beasts. But Ronnie's bellow had startled it.

It leaped forward, gobbling and flapping its wings. Eleanor reached for the thing, but she missed, as did the duchess who flung herself forward, succeeding in startling the poor creature even more.

That's a really big bird, he thought as he lay on the ground watching. Big enough to hurt a man if he were, for example, helpless on the ground.

He would not be defeated by a damned turkey. And he would not give up Mellie. So with his own muted roar, he shoved his hands down, managing to lever himself onto all fours.

That, of course, put him almost eye to eye with the bird, so he had a perfect view of the thing—running straight at him—as it fouled Ronnie's sudden charge.

Man and beast collided with much squawking and roaring. Ronnie tried to recover. He was nimble for such a big man, and he side-stepped as best he could. But he was carrying a nine-foot quarterstaff. Trevor's own six-foot one was difficult enough. The three extra feet was too much for Ronnie. He tried to use it against the bird, but ended up digging the end in the ground instead. With the quarterstaff suddenly jerking him sideways and the bird pecking at his knees, there was no hope.

Ronnie fell as all giants fall: with flailing arms, a roar of frustration, and—in this case—a bird pecking at his privates. Which—now that Trevor thought about it—was probably the reason for the high-pitched nature of Ronnie's scream.

The duchess ran forward, her truncheon raised high. She was heading for the turkey, saying something that might have been, "you poor dear," and then she gave Ronnie a big whack as she rushed past.

Ronnie might have recovered. The duchess, though fierce, had hit him on his fleshy behind, which was insulting but not really damaging.

Mr. Rausch stepped forward. He walked leisurely, which Trevor thought was rather lucky. The longer Mr. Rausch took to subdue Ronnie, the more time it gave Trevor to get to his feet.

But he'd forgotten that Rausch was a smart man, not given to ostentatious shows of fury like Ronnie. He stepped casually forward and set the silver-tipped point of his staff on Ronnie's throat.

"I win," he said.

"No," Trevor bellowed. Or he tried to. It came out more as a strangled groan. It took all his concentration to stay upright on his knees.

The crowd was deafening as they screamed abuse. No one seemed to have heard him. But he was fighting for Mellie. He couldn't let her go to the roué. He couldn't!

"No!" he tried again as he got one foot under him. Oh bloody hell, the ground was heaving about like a boiling pot of porridge.

Meanwhile, Ronnie looked like he was going to fight. There wasn't much he could do lying flat with a silver-tipped spear to his throat, but he started cursing. Apparently, the man was well versed in ways to insult his attacker. Rausch, of course, wasn't in the least bit concerned.

"Yield, Mr. Smithson."

Ronnie didn't want to. But then a little pressure to his throat had his insults sputtering to silence. A moment more—or perhaps after a deeper push from Mr. Rausch—and Ronnie gave in. He raised his hands in a gesture of surrender.

"Say it, Mr. Smithson."

Finally, Ronnie did. "Yield." It was an angry curse, but the word was clear enough.

"I don't," said Trevor.

With a Herculean effort, he surged to his feet. He would fight for Mellie.

But he'd forgotten the damned turkey. The beast was a menace. Worse, it was an easily startled menace that abruptly set to gobbling and pecking at him. And the duchess did nothing to restrain the satanic creature.

Trevor went down again, tripping over the bird on his way to Mellie, who was just now stepping into the ring. He tried to call out to her. He tried any of a thousand different things that all added up to him pleading with her to understand. To forgive him. To wait.

But none of the words came out except one. It burst forth as the turkey managed to kick him in the gut.

"Bugger!"

Then he went down beneath the creature's wings.

He rolled away. He could manage that. But by the time he got free of the maniacal creature, it was to see Mr. Rausch on one knee before Mellie. And while she stared in frozen shock, he offered her a ring.

Bloody hell, the man had just proposed.

Trevor didn't give up until he saw Mellie's nod. A slow dip of her chin that cut the heart straight out of him. Proposed. Accepted. And him flattened by a turkey.

With a moan of despair, he gave up. He closed his eyes and let unconsciousness claim him. The last thing he heard seemed fitting somehow. A final end to this charade.

"Squawk!"

He really hoped that someone had just strangled the demonic bird.

Twenty-three

If a rake once discovers he has emotions, he will be ruined forever.

THE TURKEY HAD ESCAPED. SOMETIME DURING THE END of the fight and the return to the ducal residence, the turkey and Ronnie had disappeared. She hoped the creature had run off to find a welcoming forest somewhere. She hoped Ronnie had gone off, never to be seen or heard from again.

But mostly, she didn't hope or want or feel anything at all. She just sat in a chair and stared at the fire. Trevor had failed her. She knew that wasn't a logical feeling. None of her feelings ever were. Not when she'd clutched him in a desperate need to escape London with a fake engagement. Not when she'd realized she was in love with a man who had stated at the very beginning that he didn't even like her. And certainly not when she'd decided to fight for him by giving him her virginity.

She'd been an illogical, irrational female, just like her mother. And just like her mother, she had destroyed her life. She hadn't thrown herself off a bridge, but she had done something equally disastrous. She'd accepted Mr. Rausch's ring.

Her entire goal in coming to London was to find love. Someone she loved who loved her in return. Who would marry her and raise a family with her. Mr. Rausch would do none of those things. And lest she be confused about these things, he had stated it aloud when he'd offered her his ring.

"I do not love you, Melinda, and I never will. But we can still travel the world together. And you can still give me your formula and make me rich enough to buy you anything your heart desires. If you accept these things, then I offer you honorable marriage."

She had agreed. And now, his heavy diamond ring listed sideways on her finger.

So she and Trevor had failed each other. She would have to carry on as best she could without love, which meant she had completed the transition to the aristocracy. Everywhere she looked in the *ton*, there were loveless couples. And that too Trevor had told her: my set doesn't marry for love. And now she wouldn't either.

"Hasn't the duke returned?" Mr. Rausch asked.

She looked up from the fire and mustered a smile for her fiancé. "He sent word an hour ago that he will return before the feast."

"Does he stay to watch over Mr. Anaedsley?"

She nodded. "He wrote that Trevor was drugged, not poisoned. A powerful sleeping draught."

"I told you something was off. No man goes down from a turkey kick, even one to the gut."

"Ronnie did."

Mr. Rausch smiled in obvious amusement. "Ronnie got a turkey peck in…well, in a sensitive area. That is vastly different."

She had no answer to that, and so she smiled as she might to her father. It was a vague sort of pleasant expression, which was usually enough to set her pater to prosing on without a thought to her. But Mr. Rausch was cut from a different cloth.

"For a woman newly engaged to a man as rich as Croesus, you appear remarkably downcast."

"I apologize. Was there something you wish me to do? If we are to leave soon for Africa—"

"Tell me first why you are glum."

"I'm not glum, Mr. Rausch—"

"And for God's sake, call me Carl."

She paused, then realized he was completely in the right. "Very well, Carl." She paused. She did not like the feel of his name on her tongue. It felt unwieldy in her mouth. She supposed it was one more thing she would have to adjust to. "I am merely overwhelmed, I suppose."

"Or perhaps you have given up on your dreams and are mourning the loss." Then he took her hands in his, his long fingers toying with the heavy ring he had given her. "You loved him?"

She thought about denying it, but this man was to be her husband. She would not start the relationship with a lie.

"Yes, I did. I do. But I assure you, that will not prevent me from being a good wife to you."

He patted her hand. "I never doubted it. But can you tell me why you love him?"

She frowned, wondering why he was pushing into a wound so raw.

"I find that it is the words that make a difference. If you can express things in words, it makes everything more clear."

It made sense when phrased like that, but she didn't know if she could do it. "How does one use words for a feeling?"

He squeezed her fingers. "You are of a scientific mind-set. Try analyzing the causes."

She thought back to that first day. "He makes me laugh," she said. "And so mad I want to spit at him. And then I laugh again." She thought about his hands on her body and how—when she wanted to hide away—he was there, pushing her to do something outrageous again. "He makes me live when I would much rather disappear."

"There will be a million things to see and do. And then there is what I will teach you in the bedroom. Let us disappear together into that wonderful country." He raised her fingers to his lips, but rather than press a chaste kiss to her hand, he rolled his tongue around the tip of her fourth finger before sucking it into his mouth. And when he was done, he looked into her eyes.

It was meant to be erotic, and a tiny part of her woke enough to pay attention. There were sensations tickling up her hand. Wet from his tongue. Pressure when he nipped at the tip. And a seductive heat from his eyes as he watched her reaction to everything he did.

She wanted to be aroused. She reached for the

feeling that overwhelmed her whenever she was with Trevor. She found a pale shadow of it and did her best to nurture it.

Meanwhile, he set her hand down with a fond smile. "It will take time," he reassured her. "But if you promise to try, then you will be surprised by what I can accomplish."

"Of course I will try. You will be my husband."

He nodded as if he expected no less, but there was disappointment in his eyes. She was already failing him, and their engagement was only six hours old. What would it be like in six years? Or sixteen? The idea horrified her, and yet that is what she had committed herself to do.

She struggled for something to say. She never was short of words with Trevor. And perhaps that was what she ought to say, Trevor was no more to her. She would hereafter cease thinking of the man. He was in her past, and Carl was her future.

She opened her mouth for just that purpose, but entirely different words popped out of her mouth.

"What the devil?" she said.

Her gaze had caught on someone standing in the doorway—someone who looked very much like Trevor, except that he was covered in mud, and he was carrying a bird. It was a pretty thing, somewhat reminiscent of a pigeon. But it was much larger—about a foot in size—and it had colorful green and blue plumage below the gray head and neck.

She pushed to her feet. Behind Trevor, the duke was gesturing to Carl.

"Mr. Rausch, care to share a brandy with me?"

If the man answered, Mellie didn't hear it. She was too focused on Trevor. "They said you'd been poisoned. Are you all right?"

He shrugged. "Have the devil's own headache, but Brant says that will clear by morning."

"Should you be in bed?"

He stood there looking at her. He was trailing dirt on the floor, and the pigeon on his forearm looked none too happy to be tied to him. "I should be exactly where I am, Mellie. In fact, I should have been here days ago, but..." He shrugged. "I didn't know what to say."

From beside her, Mr. Rausch's dry voice cut through the room. "Why does everyone keep bringing her birds?"

Trevor's gaze cut to Rausch, but he didn't speak. Instead, his gaze dropped to Mellie's hand and the ring that had flopped sideways again. She tucked her hands together, wanting to hide the damned thing, but he'd already seen.

Then he took a deep breath. "Mellie, would you sit down please?"

She nodded and headed toward her seat, but he shook his head.

"Not there."

"What?"

"Wait. Just a moment." Then he crossed to the chair by the window and tugged at it. It was awkward given that he still had to keep the pigeon happy. It squawked in annoyance a couple of times, but eventually, settled down. The duke stepped forward to help, but Trevor gestured him back. So everyone waited while the man balanced bird and furniture, shifting things around until the seat was facing the window.

"Will you sit down here please?"

She glanced about the room, seeing that Eleanor, the duchess, Seelye, and even a couple of the maids were crowding in the doorway to watch. She felt self-conscious sitting down with her back to everyone, but she would do what Trevor wanted. At this moment, she thought she would do anything the man wanted if only he would remain nearby a bit longer.

So she maneuvered herself into the chair and sat down. It was a tight fit given that he was standing between her and the window, and the bird did not seem to like her coming close. But she managed it and then folded her hands in her lap as she looked to him.

"I have been doing the most bizarre things lately," he said. "Things that any rational person would never contemplate much less execute."

She heard some murmuring of agreement, but with her heart beating so fast in chest, she could hardly hear Trevor or what the others were saying. "I know you were drugged. You needn't explain."

"But that's just it. I have been seized by a madness for weeks. I look at every room, and imagine it as you would arrange it with chairs facing the window, backs to the door."

So that was why he turned her chair around. "I only do that at home."

"But I want you to do that in my home. I have also broken completely with my grandfather, which everyone says is a mistake, but I cannot think that it is. And in a life with barely a schoolboy row, I have been in a duel and a fray. I've used a weapon, Mellie, short-sized though it may have been."

"Actually," inserted the duke from behind, "you didn't so much use it as fall on top of it."

Trevor shot an irritated look over her shoulder, but then refocused. "I brought you this bird too," he said, pushing the creature forward. "It's not a dodo bird, but it's the nearest relative, we think. It's called a Nicobar pigeon, and I've named him Ronnie because the first thing he did was shit on my shoes."

Mellie looked down, and yes, right there was a telltale splotch on his boot. Then when he didn't speak more, she looked up to realize he was offering her the bird.

"Oh!" she gasped, but she didn't know how to take the thing. Plus it didn't seem to like her either.

"Seelye, take him, would you?" ordered the duke.

"Take him, Your Grace? Where?"

"Well, we failed to eat Ronnie's offering. Maybe we should try Trevor's."

"Oh no!" cried Mellie, her voice tight as she grabbed the bird. "We are not eating this Ronnie!"

"Well, I doubt we should eat the other one," said Mr. Rausch. "Though I understand the desire."

Neither Trevor nor Mellie commented. They were busy handing off the bird to the appalled butler. When Mellie turned back to Trevor, he was looking at her with eyes that seemed to be stretched unnaturally wide. It was clearly a strain for him. He blinked twice, but each time seemed to push his face toward her.

"What are you doing?"

"I'm trying to be bug-eyed for you, Mellie. I'm exaggerating it now, but honestly, I've been trying to do that since you first asked me."

A giggle trembled up from inside her. She tried to hold it back because she could see he was in earnest. But he made her laugh, and she couldn't stop it. "I was teasing you, Trevor."

"I don't care." Then he opened his jacket and pulled out something from inside a pocket. "Hold out your hands."

She did, and he carefully placed a small book in her palms. Then he added two feathers to the pile. Then three more, then as many as a dozen little feathers.

"As a rule, feathers make me sneeze," he said. "I find them annoying, and they float everywhere, making a mess."

"Oh," she said.

"But these are from your dress. I have been on my knees since that day, collecting these things and sniffing them."

She frowned. "You sniffed them?"

He nodded, his expression rueful. "Made me sneeze every time, but…Mellie, they were yours. You wore them. They smell like you."

What could she say to that? She couldn't think. She didn't know what he was trying to tell her, and she couldn't bring herself to guess for fear she'd be wrong.

"And look at the book. Don't say anything. Just know that I think about that with you too."

She frowned down at the untitled book. She opened the pages, then gasped in shock before coloring up to her ears. There were couples drawn there.

In intimate poses. Instead of snapping the book shut as she ought to do, she paged through and imagined herself and Trevor doing every single picture.

"Trevor," she whispered.

"There's more."

More? She didn't think she could handle more. Already he'd said more than she'd ever hoped for except the one thing she wanted.

He dropped down onto one knee before her and reached into his pocket. Her heart lurched. He hadn't said it.

He pulled out a notebook. She recognized the journal. He carried it with him whenever he visited her father. "You were right so long ago. You called me a useless fribble who only attends parties. You said I don't care about science—"

"Trevor, I was angry."

"You were right. I've been dabbling at my studies, but here..." He flipped the book open. "I want to work more. I want to work with you."

She knew of his research. She'd overheard him talk with her father about it, but she never thought he'd want to share it with her. "But Trevor, I work with chemicals, not insects."

"You're a scientist, and I never realized how much of your father's work is actually yours. I should have. I'm sorry. All those times I was trying to get your father's advice, his clarity of mind and singular focus—I really wanted yours. Mellie, I've been an idiot."

She blinked away tears. Of all the things she should be tearing up over, this always came as a surprise. He saw her work. He knew what she did and admired her for it. "Of course," she pushed out through her tight throat. "Of course I will help."

"Thank you," he said gravely. "But that's not where I was the biggest idiot."

"Trevor, stop." She couldn't take anymore. Her heart was breaking, and yet the hope, the possibility that there might be more to his words, had her nearly dizzy with want.

He kept talking as if she hadn't interrupted. "I never understood this madness, Mellie. I've never felt it before. And my biggest idiocy was when I proposed to you—"

"What?" she gasped.

"I proposed without saying the most important part." He grabbed her fingers. "I love you, Mellie. I want to marry you and grow old together. I want to make babies with you, then argue science in the morning. But mostly, Mellie, I just love you. Please don't marry anyone else but me."

There it was. He'd said the words, and more importantly, she saw the truth in his eyes. He loved her.

"I love you too," she whispered.

"Don't answer yet," he said. "Just listen. My family will be a bother. They're *always* a bother, but you already handle my mother. And did I tell you that my investment in the mine has finally paid off? I found out just yesterday. And we can sell your cosmetic formula, so even if my grandfather does cut me off, we've got plenty of money."

"*I've* got plenty of money," she said. "I'm an heiress, remember?"

"And your father won't really cut you off. When he sees how deliriously happy I've made you—"

"I had a letter from him weeks ago. He said he was wrong."

He blinked at her, then suddenly blew out a heavy breath. "See there? It will all work out. I promise. You just have to say—"

"I love you."

"I love you too. God, Mellie, please, please don't turn me away."

She laughed, the sound light even through her tears. "Idiot! I love you *means* yes. Yes, I will marry you. Yes, I will have your babies. And yes, I will help you with your research if you will help me with mine. And you will show me how to do…" She swallowed and held up the book.

Then they were kissing. She was in his arms, and he was pulling her tight. And suddenly, she knew that everything would be all right. Despite everything, his plan had worked. And her plan had come out just right. And they were in love, so even if it hadn't, they would find a way.

Epilogue

Above all else, never lose hope.

RONNIE SAT IN THE DIRT AT A CROSSROADS AND contemplated murder. His intended victim stood nearby, happily pecking at the dirt, completely ignorant of its doom. But before Ronnie did the deed, he had to summarize in neat form the full extent of the creature's crimes.

First and most important, the bird's purpose in life had been to win Ronnie his lady fair. Far from doing that, the stupid creature had tripped him during the duel, pecked him in very private places, and covered his favorite shoes in shite. Then, to compound his crimes, the thing's demented squawking had gotten them thrown off the mail coach at this deserted crossroads too far from London for a decent inn. So here he sat contemplating murder while the afternoon sun baked his shoulders, causing the sweat under his clothes to make his wounds itch.

"What creature is that?" gasped a woman's voice.

He turned to see a tall woman with a yellow bonnet

sitting atop a cart. He had heard the thing coming, of course, and had intended to stand and make himself more presentable. But so black was his mood that he hadn't even bothered, choosing instead to think of ways to kill the hideous creature.

But now that she asked, he felt the compulsion to answer. So he pushed slowly to his feet and began his speech. "This, fair maiden, is the noblest of creatures. A rare descendent of the hitherto extinct dodo bird. It hails…" He swallowed. "I mean…" He felt his shoulders slump, his heart not in his performance.

"Sir?"

"It's a damned American turkey," he said as he kicked dust at it. "A common, cantankerous beast who—"

"An American bird! Truly?" Her cry startled him so much that he looked up in shock at her. Meanwhile, she had set the brake and scooted close to him on the bench. "Oh, I wish my brother were here to see it. A common bird, you say? But he's magnificent!" Her hands fluttered before her as she reached out, then awkwardly pulled them back to press against her full bosom. "Do you think…? Would it be possible for me to touch it?"

He blinked and wondered if she had lost her wits. But then he realized that this was exactly the reaction he had hoped for with Mellie. In truth, it had been his first thought when seeing the bird: what a magnificent creature. And then, as if sensing the topic of their discussion, the turkey ceased pecking in the dirt, lifted his head, and made that sound. Not the screeching horror of a cry that had them tossed off the mail coach, but the other sound. The soothing gobble that—

"Was that a purr? Oh sir, you must let me touch it!"

"Of course," he said, though it took him a moment to gather his wits. "Pray, give me your hand."

He helped her alight and noted for the first time how clear her skin was, how beautiful her figure. She was tall—much taller than Mellie—so he didn't feel as if he completely overwhelmed her in size. Her hair beneath her bonnet was flaxen, or so he guessed from the fair cast to her brows. And her voice was gentle.

"Come here, little bird. Oh, come here."

And to Ronnie's complete shock, the bird did. With stately movements that would put a rooster to shame, the thing walked over and allowed the girl to stroke its feathers.

"He's magnificent! How did you find him?"

She truly sounded awed, and Ronnie was so shocked that he answered without his usual embellishments. "It was a quest."

Her mouth slipped open in shock as she turned to him. "A quest?" she asked, awe in her tone. "Are you a Knight of the Round Table?"

He blinked, his mind rapidly scrambling. "What do you know of King Arthur's knights?"

"Oh heavens, but I have heard the stories since I was a little girl. My father is a scholar, you see. He studies all the old tales and thinks that the knights did not all fall when Camelot did. That there are some who yet survive. Some who demonstrate all the noble virtues first espoused by the great King Arthur."

Ronnie stared at the girl, and abruptly his heart filled with a yearning such as he had never known before. A hunger to do, to be—nay, to embody all that

Arthur's Round Table had once represented simply because she seemed to want it. But even as the desire consumed him, he realized how deeply unworthy he was. And so he looked at his shite-covered boots in dismay.

"No, sweet lady, I am not such a noble man as that." He found his words spilling from him as he might at a confessional—his sins exposed before this beautiful girl. "My quest was to find a dodo bird and nurture it with my own hand. Instead, I found this, a common American turkey from a traveling show, and pretended it was what I sought."

She gasped. "You lied?"

"I wanted my true love."

She waited a moment to answer, and in that time he felt the full weight of his idiocy on his shoulders. But then she spoke. He wasn't looking at her, so it was her gentle tone that reached him. "But you cannot catch true love with a lie, sir. Surely you know that."

He did. Or he did now. "I am a wretched soul."

"Nay, sir," she said. Then she touched his cheek, gently lifting his face until he gazed into her eyes. "You are only an imperfect one. Even Sir Galahad stumbled."

He jolted, startled by the name she uttered. Could it be possible that she mentioned that knight's name? "My lady," he whispered, dizzy with confusion.

"Do not despair," the woman said. "Shall I tell you a tale? My brother wished one thing with all his heart. One single thing when all others laughed and told him he was a fool."

Ronnie felt the blackness of his mood fade away, his heart caught by the tale. "What was his wish?"

"To become a sailor."

He frowned. "A sailor? That is not so foolish a wish."

"It is if you live in Leeds. There is no water for miles and miles, much less sailing vessels."

And for the second time, he jolted, the name of her town rocking him to the very foundation of his soul. "Leeds?"

"Yes, that is where we live. But he persisted. He bought books of nautical studies and memorized every word. By day he would work our farm until his hands bled, but by night he would dream of the sea and the day he would sail a ship."

"And his wish was granted?"

"Oh yes. Just yesterday, I waved good-bye to him. That's why we were in London. He apprenticed on a ship there and will soon sail to America."

Ronnie's mind was spinning, but somehow his question slipped out. "Will he find a turkey there and bring it home to you?"

She laughed. "Mayhaps. I asked him to bring me back a bird. I have a fondness for the creatures."

And then he saw it. She had tilted her head back when she laughed such that the sunlight fell full on her face. Her bonnet slipped, falling back from her head, and when she opened her eyes the sun burst clear and full on her eyes.

Blue. Cerulean blue. The color of clarity and purity. It called to him in the way of a holy relic. And like a gong sounding from the heavens, his soul was rocked a third and most devastating time.

"Oh!" she cried as her bonnet began to slip from

her head. She caught it, but he was faster. One hand caught a ribbon, but the other touched her face. He knew the pristine cream of her skin, and the elegant line of her jaw. And when he tilted her face again toward the sun, he saw the absolute beauty of a goddess.

And then a miracle happened. A miracle such as he had never known before. Words tumbled through his mind. Sonnets cast in iambic pentameter, but also line after line of epic poetry such as would rival that of Virgil or Homer. The words were simply there like the fountain of knowledge in his mind, and they did not stop!

Whereas before, he always had to struggle for his work. He agonized over every line, but suddenly it was all there. A well full of glorious words and all because of her.

"All yet seems well; and if it end so meet. The bitter past, more welcome is the sweet," he intoned. Why he had uttered Shakespeare's words, he had not a clue. But then she smiled at him, her lips curving into the most perfect bud of rosy beauty.

"The king's a beggar, now the play is done: All is well ended, if this suit be won."

He gaped at her while his knees turned weak. She had quoted back to him! Shakespeare's *All's Well that Ends Well*. Even Mellie had never done such a thing, as she'd no interest in reading plays, much less memorizing them enough to echo couplets back to him.

"Sir!" the woman cried as he fell to his knees before her. "Sir, are you well?"

"I am…I am…" He was flummoxed, confounded,

and perplexed. He was dizzy with all that had transpired. He saw it now, as clear as if it were laid before him on a map. The constant frustrations with Mellie. The surety that she was his glorious destiny, and yet his utter inability to win her.

It had all been for this moment now. With this woman. If he had not chased Mellie, she would not have fled to London. If he had not followed her there, she would not have given him a quest. And if it were not for the damned bird, he would not have stumbled during the duel, lost Mellie's hand, and ended up here at this crossroads where his true love would find him.

"Sir, you are unwell. Pray come up on my cart. I am heading home now, but I know of a inn close by where you can rest out of the heat."

Words continued to spill in wondrous currents. Epic poetry, sweet couplets, even a short play. They were all there in his mind, but nothing came from his lips. Nothing that would express the depth of his gratitude and awe.

"Come sir," she pressed as she helped him stagger to the cart. "And would you bring your bird too?"

Bird? The noble beast that God had used as a vehicle for his divine will? Of course he—

"Oh! Oh look. He's already in the cart."

Sure enough, the turkey had at some point pecked or fluttered or leaped his way into the back of the cart.

Ronnie smiled. "A gift for you, my lady."

"Oh sir, I am not—"

"You are to me. If I may… Could I inquire as to your name, fair goddess?"

She smiled, her blush pinking her cheeks such as the

goddess Aurora might paint on the morning sky. "It's Grace, sir. I'm—"

"My Grace."

"Sir!"

"My muse. My inspiration."

"Oh!"

He watched her then, bracing himself for the grimace of distaste or the slight roll of her eyes. That was, after all, what people did when the lyrical words fell unrestrained from his lips. But she did none of those things. Instead, her blush deepened, her eyes sparkled, and she whispered as if it were something she ought not say.

"Sit beside me, sir, if you will. And…and tell me more."

More! She wanted more! And there was more. A whole ocean of words and poetry that she inspired waiting to spill forth.

"I think I shall begin a new poem," he said as he pulled out his journal and flipped to a new page. A pristine white sheet on which he wrote these words: "To Grace on the road to Leeds."

"Oh sir!" she gasped, but he could tell she was pleased.

"When first she saw Sir Galahad," he began.

"Is that you? Sir Galahad?"

He shook his head. "No, fair lady. It is…well…" He glanced significantly behind him.

"Truly?" she cried. "The turkey? But I think that is a perfect name for him!"

He flushed, feeling embarrassed by his own fanciful notions. "I named him that when I first saw him. I thought he was a noble creature who would bring me the Holy Grail." He shook his head in wonder. "I thought he'd failed."

"Oh no, sir. Never that."

"But I see now it's true. He is Sir Galahad, and you, my grail."

"Oh sir…" she murmured, and then she cast him a coy look. A flirtatious glance from a woman who was pleased with what she saw. "Shall we on to Leeds then?"

"Anywhere you will," he answered. And from behind them, Sir Galahad added his own purr of approval.

"Gobble, gobble!"

About the Author

USA Today bestselling author Jade Lee has been scripting love stories since she first picked up a set of paper dolls. Ball gowns and rakish lords caught her attention early (thank you, Georgette Heyer), and her fascination with the Regency began. An author of more than forty romance novels and winner of dozens of industry awards, Jade Lee delights readers with her vibrant, saucy Regency romances that deliver unusual stories with a lot of heart. Lee lives in Champaign, Illinois.

WATCH FOR THE NEXT BOOK IN JADE LEE'S
RAKES AND ROGUES SERIES

One Rogue
at a Time

What the Bride Wore
by Jade Lee
USA Today bestselling author

——— ❧ ———

When all is lost

All Grant Benton, Earl of Crowle, can think of is restoring his family's fortune so he can go back to being a gentleman of leisure. But when he meets beautiful, purposeful Lady Irene Knopp, he begins to question whether there might not be a better way to live life after all...

What's left is desire

Lady Irene will never give up her fulfilling work dressing the most beautiful brides in England. She'd rather risk losing love forever than sacrifice her own life's purpose. Yet she has never met a more magnetic, attractive man than Grant. Trapped between the fleeting chance at love and passion for her work, is it possible she can have it all?

——— ❧ ———

"It's another keeper from a talented storyteller." —*RT Book Reviews*

"Readers will savor the numerous red-hot love scenes as Grant finds his way to maturity and love." —*Publishers Weekly*

For more Jade Lee, visit:

www.sourcebooks.com

What the Groom Wants

by Jade Lee

USA Today Bestselling Author

An honest love...

Radley Lyncott has been in love with Wendy Drew as long as he can remember. Now that he's returned from abroad to take up his Welsh title, he is appalled to find the Drew family in ruin, and—even worse—another man courting Wendy.

Or a dangerous attraction?

Seamstress Wendy Drew is forced to settle her brother's debt by working nights at a notorious gambling den. But her double life hasn't gone unnoticed—she has captivated Demon Damon, a nefarious rake who is hell-bent on luring Wendy into his arms.

"Strong, vibrant characters and a compelling plot that doesn't ignore the grittier aspects of Jane Austen's world will keep readers engaged." —*Booklist*

"This plot is rich from the start and thickens rapidly." —*Fresh Fiction*

For more Jade Lee, visit:

www.sourcebooks.com

It Takes Two to Tangle

by Theresa Romain

—— ❧ ——

Wooing the wrong woman...

Henry Middlebrook is back from fighting Napoleon, ready to re-enter London society where he left it. Wounded and battle weary, he decides that the right wife is all he needs. Selecting the most desirable lady in the *ton*, Henry turns to her best friend and companion to help him with his suit...

Is a terrible mistake...

Young and beautiful, war widow Frances Whittier is no stranger to social intrigue. She finds Henry Middlebrook courageous and manly, unlike the foppish aristocrats she is used to, and is inspired to exercise her considerable wit on his behalf. But she may be too clever for her own good, and Frances discovers that she has set in motion a complicated train of events that's only going to break her own heart...

—— ❧ ——

Praise for *Season for Temptation:*

"Regency romance at its best."
—*RT Book Reviews*, 4 Stars

For more Theresa Romain, visit:

www.sourcebooks.com

To Charm a
Naughty Countess
by Theresa Romain

❧

Caroline, the popular widowed Countess of Stratton, sits alone at the pinnacle of London society and has no wish to remarry. But when the brilliant, reclusive Duke of Wyverne—her counterpart in an old scandal—returns to town after a long absence, she finds herself as enthralled as ever.

Michael must save his family fortunes by wedding an heiress, but Caroline has vowed never again to sell herself in marriage. She offers him an affair, hoping to master her long-lasting fascination with him—but he remains steadfast, as always, in his dedication to purpose and his dukedom.

The only way she can keep him near is to help him find the wealthy bride he requires. As she guides him through society, Caroline realizes that she's lost her heart again. But if she pursues the only man she's ever loved, she'll lose the life she's built and on which she has pinned her sense of worth. And if Michael—who has everything to lose—ever hopes to win her hand, he must open his long-shuttered heart.

❧

For more Theresa Romain, visit:

www.sourcebooks.com

Secrets of a Scandalous Heiress
by Theresa Romain

One good proposition deserves another...

Heiress Augusta Meredith can't help herself—she stirs up gossip wherever she goes. A stranger to Bath society, she pretends to be a charming young widow, until sardonic, darkly handsome Joss Everett arrives from London and uncovers her charade.

Now they'll weave their way through the pitfalls of the polite world only if they're willing to be true to themselves...and to each other...

Praise for Theresa Romain:

"Theresa Romain writes with a delightfully romantic flair that will set your heart on fire." —Julianne MacLean, *USA Today* bestselling author

"Theresa Romain writes witty, gorgeous, and deeply emotional historical romance."
—Vanessa Kelly, award-winning author

For more Theresa Romain, visit:

www.sourcebooks.com

Between a Rake and a Hard Place

by Connie Mason and Mia Marlowe

Lady Serena's list of forbidden pleasures

Attend an exclusively male club.

Smoke a cigar.

Have a fortune told by gypsies.

Dance the scandalous waltz.

Sir Jonah Sharp thinks Lady Serena Osbourne will be just like any other debutante, and seducing her will be one of the easiest services he's ever done for the Crown. Then he catches her wearing trousers and a mustache in his gentleman's club and she demands he teach her to smoke a cigar. But what will truly be Jonah's undoing is finding out he's an item on her list too, which makes him determined to bring her all the forbidden pleasure she can handle.

"Shimmers with romance... Well-rounded characters and effortless plotting make this installment the best in the series." —*Publishers Weekly*

For more Connie Mason and Mia Marlowe, visit:

www.sourcebooks.com

Earls Just Want to Have Fun

Covent Garden Cubs

by Shana Galen

───── ❧ ─────

His heart may be the last thing she ever steals…

Marlowe runs with the Covent Garden Cubs, a gang of thieves living in the slums of London's Seven Dials. It's a fierce life, but when she's alone, Marlowe allows herself to think of a time before—a dimly remembered life when she was called Elizabeth.

Maxwell, Lord Dane, is roped into teaching Marlowe how to navigate the social morass of the *ton*, but she will not escape her past so easily. Instead, Dane is drawn into her dangerous world, where the student becomes the teacher and love is the greatest risk of all.

───── ❧ ─────

Praise for Shana Galen:

"Shana Galen has a gift for storytelling that puts her at the top of my list of authors." —*Historical Romance Lover*

"Shana Galen is brilliant at making us fall in love with her characters, their stories, their pains, heartaches, and triumphs." —*Unwrapping Romance*

For more Shana Galen, visit:

www.sourcebooks.com

The Laird

Book 3 in the Captive Hearts series

by Grace Burrowes

New York Times and *USA Today* Bestselling Author

— ❧ —

He left his bride to go to war...

After years of soldiering, Michael Brodie returns to his Highland estate to find that the bride he left behind has become a stranger. Brenna is self-sufficient, competent, confident—and furious. But despite Michael's prolonged absence, Brenna has remained loyal.

Now his most important battle will be for her heart.

Michael left Brenna when she needed him most, and then stayed away even after the war ended. Even though Michael has come home a seemingly wiser, more patient, and honorable husband, Brenna is wary of entrusting him with the truths she's been guarding.

— ❧ —

"Readers seeking a sweet, sensitive romance will savor this tale." —*RT Book Reviews*

"Burrowes's straightforward, sensual love story is intelligent and tender, rising above the crowd with deft dialogue and delightful characters." —*Publishers Weekly*

For more Grace Burrowes, visit:

www.sourcebooks.com

Mischief by Moonlight

Regency Mischief
by Emily Greenwood

Be very, very careful what you wish for…

With the night so full of romance…

Colin Pearce, the Earl of Ivorwood, never dreamed he'd desire another man's fiancée, but when his best friend goes off to war and asks Colin to look after the bewitching Josie Cardworthy, he falls under her sparkling spell.

Who can resist mischief?

Josie can't wait for the return of her long-absent fiancé. If only her beloved sister might find someone, too… someone like the handsome, reserved Colin. A gypsy's love potion gives Josie the chance to matchmake, but the wild results reveal her own rowing passion for the earl. And though fate offers them a chance, a steely honor may force him to reject what her reckless heart is offering…

Praise for *A Little Night Mischief:*

"Fun, lighthearted, engaging, and will grab you from the first page. A must-read!" —*My Book Addiction Reviews*

"Love, love, loved this book! I was up till early-morning hours finishing it." —*Books Like Breathing*

For more Emily Greenwood, visit:

www.sourcebooks.com

In Bed with a Rogue

Rival Rogues
by Samantha Grace

He's the talk of the town

The whole town is tittering about Baron Sebastian Thorne having been jilted at the altar. Every move he makes ends up in the gossip columns. Tired of being the butt of everyone's jokes, Sebastian vows to restore his family's reputation no matter what it takes.

She's the toast of the *ton*

Feted by the crème of Society, the beautiful widow Lady Prestwick is a vision of all that is proper. But Helena is no angel, and when Sebastian uncovers her dark secret, he's quick to press his advantage. In order to keep her hard-won good name, Helena will have to make a deal with the devil. But she has some tricks up her sleeves to keep this notorious rogue on his toes...

Praise for *One Rogue Too Many*:

"Filled with humor and witty repartee... Grace woos readers in true Regency style." —*Publishers Weekly*

"Charming...Grace captures the essence and atmosphere of the era." —*RT Book Reviews*

For more Samantha Grace, visit:

www.sourcebooks.com